A BOOK OF
SHORT
STORIES
1

PERSPECTIVES IN LITERATURE

A Book of Short Stories 1
A Book of Poetry 1
A Book of Drama 1
A Book of Nonfiction 1

A Book of Short Stories 2
A Book of Poetry 2
A Book of Drama 2
A Book of Nonfiction 2

A BOOK OF SHORT STORIES

1

THIRD EDITION

Secondary English Editorial Staff
Holt, Rinehart and Winston, Inc.

Holt, Rinehart and Winston, Inc.

Harcourt Brace Jovanovich, Inc.

Austin • Orlando • San Diego • Chicago • Dallas • Toronto

Printed in the United States of America
ISBN 0-03-038442-7

18 19 20 018 08 07 06

For permission to reprint copyrighted material, grateful acknowledgment is made to the following sources:

Brandt & Brandt Literary Agents, Inc.: "The Most Dangerous Game" by Richard Connell. Copyright 1924 by Richard Connell; copyright renewed © 1952 by Louise Fox Connell.

Don Congdon Associates, Inc.: "The Pedestrian" by Ray Bradbury. Copyright © 1951 and renewed 1979 by Ray Bradbury.

George Garrett: "The Confidence Man" by George Garrett from *Necessary Fictions: Selected Stories from The Georgia Review*, edited by Stanley W. Lindberg and Stephen Corey. Copyright © 1959, 1961 and copyright renewed by George Garrett.

Harcourt Brace Jovanovich, Inc.: "The Necklace" by Guy de Maupassant, translated by Newbury LeB Morse. Copyright © 1958 by Harcourt Brace Jovanovich, Inc. "The Mao Button" by Feng Jicai, translated by Susan Wilf Chen from *Chrysanthemums and Other Stories*. Copyright © 1983, 1985 by Susan Wilf Chen. "A Worn Path" from *A Curtain of Green and Other Stories* by Eudora Welty. Copyright 1941 and renewed © 1969 by Eudora Welty. "Twelve Winter" under the original title "Then He Goes Free" from *Cress Delahanty* by Jessamyn West. Copyright 1948 and renewed © 1976 by Jessamyn West.

Daniel Keyes and The Magazine of Fantasy and Science-Fiction: "Flowers for Algernon" by Daniel Keyes from *The Magazine of Fantasy and Science Fiction*. Copyright © 1959, 1987 by Daniel Keyes. Copyright © 1979 by Mercury Press, Inc.

Ashley D. Matin, Brett Deal, and Shane Townsend, on behalf of the Estate of Borden Deal: "Antaeus" by Borden Deal from *Southwest Review*, Spring 1961. Copyright © 1961 by Southern Methodist University Press.

Harold Matson Company, Inc.: "Top Man" by James Ramsey Ullman. Copyright © 1940 and renewed 1968 by James Ramsey Ullman.

REVIEWERS:

Joan M. Crimmins
Joseph A. Foran High School
Milford, CT

Flora Foss
Formerly Geneva Middle School
Geneva, IL

Mary Gail Luck
Mt. Pleasant High School
Mt. Pleasant, TX

CONTENTS

A BOOK OF
SHORT
STORIES
1

INTRODUCTION

The collection *The Arabian Nights' Entertainments*[1] contains the tales of clever Scheherazade, who saved her life by telling her husband, the king, a new story each night. By the time her stories numbered a thousand and one, the king loved her so much he could not kill her. What an enviable skill—to invent such a multitude of interesting tales. The modern short story writer might well wish for a small share of Scheherazade's talent.

The history of short prose fiction is almost as old as language itself. Through the centuries, tales, legends, myths, and fables have been enjoyed everywhere in the world. The short story was not regarded as a distinct literary form, however, until the nineteenth century, when authors in Germany, Russia, France, and the United States began to compose and define different types of fiction. The American critic, poet, and short story writer Edgar Allan Poe made an outstanding contribution to the development of the short story when he wrote that all of the details in a story should contribute to a "unique or single effect."

Today, a short story may be as brief as five hundred words or as long as several thousand words. The difference between a short story and other fictional forms, such as the novel, lies in its unity: the conversation, the action, and the idea on which a short story is based will all deliberately focus on one predominant effect.

Short stories are written to be enjoyed. Of course, you don't need to understand how a story is written in order to enjoy it. Understanding the elements of a short story, however, will

1. **The Arabian Nights' Entertainments:** a group of Oriental stories (also called *The Thousand and One Nights*) dating from the tenth century, narrated by Queen Scheherazade (shə·hĕr′ə·zäd′). The king postponed her death (the usual fate of his wives) from day to day so he could hear another of her interesting stories. Aladdin, Ali Baba, and Sinbad the Sailor are among the characters in these tales.

heighten your enjoyment because it will help you to read *critically;* that is, it will help you to evaluate and compare different stories so that you will understand why a story affects you in a certain way and why you like some stories more than others.

Elements of the Short Story

Not all short stories contain all of the following elements. Depending on the author's purpose, some factors may receive more emphasis than others; some may not be used at all.

Conflict

The reason a story grows in tension and suspense as it builds to a climax is that the pressure of conflict, the struggle between two opposing forces, is increased by each event. Conflict in a story may be (1) person against person, (2) human against nature, (3) person against self, (4) the individual against society, or (5) a combination of two or more of these types.

An example of person against person would be two people fighting for the same goal. A human against nature might involve a person caught in a storm at sea. An athlete debating the morality of accepting a bribe would illustrate one against oneself. And a doctor who meets opposition to a new medicine or vaccination would be an example of an individual against society. It is possible, obviously, to have more than one conflict within a story.

Conflict can be *external* or *internal.* Physical or external conflict is easy to recognize, especially in an adventure story which emphasizes a vivid physical struggle. Internal conflict may be represented by a character's struggle with conscience, or between what is and what should be. The character might be struggling against an impulse to commit a crime, or a tendency to be cowardly, or a fear that something disastrous is going to happen. The best stories often combine external and internal conflict.

The forces opposing each other in a conflict are labeled the *protagonist* and the *antagonist.* The protagonist is the main character who is faced with a basic problem or struggle. The antagonist is the person, place, idea, or physical force opposing the protagonist. To succeed, the protagonist must overcome the antagonist.

Plot

This is the plan of the story—the sequence of actions and events that tells what happened. In many short stories, the plot has a well-defined *beginning, middle,* and *end.*

The story begins with a situation or problem that is real and important to the protagonist (main character). Many authors try to arouse the reader's curiosity in the first sentence. The author keeps the reader in *suspense,* wondering what will happen next. Suspense is increased by withholding information that would satisfy the reader's curiosity.

The beginning of the story often introduces a *conflict* that will be important to the story. The opposing forces must seem to be so evenly matched that the reader is kept in suspense about who or what will win out. Usually the opposing forces are people, but some excellent stories have been written about internal conflict. The protagonist might be struggling against an impulse to commit a crime or a fear that something disastrous is going to happen.

In the middle of the story, the tension created in the opening situation must be increased. To maintain the reader's interest, *complications* are introduced. The goal that the protagonist wishes to attain does not appear as easy to reach as it first did, or the opponent may become more formidable. Barriers and detours are presented, creating a need for new plans and decisions.

As the main character struggles with those conflicts, the reader begins to recognize a growing tension or rising action in the plot toward a particular high point of interest called the *climax.* This is the point of highest dramatic intensity—the point toward which all of the action builds.

Following the climax comes the *dénouement,* which is the final unraveling or solution of the plot. At the end of the story, it should be clear that one side or the other triumphs, a main character meets success or failure, a mystery is solved, or some misunderstanding is cleared up. Some stories end, as conflicts in life often do, with no clear-cut answers or solutions.

Foreshadowing

This means exactly what the word implies—a hint of things to come. A word, a phrase, or a sentence can contain an important clue that has been inserted by the author to prepare the reader for a later event. Alert readers store such clues in their minds and recall them when the unexpected takes place or when a character reacts in a manner that at first appears strange or unreasonable.

Characterization

There are a number of techniques an author can use to help characters come alive. These include:

1. A physical description of a character and/or a description of the kind of person he or she is: the writer may tell you that a person is stingy and mean, or kind and considerate.
2. A description by another character.
3. The character's speech.
4. An explanation of the character's thoughts.
5. The character's actions.
6. The character's responses and reactions to other characters or to situations.
7. A combination of several of these methods.

Character and plot are closely related. A well-conceived plot involves meaningful human action, which means that characters act consciously and deliberately. A plot is believable only if the characters in a story act in a consistent and natural way. To believe in the characters, you must believe in the plot.

Everything you are told about a character should be significant. The good short story writer is selective and includes only details that are essential to the effect of the story.

Point of View

There are basically two points of view from which a writer can tell a story:

1. First-Person Narrator. Here the writer usually has a major or a minor character tell the story in his or her own words ("I said"; "I did"; "I remember"). The author, through this first-person narrator, can reveal only what the narrator might reasonably be expected to know. If a ten-year-old girl tells the story, her powers of observation and expression would naturally be limited. The use of the first-person narrator gives an illusion of immediacy and authority.

2. Third-Person Narrator. If an author feels that the reader should know more than any one person can tell, the story may be written from an *omniscient* or all-knowing point of view. Any character's actions or thoughts may be described and commented upon by an omniscient third-person narrator. A story told from a *limited* third-person point of view presents information through the eyes of a character whose knowledge of events and other characters is restricted.

Tone

Tone is a writer's attitude toward his or her subject and characters. It may be sorrowful, sentimental, angry, ironic, sympathetic, or objective and impersonal. The writer chooses and selects details that will help to set the desired tone, thus influencing how readers will react to each character.

Setting and Atmosphere

Setting—the time and place of a story's action—is most often stressed in a story of *local color,* which emphasizes the particular characteristics of a region and its inhabitants. It is also important in *science fiction* stories, where the author has to create an impression of reality to make imagined scientific changes of the future real to present-day readers. When evaluating the role of setting in a short story, ask yourself what the setting contributes to the story and if it could possibly be eliminated as an essential element in the story.

As a rule, setting is not a dominant element, but it does serve to establish or heighten atmosphere. This is especially evident in stories where the author wants to create a special feeling or mood.

Atmosphere, an integral part of plot, theme, and character, is something you sense or feel. Descriptive details give an emotional coloring to a story, but there are many other ways of obtaining atmosphere. For example, *style*—the author's choice of words, the kind and quantity of verbs, adjectives, and adverbs, and the length and rhythmical pattern of sentences—helps to create atmosphere.

Symbol

A symbol is something that represents or suggests a relationship or association. For example, a flag symbolizes patriotism; a lamp represents knowledge; a cross stands for the Christian Church.

In fiction, symbols are often concrete objects used to represent abstract ideas. A stack of gold coins might, during the course of a story, come to stand for greed; or a lovely rose, for beauty.

Characters' names may also be symbolic. "Red," for example, could be a name associated with a hotheaded person. A "Mrs. Oakwood" might manifest both physical and moral strength.

Theme

Another important element is the theme, the central insight or idea on which the story is based. A theme is rarely stated; usually it is implied. Generally, a theme is a significant insight about human life.

The central insight or underlying idea of a story can often be stated in one or two sentences. For example, the theme might be "Honesty is the best policy." Or the theme might be that all persons are responsible beings who must someday answer for their acts. Not every story has a theme, but in some stories, the theme is more important than the plot. In general, the most memorable stories have a serious idea or comment about life underlying the plot.

Analysis of a Short Story

In order to discover the underlying meaning of a story, you need to learn to read more than just the printed words. Much of the pleasure of reading comes from being able to supply what the author does not say but only suggests. For example, when you read "The Secret Life of Walter Mitty," notice that Walter Mitty never says he is deathly tired of being nagged and henpecked; but listen as Mrs. Mitty talks at him. Every word is a pin in a balloon, a pop in his soap-bubble world.

The key to a story will most often be found by asking the question "Why?" Of each story, ask two *why's*. The first *why* is directed toward the characters' motivations. Why do the characters act and speak as they do? What motives do they have for their choices and decisions? These decisions are what bring the action or plot to its climax. The dénouement should be determined by the nature of the characters. You should be able to believe that certain characters would make the kinds of choices they do. Through their characters, authors are able to tell their readers something about human beings—what pressures they face and how they react, or what they will live or die for.

The second *why* will help relate the different parts or elements of the story. Short stories are limited. They do not include "extras." Ask then, why did the author use this type of setting, this kind of dialogue, these events, these characters, this particular point of view? Asking these questions will help you to understand how the story's meaning is conveyed through the relationship of all the parts of the story: that is, the method of this particular writer in this particular story. In every well-written story, there will be good reasons for the author's selection and arrangement of material.

GEORGE GARRETT

(born 1929)

Although George Garrett is best known for his historical fiction, his talent and imagination span many types of writing. His works include seven books of poems, six novels, five collections of short stories, a number of plays and screenplays, and many scholarly studies.

Born in Orlando, Florida, Garrett received his undergraduate and graduate degrees from Princeton University. He continued his studies at Columbia University and then served in the Army from 1952-1955. In the late 1950s, he began his teaching career and also began publishing his stories and poems.

In addition to developing his own writing craft, Garrett has devoted much of his creative energy toward nurturing the talents of young writers. He has taught and lectured at a number of colleges and universities, including the University of Virginia, where he has been a Professor of Creative Writing since 1984.

THE CONFIDENCE MAN

Foreshadowing of conflict.

Major character introduced.

Major character described.

The motorcycle, flaring a roar of sound behind its improbable, tilting forward rush, was the first sign of the change. Through years the summer visitors to Gulfport had become accustomed to the spectacle of Miss Alma, prim on her bicycle, twisting in and out of the shiny herd of traffic on the main street, Palm Boulevard, and precariously descending the slight slope down to the wharf where the fish market used to be. There she'd dismount, carefully lock her bicycle, and be seen, a slight gray-haired woman in a high-collared cotton dress, moving among the tall tanned fishermen, boys with their eyes still squinted against the shifting winds and the shiny brass of the waves, awkward and heavy-footed as ducks on dry land. There amid the clatter of unloading, the sagging nets hoisting the squirm and silver of the catch from the boats, the coarse laughter, the rich odor of the deep sea, she'd be like a thin ghost edging her way to examine, haggle, poke, and finally buy a single fish for dinner. She was the only person in the world still allowed to market right there where the boats came in instead of uptown at the Fish Market. Nobody had the heart or the inclination to tell her that long ago all that had changed. Would it have made any difference if they *had* told her? Not a bit. She'd stiffen and go right on about her business. She'd buy a fish and one of the fishermen would produce a paper bag from somewhere and write the price, still the same price, on it with a black grease pencil. She'd open her formidable purse, rummage, count the money out. He'd pocket the coins and, more than likely, tip his hat.

Characterization by actions.

Others' attitude toward major character indicated.

"Thank you very much, Miss Alma," he'd say as if she had conferred a special favor on him by the purchase.

She'd mount her bicycle and pedal away. The summer visitors found it very amusing. It was almost absurd enough to make up for the fact that she was anything but helpless when it came to renting the summer cottage she owned along the beach. She made them pay for the privilege of renting beach cottages in her town with a fine view of her ocean. When it came to real estate, not the least, most subtle variation in the national economic structure escaped her attention.

Conflict foreshadowed: contradiction between others' perception of Alma and her actual behavior.

Miss Alma lived in a fine old Florida house, long, high-ceilinged, rambling, with only a bit of the roof visible above a green jungle of pines and palms and live oaks, and with ragged shrubs like wild beasts crouching on what had been a lawn. You passed the driveway with its peeling signboard, *Capt. T.R. Drinkwater, Esq.*, but you

Characterization by setting.

didn't go in. If you had business you conducted it in a paintless lean-to at the edge of the driveway that looked like a child's lemonade stand. Which in fact was what it was. When The Old Fraud died, Miss Alma made it her office.

"Didn't I build this myself?" she'd holler. "Shoo! children. Shoo!"

Dialogue used for characterization.

Sure enough she had built it. She had sat there, longer than was respectable some said, selling lemonade to passers-by, unsmiling, condescending, until her mother died and she was busy from then on leaping about the house like an acrobat to the raging commands of the captain.

Father characterized.

That he was mad, that he had never been to sea as the captain of anything, tugboat or Titanic[1], did not lessen the authority of the myth he had found for himself, believed in with all his heart until, at last, even Gulfport accepted it without question. You could hear him and he *did* sound like a foghorn in foul weather. You might have seen him then on the sidewalk, leaning down as if he were bucking the breeze of a gale, rolling-gated[2] in the plenty of space that cleared without a whisper or the raising of an eyebrow in front of him no matter how crowded the time or the day, talking to no one but himself. To be in the real-estate business! To be a seaman condemned to the parceling out of little pieces of dry land to a flock of ridiculous spineless figures in piratical costumes who thought the Gulf of Mexico was something to look at, for children to splash brightly in, to cast a fishing line or to sail on, safe and clumsy in their rented boats—rented from him—cramming the pure calm of the bay with the cursed diagonals of their sails! It's no wonder there was a strong odor of bourbon whiskey in his wake. No wonder the children followed behind,

---

1. Titanic: a huge passenger ship; advertised as "unsinkable," it hit an iceberg and sank on its maiden voyage.

2. rolling-gated: walking in a manner typical of sailors who adapt their movements to heaving ship decks.

shrill and active like a flight of gulls. And naturally everybody said, "Poor Alma."

Others' reaction to Alma.

Yes, no one was ready for the motorcycle. That day the fishing boats churned into the little bay, the tourists assembled with cameras, and the gulls coaxed with bleak cries overhead. One or two heads might have turned casually to the place where the road comes into view to see her strict, indignant pedaling. Then they heard the motorcycle. It careened into sight, skidding on the curve, a lank man in a straw hat holding the longhorned handlebars, and behind him, clinging to his waist, unabashed, Miss Alma, her skirt misbehaving in the wind and her laughter as naked and shrill as a girl's. They were so still they might have been a photograph themselves, those tourists with cameras, when the motorcycle shot onto the dock, came to a screeching halt. The tall man rolled down his pants legs, took off the goggles he'd been wearing, cocked his straw hat at a wry angle, and, openly, for all the world to see, bought two nice bluefish while Miss Alma, breathless still from the wild ride, held his motorcycle for him. The fisherman even had to make change for him. When he walked back to her with the paper bag, the taps on his heels clicked arrogantly on the dock. He rolled up his pants legs again, revealing red silk socks and a wide garter. He put the goggles on, adjusted them, pulled his hat far down over his ears, and stamped down on the starter. And they were off in a coughing growl, propelled out of sight at an unbelievable speed, never even slowing at the curve.

Beginning of conflict.

New character introduced.

Contrast to Alma's usual manner.

Contrast to earlier scene at wharf.

It was the fisherman who spoke first.

"He's from Georgia," he said. "I can always tell a Georgia accent."

"Pocket full of money. Did you see all those bills?"

"I didn't know Miss Alma had any family in Georgia."

"As far as I know, she don't," someone said.

Dialogue develops impression of the stranger.

"Anyway, that fellow don't have the Drinkwater nose."

"Might be on the Cawley side."

"Doubt it."

Conflict builds.

It wasn't long before everybody was concerned about poor Miss Alma. It didn't take long to figure out what *he* was up to. What if he *did*

Characterization by actions.

have such fine manners, would move aside for a lady on the sidewalk with even the subtle indication of an old-fashioned bow, tipping his straw hat high and wide!

Description used to characterize.

What if he had an alligator wallet crisp with the money he was quick to spend everywhere, for flowers, for a bottle of wine, for a Brownie camera and several rolls of film, for a box of fine linen handkerchiefs, initialed? If his summer suits were neat and clean, creased to perfection, if his pointed tapping two-toned shoes gleamed with white and brown where they ought to, there was nevertheless no doubt that he was an opportunist.

Larry Thompson, the plainclothes policeman, patted his stomach and noted that this Mr. Hunter from Atlanta, Georgia, was a type well known to him.

Dialogue used for characterization.

"You can see him by the battalion at most any race track," he said.

"I expect if you was to turn him upside down and give him a fair shake there'd be a regular shower of ticket stubs."

Others' perception of Alma's situation.

"It's a shame," everybody was saying, "to see a sweet, lonely, eccentric woman like Miss Alma taken advantage of."

At any rate, whatever was being said, there he was all smiles, bug-eyed in goggles, Miss Alma likewise smiling, zooming around the countryside on the devilish machine. They were seen together. They appeared together one fine day on the beach. Who can honestly remember

Actions used for characterization.

seeing Miss Alma on the beach? But there they were with a bright umbrella and a striped beach ball that bounced like a joyful planet above the clear bells of her laughter. Oh, yes, and she had been heard whistling, both of them whistling what might have been most any tune as they lunged past baffled spectators in lean profile on the motorcycle.

"I'll keep my eye on that fellow," promised Everett Meriwether, the lawyer. If something—something that we all expected—happened, he'd know first. He would have had a hard time if he meant this literally. They were all over the county. They were seen bidding at an auction, right in the midst of the tourists. Someone with a pair of binoculars and the time to use them swore he saw the two of them heeling along in a swift white tack in a catboat[3] on the bay.

Foreshadowing of later conflict.

"It's dangerous for a woman of middle age to carry on that way" began to be the sentiment among the women.

Others' reaction to Alma's actions.

This seemed to be confirmed by what happened at the El Tropitan nightclub. They were there too, all right, the report was, starting the evening with cocktails and rock lobster dinner, oblivious of any eyebrows. They stayed on for an evening of it, and he became expansive, hiring the orchestra to play a medley of waltzes for her, having their picture taken a half-dozen times, ordering the tall, ice-packed, colored drinks that put the bartender into a frenzy. They laughed and he waved his hands grandiloquently, his diamond ring flashing in the light, as he told her stories. He tried on her glasses, made faces for her, and they sang loudly and off key without much provocation. It might, they said, have gone on marvelously forever if she hadn't slipped and, head over heels no less, fallen with a memorable clatter in the midst of the dance floor while he was teaching her the samba[4].

Description of actions used to characterize.

3. **catboat:** a broad-beamed sailboat with a single mast set near the ship's bow.
4. **samba:** a South American dance whose characteristic movement is a bend of the knee, a dip downward, and a spring back up on each beat of the music.

Conflict between townspeople and stranger deepens.

It was at this point that Lawyer Meriwether decided to step boldly forward. He arranged for a little talk with Mr. Hunter. And so, they say, the two of them sat in Meriwether's office above the bank, the lawyer peering behind thick lenses at his prey, trying, in all fairness, to conceal his stern distaste. They talked for a while of this and that, feeling their way like crabs in a wavering submarine light. This gentleman from Georgia spun his fine straw hat like a gypsy's tambourine on his index finger while he spoke a little and listened more.

Confrontation between lawyer and Rodney Hunter.

"About Miss Alma. . . ." Meriwether finally began.

"The flower of the state of Florida," Hunter interrupted.

"That may be. There may be truth in that," the lawyer said. "She is my client, however, and I have the duty and pleasure of protecting her interests."

"I should say so," Hunter said.

"Now, Mr. Hunter, you've been most kind to the lady during this summer season. . . ."

"I've done nothing at all."

Lawyer expresses community's view of Alma as pitiable spinster.

"On the contrary. You've squired her around. You've offered her a kind of joy and pleasure she's usually been deprived of by virtue of her position in town."

"Really, I have done nothing at all," Hunter said, modestly enough, staring at the sharp points of his shoes.

"It isn't often that a woman of middle age has the good fortune of an admirer years younger than herself."

"What are years, after all?" Hunter said in a whisper. "Alma has the spirit of a thoroughbred."

Meriwether winced at the allusion to the race track and bore down.

"And where will it all be at the end of the summer season?"

Hunter smiled broadly, triumphantly, spun the hat like a potter's wheel on his finger.

"Who knows?" he said. "Who can tell?"

"I'll be frank with you, " the lawyer said. "I don't know for sure what you're up to, but I know you're up to something and I mean to tell you that I intend to protect my client."

"Indeed!" Hunter said, rising, tipping a parody of his sidewalk bow. "I can't say I thank you for your concern, though I thank you enough for being honest with me. Honesty is not to be despised, never, not even when its advocate is no gentleman."

Conflict reaches a peak.

So in a crisp huff he was gone, and Meriwether was left to consider, puzzled, the neat rhythm of the tapped heels as they clicked down the hall. He spun his swivel chair around and looked through the window as Hunter, stiff-backed as a cadet, bowed his bow for the ladies, smiled his smile, and mounted the waiting motorcycle—so indignant, it seemed, at the suggestion that his motives were not wholly honorable, that he forgot to roll up his trousers or put on his goggles.

Meriwether decided to give him a week before he approached Miss Alma on the delicate subject. A week was too long. By the time he'd dressed in a dark suit and slicked down his hair and was walking up the quiet dust of the driveway to call on the lady, the other one, irresponsible, yet shrewd as a cat, had vanished into thin air. The lawyer arrived at least in time to console. He sat stiffly in the living room, vaguely afraid of the close fragility of old things around him, and listened to the sad, inevitable tale of how the confidence man had roared away on his motorcycle, his alligator wallet bulging with new money—not all of it, of course, but all that had been hidden even from the lawyer's knowledge in a copper pitcher for years and years going back to the days of the lemonade stand.

Lawyer assumes Alma is heartbroken.

*Indication
of Alma's
independence.*

*Alma reacts in
an unexpected
way.*

"It was money that I had secreted from Father and from you as well," she said simply.

He decided he would have felt better, more at ease, if she hadn't been so tearless, rational, unperturbed (the women would say, and do, *unrepentant*). She asked him not for pity, not even advice. She was just telling him what had happened.

"I'm sorry, Miss Alma, very sorry."

*Dialogue used to
characterize.*

"Sorry? Why, Everett, what is there to be sorry about? I was duped out of my money by a clever and charming man. Oh, he certainly was *that*—not clever I mean, not terribly clever—but charming, oh, yes, in his own way, quite a charming man."

"Well, we'll certainly catch up with him sooner or later."

*Dialogue reveals
character: Alma
pities Rodney.*

"I think not," she said, standing up. "I rather hope not. That makes me feel a little sad. What would a man like Mr. Rodney Hunter, if that *is* his name, do in jail?"

"Do you know," she said, "it's going to be a little difficult to go back to my bicycle again. There was such a breeze and such a sound. There was so much speed on the motorcycle."

*Characterization
by contrast:
lawyer is more
conservative
than Alma.*

"The bike's a lot safer," he said. "You're more likely to get where you're going even if it takes a little longer."

"Oh, yes," she said. "But not nearly as much fun. I may even buy myself a motorcycle. Do you know how to drive one, Everett? Could you teach me? Have you ever been on one?"

*Lawyer puzzled
by "new" Alma.*

"No ma'am," he said quickly, and he hurried away down the still drive.

Story Analysis

To understand a story and get the most from it, you should probably read it twice. On the first reading you might form a mental picture of the characters, notice the setting and atmosphere, and watch the action build, peak, and fall. On the second reading you may notice details that you missed the first time, and you will gain a better sense of the conflicts in the story and how the author resolves them. After reading a story twice, you will probably have a clearer understanding of its central theme, and you will have begun to recognize how the author uses the elements of the short story.

The following discussion examines the elements of *plot, character, setting, atmosphere, point of view,* and *theme* in "The Confidence Man." As you read the analysis, think about how these elements work together to create an overall effect.

Plot

In analyzing the *plot,* or sequence of events, of "The Confidence Man," the reader might think about the following questions.

- What events make up the plot, and what significance do these events have?
- What *conflicts* complicate the plot?
- What is the *climax,* or turning point, of the story, and how does the plot build toward it?
- What is the resolution of the story?

There are fewer events in "The Confidence Man" than in some other stories, but every event is important. The story's opening sentences introduce the plot: A motorcycle, rushing through the town of Gulfport, is a "first sign" of change. The story then pauses a little to give the reader some background information about Alma Drinkwater, a prominent and eccentric citizen of the small, conservative town.

Development of Conflicts

Both the townsfolk and the tourists think of "Miss Alma" as an eccentric but harmless spinster who is set in her ways. Thus her public appearance with the "charming" and much younger Rodney Hunter—on the back of a motorcycle, no less—introduces a major conflict into the story: the townspeople's image and opinion of Alma is at odds with her uncharacteristic, shocking behavior. The townspeople begin to gossip about Alma and Rodney, who are seen together "all over the county." Their gossip introduces an additional conflict: Rodney versus the townspeople, who are "concerned about poor Miss Alma" and believe that the stranger is "up to" something.

Deepening of Conflicts

The conflicts deepen as Alma continues to "carry on" with the stranger. Everett Meriwether, Alma's lawyer, vows to "keep an eye on" Rodney Hunter, and others comment that Alma's behavior is "dangerous" for a woman her age. At this point in the story, the reader is probably suspicious of Rodney Hunter and concerned about how he might take advantage of Alma.

The townspeople's disapproval of Alma's behavior is "confirmed" by an incident at a local nightclub, where Alma slips and falls while dancing with Rodney. This event compels Alma's lawyer to intervene to "protect" Alma, and he makes an appointment to speak privately with Rodney Hunter. Anticipation of this meeting creates *suspense* for the reader: What will happen when the lawyer confronts the stranger?

The conflict between the townspeople and Rodney Hunter comes to a peak in the next scene, when Rodney Hunter and Everett Meriwether (who represents the town's opinion) meet in the lawyer's office. Although they chat politely at first, both men are braced for a confrontation. The lawyer hints that Rodney is not interested in Alma for herself and that he has dishonorable motives for paying attention to her. Rodney insists that he thinks highly of Alma, and he reacts indignantly to the lawyer's accusations. The reader is left to wonder whether Rodney is sincere. Does he really care for Alma, or is he "up to something"?

Climax

The climax of the story occurs when, one week later, the lawyer visits Alma and discovers that Rodney Hunter has "vanished into thin air" with some of Alma's money. At this point, the conflicts in the story seem to have been resolved: Rodney Hunter was an opportunist as the townsfolk suspected, and his betrayal of Alma has proven that her behavior was "dangerous." However, the story ends with a twist. Far from being heartbroken, Alma is "tearless," "unperturbed," and matter-of-fact about the whole affair. She calmly accepts the consequences of her actions, and she shocks the lawyer (and, perhaps, the reader) by deciding to buy a motorcycle of her own.

Resolution

The resolution of the plot consists of Alma's subtle triumph over both Rodney Hunter and the townspeople. She was duped by the "charming" but "not terribly clever" Rodney (whom she actually feels sorry for), but she feels that the wonderful time she had was worth the price she paid. She is also "unrepentant," which suggests that she cares little for the townspeople's opinion of her and will continue to do as she pleases.

Characterization

Because characterization is one of the most important elements in "The Confidence Man," you will want to think about how the author develops his characters and how he influences the reader's opinion of them. Review the discussion of characterization on page 4 of this book, and then consider the following questions.

- Who is the main character of the story?
- What other characters are important in the story?
- What techniques does the author use to portray the main character?

The main character is Alma Drinkwater. Everett Meriwether and Rodney Hunter also play important roles in the story, but their main function is to help reveal two facets of Alma: the side of her character that the townspeople see and the more complex aspects of her character that Rodney Hunter brings to the forefront.

The author uses the following methods to characterize Alma and to contrast her true character with the townspeople's perceptions of her.

1. He tells the reader what Alma looks like and what her background is. These details, combined with the townspeople's comments, characterize Alma as an eccentric, stubborn, pitiable spinster.

2. He gives the townspeople's perceptions and opinions of Alma and shows their reactions to her behavior. The reader gradually realizes that the townsfolk's view is not objective; they have stereotyped Alma and don't recognize her complexity or her strength of character.

3. He uses dialogue to present the townspeople's comments about Alma and, at the end of the story, to report Alma's conversation with her lawyer. The townspeople's dialogue shows how others see and judge Alma; but Alma's comments about her experiences with Rodney Hunter show the kind of person she actually is.

4. He contrasts Alma's usual actions (such as riding primly on her bicycle and haggling over fish at the wharf) with the unexpected actions that shock the townspeople (such as riding on the back of Rodney Hunter's motorcycle and dancing at a nightclub).

5. He shows Alma's reaction to Rodney Hunter's betrayal of her. Alma's calm matter-of-factness about Rodney's disappearance shows the reader her true character: she has the strength and self-assurance to emerge unharmed from the whole affair, and she has the insight and compassion to feel sorry for Rodney.

Setting and Atmosphere

Setting and atmosphere contribute to the overall effect "The Confidence Man" has for the reader. To determine the role these elements play in the story, you might think about the following questions.

- Where does the story take place?
- What details indicate the kind of community Alma lives in?
- How does the description of Alma's home help to characterize Alma and show how the community sees her?

- How does the atmosphere of the second scene on the main street and the wharf contrast with the first scene set in these places?
- How does this contrast contribute to the overall atmosphere of the story?

Setting

The story takes place in a seaside Florida community. The author gives a variety of details to suggest the type of community it is and to establish the community's view of Alma's role in their town.

For example, the story begins on the town's main street. Since the main street of a small town is generally the center of activity, this setting helps to establish Alma's relationship to the mainstream of the community. Details of setting, which include a "shiny herd of traffic" through which "prim" Alma rides her bicycle, make Alma seem out of place in the town. Descriptions of the wharf also indicate how out of place Alma looks. The hearty, coarse fishermen and their lively, wiggling fish provide a sharp contrast to Alma as she haggles over a fish for her dinner.

The description of Alma's home further establishes her character and helps show how the community sees her. She lives in "a fine old Florida house," which suggests her relative wealth and her standing in the town. But the house is hidden behind "a green jungle of pines and palms and live oaks," and Alma conducts her business with the townsfolk and tourists in an unpainted old lemonade stand at the edge of her property. These details reveal Alma's longstanding isolation from the rest of the community.

The description of Alma's property also hints at her hidden qualities. The overgrown yard is more than evidence of eccentricity: it suggests that Alma cares little about appearances or about impressing the community. The old lemonade stand, which the townspeople see as a pointless eccentricity, actually demonstrates Alma's stubborn independence: instead of conducting business in the house she inherited from her father, she keeps people at a distance and uses as an office something that she built with her own hands.

Atmosphere

The two scenes that take place on the main street and the wharf use the same setting, but they contrast greatly in atmosphere. In the first scene, Alma is silently dodging traffic on her way to the wharf. The noise in the scene comes from the traffic and from the fishermen's activity on the boats. The atmosphere suggests a routine day in which the characters follow established patterns of behavior. In the second scene, however, Alma and Rodney are the focus of attention. The roar of Rodney's motorcycle announces their arrival, and they skid dramatically around the corner as they burst into sight. Now the townspeople and tourists are struck silent—they are speechless with shock. Alma, in contrast, has come alive, her laughter "naked and shrill" as she clings to Rodney on the motorcycle. This scene has an atmosphere of excited change, of surprise and broken routine.

The prevailing feeling in each of these scenes—one calm and relaxed and the other unsettled and shocking—contributes to the overall atmosphere of the story by showing a clear contrast between Alma's usual role in the town and her greatly changed behavior.

Point of View

Point of view—the vantage point from which a story is told—is critically important in "The Confidence Man." Thinking about the following questions will help you to determine how point of view influences the development of the story.
- What is the point of view of the story?
- What aspects of the story are enhanced by the point of view?
- How would the story be different if it were told from Alma's point of view?

The author uses a limited third-person point of view. In other words, the story is told by someone who stands outside of the narrative but whose knowledge of the events and characters is restricted. The reader sees the events of the story exclusively through the townspeople's eyes.

The limited point of view allows the development of the story's central conflict: the conflict between the townspeople's view of Alma and Alma's true character. Because the story is told from the townspeople's point of view, the reader must infer what Alma is really like. If the story were told from the first-person point of view by Alma, there would be no conflict and therefore no story.

Theme

An understanding of a story's theme usually depends on a thoughtful analysis of the story as a whole. Now that you have examined the elements of plot, character, setting, atmosphere, and point of view in "The Confidence Man," you probably have a better grasp of the story's meaning.

• How might you briefly state the story's theme?

Like most well-crafted stories, "The Confidence Man" has an implicit theme—a theme that is not expressed directly. However, the reader might sum up the underlying message of the story in the following way:

People often judge others—particularly those who are different—by appearances and expected patterns of behavior. Such judgments are misleading; to learn the true character and worth of a person, one must abandon stereotypes and get to know the person as an individual.

JAMES RAMSEY ULLMAN
(1907–1971)

James Ramsey Ullman was born in New York and died in Boston, but much of his life was spent in exotic places mountain climbing or beachcombing. He was a freelance writer and journalist who wrote about what he knew firsthand. During the 1930s he wrote and produced plays; after that period he became increasingly interested in mountain climbing and exploring, and his books reflected those interests. In 1963, he was a member of the American Mount Everest expedition. His life appears to have been as exciting as his stories. Among his many books are: *The Other Side of the Mountain, High Conquest, The White Tower, Island of the Blue Macaws, Banner in the Sky, The Age of Mountaineering, Down the Colorado with Major Powell,* and *Americans on Everest.*

TOP MAN

The gorge bent. The walls fell suddenly away, and we came out on the edge of a bleak, boulder-strewn valley. . . . *And there it was.*

Osborn saw it first. He had been leading the column, threading his way slowly among the huge rock masses of the gorge's mouth. Then he came to the first flat bare place and stopped. He neither pointed nor cried out, but every man behind him knew instantly what it was. The long file sprang taut, like a jerked rope. As swiftly as we could, but in complete silence, we came out one by one into the open space where Osborn stood, and we raised our eyes with his.

In the records of the Indian Topographical Survey it says: "Kalpurtha: altitude 27,930 feet. The highest peak in the Garhwal Himalayas and probably fourth highest in the world. Also known as K3. A Tertiary formation of sedimentary limestone. . . ."

There were men among us who had spent months of their lives—in some cases years—reading, thinking, planning about what now lay before us; but at that moment statistics and geology, knowledge, thought, and plans, were as remote and forgotten as the faraway western cities from which we had come. We were men bereft of everything but eyes, everything but the single electric perception: *there it was!*

Before us the valley stretched into miles of rocky desolation. To right and left it was bounded by low ridges, which, as the eye followed them, slowly mounted and drew closer together, until the valley was no longer a valley at all, but a narrowing, rising corridor between the cliffs. What happened then I can describe only as a stupendous crash of music. At the end of the corridor and above it—so far above it that it shut out half the sky—hung the blinding white mass of K3.

It was like the many pictures I had seen, and at the same time utterly unlike them. The shape was there, and the familiar distinguishing features: the sweeping skirt of glaciers; the monstrous vertical precipices of the face and the jagged ice-line of the east ridge; finally, the symmetrical summit pyramid that transfixed the sky. But whereas in the pictures the mountain had always seemed unreal—a dream-image of cloud, snow, and crystal—it was now no longer an image at all. It was a mass: solid, immanent, appalling. We were still too far away to see the windy whipping of its snow plumes or to hear the cannonading of its avalanches, but in that sudden silent moment every man of us was for the first time aware of it not as a picture in his mind, but as a thing, an antagonist. For all its twenty-eight thousand feet of lofty grandeur it seemed, somehow, less to tower than to crouch—a white-hooded giant, secret and remote, but living. Living and on guard.

I turned my eyes from the dazzling glare and looked at my companions. Osborn still stood a little in front of the others. He was absolutely motionless, his young face tense and shining, his eyes devouring the mountain as a lover's might devour the form of his beloved. One could feel in the very set of his body the overwhelming desire that swelled in him to act, to come to grips, to conquer. A little behind him were ranged the other white men of the expedition: Randolph, our leader, Wittmer and Johns, Dr. Schlapp and Bixler. All were still, their eyes cast upward. Off to one side a little stood Nace, the Englishman, the only one among us who was not staring at K3 for the first time. He had been the last to come up out of the gorge and stood now with arms folded on his chest, squinting at the great peak he had known so long and fought so tirelessly and fiercely. His lean British face, under its mask of stubble and windburn, was expressionless. His lips were a thin line, and his eyes seemed almost shut. Behind the sahibs[1] ranged the porters, bent forward over their staffs, their brown seamed faces straining upward from beneath their loads.

For a long while no one spoke or moved. The only sounds between earth and sky were the soft hiss of our breathing and the pounding of our hearts.

Through the long afternoon we wound slowly between the great boulders of the valley and at sundown pitched camp in the bed of a dried-up stream. The porters ate their rations in silence, wrapped themselves in their blankets, and fell asleep under the stars. The rest of us, as was our custom, sat close about the fire that blazed in the circle of tents, discussing the events of the day and the plans for the next. It was a flawlessly clear Himalayan night, and K3 tiered up[2] into the blackness like a monstrous beacon lighted from within. There was no wind, but a great tide of cold air crept down the valley from the ice fields above, penetrating our clothing, pressing gently against the canvas of the tents.

"Another night or two and we'll be needing the sleeping bags," commented Randolph.

Osborn nodded. "We could use them tonight would be my guess."

Randolph turned to Nace. "What do you say, Martin?"

The Englishman puffed at his pipe a moment. "Rather think it might be better to wait," he said at last.

"Wait? Why?" Osborn jerked his head up.

"Well, it gets pretty nippy high up, you know. I've seen it thirty below at twenty-five thousand on the east ridge. Longer we wait for the bags, better acclimated we'll get."

Osborn snorted. "A lot of good being acclimated will do, if we have frozen feet."

"Easy, Paul, easy," cautioned Randolph. "It seems to me Martin's right."

Osborn bit his lip, but said nothing. The other men entered the conversation, and soon it had veered to other matters: the weather, the porters and pack animals, routes, camps, and strategy, the inevitable, inexhaustible topics of the climber's world.

There were all kinds of men among the eight of us, men with a great diversity of background and interest. Sayre Randolph,

1. **sahibs** (sä′ĭbs): a word used in India to refer to people of high rank.
2. **tiered** (tērd) **up:** rose upward in rows or *tiers.*

whom the Alpine Club had named leader of our expedition, had for years been a well-known explorer and lecturer. Now in his middle fifties, he was no longer equal to the grueling physical demands of high climbing, but served as planner and organizer of the enterprise. Wittmer was a Seattle lawyer, who had recently made a name for himself by a series of difficult ascents in the Coast Range of British Columbia. Johns was an Alaskan, a fantastically strong, able sourdough,[3] who had been a ranger in the U.S. Forestry Service and had accompanied many famous Alaskan expeditions. Schlapp was a practicing physician from Milwaukee, Bixler a government meteorologist with a talent for photography. I, at the time, was an assistant professor of geology at an eastern university.

Finally, and preeminently, there were Osborn and Nace. I say "preeminently" because, even at this time, when we had been together as a party for little more than a month, I believe all of us realized that these were the two key men of our venture. None, to my knowledge, ever expressed it in words, but the conviction was none the less there that if any of us were eventually to stand on the summit of K3, it would be one of them, or both. They were utterly dissimilar men. Osborn was twenty-three and a year out of college, a compact, buoyant mass of energy and high spirits. He seemed to be wholly unaffected by either the physical or mental hazards of mountaineering and had already, by virtue of many spectacular ascents in the Alps and Rockies, won a reputation as the most skilled and audacious of younger American climbers. Nace was in his forties—lean, taciturn,[4] introspective. An official in the Indian Civil Service, he had explored and climbed in the Himalayas for twenty years. He had been a member of all five of the unsuccessful British expeditions to K3, and in his last attempt had attained to within five hundred feet of the summit, the highest point which any man had reached on the unconquered giant. This had been the famous, tragic attempt in which his fellow climber and lifelong friend, Captain Furness, had slipped and fallen ten thousand feet to his death. Nace rarely mentioned his name, but on the steel head of his ice ax were engraved the words: TO MARTIN FROM JOHN. If fate were to grant that the ax of any one of us should be planted upon the summit of K3, I hoped it would be this one.

3. **sourdough:** *slang,* pioneer or prospector.
4. **taciturn** (tas'ə·tûrn): reserved, quiet.

Such were the men who huddled about the fire in the deep, still cold of a Himalayan night. There were many differences among us, in temperament as well as in background. In one or two cases, notably that of Osborn and Nace, there had already been a certain amount of friction, and as the venture continued and the struggles and hardships of the actual ascent began, it would, I knew, increase. But differences were unimportant. What mattered—all that mattered—was that our purpose was one: to conquer the monster of rock and ice that now loomed above us in the night; to stand for a moment where no man, no living thing, had ever stood before. To that end we had come from half a world away, across oceans and continents to the fastnesses[5] of inner Asia. To that end we were prepared to endure cold, exhaustion, and danger, even to the very last extremity of human endurance. . . . Why? There is no answer, and at the same time every man among us knew the answer; every man who has ever looked upon a great mountain and felt the fever in his blood to climb and conquer knows the answer. George Leigh Mallory, greatest of mountaineers, expressed it once and for all when he was asked why he wanted to climb unconquered Everest.

"I want to climb it," said Mallory, "because it is there."

Day after day we crept on and upward. Sometimes the mountain was brilliant above us, as it had been when we first saw it; sometimes it was partially or wholly obscured by tiers of clouds. The naked desolation of the valley was unrelieved by any motion, color, or sound; and as we progressed, the great rock walls that enclosed it grew so high and steep that its floor received the sun for less than two hours each day. The rest of the time it lay in ashen half-light, its gloom intensified by the dazzling brilliance of the ice slopes above. As long as we remained there we had the sensation of imprisonment; it was like being trapped at the bottom of a deep well or in a sealed court between great skyscrapers. Soon we were thinking of the ascent of the shining mountain not only as an end in itself, but as an escape.

In our nightly discussions around the fire our conversation narrowed more and more to the immediate problems confronting us, and during them I began to realize that the tension between Osborn and Nace went deeper than I had at first surmised. There

5. **fastnesses:** fortresses or strongholds.

was rarely any outright argument between them—they were both far too able mountain men to disagree on fundamentals—but I saw that at almost every turn they were rubbing each other the wrong way. It was a matter of personalities, chiefly. Osborn was talkative, enthusiastic, optimistic, always chafing to be up and at it, always wanting to take the short straight line to the given point. Nace, on the other hand, was matter-of-fact, cautious, slow. He was the apostle of trial-and-error and watchful waiting. Because of his far greater experience and intimate knowledge of K3, Randolph almost invariably followed his advice, rather than Osborn's, when a difference of opinion arose. The younger man usually capitulated with good grace, but I could tell that he was irked.

During the days in the valley I had few occasions to talk privately with either of them, and only once did either mention the other in any but the most casual manner. Even then, the remarks they made seemed unimportant and I remember them only in view of what happened later.

My conversation with Osborn occurred first. It was while we were on the march, and Osborn, who was directly behind me, came up suddenly to my side. "You're a geologist, Frank," he began without preamble. "What do you think of Nace's theory about the ridge?"

"What theory?" I asked.

"He believes we should traverse[6] under it from the glacier up. Says the ridge itself is too exposed."

"It looks pretty mean through the telescope."

"But it's been done before. He's done it himself. All right, it's tough—I'll admit that. But a decent climber could make it in half the time the traverse will take."

"Nace knows the traverse is longer," I said. "But he seems certain it will be much easier for us."

"Easier for *him* is what he means." Osborn paused, looking moodily at the ground. "He was a great climber in his day. It's a shame a man can't be honest enough with himself to know when he's through." He fell silent and a moment later dropped back into his place in line.

It was that same night, I think, that I awoke to find Nace sitting up in his blanket and staring at the mountain.

"How clear it is!" I whispered.

---

6. **traverse** (trăv'ərs): In climbing, to crisscross instead of going straight up.

The Englishman pointed. "See the ridge?"

I nodded, my eyes fixed on the great, twisting spine of ice that climbed into the sky. I could see now, more clearly than in the blinding sunlight, its huge indentations and jagged, wind-swept pitches. "It looks impossible," I said.

"No, it can be done. Trouble is, when you've made it you're too done in for the summit."

"Osborn seems to think its shortness would make up for its difficulty."

Nace was silent a long moment before answering. Then for the first and only time I heard him speak the name of his dead companion. "That's what Furness thought," he said quietly. Then he lay down and wrapped himself in his blanket.

For the next two weeks the uppermost point of the valley was our home and workshop. We established our base camp as close to the mountain as we could, less than half a mile from the tongue of its lowest glacier, and plunged into the arduous tasks of preparation for the ascent. Our food and equipment were unpacked, inspected and sorted, and finally repacked in lighter loads for transportation to more advanced camps. Hours were spent poring over maps and charts and studying the monstrous heights above us through telescope and binoculars. Under Nace's supervision, a thorough reconnaissance of the glacier was made and the route across it laid out; then began the backbreaking labor of moving up supplies and establishing the chain of camps.

Camps I and II were set up on the glacier itself, in the most sheltered sites we could find. Camp III we built at its upper end, as near as possible to the point where the great rock spine of K3 thrust itself free of ice and began its precipitous ascent. According to our plans, this would be the advance base of operations during the climb. The camps to be established higher up, on the mountain proper, would be too small and too exposed to serve as anything more than one or two nights' shelter. The total distance between the base camp and Camp III was only fifteen miles, but the utmost daily progress of our porters was five miles, and it was essential that we should never be more than twelve hours' march from food and shelter. Hour after hour, day after day, the long file of men wound up and down among the hummocks[7] and crevasses of the

7. **hummocks:** here, mounds of ice.

glacier, and finally the time arrived when we were ready to advance.

Leaving Dr. Schlapp in charge of eight porters at the base camp, we proceeded easily and on schedule, reaching Camp I the first night, Camp II the second, and the advance base the third. No men were left at Camps I and II, inasmuch as they were designed simply as caches for food and equipment; and furthermore we knew we would need all the manpower available for the establishment of the higher camps on the mountain proper.

For more than three weeks now the weather had held perfectly, but on our first night at the advance base, as if by malignant prearrangement of nature, we had our first taste of the fury of a high Himalayan storm. It began with great streamers of lightning that flashed about the mountain like a halo; then heavily through the weird glare, snow began to fall. The wind rose. At first it was only sound—a remote, desolate moaning in the night high above us—but soon it descended, sucked down the deep valley as if into a gigantic funnel. Hour after hour it howled about the tents with hurricane frenzy, and the wild flapping of the canvas dinned in our ears like machine-gun fire.

There was no sleep for us that night or the next. For thirty-six hours the storm raged without lull, while we huddled in the icy gloom of the tents, exerting our last ounce of strength to keep from being buried alive or blown into eternity. At last, on the third morning, it was over, and we came out into a world transformed by a twelve-foot cloak of snow. No single landmark remained as it had been before, and our supplies and equipment were in the wildest confusion. Fortunately there had not been a single serious injury, but it was another three days before we had regained our strength and put the camp in order.

Then we waited. The storm did not return, and the sky beyond the ridges gleamed flawlessly clear; but night and day we could hear the roaring thunder of avalanches on the mountain above us. To have ventured so much as one step into that savage vertical wilderness before the new-fallen snow froze tight would have been suicidal. We chafed or waited patiently, according to our individual temperaments, while the days dragged by.

It was late one afternoon that Osborn returned from a short reconnaissance up the ridge. His eyes were shining and his voice jubilant.

"It's tight!" he cried. "Tight as a drum. We can go!" All of us stopped whatever we were doing. His excitement leaped like an electric spark from one to another. "I went about a thousand feet, and it's sound all the way. What do you say, Sayre? Tomorrow?"

Randolph hesitated, then looked at Nace.

"Better give it another day or two," said the Englishman.

Osborn glared at him. "Why?" he challenged.

"It's usually safer to wait till—"

"Wait! Wait!" Osborn exploded. "Don't you ever think of anything but waiting? My God, man, the snow's firm, I tell you!"

"It's firm down here," Nace replied quietly, "because the sun hits it only two hours a day. Up above it gets the sun twelve hours. It may not have frozen yet."

"The avalanches have stopped."

"That doesn't necessarily mean it will hold a man's weight."

"It seems to me Martin's point—" Randolph began.

Osborn wheeled on him. "Sure," he snapped. "I know. Martin's right. The cautious bloody English are always right. Let him have his way, and we'll be sitting here chewing our nails until the mountain falls down on us." His eyes flashed to Nace. "Maybe with a little less of that bloody cautiousness you English wouldn't have made such a mess of Everest. Maybe your pals Mallory and Furness wouldn't be dead."

"Osborn!" commanded Randolph sharply.

The youngster stared at Nace for another moment, breathing heavily. Then abruptly he turned away.

The next two days were clear and windless, but we still waited, following Nace's advice. There were no further brushes between him and Osborn, but an unpleasant air of restlessness and tension hung over the camp. I found myself chafing almost as impatiently as Osborn himself for the moment when we would break out of that maddening inactivity and begin the assault.

At last the day came. With the first paling of the sky a roped file of men, bent almost double beneath heavy loads, began slowly to climb the ice slope, just beneath the jagged line of the great east ridge. In accordance with prearranged plan, we proceeded in relays, this first group consisting of Nace, Johns, myself, and eight porters. It was our job to ascend approximately two thousand feet in a day's climbing and establish Camp IV at the most level and sheltered site we could find. We would spend the night there and return to the advance base next day, while the second relay, consisting of Osborn, Wittmer, and eight more porters, went up with their loads. This process was to continue until all necessary supplies were at Camp IV, and then the whole thing would be repeated between Camps IV and V and V and VI. From VI, at an altitude of about twenty-six thousand feet, the ablest and fittest men—presumably Nace and Osborn—would make the direct assault on the summit. Randolph and Bixler were to remain at the advance base throughout the operations, acting as directors and co-ordinators. We were under the strictest orders that any man—sahib or porter—who suffered illness or injury should be brought down immediately.

How shall I describe those next two weeks beneath the great ice ridge of K3? In a sense there was no occurrence of importance, and at the same time everything happened that could possibly happen, short of actual disaster. We established Camp IV, came down again, went up again, came down again. Then we crept laboriously higher. With our axes we hacked uncountable thousands of steps in the gleaming walls of ice. Among the rocky outcroppings of the cliffs we clung to holds and strained at ropes until we thought our arms would spring from their sockets. Storms swooped down on us, battered us, and passed. The wind increased, and the air grew steadily colder and more difficult to breathe. One morning two of the porters awoke with their feet frozen black; they had to be sent down. A short while later Johns developed an uncontrollable nosebleed and was forced to descend to a lower camp. Wittmer was suffering from racking headaches and I from a continually dry throat. But providentially, the one enemy we feared the most in that icy gale-lashed hell did not again attack us. No snow fell. And day by day, foot by foot, we ascended.

It is during ordeals like this that the surface trappings of a man are shed and his secret mettle[8] laid bare. There were no shirkers or quitters among us—I had known that from the beginning—but now, with each passing day, it became more manifest which were the strongest and ablest among us. Beyond all argument, these were Osborn and Nace.

Osborn was magnificent. All the boyish impatience and

8. mettle (mĕt′l): courage, spirit.

moodiness which he had exhibited earlier were gone, and, now that he was at last at work in his natural element, he emerged as the peerless mountaineer he was. His energy was inexhaustible, his speed, both on rock and ice, almost twice that of any other man in the party. He was always discovering new routes and short cuts. Often he ascended by the ridge itself, instead of using the traverse beneath it, as had been officially prescribed; but his craftsmanship was so sure and his performance so brilliant that no one ever thought of taking him to task. Indeed, there was such vigor, buoyancy, and youth in everything he did that it gave heart to all the rest of us.

In contrast, Nace was slow, methodical, unspectacular. Since he and I worked in the same relay, I was with him almost constantly, and to this day I carry in my mind the clear image of the man: his tall body bent almost double against endless shimmering slopes of ice; his lean brown face bent in utter concentration on the problem in hand, then raised searchingly to the next; the bright prong of his ax rising, falling, rising, falling, with tireless rhythm, until the steps in the glassy incline were so wide and deep that the most clumsy of the porters could not have slipped from them had he tried. Osborn attacked the mountain head on. Nace studied it, sparred with it, wore it down. His spirit did not flap from his sleeve like a pennon;[9] it was deep inside him—patient, indomitable.

The day soon came when I learned from him what it is to be a great mountaineer. We were making the ascent from Camp IV to V, and an almost perpendicular ice wall had made it necessary for us to come out for a few yards on the exposed crest of the ridge. There were six of us in the party, roped together, with Nace leading, myself second, and four porters bringing up the rear. The ridge at this particular point was free of snow, but razor-thin, and the rocks were covered with a smooth glaze of ice. On either side the mountain dropped away in sheer precipices of five thousand feet.

Suddenly the last porter slipped. I heard the ominous scraping of boot nails behind me and, turning, saw a gesticulating figure plunge sideways into the abyss. There was a scream as the next porter was jerked off too. I remember trying frantically to dig into the ridge with my ax, realizing at the same time it would no more

9. **pennon** (pĕn′ən): flag.

hold against the weight of the falling men than a pin stuck in a wall. Then I heard Nace shout, "Jump!" As he said it, the rope went tight about my waist, and I went hurtling after him into space on the opposite side of the ridge. After me came the nearest porter. . . .

What happened then must have happened in five yards and a fifth of a second. I heard myself cry out, and the glacier, a mile below, rushed up at me, spinning. Then both were blotted out in a violent spasm, as the rope jerked taut. I hung for a moment, an inert mass, feeling that my body had been cut in two; then I swung in slowly to the side of the mountain. Above me the rope lay tight and motionless across the crest of the ridge, our weight exactly counterbalancing that of the men who had fallen on the far slope.

Nace's voice came up from below. "You chaps on the other side!" he shouted. "Start climbing slowly. We're climbing too."

In five minutes we had all regained the ridge. The porters and I crouched panting on the jagged rocks, our eyes closed, the sweat beading our faces in frozen drops. Nace carefully examined the rope that again hung loosely between us.

"All right, men," he said presently. "Let's get on to camp for a cup of tea."

Above Camp V the whole aspect of the ascent changed. The angle of the ridge eased off, and the ice, which lower down had covered the mountain like a sheath, lay only in scattered patches between the rocks. Fresh enemies, however, instantly appeared to take the place of the old. We were now laboring at an altitude of more than twenty-five thousand feet—well above the summits of the highest surrounding peaks—and day and night, without protection or respite, we were buffeted by the fury of the wind. Worse than this was that the atmosphere had become so rarefied it could scarcely support life. Breathing itself was a major physical effort, and our progress upward consisted of two or three painful steps followed by a long period of rest in which our hearts pounded wildly and our burning lungs gasped for air. Each of us carried a small cylinder of oxygen in his pack, but we used it only in emergencies and found that, while its immediate effect was salutary, it left us later even worse off than before. My throat dried and contracted until it felt as if it were lined with brass. The faces of all of us, under our beards and windburn, grew haggard and strained.

But the great struggle was now mental as much as physical. The lack of air induced a lethargy of mind and spirit; confidence and the powers of thought and decision waned, and dark foreboding crept out from the secret recesses of the subconscious. The wind seemed to carry strange sounds, and we kept imagining we saw things which we knew were not there. The mountain, to all of us, was no longer a mere giant of rock and ice; it had become a living thing, an enemy, watching us, waiting for us, hostile, relentless, and aware. Inch by inch we crept upward through that empty forgotten world above the world, and only one last thing remained to us of human consciousness and human will: to go on. To go on.

On the fifteenth day after we had first left the advance base we pitched Camp VI at an altitude of almost twenty-six thousand feet. It was located near the uppermost extremity of the great east ridge, directly beneath the so-called shoulder of the mountain. On the far side of the shoulder the monstrous north face of K3 fell sheer to the glaciers, two miles below. And above it and to the left rose the symmetrical bulk of the summit pyramid. The topmost rocks of its highest pinnacle were clearly visible from the shoulder, and the intervening two thousand feet seemed to offer no insuperable obstacles.

Camp VI, which was in reality no camp at all, but a single tent, was large enough to accommodate only three men. Osborn established it with the aid of Wittmer and one porter; then, the following morning, Wittmer and the porter descended to Camp V, and Nace and I went up. It was our plan that Osborn and Nace should launch the final assault—the next day, if the weather held—with myself in support, following their progress through binoculars and going to their aid or summoning help from below if anything went wrong. As the three of us lay in the tent that night, the summit seemed already within arm's reach, victory securely in our grasp.

And then the blow fell. With malignant timing, which no power on earth could have made us believe was a simple accident of nature, the mountain hurled at us its last line of defense. It snowed.

For a day and a night the great flakes drove down on us, swirling and swooping in the wind, blotting out the summit, the shoulder, everything beyond the tiny white-walled radius of our tents. Hour after hour we lay in our sleeping bags, stirring only to eat or to secure the straining rope and canvas. Our feet froze under their thick layers of wool and rawhide. Our heads and bodies throbbed with a dull nameless aching, and time crept over our numbed minds like a glacier. At last, during the morning of the following day, it cleared. The sun came out in a thin blue sky, and the summit pyramid again appeared above us, now whitely robed in fresh snow. But still we waited. Until the snow either froze or was blown away by the wind it would have been the rashest courting of destruction for us to have ascended a foot beyond the camp. Another day passed. And another.

By the third nightfall our nerves were at the breaking point. For hours on end we had scarcely moved or spoken, and the only sounds in all the world were the endless moaning of the wind outside and the harsh sucking noise of our breathing. I knew that, one way or another, the end had come. Our meager food supply was running out; even with careful rationing there was enough left for only two more days.

Presently Nace stirred in his sleeping bag and sat up. "We'll have to go down tomorrow," he said quietly.

For a moment there was silence in the tent. Then Osborn struggled to a sitting position and faced him.

"No," he said.

"There's still too much loose snow above. We can't make it."

"But it's clear. As long as we can see—"

Nace shook his head. "Too dangerous. We'll go down tomorrow and lay in a fresh supply. Then we'll try again."

"Once we go down we're licked. You know it."

Nace shrugged. "Better to be licked than . . ." The strain of speech was suddenly too much for him and he fell into a violent paroxysm of coughing. When it had passed there was a long silence.

Then suddenly Osborn spoke again. "Look, Nace," he said, "I'm going up tomorrow."

The Englishman shook his head.

"I'm going—understand?"

For the first time since I had known him I saw Nace's eyes flash in anger. "I'm the senior member of this group," he said. "I forbid you to go!"

Osborn jerked himself to his knees, almost upsetting the tiny tent. "You forbid me? This may be your sixth time on this mountain, and all that, but you don't *own* it! I know what you're up to.

You haven't got it in you to make the top yourself, so you don't want anyone else to make it. That's it, isn't it? Isn't it?" He sat down again suddenly, gasping for breath.

Nace looked at him with level eyes. "This mountain has beaten me five times," he said softly. "It killed my best friend. It means more to me to climb it than anything else in the world. Maybe I'll make it and maybe I won't. But if I do, it will be as a rational intelligent human being—not as a fool throwing my life away. . . ."

He collapsed into another fit of coughing and fell back in his sleeping bag. Osborn, too, was still. They lay there inert, panting, too exhausted for speech.

It was hours later that I awoke from dull, uneasy sleep. In the faint light I saw Nace fumbling with the flap of the tent.

"What is it?" I asked.

"Osborn. He's gone."

The words cut like a blade through my lethargy. I struggled to my feet and followed Nace from the tent.

Outside, the dawn was seeping up the eastern sky. It was very cold, but the wind had fallen and the mountain seemed to hang suspended in a vast stillness. Above us the summit pyramid climbed bleakly into space, like the last outpost of a spent and lifeless planet. Raising my binoculars, I swept them over the gray waste. At first I saw nothing but rock and ice; then, suddenly, something moved.

"I've got him," I whispered.

As I spoke, the figure of Osborn sprang into clear focus against a patch of ice. He took three or four slow upward steps, stopped, went on again. I handed the glasses to Nace.

The Englishman squinted through them, returned them to me, and reentered the tent. When I followed, he had already laced his boots and was pulling on his outer gloves.

"He's not far," he said. "Can't have been gone more than half an hour." He seized his ice ax and started out again.

"Wait," I said. "I'm going with you."

Nace shook his head. "Better stay here."

"I'm going with you," I said.

He said nothing further, but waited while I made ready. In a few moments we left the tent, roped up, and started off.

Almost immediately we were on the shoulder and confronted with the paralyzing two-mile drop of the north face; but we negotiated the short exposed stretch without mishap, and in ten minutes were working up the base of the summit pyramid. The going here was easier, in a purely climbing sense: the angle of ascent was not steep, and there was firm rock for hand- and footholds between the patches of snow and ice. Our progress, however, was creepingly slow. There seemed to be literally no air at all to breathe, and after almost every step we were forced to rest, panting and gasping as we leaned forward against our axes. My heart swelled and throbbed with every movement until I thought it would explode.

The minutes crawled into hours and still we climbed. Presently the sun came up. Its level rays streamed across the clouds, far below, and glinted from the summits of distant peaks. But, although the pinnacle of K3 soared a full three thousand feet above anything in the surrounding world, we had scarcely any sense of height. The wilderness of mountain valley and glacier that spread beneath us to the horizon was flattened and remote, an unreal, insubstantial landscape seen in a dream. We had no connection with it, or it with us. All living, all awareness, purpose, and will, was concentrated in the last step and the next: to put one foot before the other; to breathe; to ascend. We struggled on in silence.

I do not know how long it was since we had left the camp—it might have been two hours, it might have been six—when we suddenly sighted Osborn. We had not been able to find him again since our first glimpse through the binoculars; but now, unexpectedly and abruptly, as we came up over a jagged outcropping of rock, there he was. He was at a point, only a few yards above us, where the mountain steepened into an almost vertical wall. The smooth surface directly in front of him was obviously unclimbable, but two alternate routes were presented. To the left, a chimney[10] cut obliquely across the wall, forbiddingly steep, but seeming to offer adequate holds. To the right was a gentle slope of snow that curved upward and out of sight behind the rocks. As we watched, Osborn ascended to the edge of the snow, stopped, and probed it with his ax. Then, apparently satisfied that it would bear his weight he stepped out on the slope.

I felt Nace's body tense. "Paul!" he cried out.

His voice was too weak and hoarse to carry. Osborn continued his ascent.

---

10. **chimney:** formation of rock resembling a chimney.

Nace cupped his hands and called his name again, and this time Osborn turned. "Wait!" cried the Englishman.

Osborn stood still, watching us, as we struggled up the few yards to the edge of the snow slope. Nace's breath came in shuddering gasps, but he climbed faster than I had ever seen him climb before.

"Come back!" he called. "Come off the snow!"

"It's all right. The crust is firm," Osborn called back.

"But it's melting. There's . . ." Nace paused, fighting for air. "There's nothing underneath!"

In a sudden sickening flash I saw what he meant. Looked at from directly below, at the point where Osborn had come to it, the slope on which he stood appeared as a harmless covering of snow over the rocks. From where we were now, however, a little to one side, it could be seen that it was in reality no covering at all, but merely a cornice or unsupported platform clinging to the side of the mountain. Below it was not rock, but ten thousand feet of blue air.

"Come back!" I cried. "Come back!"

Osborn hesitated, then took a downward step. But he never took the next. For in that same instant the snow directly in front of him disappeared. It did not seem to fall or to break away. It was just soundlessly and magically no longer there. In the spot where Osborn had been about to set his foot there was now revealed the abysmal drop of the north face of K3.

I shut my eyes, but only for a second, and when I reopened them Osborn was still, miraculously, there. Nace was shouting, "Don't move! Don't move an inch!"

"The rope—" I heard myself saying.

The Englishman shook his head. "We'd have to throw it, and the impact would be too much. Brace yourself and play it out." As he spoke, his eyes were traveling over the rocks that bordered the snow bridge. Then he moved forward.

I wedged myself into a cleft in the wall and let out the rope which extended between us. A few yards away Osborn stood in the snow, transfixed, one foot a little in front of the other. But my eyes now were on Nace. Cautiously, but with astonishing rapidity, he edged along the rocks beside the cornice. There was a moment when his only support was an inch-wide ledge beneath his feet, another where there was nothing under his feet at all, and he supported himself wholly by his elbows and hands. But he advanced steadily and at last reached a shelf wide enough for him to turn around on. At this point he was perhaps six feet away from Osborn.

"It's wide enough here to hold both of us," he said in a quiet voice. "I'm going to reach out my ax. Don't move until you're sure you have a grip on it. When I pull, jump."

He searched the wall behind him and found a hold for his left hand. Then he slowly extended his ice ax, head foremost, until it was within two feet of Osborn's shoulder. "Grip it!" he cried suddenly. Osborn's hands shot out and seized the ax. "Jump!"

There was a flash of steel in the sunlight and a hunched figure hurtled inward from the snow to the ledge. Simultaneously another figure hurtled out. The haft[11] of the ax jerked suddenly from Nace's hand, and he lurched forward and downward. A violent spasm convulsed his body as the rope went taut. Then it was gone. Nace did not seem to hit the snow; he simply disappeared through it, soundlessly. In the same instant the snow itself was gone. The frayed, yellow end of broken rope spun lazily in space. . . .

Somehow my eyes went to Osborn. He was crouched on the ledge where Nace had been a moment before, staring dully at the ax he held in his hands. Beyond his head, not two hundred feet above, the white untrodden pinnacle of K3 stabbed the sky.

Perhaps ten minutes passed, perhaps a half hour. I closed my eyes and leaned forward motionless against the rock, my face against my arm. I neither thought nor felt; my body and mind alike were enveloped in a suffocating numbness. Through it at last came the sound of Osborn moving. Looking up, I saw he was standing beside me.

"I'm going to try for the top," he said tonelessly.

I merely stared at him.

"Will you come?"

"No," I said.

Osborn hesitated; then turned and began slowly climbing the steep chimney above us. Halfway up he paused, struggling for breath. Then he resumed his laborious upward progress and presently disappeared beyond the crest.

I stayed where I was, and the hours passed. The sun reached its zenith above the peak and sloped away behind it. And at last I

11. **haft:** handle.

heard above me the sound of Osborn returning. As I looked up, his figure appeared at the top of the chimney and began the descent. His clothing was in tatters, and I could tell from his movements that only the thin flame of his will stood between him and collapse. In another few minutes he was standing beside me.

"Did you get there?" I asked dully.

He shook his head. "I couldn't make it," he answered. "I didn't have what it takes."

We roped together silently and began the descent to the camp.

There is nothing more to be told of the sixth assault on K3—at least not from the experiences of the men who made it. Osborn and I reached Camp V in safety, and three days later the entire expedition gathered at the advance base. It was decided, in view of the tragedy that had occurred, to make no further attempt on the summit, and by the end of the week we had begun the evacuation of the mountain.

It remained for another year and other men to reveal the epilogue.

The summer following our attempt a combined English-Swiss expedition stormed the peak successfully. After weeks of hardship and struggle they attained the topmost pinnacle of the giant, only to find that what should have been their great moment of triumph was, instead, a moment of the bitterest disappointment. For when they came out at last upon the summit they saw that they were *not* the first. An ax stood there. Its haft was embedded in rock and ice and on its steel head were the engraved words: TO MARTIN FROM JOHN.

They were sporting men. On their return to civilization they told their story, and the name of the conqueror of K3 was made known to the world.

Meaning

1. Most fiction tries to *show* rather than to describe. How does the author demonstrate the differences between Nace and Osborn before he describes them?

2. *Conflict* in a short story may be **a.** person against person, **b.** individual against society, **c.** human against nature, or **d.** persons against themselves. Which of these conflicts occur in "Top Man"? Justify your answer with specific references to the story.
3. Moments of decision often reveal what a person is really like. In "Top Man," how do the two central characters act at times of decision? Cite examples. Which character do you most admire?

Method

1. The *climax* is the highest point of interest or suspense in a story. It usually marks the turning point, at which the reader can foresee how the struggle will end. What point in this story would you consider the climax? How did the author build toward it?
2. How does the setting of this story become an integral part of the plot? What does it add to the story?
3. *Characterization* may be achieved by **a.** physical description of a character by the author, **b.** a description by another character, **c.** the use of dialogue or conversation, **d.** an explanation of a character's inner thoughts, **e.** the behavior or actions of a character, or **f.** the reactions of a character to another character or to a situation. Which of these methods does Ullman employ? Illustrate your choices with examples from the text.

Language: Meaning from Context

In your reading, you will come across words that are either completely new to you or that you have not noticed before. There are several ways to unlock the meanings of these words. You can consult a dictionary, ask another person, try to relate these words to words you already know, or attack the meaning through context.

Context comes from the Latin prefix *con* (together with) and the Latin verb *texere* (to weave). Applied here, context means the parts of a sentence, paragraph, or speech occurring just before and after a specified word. These words form a setting (a context) which can help to determine the meaning of a particular word when it is used in their company.

For example, look at the following sentences:

1. She flew into a *rage* when she saw her broken vase.
2. Hoop skirts were the *rage* in my grandmother's day.

In the first example, *rage* means "violent anger"; in the second, it means "fashion" or "fad."

However, it is not unusual for an author to suggest ambiguity by using a word with more than one meaning. How might this be true of the title "Top Man"?

When you study a word in context, try to identify the place, time, situation, and speaker or writer associated with each problem word.

Try to define the italicized words in the following sentences, using contextual clues. Then check your definitions with a dictionary.

1. "Osborn was twenty-three and a year out of college, a compact, *buoyant* mass of energy and high spirits."
2. "Osborn was talkative, enthusiastic, optimistic, always *chafing* to be up and at it, always wanting to take the short straight line to a given point."
3. "There were no shirkers or quitters among us—I had known that from the beginning—but now, with each passing day, it became more *manifest* which were the strongest and ablest among us."
4. "The lack of air induced a lethargy of mind and spirit; confidence and the powers of thought and decision waned, and dark *foreboding* crept out from the secret recesses of the subconscious."

Composition

1. In "Top Man," the author uses a number of imaginative comparisons to make scenes vivid to the reader. Write a composition explaining how several of the similes and metaphors that Ullman uses appeal to your senses and emotions and make a scene especially vivid to you. You might first review the definitions of *simile* and *metaphor* in the Glossary of Literary Terms at the back of this textbook. Then reread the story with an eye for similes and metaphors. Focus your discussion on a specific scene in the story.

2. Write a character sketch of one of the two main characters in "Top Man" so that your reader has a clear picture of the man—of

what he looks like and what kind of person he is. As you plan your sketch, list details about the character's physical appearance, personality traits, and actions. From your list, choose the details that will help to create a strong, accurate characterization in your sketch.

JACK LONDON
(1876–1916)

The life story of Jack London is as exciting as any of the novels and stories he wrote. He grew up on the waterfront of Oakland, California. He worked in a bowling alley, a mill, a cannery, and a laundry, led a boy's gang, ran away to sea, traveled over most of the United States as a tramp, prospected for gold in Alaska, and sailed home 1,900 miles in an open boat, all before he was twenty-two years old.

London educated himself primarily at public libraries. He attended high school for one year and the University of California for one year. In *Martin Eden* (1909), his autobiographical novel, he tells how he trained himself to be a professional author, daily studying and producing every kind of writing on a rigid schedule that he set for himself.

London's stories earned him a million dollars and great popularity at the height of his short career. Today he is not considered to be among the greatest of American authors, but his use of realistic detail influenced many other writers.

"To Build a Fire" is typical of London's best work. Here he depicts the splendor and terror of nature, and reveals his ideas about the superiority of animal instinct over human reason.

TO BUILD A FIRE

Day had broken cold and gray, exceedingly cold and gray, when the man turned aside from the main Yukon trail and climbed the high earth bank, where a dim and little-traveled trail led eastward through the fat spruce timberland. It was a steep bank, and he paused for breath at the top, excusing the act to himself by looking at his watch. It was nine o'clock. There was no sun or hint of sun, though there was not a cloud in the sky. It was a clear day, and yet there seemed an intangible pall[1] over the face

---

1. **pall** (pôl): a dark covering, usually a cloth draped over a coffin. Here it refers to the gloomy atmosphere.

of things, a subtle gloom that made the day dark, and that was due to the absence of sun. This fact did not worry the man. He was used to the lack of sun. It had been days since he had seen the sun, and he knew that a few more days must pass before that cheerful orb, due south, would just peep above the skyline and dip immediately from view.

The man flung a look back along the way he had come. The Yukon lay a mile wide and hidden under three feet of ice. On top of this ice were as many feet of snow. It was all pure white, rolling in gentle undulations[2] where the ice jams of the freeze-up had formed. North and south, as far as his eye could see, it was unbroken white, save for a dark hairline that curved and twisted from around the spruce-covered island to the south, and that curved and twisted away into the north, where it disappeared behind another spruce-covered island. This dark hairline was the trail—the main trail—that led south five hundred miles to the Chilkoot Pass, Dyea,[3] and salt water; and that led north seventy miles to Dawson, and still on to the north a thousand miles to Nulato, and finally to St. Michael on the Bering Sea, a thousand miles and half a thousand more.

But all this—the mysterious, far-reaching hairline trail, the absence of sun from the sky, the tremendous cold, and the strangeness and weirdness of it all—made no impression on the man. It was not because he was long used to it. He was a newcomer in the land, a cheechako,[4] and this was his first winter. The trouble with him was that he was without imagination. He was quick and alert in the things of life, but only in the things, and not in the significances. Fifty degrees below zero meant eighty-odd degrees of frost. Such fact impressed him as being cold and uncomfortable, and that was all. It did not lead him to meditate upon his frailty as a creature of temperature, and upon man's frailty in general, able only to live within certain narrow limits of heat and cold, and from there on it did not lead him to the conjectural[5] field of

---

2. **undulations** (ŭn′dyə·lā′shəns): waves. The snow had a rolling appearance.
3. **Dyea** (dī′ā): a former village in southeast Alaska. When gold was discovered in 1896 in the Klondike region, Dyea became the supply center and starting point for the trail over the Chilkoot Pass to the northern mining fields and towns such as Dawson and Nulato.
4. **cheechako** (chē·chä′kō): in Alaska, a newcomer; a tenderfoot.
5. **conjectural** (kən·jĕk′chər·əl): based on surmise or guesswork. To conjecture is to come to conclusions using incomplete or merely probable evidence.

immortality and man's place in the universe. Fifty degrees below zero stood for a bite of frost that hurt and that must be guarded against by the use of mittens, ear flaps, warm moccasins, and thick socks. Fifty degrees below zero was to him just precisely fifty degrees below zero. That there should be anything more to it than that was a thought that never entered his head.

As he turned to go on, he spat speculatively. There was a sharp, explosive crackle that startled him. He spat again. And again, in the air, before it could fall to the snow, the spittle crackled. He knew that at fifty below, spittle crackled on the snow, but this spittle had crackled in the air. Undoubtedly it was colder than fifty below—how much colder he did not know. But the temperature did not matter. He was bound for the old claim on the left fork of Henderson Creek, where the boys were already. They had come over across the divide from the Indian Creek country, while he had come the roundabout way to take a look at the possibilities of getting out logs in the spring from the islands in the Yukon. He would be into camp by six o'clock; a bit after dark, it was true, but the boys would be there, a fire would be going, and a hot supper would be ready. As for lunch, he pressed his hand against the protruding bundle under his jacket. It was also under his shirt, wrapped up in a handkerchief and lying against the naked skin. It was the only way to keep the biscuits from freezing. He smiled agreeably to himself as he thought of those biscuits, each cut open and sopped in bacon grease, and each enclosing a generous slice of fried bacon.

He plunged in among the big spruce trees. The trail was faint. A foot of snow had fallen since the last sled had passed over, and he was glad he was without a sled, traveling light. In fact, he carried nothing but the lunch wrapped in the handkerchief. He was surprised, however, at the cold. It certainly was cold, he concluded, as he rubbed his numb nose and cheekbones with his mittened hand. He was a warm-whiskered man, but the hair on his face did not protect the high cheekbones and the eager nose that thrust itself aggressively into the frosty air.

At the man's heels trotted a dog, a big native husky, the proper wolf dog, gray-coated and without any visible or temperamental difference from its brother, the wild wolf. The animal was depressed by the tremendous cold. It knew that it was no time for traveling. Its instinct told it a truer tale than was told to the man by the man's judgment. In reality, it was not merely colder than fifty above zero, it meant that one hundred and seven degrees of frost obtained. The dog did not know anything about thermometers. Possibly in its brain there was no sharp consciousness of a condition of very cold such as was in the man's brain. But the brute had its instinct. It experienced a vague but menacing apprehension that subdued it and made it slink along at the man's heels and that made it question eagerly every unwonted[6] movement of the man, as if expecting him to go into camp or to seek shelter somewhere and build a fire. The dog had learned fire, and it wanted fire, or else to burrow under the snow and cuddle its warmth away from the air.

The frozen moisture of its breathing had settled on its fur in a fine powder of frost, and especially were its jowls, muzzle, and eyelashes whitened by its crystaled breath. The man's red beard and mustache were likewise frosted, but more solidly, the deposit taking the form of ice and increasing with every warm, moist breath he exhaled. Also, the man was chewing tobacco, and the muzzle of ice held his lips so rigidly that he was unable to clear his chin when he expelled the juice. the result was that a crystal beard of the color and solidity of amber[7] was increasing its length on his chin. If he fell down it would shatter itself, like glass, into brittle fragments. But he did not mind the appendage. It was the penalty all tobacco chewers paid in that country, and he had been out before in two cold snaps. They had not been so cold as this, he knew, but by the spirit thermometer[8] at Sixty Mile he knew they had been registered at fifty below and at fifty-five.

He held on through the level stretch of woods for several miles, crossed a wide flat, and dropped down a bank to the frozen bed of a small stream. This was Henderson Creek, and he knew he was ten miles from the forks. He looked at his watch. It was ten o'clock. He was making four miles an hour, and he calculated that he would arrive at the forks at half-past twelve. He decided to celebrate that event by eating his lunch there.

The dog dropped in again at his heels, with a tail drooping discouragement, as the man swung along the creek bed. The fur-

6. **unwonted** (ŭn′·wŭn′tĭd): unusual, unfamiliar.
7. **amber:** a reddish- or brownish-yellow vegetable resin used in making beads.
8. **spirit thermometer:** an alcohol thermometer used particularly in severe cold.

row of the old sled trail was plainly visible, but a dozen inches of snow covered the marks of the last runners. In a month no man had come up or down that silent creek. The man held steadily on. He was not much given to thinking, and just then particularly he had nothing to think about save that he would eat lunch at the forks and that at six o'clock he would be in camp with the boys. There was nobody to talk to, and had there been, speech would have been impossible because of the ice muzzle on his mouth. So he continued monotonously to chew tobacco and to increase the length of his amber beard.

Once in a while the thought reiterated itself that it was very cold and that he had never experienced such cold. As he walked along he rubbed his cheekbones and nose with the back of his mittened hand. He did this automatically, now and again changing hands. But rub as he would, the instant he stopped his cheekbones went numb, and the following instant the end of his nose went numb. He was sure to frost his cheeks; he knew that, and experienced a pang of regret that he had not devised a nose strap of the sort Bud wore in cold snaps. Such a strap passed across the cheeks, as well, and saved them. But it didn't matter much, after all. What were frosted cheeks? A bit painful, that was all; they were never serious.

Empty as the man's mind was of thought, he was keenly observant, and he noticed the changes in the creek, the curves and bends and timber jams, and always he sharply noted where he placed his feet. Once, coming around a bend, he shied abruptly, like a startled horse, curved away from the place where he had been walking, and retreated several paces back along the trail. The creek, he knew, was frozen clear to the bottom—no creek could contain water in that arctic winter—but he knew also that there were springs that bubbled out from the hillsides and ran along under the snow and on top of the ice of the creek. He knew that the coldest snaps never froze these springs, and he knew likewise their danger. They were traps. They hid pools of water under the snow that might be three inches deep, or three feet. Sometimes a skin of ice half an inch thick covered them, and in turn was covered by the snow. Sometimes there were alternate layers of water and ice skin, so that when one broke through he kept on breaking through for a while, sometimes wetting himself to the waist.

That was why he had shied in such panic. He had felt the give under his feet and heard the crackle of a snow-hidden ice skin. And to get his feet wet in such a temperature meant trouble and danger. At the very least it meant delay, for he would be forced to stop and build a fire, and under its protection to bare his feet while he dried his socks and moccasins. He stood and studied the creek bed and its banks, and decided that the flow of water came from the right. He reflected a while, rubbing his nose and cheeks, then skirted to the left, stepping gingerly and testing the footing for each step. Once clear of the danger, he took a fresh chew of tobacco and swung along at his four-mile gait.

In the course of the next two hours he came upon several similar traps. Usually the snow above the hidden pools had a sunken, candied appearance that advertised the danger. Once again, however, he had a close call; and once, suspecting danger, he compelled the dog to go on in front. The dog did not want to go. It hung back until the man shoved it forward, and then it went quickly across the white, unbroken surface. Suddenly it broke through, floundered to one side, and got away to firmer footing. It had wet its forefeet and legs, and almost immediately the water that clung to it turned to ice. It made quick efforts to lick the ice off its legs, then dropped down in the snow and began to bite out the ice that had formed between the toes. This was a matter of instinct. To permit the ice to remain would mean sore feet. It did not know this. It merely obeyed the mysterious prompting that arose from the deep crypts[9] of its being. But the man knew, having achieved a judgment on the subject, and he removed the mitten from his right hand and helped tear out the ice particles. He did not expose his fingers more than a minute, and was astonished at the swift numbness that smote[10] them. It certainly was cold. He pulled on the mitten hastily, and beat the hand savagely across his chest.

At twelve o'clock the day was at its brightest. Yet the sun was too far south on its winter journey to clear the horizon. The bulge of the earth intervened between it and Henderson Creek, where

---

9. crypts (krĭpts): usually chambers or vaults wholly or partly underground, used for burial. As used here, the word refers to something deep and unknown in an animal's nature that causes it to act instinctively to protect itself.

10. smote (smōt): past tense of the verb *smite*, which means to strike, often suddenly and with great force.

the man walked under a clear sky at noon and cast no shadow. At half-past twelve, to the minute, he arrived at the forks of the creek. He was pleased at the speed he had made. If he kept it up, he would certainly be with the boys by six. He unbuttoned his jacket and shirt and drew forth his lunch. The action consumed no more than a quarter of a minute, yet in that brief moment the numbness laid hold of the exposed fingers. He did not put the mitten on, but instead struck the fingers a dozen sharp smashes against his leg. Then he sat down on a snow-covered log to eat. The sting that followed upon the striking of his fingers against his leg ceased so quickly that he was startled. He had had no chance to take a bite of biscuit. He struck the fingers repeatedly and returned them to the mitten, baring the other hand for the purpose of eating. He tried to take a mouthful, but the ice muzzle prevented. He had forgotten to build a fire and thaw out. He chuckled at his foolishness, and as he chuckled he noted the numbness creeping into the exposed fingers. Also, he noted that the stinging which had first come to his toes when he sat down was already passing away. He wondered whether the toes were warm or numb. He moved them inside the moccasins and decided that they were numb.

He pulled the mitten on hurriedly and stood up. He was a bit frightened. He stamped up and down until the stinging returned into the feet. It certainly was cold, was his thought. That man from Sulfur Creek had spoken the truth when telling how cold it sometimes got in the country. And he had laughed at him at the time! That showed one must not be too sure of things. There was no mistake about it, it *was* cold. He strode up and down, stamping his feet and threshing his arms, until reassured by the returning warmth. Then he got out matches and proceeded to make a fire. From the undergrowth, where high water of the previous spring had lodged a supply of seasoned twigs, he got his firewood. Working carefully from a small beginning, he soon had a roaring fire, over which he thawed the ice from his face and in the protection of which he ate his biscuits. For the moment the cold of space was outwitted. The dog took satisfaction in the fire, stretching out close enough for warmth and far enough away to escape being singed.

When the man had finished, he filled his pipe and took his comfortable time over a smoke. Then he pulled on his mittens, settled the ear flaps of his cap firmly about his ears, and took the creek trail up the left fork. The dog was disappointed and yearned back toward the fire. This man did not know cold. Possibly all the of cold one hundred and seven degrees below freezing point. But the dog knew; all its ancestry knew, and it had inherited the knowledge. And it knew that it was not good to walk abroad in such fearful cold. It was the time to lie snug in a hole in the snow and wait for a curtain of cloud to be drawn across the face of outer space whence this cold came. On the other hand, there was no keen intimacy between the dog and the man. The one was the toil-slave of the other, and the only caresses it had ever received were the caresses of the whiplash and of harsh and menacing throat sounds that threatened the whiplash. So the dog made no effort to communicate its apprehension to the man. It was not concerned in the welfare of the man; it was for its own sake that it yearned back toward the fire. But the man whistled, and spoke to it with the sound of whiplashes, and the dog swung in at the man's heels and followed after.

The man took a chew of tobacco and proceeded to start a new amber beard. Also, his moist breath quickly powdered with white his mustache, eyebrows, and lashes. There did not seem to be so many springs on the left fork of the Henderson, and for half an hour the man saw no signs of any. And then it happened. At a place where there were no signs, where the soft, unbroken snow seemed to advertise solidity beneath, the man broke through. It was not deep. He wet himself halfway to the knees before he floundered out to the firm crust.

He was angry, and cursed his luck aloud. He had hoped to get into camp with the boys at six o'clock, and this would delay him an hour, for he would have to build a fire and dry out his footgear. This was imperative at that low temperature—he knew that much; and he turned aside to the bank, which he climbed. On top, tangled in the underbrush about the trunks of several small spruce trees, was a highwater deposit of dry firewood—sticks and twigs, principally, but also larger portions of seasoned branches and fine, dry, last year's grasses. He threw down several large pieces on top of the snow. This served for a foundation and prevented the young flame from drowning itself in the snow it otherwise would melt. The flame he got by touching a match to a small shred of birch bark that he took from his pocket. This burned even more readily than paper. Placing it on the foundation, he fed the young flame with wisps of dry grass and with the tiniest dry twigs.

He worked slowly and carefully, keenly aware of his danger. Gradually, as the flame grew stronger, he increased the size of the twigs with which he fed it. He squatted in the snow, pulling the twigs out from their entanglement in the brush and feeding directly to the flame. He knew there must be no failure. When it is seventy-five below zero, a man must not fail in his first attempt to build a fire—that is, if his feet are wet. If his feet are dry, and he fails, he can run along the trail for a half a mile and restore his circulation. But the circulation of wet and freezing feet cannot be restored by running when it is seventy-five below. No matter how fast he runs, the wet feet will freeze the harder.

All this the man knew. The old-timer on Sulfur Creek had told him about it the previous fall, and now he was appreciating the advice. Already all sensation had gone out of his feet. To build the fire, he had been forced to remove his mittens, and the fingers had quickly gone numb. His pace of four miles an hour had kept his heart pumping blood to the surface of his body and to all the extremities. But the instant he stopped, the action of the pump eased down. The cold of space smote the unprotected tip of the planet, and he, being on that unprotected tip, received the full force of the blow. The blood of his body recoiled before it. The blood was alive, like the dog, and like the dog it wanted to hide away and cover itself up from the fearful cold. So long as he walked four miles an hour, he pumped that blood, willy-nilly, to the surface; but now it ebbed away and sank down into the recesses of his body. The extremities were the first to feel its absence. His wet feet froze the faster, and his exposed fingers numbed the faster, though they had not yet begun to freeze. Nose and cheeks were already freezing, while the skin of all his body chilled as it lost its blood.

But he was safe. Toes and nose and cheeks would be only touched by the frost, for the fire was beginning to burn with strength. He was feeding it with twigs the size of his finger. In another minute he would be able to feed it with branches the size of his wrist, and then he could remove his wet footgear, and, while it dried, he could keep his naked feet warm by the fire, rubbing them at first, of course, with snow. The fire was a success. He was safe. He remembered the advice of the old-timer on Sulfur Creek, and smiled. The old-timer had been very serious in laying down the law that no man must travel alone in the Klondike after fifty below. Well, here he was; he had had the accident; he was alone;

and he had saved himself. Those old-timers were rather womanish, some of them, he thought. All a man had to do was to keep his head and he was all right. Any man who was a man could travel alone. But it was surprising, the rapidity with which his cheeks and nose were freezing. And he had not thought his fingers could go lifeless in so short a time. Lifeless they were, for he could scarcely make them move together to grip a twig, and they seemed remote from his body and from him. When he touched a twig he had to look and see whether or not he had hold of it. The wires were pretty well down between him and his finger ends.

All of which counted for little. There was the fire, snapping and crackling and promising life with every dancing flame. He started to untie his moccasins. They were coated with ice; the thick German socks were like sheaths of iron halfway to the knees; and the moccasin strings were like rods of steel all twisted and knotted as by some conflagration.[11] For a moment he tugged with his numb fingers, then, realizing the folly of it, he drew his sheath knife.

But before he could cut the strings, it happened. It was his own fault, or, rather, his mistake. He should not have built the fire under the spruce tree. He should have built it in the open. But it had been easier to pull the twigs from the bush and drop them directly on the fire. Now the tree under which he had done this carried a weight of snow on its boughs. No wind had blown for weeks, and each bough was fully freighted. Each time he had pulled a twig he had communicated a slight agitation to the tree—an imperceptible agitation, so far as he was concerned, but an agitation sufficient to bring about the disaster. High up in the tree one bough capsized its load of snow. This fell on the boughs beneath, capsizing them. This process continued, spreading out and involving the whole tree. It grew like an avalanche, and it descended without warning upon the man and the fire, and the fire was blotted out! Where it had burned was a mantle of fresh and disordered snow.

The man was shocked. It was as though he had just heard his own sentence of death. For a moment he sat and stared at the spot where the fire had been. Then he grew very calm. Perhaps the old-timer on Sulfur Creek was right. If he had only had a trail-mate, he would have been in no danger now. The trailmate could

11. **conflagration** (kŏn'flə·grā'shən): a large, disastrous fire.

have built the fire. Well, it was up to him to build the fire over again, and this second time there must be no failure. Even if he succeeded, he would most likely lose some toes. His feet must be badly frozen by now, and there would be some time before the second fire was ready.

Such were his thoughts, but he did not sit and think them. He was busy all the time they were passing through his mind. He made a new foundation for a fire, this time in the open, where no treacherous tree could blot it out. Next he gathered dry grasses and tiny twigs from the high-water flotsam.[12] He could not bring his fingers together to pull them out, but he was able to gather them by the handful. In this way he got many rotten twigs and bits of green moss that were undesirable, but it was the best he could do. He worked methodically, even collecting an armful of the larger branches to be used later when the fire gathered strength. And all the while the dog sat and watched him, a certain yearning wistfulness in its eyes, for it looked upon him as the fire provider, and the fire was slow in coming.

When all was ready, the man reached in his pocket for a second piece of birch bark. He knew the bark was there, and, though he could not feel it with his fingers, he could hear its crisp rustling as he fumbled for it. Try as he would, he could not clutch hold of it. And all the time, in his consciousness, was the knowledge that each instant his feet were freezing. This thought tended to put him in a panic, but he fought against it and kept calm. He pulled on his mittens with his teeth, and threshed his arms back and forth, beating his hands with all his might against his sides. He did this sitting down, and he stood up to do it; and all the while the dog sat in the snow, its wolf brush of a tail curled around warmly over its forefeet, its sharp wolf ears pricked forward intently as it watched the man. And the man, as he beat and threshed with his arms and hands, felt a great surge of envy as he regarded the creature that was warm and secure in its natural covering.

After a time he was aware of the first faraway signals of sensation in his beaten fingers. The faint tingling grew stronger till it evolved into a stinging ache that was excruciating,[13] but which

---

12. **flotsam** (flŏt′səm): the floating wreckage of a ship or its cargo; hence, anything drifting about on a body of water. The word is derived from the Old English verb *flotian,* to float.
13. **excruciating** (ĭks·kroo′shē·ā′ting): causing great pain.

the man hailed with satisfaction. He stripped the mitten from his right hand and fetched forth the birch bark. The exposed fingers were quickly going numb again. Next he brought out his bunch of sulfur matches. But the tremendous cold had already driven the life out of his fingers. In his effort to separate one match from the others, the whole bunch fell in the snow. He tried to pick it out of the snow, but failed. The dead fingers could neither touch nor clutch. He was very careful. He drove the thought of his freezing feet, and nose, and cheeks, out of his mind, devoting his whole soul to the matches. He watched, using the sense of vision in place of that of touch, and when he saw his fingers on each side of the bunch, he closed them—that is, he willed to close them, for the wires were down, and the fingers did not obey. He pulled the mitten on the right hand, and beat it fiercely against his knee. Then, with both mittened hands, he scooped the bunch of matches, along with much snow, into his lap. Yet he was no better off.

After some manipulation he managed to get the bunch between the heels of his mittened hands. In this fashion he carried it to his mouth. The ice crackled and snapped when by a violent effort he opened his mouth. He drew the lower jaw in, curled the upper lip out of the way, and scraped the bunch with his upper teeth in order to separate a match. He succeeded in getting one, which he dropped on his lap. He was no better off. He could not pick it up. Then he devised a way. He picked it up in his teeth and scratched it on his leg. Twenty times he scratched before he succeeded in lighting it. As it flamed he held it with his teeth to the birch bark. But the burning brimstone[14] went up his nostrils and into his lungs, causing him to cough spasmodically.[15] The match fell into the snow and went out.

The old-timer on Sulfur Creek was right, he thought in the moment of controlled despair that ensued: after fifty below, a man should travel with a partner. He beat his hands, but failed in exciting any sensation. Suddenly he bared both hands, removing the mittens with his teeth. He caught the whole bunch between the heels of his hands. His arm muscles, not being frozen, enabled him to press the hand heels tightly against the matches. Then he scratched the bunch along his leg. It flared into flame, seventy

14. **brimstone:** sulfur.
15. **spasmodically** (spăz·mŏd'i·kə·lē): suddenly and violently.

sulfur matches at once! There was no wind to blow them out. He kept his head to one side to escape the strangling fumes, and held the blazing bunch to the birch bark. As he so held it, he became aware of sensation in his hand. His flesh was burning. He could smell it. Deep down below the surface he could feel it. The sensation developed into pain that grew acute. And still he endured it, holding the flame of the matches clumsily to the bark that would not light readily because his own burning hands were in the way, absorbing most of the flame.

At last, when he could endure no more, he jerked his hands apart. The blazing matches fell sizzling into the snow, but the birch bark was alight. He began laying dry grass and the tiniest twigs on the flame. He could not pick and choose, for he had to lift the fuel between the heels of his hands. Small pieces of rotten wood and green moss clung to the twigs, and he bit them off as well as he could with his teeth. He cherished the flame carefully and awkwardly. It meant life, and it must not perish. The withdrawal of blood from the surface of his body now made him begin to shiver, and he grew more awkward. A large piece of green moss fell squarely on the little fire. He tried to poke it out with his fingers, but his shivering frame made him poke too far, and he disrupted the nucleus of the little fire, the burning grasses and tiny twigs separating and scattering. He tried to poke them together again, but in spite of the tenseness of the effort, his shivering got away with him, and the twigs were hopelessly scattered. Each twig gushed a puff of smoke and went out. The fire provider had failed. As he looked apathetically[16] about him, his eyes chanced on the dog, sitting across the ruins of the fire from him, in the snow, making restless, hunching movements, slightly lifting one forefoot and then the other, shifting its weight back and forth on them with wistful eagerness.

The sight of the dog put a wild idea into his head. He remembered the tale of the man, caught in a blizzard, who killed a steer and crawled inside the carcass, and so was saved. He would kill the dog and bury his hands in the warm body until the numbness went out of them. Then he could build another fire. He spoke to the dog, calling it to him; but in his voice was a strange note of fear that frightened the animal, who had never known the man to speak in such a way before. Something was the matter, and its

16. **apathetically** (ăp′ə·thĕt′ĭ·kə·lē): without interest or emotion.

suspicious nature sensed danger—it knew not what danger, but somewhere, somehow, in its brain arose an apprehension of the man. It flattened its ears down at the sound of the man's voice, and its restless, hunching movements and the liftings and shiftings of its forefeet became more pronounced; but it would not come to the man. He got on his hands and knees and crawled toward the dog. This unusual posture again excited suspicion, and the animal sidled[17] mincingly[18] away.

The man sat up in the snow for a moment and struggled for calmness. Then he pulled on his mittens, by means of his teeth, and got up on his feet. He glanced down at first in order to assure himself that he was really standing up, for the absence of sensation in his feet left him unrelated to the earth. His erect position in itself started to drive the webs of suspicion from the dog's mind; and when he spoke peremptorily,[19] with the sound of whiplashes in his voice, the dog rendered its customary allegiance and came to him. As it came within reaching distance, the man lost his control. His arms flashed out to the dog, and he experienced genuine surprise when he discovered that his hands could not clutch, that there was neither bend nor feeling in the fingers. He had forgotten for the moment that they were frozen and that they were freezing more and more. All this happened quickly, and before the animal could get away, he encircled its body with his arms. He sat down in the snow, and in this fashion held the dog, while it snarled and whined and struggled.

But it was all he could do, hold its body encircled in his arms and sit there. He realized that he could not kill the dog. There was no way to do it. With his helpless hands he could neither draw nor hold his sheath knife nor throttle[20] the animal. He released it, and it plunged wildly away, its tail between its legs and still snarling. It halted forty feet away and surveyed him curiously, with ears sharply pricked forward. The man looked down at his hands in order to locate them, and found them hanging on the ends of his arms. It struck him as curious that one should have to use his eyes in order to find out where his hands were. He began threshing his arms back and forth, beating the mittened hands against his sides.

17. **sidled** (sīd'əld): moved sideways in a cautious manner.
18. **mincingly** (mĭn'sĭng·lē): with short steps in a dainty, affected manner.
19. **peremptorily** (pə·rĕmp'tə·rə·lē): in a commanding manner.
20. **throttle** (thrŏt'l): choke or strangle. What is the mechanical meaning of this word?

He did this for five minutes, violently, and his heart pumped enough blood up to the surface to put a stop to his shivering. But no sensation was aroused in his hands. He had an impression that they hung like weights on the ends of his arms, but when he tried to run the impression down, he could not find it.

A certain fear of death, dull and oppressive, came to him. This fear quickly became poignant[21] as he realized that it was no longer a mere matter of freezing his fingers and toes, or of losing his hands and feet, but that it was a matter of life and death, with the chances against him. This threw him into a panic, and he turned and ran up the creek bed along the old, dim trail. The dog joined in behind and kept up with him. He ran blindly, without intention, in fear such as he had never known in his life. Slowly, as he plowed and floundered through the snow, he began to see things again—the banks of the creek, the old timber jams, the leafless aspens, and the sky. The running made him feel better. He did not shiver. Maybe, if he ran on, his feet would thaw out; and, anyway, if he ran far enough, he would reach the camp and the boys. Without doubt he would lose some fingers and toes and some of his face; but the boys would take care of him, and save the rest of him when he got there. And at the same time there was another thought in his mind that said he would never get to the camp and the boys; that it was too many miles away, that the freezing had too great a start on him, and that he would soon be stiff and dead. This thought he kept in the background and refused to consider. Sometimes it pushed itself forward and demanded to be heard, but he thrust it back and strove to think of other things.

It struck him as curious that he could run at all on feet so frozen that he could not feel them when they struck the earth and took the weight of his body. He seemed to himself to skim along above the surface, and to have no connection with the earth. Somewhere he had once seen a winged Mercury,[22] and he wondered if Mercury felt as he felt when skimming over the earth.

His theory of running until he reached camp and the boys had one flaw in it: he lacked the endurance. Several times he stumbled, and finally he tottered, crumpled up, and fell. When he tried to rise, he failed. He must sit and rest, he decided, and next

21. **poignant** (poin′yənt): painfully affecting the feelings; piercing.
22. **Mercury:** in Roman mythology, the herald and messenger of the gods. He is depicted as having winged feet.

time he would merely walk and keep on going. As he sat and regained his breath, he noted that he was feeling quite warm and comfortable. He was not shivering, and it even seemed that a warm glow had come to his chest and trunk. And yet, when he touched his nose or cheeks, there was no sensation. Running would not thaw them out. Nor would it thaw out his hands and feet. Then the thought came to him that the frozen portions of his body must be extending. He tried to keep this thought down, to forget it, to think of something else; he was aware of the panicky feeling that it caused, and he was afraid of the panic. But the thought asserted itself, and persisted, until it produced a vision of his body totally frozen. This was too much, and he made another wild run along the trail. Once he slowed down to a walk, but the thought of the freezing extending itself made him run again.

And all the time the dog ran with him, at his heels. When he fell down a second time, it curled its tail over its forefeet and sat in front of him, facing him, curiously eager and intent. The warmth and security of the animal angered him, and he cursed it till it flattened down its ears appeasingly.[23] This time the shivering came more quickly upon the man. He was losing in his battle with the frost. It was creeping into his body from all sides. The thought of it drove him on, but he ran no more than a hundred feet when he staggered and pitched headlong. It was his last panic. When he had recovered his breath and control, he sat up and entertained in his mind the conception of meeting death with dignity. However, the conception did not come to him in such terms. His idea of it was that he had been making a fool of himself, running around like a chicken with its head cut off—such was the simile that occurred to him. Well, he was bound to freeze anyway, and he might as well take it decently. With this new-found peace of mind came the first glimmerings of drowsiness. A good idea, he thought, to sleep off to death. It was like taking an anesthetic.[24] Freezing was not so bad as people thought. There were lots worse ways to die.

He pictured the boys finding his body next day. Suddenly he found himself with them, coming along the trail and looking for himself. And, still with them, he came around a turn in the trail and found himself lying in the snow. He did not belong with

23. **appeasingly:** trying to make peace.
24. **anesthetic** (ăn'ĭs·thĕt'ĭk): a drug or gas that causes loss of physical sensation or pain.

himself any more, for even then he was out of himself, standing with the boys and looking at himself in the snow. It certainly was cold, was his thought. When he got back to the States, he could tell the folks what real cold was. He drifted on from this to a vision of the old-timer on Sulfur Creek. He could see him quite clearly, warm and comfortable, and smoking a pipe.

"You were right, old hoss; you were right," the man mumbled to the old-timer of Sulfur Creek.

Then the man drowsed off into what seemed to him the most comfortable and satisfying sleep he had ever known. The dog sat facing him and waiting. The brief day drew to a close in a long, slow twilight. There were no signs of a fire to be made, and, besides, never in the dog's experience had it known a man to sit like that in the snow and make no fire. As the twilight drew on, its eager yearning for the fire mastered it, and with a great lifting and shifting of forefeet, it whined softly, then flattened its ears down in anticipation of being chidden[25] by the man. But the man remained silent. Later, the dog whined loudly. And still later it crept close to the man and caught the scent of death. This made the animal bristle[26] and back away. A little longer it delayed, howling under the stars that leaped and danced and shone brightly in the cold sky. Then it turned and trotted up the trail in the direction of the camp it knew, where were the other food providers and fire providers.

25. chidden (chĭd'n): scolded.
26. bristle: become agitated; take on an aggressive appearance.

Meaning

1. Cite incidents in the story that indicate the dog's instinct for survival. In what way is the animal's instinct more accurate and effective than the man's judgment?
2. What force defeats the man's attempts to build a fire? To what extent did the man defeat himself?
3. With the understanding you have gained from reading the entire story, list those things that could have made the man victorious in his struggle with the elements.

Method

1. The *protagonist* is the main character in a story. The *antagonist* is the person, place, idea, or force that opposes the protagonist. Identify the protagonist and the antagonist in this story. List some incidents that will support your answer.
2. What point in the story do you consider the climax? What descriptive details help to heighten the climax?
3. Why do you think the author did not name his main character?
4. What feeling or mood does London arouse by his repetition of the words *cold* and *gray* in his opening sentence? How is this mood sustained throughout the story?
5. Would the story have been less realistic and less interesting if London had chosen to have the man survive his ordeal in the Yukon? Why or why not?
6. Is there any foreshadowing of the final outcome of the story in the first paragraph? How does it contribute to suspense?

Language: Finding the Exact Meaning

The *context* of an unfamiliar word will often give you its general meaning; thus, you can read most stories and get a general understanding of what is happening without looking up a single word in the dictionary. However, to appreciate the author's choice of words, and to make a word part of your own vocabulary, you should look up the exact meaning of any unfamiliar word.

Use a dictionary to find the exact definitions of the italicized words in the following sentences from "To Build a Fire."

1. "It was a clear day, and yet there seemed an *intangible* pall over the face of things . . ."
2. "It experienced a vague but menacing *apprehension* that subdued it . . ."
3. ". . . the thick German socks were like *sheaths* of iron halfway to the knees . . ."
4. ". . . there was no keen *intimacy* between the dog and the man."
5. ". . . he disrupted the *nucleus* of the little fire . . ."
6. "The faint tingling grew stronger till it evolved into a stinging ache that was *excruciating* . . ."

Discussion and Composition

1. When the implied meaning is quite different from the surface meaning, a statement is said to be ironic. For example, you might say "Nice going" or "Well done" after a friend has broken one of your prized possessions. Situations can also be ironic—for example, when something happens that is the opposite of what is expected. What ironies are there in the outcome of "To Build a Fire"?

2. Write a composition in which you compare and contrast the man in "To Build a Fire" with one of the main characters in "Top Man" (page 24). Discuss the problems each man faces and how he goes about solving them. For example, you might compare the two characters' methods of dealing with a hostile, life-threatening environment, giving examples from each story of these methods and their relative success.

3. Imagine an outcome in which the man survives his ordeal. Rewrite the first paragraph of the story to hint at, or foreshadow, this new ending. As you re-read London's paragraph, pay special attention to the descriptive words and phrases he uses to create a threatening, gloomy atmosphere. Then rework these descriptions to create a more hopeful tone.

JAMES THURBER
(1894–1961)

Thurber was the man who left the world "a magnificent legacy of laughter" in his writings and cartoons. His drawings of flop-eared dogs, aggressive females, and timid husbands had universal appeal. He drew rapidly but worked slowly and carefully in composing his stories and essays, for which he is primarily known. Because of a boyhood accident, he was almost completely blind by the time he was fifty. Yet he continued to write and rewrite, sometimes with heavy black pencil on long yellow sheets.

In 1926, Thurber joined the staff of *The New Yorker,* for which he wrote and drew throughout the rest of his life. His experiences on the magazine and with its editor and founder, Harold Ross, are recounted in *The Years with Ross* (1959).

Thurber's writing is almost never just amusing. Like most of his work, "The Secret Life of Walter Mitty" is funny, yet it makes a serious comment on modern life.

THE SECRET LIFE
OF WALTER MITTY

"We're going through!" The Commander's voice was like thin ice breaking. He wore his full-dress uniform, with the heavily braided white cap pulled down rakishly over one cold gray eye. "We can't make it, sir. It's spoiling for a hurricane, if you ask me." "I'm not asking you, Lieutenant Berg," said the Commander. "Throw on the power light! Rev her up to 8,500! We're going through!" The pounding of the cylinders increased: ta-pocketa-pocketa-pocketa-*pocketa-pocketa.* The Commander stared at the ice forming on the pilot window. He walked over and twisted a row of complicated dials. "Switch on No. 8 auxiliary!" he shouted. "Switch on No. 8 auxiliary!" repeated Lieutenant Berg. "Full strength in No. 3 turret!"[1] shouted the Commander. "Full

---

1. **turret:** the enclosure in an airplane for the gun and/or gunners.

strength in No. 3 turret!" The crew, bending to their various tasks in the huge, hurtling[2] eight-engined navy hydroplane,[3] looked at each other and grinned. "The Old Man'll get us through," they said to one another. "The Old Man ain't afraid of Hell! . . ."

"Not so fast! You're driving too fast!" said Mrs. Mitty. "What are you driving so fast for?"

"Hmm?" said Walter Mitty. He looked at his wife, in the seat beside him, with shocked astonishment. She seemed grossly unfamiliar, like a strange woman who had yelled at him in a crowd. "You were up to fifty-five," she said. "You know I don't like to go more than forty. You were up to fifty-five." Walter Mitty drove on toward Waterbury in silence, the roaring of the SN202 through the worst storm in twenty years of Navy flying fading in the remote, intimate airways of his mind. "You're tensed up again," said Mrs. Mitty. "It's one of your days. I wish you'd let Dr. Renshaw look you over."

Walter Mitty stopped the car in front of the building where his wife went to have her hair done. "Remember to get those overshoes while I'm having my hair done," she said. "I don't need overshoes," said Mitty. She put her mirror back into her bag. "We've been all through that," she said, getting out of the car. "You're not a young man any longer." He raced the engine a little. "Why don't you wear your gloves? Have you lost your gloves?" Walter Mitty reached into a pocket and brought out the gloves. He put them on, but after she had turned and gone into the building and he had driven on to a red light, he took them off again. "Pick it up, brother!" snapped a cop as the light changed, and Mitty hastily pulled on his gloves and lurched ahead. He drove around the streets aimlessly for a time, and then he drove past the hospital on his way to the parking lot.

. . . "It's the millionaire banker, Wellington McMillan," said the pretty nurse. "Yes?" said Walter Mitty, removing his gloves slowly. "Who has the case?" "Dr. Renshaw and Dr. Benbow, but there are two specialists here, Dr. Remington from New York and Dr. Pritchard-Mitford from London. He flew over." A door opened down a long, cool corridor and Dr. Renshaw came out. He looked distraught[4] and haggard.

---

2. hurtling (hûrt′ling): moving with a rushing or crashing sound.
3. hydroplane (hī′drə·plān′): an airplane that can land or take off from the water; it moves at great speed on the water.
4. distraught (dĭs·trôt′): worried and tense.

McMillan, the millionaire banker and close personal friend of Roosevelt. Obstreosis[5] of the ductal tract. Tertiary. Wish you'd take a look at him." "Glad to," said Mitty.

In the operating room there were whispered introductions: "Dr. Remington, Dr. Mitty. Dr. Pritchard-Mitford, Dr. Mitty." "I've read your book on streptothricosis," said Pritchard-Mitford, shaking hands. "A brilliant performance, sir." "Thank you," said Walter Mitty. "Didn't know you were in the States, Mitty," grumbled Remington. "Coals to Newcastle,[6] bringing Mitford and me up here for a tertiary." "You are very kind," said Mitty. A huge, complicated machine, connected to the operating table, with many tubes and wires, began at this moment to go pocketa-pocketa-pocketa. "The new anesthetizer[7] is giving way!" shouted an intern. "There is no one in the East who knows how to fix it!" "Quiet, man!" said Mitty, in a low, cool voice. He sprang to the machine, which was now going pocketa-pocketa-queep-pocketa-queep. He began fingering delicately a row of glistening dials. "Give me a fountain pen!" he snapped. Someone handed him a fountain pen. He pulled a faulty piston out of the machine and inserted the pen in its place. "That will hold for ten minutes," he said. "Get on with the operation." A nurse hurried over and whispered to Renshaw, and Mitty saw the man turn pale. "Coreopsis has set in," said Renshaw nervously. "If you would take over, Mitty?" Mitty looked at him and at the craven[8] figure of Benbow, who drank, and at the grave, uncertain faces of the two great specialists. "If you wish," he said. They slipped a white gown on him; he adjusted a mask and drew on thin gloves; nurses handed him shining. . . .

"Back it up, Mac! Look out for that Buick!" Walter Mitty jammed on the brakes. "Wrong lane, Mac," said the parking-lot attendant, looking at Mitty closely. "Gee. Yeh," muttered Mitty.

---

5. **obstreosis** (əb·strē·ō′sĭs): Some of these medical terms are legitimate; others are not.

6. **Coals to Newcastle:** Newcastle is a city in England noted for its production of coal. "To carry coals to Newcastle" means to take things to a place where they are already in abundant supply; to waste labor.

7. **anesthetizer** (ə·nĕs′thə·tīz′ər): from the verb *anesthetize*, to make insensitive to pain, especially by the use of an **anesthetic** (ăn′ĭs·thĕt′ĭk), a drug or gas that deadens sensation.

8. **craven** (krā′vən): noticeably lacking in courage; afraid.

He began cautiously to back out of the lane marked "Exit Only." "Leave her sit there," said the attendant. "I'll put her away." Mitty got out of the car. "Hey, better leave the key." "Oh," said Mitty, handing the man the ignition key. The attendant vaulted into the car, backed it up with insolent skill, and put it where it belonged.

They're so darn cocky, thought Walter Mitty, walking along Main Street; they think they know everything. Once he had tried to take his chains off, outside New Milford, and he had got them wound around the axles. A man had had to come out in a wrecking car and unwind them, a young, grinning garageman. Since then Mrs. Mitty always made him drive to a garage to have the chains taken off. The next time, he thought, I'll wear my right arm in a sling; they won't grin at me then. I'll have my right arm in a sling and they'll see I couldn't possibly take the chains off myself. He kicked at the slush on the sidewalk. "Overshoes," he said to himself, and he began looking for a shoe store.

When he came out into the street again, with the overshoes in a box under his arm, Walter Mitty began to wonder what the other thing was his wife had told him to get. She had told him twice before they set out from their house for Waterbury. In a way he hated these weekly trips to town—he was always getting something wrong. Kleenex, he thought, Squibb's, razor blades? No. Toothpaste, toothbrush, bicarbonate, carborundum,[9] initiative,[10] and referendum?[11] He gave it up. But she would remember it. "Where's the what's-its-name?" she would ask. "Don't tell me you forgot the what's-its-name." A newsboy went by shouting something about the Waterbury trial.

. . . "Perhaps this will refresh your memory." The District Attorney suddenly thrust a heavy automatic at the quiet figure on the witness stand. "Have you ever seen this before?" Walter Mitty took the gun and examined it expertly. "This is my Webley-

---

9. carborundum (kär′bə·rŭn′dəm): a technical trade name for an abrasive used to wear or grind down something.

10. initiative (ĭn·ĭsh′ē·ə·tĭv): in government, the right of the voters to propose legislative matters by getting together a petition and submitting it to popular vote or to the legislature for approval.

11. referendum (rĕf′ə·rĕn′dəm): in government, the practice of submitting a measure passed upon by a legislative body or by popular initiative to a vote of the people for ratification or rejection.

Vickers 50.80,"[12] he said calmly. An excited buzz ran around the courtroom. The Judge rapped for order. "You are a crack shot with any sort of firearms, I believe?" said the District Attorney, insinuatingly.[13] "Objection!" shouted Mitty's attorney. "We have shown that the defendant could not have fired the shot. We have shown that he wore his right arm in a sling on the night of the fourteenth of July." Walter Mitty raised his hand briefly, and the bickering attorneys were stilled. "With any known make of gun," he said evenly, "I could have killed Gregory Fitzhurst at three hundred feet *with my left hand.*" Pandemonium broke loose in the courtroom. A woman's scream rose above the bedlam, and suddenly a lovely, dark-haired girl was in Walter Mitty's arms. The District Attorney struck at her savagely. Without rising from his chair, Mitty let the man have it on the point of the chin. "You miserable cur!"[14] . . .

·"Puppy biscuit," said Walter Mitty. He stopped walking, and the buildings of Waterbury rose up out of the misty courtroom and surrounded him again. A woman who was passing laughed. "He said 'Puppy biscuit,'" she said to her companion. "That man said 'Puppy biscuit' to himself." Walter Mitty hurried on. He went into an A&P, not the first one he came to but a smaller one farther up the street. "I want some biscuit for small, young dogs," he said to the clerk. "Any special brand, sir?" The greatest pistol shot in the world thought a moment. "It says 'Puppies Bark for It' on the box," said Walter Mitty.

His wife would be through at the hairdresser's in fifteen minutes, Mitty saw in looking at his watch, unless they had trouble drying it; sometimes they had trouble drying it. She didn't like to get to the hotel first; she would want him to be there waiting for her as usual. He found a big leather chair in the lobby, facing the window, and he put the overshoes and the puppy biscuit on the floor beside it. He picked up an old copy of *Liberty* and sank down into the chair. "Can Germany Conquer the World Through the Air?" Walter Mitty looked at the pictures of bombing planes and of ruined streets.

. . . "The cannonading has got the wind up in young

12. **Webley-Vickers 50.80:** Mitty invents an impressive name and unlikely caliber for his obviously exceptional weapon.
13. **insinuatingly** (ĭn·sĭn′yo͞o·āt′ĭng·lē): in a sly or indirect manner.
14. **cur:** a mongrel dog; a contemptible person.

Raleigh, sir," said the sergeant. Captain Mitty looked at him through tousled hair. "Get him to bed," he said wearily. "With the others. I'll fly alone." "But you can't, sir," said the sergeant anxiously. "It takes two men to handle that bomber, and the Archies[15] are pounding hell out of the air. Von Richtman's circus is between here and Saulier." "Somebody's got to get that ammunition dump," said Mitty. "I'm going over. Spot of brandy?" He poured a drink for the sergeant and one for himself. War thundered and whined around the dugout and battered at the door. There was a rending of wood, and splinters flew through the room. "A bit of a near thing," said Captain Mitty carelessly. "The box barrage is closing in," said the sergeant. "We only live once, Sergeant," said Mitty, with his faint, fleeting smile. "Or do we?" He poured another brandy and tossed it off. "I never see a man could hold his brandy like you, sir," said the sergeant. "Begging your pardon, sir." Captain Mitty stood up and strapped on his huge Webley-Vickers automatic. "It's forty kilometers through hell, sir," said the sergeant. Mitty finished one last brandy. "After all," he said softly, "what isn't?" The pounding of the cannon increased; there was the rat-tat-tatting of machine guns, and from somewhere came the menacing pocketa-pocketa-pocketa of the new flamethrowers. Walter Mitty walked to the door of the dugout humming "Auprès de Ma Blonde."[16] He turned and waved to the sergeant. "Cheerio!" he said. . . .

Something struck his shoulder. "I've been looking all over this hotel for you," said Mrs. Mitty. "Why do you have to hide in this old chair? How did you expect me to find you?" "Things close in," said Walter Mitty vaguely. "What?" Mrs. Mitty said. "Did you get the what's-its-name? The puppy biscuit? What's in that box?" "Overshoes," said Mitty. "Couldn't you have put them on in the store?" "I was thinking," said Walter Mitty. "Does it ever occur to you that I am sometimes thinking?" She looked at him. "I'm going to take your temperature when I get you home," she said.

They went out through the revolving doors that made a faintly derisive[17] whistling sound when you pushed them. It was

15. **Archies:** a term used by the Allied troops in World War I for antiaircraft guns.
16. **"Auprès de Ma Blonde"** (ŏ·prē·də·mə·blŏnde′): A French World War I song, "Close to My Blonde."
17. **derisive** (dĭ·rī′sĭv): expressing ridicule or scorn.

two blocks to the parking lot. At the drugstore on the corner she said, "Wait here for me. I forgot something. I won't be a minute." She was more than a minute. Walter Mitty lighted a cigarette. It began to rain, rain with sleet in it. He stood up against the wall of the drugstore, smoking. . . . He put his shoulders back and his heels together. "To hell with the handkerchief," said Walter Mitty scornfully. He took one last drag on his cigarette and snapped it away. Then, with that faint, fleeting smile playing about his lips, he faced the firing squad; erect and motionless, proud and disdainful, Walter Mitty the Undefeated, inscrutable[18] to the last.

18. **inscrutable** (ĭn·skro͞o′tə·bəl): mysterious; not easily understood.

Meaning

1. Make a list of the settings Mitty sees himself in and the characters he becomes. In what general type of role does he see himself in his dreams?
2. This story is humorous, but it has its serious side too. Why does Mitty daydream so much? What serious comment about life is Thurber making?
3. Mitty's last daydream concerns a firing squad, which he faces "erect and motionless, proud and disdainful, Walter Mitty the Undefeated, inscrutable to the last." Are the words *undefeated* and *inscrutable* ironic, or could they really describe Mitty?

Method

1. Mitty's daydreams are the result of a process of association; they are related to the everyday world. For example, as he passes the hospital he imagines himself a surgeon. List some of the things and places in Mitty's life that start and end his daydreaming.
2. What is the effect of beginning the story with a daydream sequence rather than an actual event?
3. How would you describe Mrs. Mitty? In what ways is she a contrast to her husband? Give specific examples from the text to support your statements.

4. Second-rate movie and television stories often have stock characters who always have the same traits and whose actions are quite predictable; at a crucial moment, the beautiful young girl will be rescued by the dashing hero. By presenting Mitty's daydreams as stereotyped adventure situations, with hackneyed dialogue and stock characters, Thurber makes fun of such stories. What comment do you think Thurber is making about Mitty's imagination?

5. There are various ways in which a writer can create humor. One is to present something that is incongruous, i.e., something that is not suitable, reasonable, or proper to the situation. Such an incongruity occurs in this story when the commander wears a full-dress uniform in the midst of battle.

Another way to create humor is to use names (such as Gregory Fitzhurst) that sound amusing, and to exaggerate descriptions (as in "huge, hurtling eight-engined navy hydroplane"). Still another method is to create nonsense words and expressions such as "obstreosis of the ductal tract."

Find two more examples each of incongruity, amusing names, exaggeration, and nonsense words or expressions in the story.

Language: Onomatopoeia—a Word from a Sound

Thurber uses the word *pocketa* several times in the story. It is impossible to find this word in a dictionary, even a very large one, since it exists and has meaning only in the context of this story. Where did the author get the word? He made it up by writing an imitation of a sound, first a pounding cylinder in a hydroplane, and later the failing equipment in a hospital operating room. When spoken very rapidly, "pocketa-pocketa" sounds like the sputtering of a motor. What other machines can it be used to describe?

Words which sound like the things they describe are called onomatopoetic (ŏn'ə·măt'ə·pō·ĕt'ĭk) words. *Pop, zip, buzz, bow-wow,* and *splash* are examples of well known onomatopoeias (ŏn'ə·măt'ə·pē'əs). Name five other words that are onomatopoetic. Then make up five onomatopoetic words of your own and tell what they mean.

Discussion and Composition

1. Researchers into dreams claim that dreaming is essential to mental health. Why do you think this might be so? How are daydreams different from the dreams one has at night?

2. Create a "daydream" scene in which you, as the hero or heroine, perform feats of courage, daring, and skill. Focus your scene on a specific incident or situation. Write appropriate dialogue and include descriptive details to help the reader visualize your heroic exploits.

O. HENRY

(1862–1910)

William Sydney Porter first used the pen name O. Henry to hide his true identity when he wrote stories while serving a prison term. Born in Greensboro, North Carolina, Porter had left school at fifteen to work in his uncle's drugstore. When he was twenty, he went to Texas, where he worked on a ranch and later in a bank.

The bank job resulted in the tragedy of Porter's life; yet out of his trouble came the warm sympathy for people down on their luck which underlies his best work. The bank was so poorly managed that it is not clear to this day exactly what happened. Some accounts were found short, and Porter was accused of embezzlement. Instead of waiting for a trial, he fled to Honduras. He returned to face trial when he learned that his wife was dying of tuberculosis.

During his three-year prison term, Porter worked as a night druggist in the prison hospital. During the day, he wrote adventure stories to earn the money that he needed to support his daughter.

After his release, Porter went to New York and worked for the *New York World,* for which he wrote a number of stories. He died of tuberculosis at the age of forty-eight.

O. Henry was influential in creating a pattern for a particular type of short story. He wrote quickly, primarily for newspaper readers who wanted their stories exciting and easy to understand. His stories, which have great popular appeal, tend to be sentimental and filled with unlikely coincidences. At times, the surprise or trick ending (at which he excelled) seems a bit forced. Nevertheless, his popularity is deserved, for he was a master storyteller.

THE RANSOM
OF RED CHIEF

It looked like a good thing: but wait till I tell you. We were down South, in Alabama—Bill Driscoll and myself—when this kidnapping idea struck us. It was, as Bill afterward expressed it, "during a moment of temporary mental apparition";[1] but we didn't find that out till later.

There was a town down there, as flat as a flannel-cake, and called Summit, of course. It contained inhabitants of as undeleterious[2] and self-satisfied a class of peasantry as ever clustered around a Maypole.

Bill and me had a joint capital of about six hundred dollars, and we needed just two thousand dollars more to pull off a fraudulent town-lot scheme in western Illinois with. We talked it over on the front steps of the hotel. Philoprogenitiveness,[3] says we, is strong in semi-rural communities; therefore, and for other reasons, a kidnapping project ought to do better there than in the radius of newspapers that send reporters out in plain clothes to stir up talk about such things. We knew that Summit couldn't get after us with anything stronger than constables and, maybe, some lackadaisical bloodhounds and a diatribe[4] or two in the *Weekly Farmers' Budget*. So, it looked good.

We selected for our victim the only child of a prominent citizen named Ebenezer Dorset. The father was respectable and tight, a mortgage fancier and a stern, upright collection-plate passer and forecloser. The kid was a boy of ten, with bas-relief[5] freckles, and hair the color of the cover of the magazine you buy at the newsstand when you want to catch a train. Bill and me figured

---

1. **apparition** (ăp'ə·rĭsh'ən): mispronunciation of *aberration* (ab'ə·rā'shən), disorder or insanity.
2. **undeleterious** (ŭn·dĕl'ə·tĭr'ē·əs): nondestructive, harmless.
3. **philoprogenitiveness** (fĭl'ō·prō·jĕn'ə·tĭv·nĭs): love of parents for their children.
4. **diatribe** (dī'ə·trīb): a bitter criticism or denunciation, as in an angry editorial.
5. **bas-relief** (bä'rĭ·lĕf'): projecting slightly from the background; usually refers to a carving or sculpture.

that Ebenezer would melt down for a ransom of two thousand dollars to a cent. But wait till I tell you.

About two miles from Summit was a little mountain, covered with a dense cedar brake. On the rear elevation of this mountain was a cave. There we stored provisions.

One evening after sundown, we drove in a buggy past old Dorset's house. The kid was in the street, throwing rocks at a kitten on the opposite fence.

"Hey, little boy!" says Bill. "Would you like to have a bag of candy and a nice ride?"

The boy catches Bill neatly in the eye with a piece of brick.

"That will cost the old man an extra five hundred dollars," says Bill, climbing over the wheel.

That boy put up a fight like a welterweight cinnamon bear; but, at last, we got him down in the bottom of the buggy and drove away. We took him up to the cave, and I hitched the horse in the cedar brake. After dark I drove the buggy to the little village, three miles away, where we had hired it, and walked back to the mountain.

Bill was pasting court plaster[6] over the scratches and bruises on his features. There was a fire burning behind the big rock at the entrance of the cave, and the boy was watching a pot of boiling coffee, with two buzzard tail feathers stuck in his red hair. He points a stick at me when I come up, and says:

"Ha! cursèd paleface, do you dare to enter the camp of Red Chief, the terror of the plains?"

"He's all right now," says Bill, rolling up his trousers and examining some bruises on his shins. "We're playing Indian. We're making Buffalo Bill's show look like magic-lantern views of Palestine in the town hall. I'm Old Hank the Trapper, Red Chief's captive, and I'm to be scalped at daybreak. By Geronimo! That kid can kick hard!"

Yes, sir, that boy seemed to be having the time of his life. The fun of camping out in a cave had made him forget that he was a captive himself. He immediately christened me Snake-Eye the Spy, and announced that, when his braves returned from the war-path, I was to be broiled at the stake at the rising of the sun.

6. **court plaster:** cloth covered on one side with sticky material; formerly used to protect cuts in the skin. This was the forerunner of today's adhesive bandage.

Then we had supper; and he filled his mouth full of bacon and bread and gravy, and began to talk. He made a during-dinner speech something like this:

"I like this fine. I never camped out before; but I had a pet possum once, and I was nine last birthday. I hate to go to school. Rats ate up sixteen of Jimmy Talbot's aunt's speckled hen's eggs. Are there any real Indians in these woods? I want some more gravy. Does the trees moving make the wind blow? We had five puppies. What makes your nose so red, Hank? My father has lots of money. Are the stars hot? I whipped Ed Walker twice, Saturday. I don't like girls. You dassent catch toads unless with a string. Do oxen make any noise? Why are oranges round? Have you got beds to sleep on in this cave? Amos Murray has got six toes. A parrot can talk, but a monkey or a fish can't. How many does it take to make twelve?"

Every few minutes he would remember that he was a pesky redskin and pick up his stick rifle and tiptoe to the mouth of the cave to rubber[7] for the scouts of the hated paleface. Now and then he would let out a war whoop that made Old Hank the Trapper shiver. That boy had Bill terrorized from the start.

"Red Chief," says I to the kid, "would you like to go home?"

"Aw, what for?" says he. "I don't have any fun at home. I hate to go to school. I like to camp out. You won't take me back home again, Snake-Eye, will you?"

"Not right away," says I. "We'll stay here in the cave a while."

"All right!" says he. "That'll be fine. I never had such fun in all my life."

We went to bed about eleven o'clock. We spread down some wide blankets and quilts and put Red Chief between us. We weren't afraid he'd run away. He kept us awake for three hours, jumping up and reaching for his rifle and screeching: "Hist! pard," in mine and Bill's ears, as the fancied crackle of a twig or the rustle of a leaf revealed to his young imagination the stealthy approach of the outlaw band. At last, I fell into a troubled sleep and dreamed that I had been kidnaped and chained to a tree by a ferocious pirate with red hair.

---

7. **rubber:** short for *rubberneck,* to stretch one's neck while looking for something.

Just at daybreak, I was awakened by a series of awful screams from Bill. They weren't yells, or howls, or shouts, or whoops, or yawps, such as you'd expect from a manly set of vocal organs— they were simply indecent, terrifying, humiliating screams, such as women emit when they see ghosts or caterpillars. It's an awful thing to hear a strong, desperate, fat man scream incontinently[8] in a cave at daybreak.

I jumped up to see what the matter was. Red Chief was sitting on Bill's chest, with one hand twined in Bill's hair. In the other he had the sharp case knife we used for slicing bacon, and he was industriously and realistically trying to take Bill's scalp, according to the sentence that had been pronounced upon him the evening before.

I got the knife away from the kid and made him lie down again. But, from that moment, Bill's spirit was broken. He laid down on his side of the bed, but he never closed an eye again in sleep as long as that boy was with us. I dozed off for a while, but along toward sunup I remembered that Red Chief had said I was to be burned at the stake at the rising of the sun. I wasn't nervous or afraid; but I sat up and lit my pipe and leaned against a rock.

"What you getting up so soon for, Sam?" asked Bill.

"Me?" says I. "Oh, I got a kind of a pain in my shoulder. I thought sitting up would rest it."

"You're a liar!" says Bill. "You're afraid. You was to be burned at sunrise, and you was afraid he'd do it. And he would, too, if he could find a match. Ain't it awful, Sam? Do you think anybody will pay out money to get a little imp like that back home?"

"Sure," said I. "A rowdy kid like that is just the kind that parents dote on. Now, you and the Chief get up and cook breakfast, while I go up on the top of this mountain and reconnoiter."

I went up on the peak of the little mountain and ran my eye over the contiguous[9] vicinity. Over toward Summit I expected to see the sturdy yeomanry[10] of the village, armed with scythes and pitchforks, beating the countryside for the dastardly kidnapers. But what I saw was a peaceful landscape dotted with one man plowing with a dun mule. Nobody was dragging the creek; no couriers dashed hither and yon, bringing tidings of no news to the

---

8. **incontinently:** without self-restraint.
9. **contiguous** (kən·tĭg′yōō·əs): bordering.
10. **yeomanry** (yō′mən·rē): people who own a small amount of land.

distracted parents. There was a sylvan[11] attitude of somnolent[12] sleepiness pervading that section of the external outward surface of Alabama that lay exposed to my view. "Perhaps," says I to myself, "it has not yet been discovered that the wolves have borne away the tender lambkin from the fold. Heaven help the wolves!" says I, and I went down the mountain to breakfast.

When I got to the cave, I found Bill backed up against the side of it, breathing hard, and the boy threatening to smash him with a rock half as big as a coconut.

"He put a red-hot boiled potato down my back," explained Bill, "and then mashed it with his foot; and I boxed his ears. Have you got a gun about you, Sam?"

I took the rock away from the boy and kind of patched up the argument. "I'll fix you," says the kid to Bill. "No man ever yet struck the Red Chief but he got paid for it. You better beware!"

After breakfast the kid takes a piece of leather with strings wrapped around it out of his pocket and goes outside the cave unwinding it.

"What's he up to now?" says Bill anxiously. "You don't think he'll run away, do you, Sam?"

"No fear of it," says I. "He don't seem to be much of a homebody. But we've got to fix up some plan about the ransom. There don't seem to be much excitement around Summit on account of his disappearance, but maybe they haven't realized yet that he's gone. His folks may think he's spending the night with Aunt Jane or one of the neighbors. Anyhow, he'll be missed today. Tonight we must get a message to his father demanding the two thousand dollars for his return."

Just then we heard a kind of war whoop, such as David might have emitted when he knocked out the champion Goliath. It was a sling that Red Chief had pulled out of his pocket, and he was whirling it around his head.

I dodged and heard a heavy thud and a kind of a sigh from Bill, like a horse gives out when you take his saddle off. A rock the size of an egg had caught Bill just behind his left ear. He loosened himself all over and fell in the fire across the frying pan of hot

11. **sylvan:** woodsy. Silvanus in Roman mythology was a god of forests, fields and herds; and represented a simple, uncomplicated life.
12. **somnolent** (sŏm'nə·lənt): drowsy.

water for washing the dishes. I dragged him out and poured cold water on his head for half an hour.

By and by, Bill sits up and feels behind his ear and says: "Sam, do you know who my favorite Biblical character is?"

"Take it easy," says I. "You'll come to your senses presently."

"King Herod,"[13] says he. "You won't go away and leave me here alone, will you, Sam?"

I went out and caught that boy and shook him until his freckles rattled.

"If you don't behave," says I, "I'll take you straight home. Now, are you going to be good or not?"

"I was only funning," says he, sullenly. "I didn't mean to hurt Old Hank. But what did he hit me for? I'll behave, Snake-Eye, if you won't send me home, and if you'll let me play the Black Scout today."

"I don't know the game," says I. "That's for you and Mr. Bill to decide. He's your playmate for the day. I'm going away for a while, on business. Now, you come in and make friends with him and say you are sorry for hurting him, or home you go, at once."

I made him and Bill shake hands, and then I took Bill aside and told him I was going to Poplar Grove, a little village three miles from the cave, and find out what I could about how the kidnapping had been regarded in Summit. Also, I thought it best to send a peremptory[14] letter to old man Dorset that day, demanding the ransom and dictating how it should be paid.

"You know, Sam," says Bill, "I've stood by you without batting an eye in earthquakes, fire, and flood—in poker games, dynamite outrages, police raids, train robberies, and cyclones. I never lost my nerve yet till we kidnaped that two-legged sky-rocket of a kid. He's got me going. You won't leave me long with him, will you, Sam?"

"I'll be back some time this afternoon," says I. "You must keep the boy amused and quiet till I return. And now we'll write the letter to old Dorset."

Bill and I got paper and pencil and worked on the letter while Red Chief, with a blanket wrapped around him, strutted up

---

13. King Herod: King of Judea who tried to kill the infant Jesus by ordering the slaying of all male children under the age of two in Bethlehem.
14. peremptory (pə·rĕmp′tər·ē): sternly decisive.

and down, guarding the mouth of the cave. Bill begged me tearfully to make the ransom fifteen hundred dollars instead of two thousand. "I ain't attempting," says he, "to decry the celebrated moral aspect of parental affection, but we're dealing with humans, and it ain't human for anybody to give up two thousand dollars for that forty pound chunk of freckled wildcat. I'm willing to take a chance at fifteen hundred dollars. You can charge the difference up to me."

So, to relieve Bill, I acceded, and we collaborated a letter that ran this way:

> *Ebenezer Dorset, Esq.:*
> We have your boy concealed in a place far from Summit. It is useless for you or the most skillful detectives to attempt to find him. Absolutely, the only terms on which you can have him restored to you are these: We demand fifteen hundred dollars in large bills for his return; the money to be left at midnight tonight at the same spot and in the same box as your reply—as hereinafter described. If you agree to these terms, send your answer in writing by a solitary messenger tonight at half-past eight o'clock. After crossing Owl Creek on the road to Poplar Grove, there are three large trees about a hundred yards apart, close to the fence of the wheat field on the right-hand side. At the bottom of the fence post, opposite the third tree, will be found a small pasteboard box.
>
> The messenger will place the answer in this box and return immediately to Summit.
>
> If you attempt any treachery or fail to comply with our demand as stated, you will never see your boy again.
>
> If you pay the money as demanded, he will be returned to you safe and well within three hours. These terms are final, and if you do not accede to them, no further communication will be attempted.
>
> *Two Desperate Men*

I addressed this letter to Dorset and put it in my pocket. As I was about to start, the kid comes up to me and says:

"Aw, Snake-Eye, you said I could play the Black Scout while you was gone."

"Play it, of course," says I. "Mr. Bill will play with you. What kind of a game is it?"

"I'm the Black Scout," says Red Chief, "and I have to ride to the stockade to warn the settlers that the Indians are coming. I'm tired of playing Indian myself. I want to be the Black Scout."

"All right," says I. "It sounds harmless to me. I guess Mr. Bill will help you foil the pesky savages."

"What am I to do?" asks Bill, looking at the kid suspiciously.

"You are the hoss," says Black Scout. "Get down on your hands and knees. How can I ride to the stockade without a hoss?"

"You'd better keep him interested," said I, "till we get the scheme going. Loosen up."

Bill gets down on his all fours, and a look comes in his eye like a rabbit's when you catch it in a trap.

"How far is it to the stockade, kid?" he asks, in a husky manner of voice.

"Ninety miles," says the Black Scout. "And you have to hump yourself to get there on time. Whoa, now!"

The Black Scout jumps on Bill's back and digs his heels in his side.

"For Heaven's sake," says Bill, "hurry back, Sam, as soon as you can. I wish we hadn't made the ransom more than a thousand. Say, you quit kicking me or I'll get up and warm you good."

I walked over to Poplar Grove and sat around the post office and store talking with the chaw-bacons that came in to trade. One whiskerando says that he hears Summit is all upset on account of Elder Ebenezer Dorset's boy having been lost or stolen. That was all I wanted to know. I bought some smoking tobacco, referred casually to the price of black-eyed peas, posted my letter surreptitiously,[15] and came away. The postmaster said the mail carrier would come by in an hour to take the mail to Summit.

When I got back to the cave, Bill and the boy were not to be found. I explored the vicinity of the cave and risked a yodel or two, but there was no response.

So I lighted my pipe and sat down on a mossy bank to await developments.

In about half an hour I heard the bushes rustle, and Bill wabbled out into the little glade in front of the cave. Behind him was the kid, stepping softly like a scout, with a broad grin on his

---

15. **surreptitiously** (sŭr'əp·tĭsh'əs·lē): secretly.

face. Bill stopped, took off his hat, and wiped his face with a red handkerchief. The kid stopped about eight feet behind him.

"Sam," says Bill, "I suppose you'll think I'm a renegade, but I couldn't help it. I'm a grown person with masculine proclivities[16] and habits of self-defense, but there is a time when all systems of egotism and predominance[17] fail. The boy is gone. I have sent him home. All is off. There was martyrs in old times," goes on Bill, "that suffered death rather than give up the particular graft they enjoyed. None of 'em ever was subjugated to such supernatural tortures as I have been. I tried to be faithful to our articles of depredation,[18] but there came a limit."

"What's the trouble, Bill?" I asks him.

"I was rode," says Bill, "the ninety miles to the stockade, not barring an inch. Then, when the settlers was rescued, I was given oats. Sand ain't a palatable substitute. And then, for an hour I had to try to explain to him why there was nothin' in holes, how a road can run both ways, and what makes the grass green. I tell you, Sam, a human can only stand so much. I takes him by the neck of his clothes and drags him down the mountain. On the way, he kicks my legs black-and-blue from the knees down; and I've got to have two or three bites on my thumb and hand cauterized.

"But he's gone"—continues Bill—"gone home. I showed him the road to Summit and kicked him about eight feet nearer there at one kick. I'm sorry we lose the ransom, but it was either that or Bill Driscoll to the madhouse."

Bill is puffing and blowing, but there is a look of ineffable peace and growing content on his rose-pink features.

"Bill," says I, "there isn't any heart disease in your family, is there?"

"No," says Bill, "nothing chronic except malaria and accidents. Why?"

"Then you might turn around," says I, "and have a look behind you."

Bill turns and sees the boy, and loses his complexion and sits down plump on the ground and begins to pluck aimlessly at grass

---

16. **proclivities** (prō·klĭv'ə·tēz): inclinations or traits.
17. **systems of egotism and predominance**: here, self-confidence and authority.
18. **depredation** (dĕp'rə·dā'shən): plundering, robbery.

and little sticks. For an hour I was afraid for his mind. And then I told him that my scheme was to put the whole job through immediately and that we would get the ransom and be off with it by midnight if old Dorset fell in with our proposition. So Bill braced up enough to give the kid a weak sort of a smile and a promise to play the Russian in a Japanese war with him as soon as he felt a little better.

I had a scheme for collecting that ransom without danger of being caught by counterplots that ought to commend itself to professional kidnappers. The tree under which the answer was to be left—and the money later on—was close to the road fence with big, bare fields on all sides. If a gang of constables should be watching for anyone to come for the note, they could see him a long way off crossing the fields or in the road. But no, siree! At half-past eight I was up in that tree, as well-hidden as a tree toad, waiting for the messenger to arrive.

Exactly on time, a half-grown boy rides up the road on a bicycle, locates the pasteboard box at the foot of the fence post, slips a folded piece of paper into it, and pedals away again back toward Summit.

I waited an hour and then concluded the thing was square. I slid down the tree, got the note, slipped along the fence till I struck the woods, and was back at the cave in another half an hour. I opened the note, got near the lantern, and read it to Bill. It was written with a pen in a crabbed hand, and the sum and substance of it was this:

Two Desperate Men:
Gentlemen, I received your letter today by post, in regard to the ransom you ask for the return of my son. I think you are a little high in your demands, and I hereby make you a counterproposition, which I am inclined to believe you will accept. You bring Johnny home and pay me two hundred and fifty dollars in cash, and I agree to take him off your hands. You had better come at night, for the neighbors believe he is lost, and I couldn't be responsible for what they would do to anybody they saw bringing him back.

Very respectfully,
Ebenezer Dorset

"Great pirates of Penzance!"[19] says I; "of all the impudent—"
But I glanced at Bill and hesitated. He had the most appealing
look in his eyes I ever saw on the face of a dumb or a talking brute.

"Sam," says he, "what's two hundred and fifty dollars, after
all? We've got the money. One more night of this kid will send me
to a bed in Bedlam.[20] Besides being a thorough gentleman, I think
Mr. Dorset is a spendthrift for making us such a liberal offer. You
ain't going to let the chance go, are you?"

"Tell you the truth, Bill," says I, "this little he ewe lamb has
somewhat got on my nerves, too. We'll take him home, pay the
ransom, and make our getaway."

We took him home that night. We got him to go by telling
him that his father had bought a silver-mounted rifle and a pair of
moccasins for him and that we were going to hunt bears the next
day.

It was just twelve o'clock when we knocked at Ebenezer's
front door. Just at the moment when I should have been abstract-
ing the fifteen hundred dollars from the box under the tree, according to the original proposition, Bill was counting out two
hundred and fifty dollars into Dorset's hand.

When the kid found out we were going to leave him at
home, he started up a howl like a calliope[21] and fastened himself as
tight as a leech to Bill's leg. His father peeled him away gradually,
like a porous plaster.

"How long can you hold him?" asks Bill.

"I'm not as strong as I used to be," says old Dorset, "but I
think I can promise you ten minutes."

"Enough," says Bill. "In ten minutes I shall cross the Central,
Southern, and Middle-Western states and be legging it trippingly
for the Canadian border."

And, as dark as it was, and as fat as Bill was, and as good a
runner as I am, he was a good mile and a half out of Summit
before I could catch up with him.

---

19. **Penzance** (pĕn·zăns′): seaport in England. *The Pirates of Penzance* (1879) is
a comic operetta by Gilbert and Sullivan.
20. **Bedlam:** slang for St. Mary of Bethlehem, a hospital for the insane in
London.
21. **calliope** (kə·lī′ə·pē): a mechanical organ consisting of a series of whistles.
In Greek mythology, Calliope was the Muse of eloquence and heroic poetry.

Meaning

1. A situation or event that turns out to be in strange contrast to what was intended or expected is said to be *ironic*. What is ironic about the actions of Sam and Bill in this story?
2. How much ransom is paid for Red Chief? Who pays it?
3. In literature, *conflict* is a clash between opposing forces, people, or ideas. What are the conflicts in this story?

Method

1. To be effective, a surprise ending must be foreshadowed. How does O. Henry prepare the reader for the final turn of events?
2. What is the *climax* of this story, the point at which you could predict its outcome?
3. Which element of the story will you probably remember the longest: character, theme, or plot? Why?
4. Why do you think O. Henry chose to tell this story through the eyes of Sam? Do you think it would have been more or less amusing or effective if it had been told from Red Chief's point of view? Why?

Language: Formal and Colloquial Usage

O. Henry uses formal and colloquial language together for humorous effect. Formal English is used most often in serious, scholarly writing. It seems incongruous for "desperate kidnappers" such as Sam, and occasionally Bill, to use many-syllabled words (such as "philoprogenitiveness") which are rarely heard in conversation. Along with this highly formal language, however, Bill and Sam use colloquial words—informal slang expressions (such as "Wait till I tell you") that are typical of everyday speech. The kidnappers' errors in pronunciation and grammar make their attempts at fancy English even funnier.

Decide whether the following expressions from "The Ransom of Red Chief" are formal or colloquial. Note where errors have been made in pronunciation or grammar.

1. ". . . the fancied crackle of a twig or the rustle of a leaf revealed to his young imagination the stealthy approach of the outlaw band."

2. "We were down South, in Alabama—Bill Driscoll and myself—when this kidnapping idea struck us."
3. There was a sylvan attitude of somnolent sleepiness pervading that section of the external outward surface of Alabama that lay exposed to my view."
4. "The kid was a boy of ten. . . ."
5. "Bill and me figured that Ebenezer would melt down for a ransom of two thousand dollars to a cent."

Discussion and Composition

1. Discuss the character of Red Chief and the attempts of Bill and Sam to get along with him. In Bill and Sam's place, what would you have done to change and improve Red Chief's behavior? Explain why.

2. In the character of Red Chief, O. Henry humorously exaggerates qualities that might be typical of a nine-year-old child. Write a composition in which you compare Red Chief to children you have known. In what ways is his behavior typical of a child his age? What aspects of his character are exaggerated for comic effect? Give examples to support your discussion.

DANIEL KEYES
(born 1927)

Novelist and short story writer Daniel Keyes was born in Brooklyn, New York. After graduating from high school, he enlisted in the United States Maritime Service. He was a merchant seaman and then a ship's purser before he entered Brooklyn College (now part of the City University of New York), where he received his bachelor's and master's degrees. He has worked as a fiction editor and a high school teacher, and is presently a professor of English at Ohio University in Athens, Ohio.

"Flowers for Algernon" (1959), which was originally published in a science fiction magazine, has appeared in more than twenty collections of short stories and has been translated into several languages. Mr. Keyes expanded the story into a novel which was published in 1966. It has also been a television play and a movie (retitled *Charly*).

FLOWERS FOR ALGERNON

PROGRIS RIPORT 1—MARTCH 5, 1965

Dr. Strauss says I shud rite down what I think and evrey thing that happins to me from now on. I dont know why but he says its importint so they will see if they will use me. I hope they use me. Miss Kinnian says maybe they can make me smart. I want to be smart. My name is Charlie Gordon. I am 37 years old. I have nuthing more to rite now so I will close for today.

PROGRIS RIPORT 2—MARTCH 6

I had a test today. I think I faled it. And I think maybe now they wont use me. What happind is a nice young man was in the room and he had some white cards and ink spillled all over them. He sed Charlie what do yo see on this card. I was very skared even tho I had my rabits foot in my pockit because when I was a kid I always faled tests in school and I spillled ink to.

I told him I saw a inkblot. He said yes and it made me feel good. I thot that was all but when I got up to go he said Charlie we are not thru yet. Then I dont remember so good but he wantid me to say what was in the ink. I dint see nuthing in the ink but he said there was picturs there other pepul saw some picturs. I couldnt see any picturs. I reely tryed. I held the card close up and then far away. Then I said if I had my glases I coud see better I usally only ware my glases in the movies or TV but I said they are in the closit in the hall. I got them. Then I said let me see that card agen I bet Ill find it now.

I tryed hard but I only saw the ink. I told him maybe I need new glases. He rote something down on a paper and I got skared of faling the test. I told him it was a very nice inkblot with littel points all around the edges. He looked very sad so that wasnt it. I said please let me try agen. Ill get it in a few minits becaus Im not so fast somtimes. Im a slow reeder too in Miss Kinnians class for slow adults but I'm trying very hard.

He gave me a chance with another card that had 2 kinds of ink spilled on it red and blue.

He was very nice and talked slow like Miss Kinnian does and he explaned it to me that it was a *raw shok*.[1] He said pepul see things in the ink. I said show me where. He said think. I told him I think a inkblot but that wasn't rite eather. He said what does it remind you—pretend something. I closed my eyes for a long time to pretend. I told him I pretend a fowntan pen with ink leeking all over a table cloth.

I dont think I passed the *raw shok* test

PROGRIS RIPORT 3—MARTCH 7

Dr Strauss and Dr Nemur say it dont matter about the inkblots. They said that maybe they will still use me. I said Miss Kinnian never gave me tests like that one only spelling and reading. They said Miss Kinnian told that I was her bestist pupil in the adult nite school becaus I tryed the hardist and I reely wantid to lern. They said how come you went to the adult nite scool all by yourself Charlie. How did you find it. I said I asked pepul and sumbody told me where I shud go to lern to read and spell good. They said why did you want to. I told them becaus all my life I wantid to be smart and not dumb. But its very hard to be smart.

---

1. **raw shok:** Rorschach personality test, analyzes a subject's response to a series of inkblots. The test was devised by Hermann Rorschach (1884–1922), a Swiss psychiatrist.

They said you know it will probly be tempirery. I said yes. Miss Kinnian told me. I dont care if it herts.

Later I had more crazy tests today. The nice lady who gave it to me told me the name and I asked her how do you spellit so I can rite it my progris riport. THEMATIC APPERCEPTION TEST.[2] I dont know the frist 2 words but I know what *test* means. You got to pass it or you get bad marks. This test lookd easy becaus I coud see the picturs. Only this time she dint want me to tell her the picturs. That mixed me up. She said make up storys about the pepul in the picturs.

I told her how can you tell storys about pepul you never met. I said why shud I make up lies. I never tell lies any more becaus I always get caut.

She told me this test and the other one the raw-shok was for getting personality. I laffed so hard. I said how can you get that thing from inkblots and fotos. She got sore and put her picturs away. I don't care. It was sily. I gess I faled that test too.

Later some men in white coats took me to a difernt part of the hospitil and gave me a game to play. It was like a race with a white mouse. They called the mouse Algernon. Algernon was in a box with a lot of twists and turns like all kinds of walls and they gave me a pencil and a paper with lines and lots of boxes. On one side it said START and on the other end it said FINISH. They said it was *amazed* and that Algernon and me had the same *amazed* to do. I dint see how we could have the same *amazed* if Algernon had a box and I had a paper but I dint say nothing. Anyway there wasnt time because the race started.

One of the men had a watch he was trying to hide so I wouldnt see it so I tryed not to look and that made me nervus.

Anyway that test made me feel worser than all the others because they did it over 10 times with different *amazeds* and Algernon won every time. I dint know that mice were so smart. Maybe thats because Algernon is a white mouse. Maybe white mice are smarter than other mice.

PROGRIS RIPORT 4—MAR 8

Their going to use me! Im so exited I can hardly write. Dr Nemur and Dr Strauss had a argament about it first. Dr Nemur

---

2. Thematic Apperception Test: another popular test of personality. The subject is asked to make up stories about a series of pictures.

was in the office when Dr Strauss brot me in. Dr Nemur was worryed about using me but Dr Strauss told him Miss Kinnian rekemmended me the best from all the people who she was teaching. I like Miss Kinnian becaus shes a very smart teacher. And she said Charlie your going to have a second chance. If you volenteer for this experament you mite get smart. They dont know if it will be perminint but theirs a chance. Thats why I said ok even when I was scared because she said it was an operashun. She said dont be scared Charlie you done so much with so little I think you deserv it most of all.

So I got scaird when Dr. Nemur and Dr. Strauss argud about it. Dr. Strauss said I had something that was very good. He said I had a good *motorvation*. I never even knew I had that. I felt proud when he said that not every body with an eye-q[3] of 68 had that thing. I dont know what it is or where I got it but he said Algernon had it too. Algernons *motor-vation* is the cheese they put in his box. But it cant be that because I didn't eat any cheese this week.

Then he told Dr Nemur something I dint understand so while they were talking I wrote down some of the words.

He said Dr. Nemur I know Charlie is not what you had in mind as the first of your new brede of intelek* * (coudnt get the word) superman. But most people of his low ment* * are host* * and uncoop* * they are usually dull apath* * and hard to reach. He has a good natcher hes intristed and eager to please.

Dr Nemur said remember he will be the first human beeng ever to have his intellijence tripled by surgicle meens.

Dr. Strauss said exakly. Look at how well hes lerned to read and write for his low mentel age its as grate an acheve* * as you and I lerning einstines therey of * *vity[4] without help. That shows the inteness motor-vation. Its comparat* * a tremen* * achev* * I say we use Charlie.

I dint get all the words but it sounded like Dr Strauss was on my side and like the other one wasnt.

---

3. eye-q: I.Q. or intelligence quotient, a number arrived at by dividing a person's mental age (as determined by a standardized intelligence test) by his or her chronological age, and multiplying the result by 100. A score of 100 is considered average; 125–140 or above, gifted; below 70, mentally deficient (50–75 is considered educable). There is much controversy over how I.Q. tests are constructed and standardized.

4. einstines therey of * *vity: Einstein's theory of relativity. Albert Einstein (1879–1955). His theory of relativity revolutionized physics.

Then Dr Nemur nodded he said all right maybe your right. We will use Charlie. When he said that I got so exited I jumped up and shook his hand for being so good to me. I told him thank you doc you wont be sorry for giving me a second chance. And I mean it like I told him. After the operashun Im gonna try to be smart. Im gonna try awful hard.

PROGRIS RIPORT 5—MAR 10

Im skared. Lots of the nurses and the people who gave me the tests came to bring me candy and wish me luck. I hope I have luck. I got my rabits foot and my lucky penny. Only a black cat crossed me when I was comming to the hospitil. Dr Strauss says dont be supersitis Charlie this is science. Anyway Im keeping my rabits foot with me.

I asked Dr Strauss if Ill beat Algernon in the race after the operashun and he said maybe. If the operashun works Ill show that mouse I can be as smart as he is. Maybe smarter. Then Ill be abel to read better and spell the words good and know lots of things and be like other people. I want to be smart like other people. If it works perminint they will make everybody smart all over the wurld.

They dint give me anything to eat this morning. I dont know what that eating has to do with getting smart. Im very hungry and Dr. Nemur took away my box of candy. That Dr Nemur is a grouch. Dr Strauss says I can have it back after the operashun. You cant eat befor a operashun . . .

PROGRESS REPORT 6—MAR 15

The operashun dint hurt. He did it while I was sleeping. They took off the bandijis from my head today so I can make a PROGRESS REPORT. Dr. Nemur who looked at some of my other ones says I spell PROGRESS wrong and told me how to spell it and REPORT too. I got to try and remember that.

I have a very bad memary for spelling. Dr Strauss says its ok to tell about all the things that happin to me but he says I should tell more about what I feel and what I think. When I told him I dont know how to think he said try. All the time when the bandijis were on my eyes I tryed to think. Nothing happened. I dont know what to think about. Maybe if I ask him he will tell me how I can think now that Im suppose to get smart. What do smart people think about. Fancy things I suppose. I wish I knew some fancy things alredy.

PROGRESS REPORT 7—MAR 19

Nothing is happining. I had lots of tests and different kinds of races with Algernon. I hate that mouse. He always beats me. Dr. Strauss said I got to play those games. And he said some time I got to take those tests over again. Those inkblots are stupid. And those pictures are stupid too. I like to draw a picture of a man and a woman but I wont make up lies about people.

I got a headache from trying to think so much. I thot Dr Strauss was my frend but he dont help me. He dont tell me what to think or when Ill get smart. Miss Kinnian dint come to see me. I think writing these progress reports are stupid too.

PROGRESS REPORT 8—MAR 23

Im going back to work at the factory. They said it was better I shud go back to work but I cant tell anyone what the operashun was for and I have to come to the hospitil for an hour evry night after work. They are gonna pay me mony every month for learning to be smart.

Im glad Im going back to work because I miss my job and all my frends and all the fun we have there.

Dr Strauss says I shud keep writing things down but I dont have to do it every day just when I think of something or something speshul happins. He says dont get discoridged because it takes time and it happins slow. He says it took a long time with Algernon before he got 3 times smarter than he was before. Thats why Algernon beats me all the time because he had that operashun too. That makes me feel better. I coud probly do that *amazed* faster than a reglar mouse. Maybe some day Ill beat him. That would be something. So far Algernon looks smart perminent.

MAR 25   (I dont have to write PROGRESS REPORT on top any more just when I hand it in once a week for Dr Nemur. I just have to put the date on. That saves time)

We had a lot of fun at the factery today. Joe Carp said hey look where Charlie had his operashun what did they do Charlie put some brains in. I was going to tell him but I remembered Dr Strauss said no. Then Frank Reilly said what did you do

Charlie forget your key and open your door the hard way. That made me laff. Their really my friends and they like me.

Sometimes somebody will say hey look at Joe or Frank or George he really pulled a Charlie Gordon. I dont know why they say that but they always laff. This morning Amos Borg who is the 4 man at Donnegans used my name when he shouted at Ernie the office boy. Ernie lost a packige. He said Ernie for godsake what are you trying to be a Charlie Gordon. I dont understand why he said that.

MAR 28   Dr Strauss came to my room tonight to see why I dint come in like I was suppose to. I told him I dont like to race with Algernon any more. He said I dont have to for a while but I shud come in. He had a present for me. I thot it was a little television but it wasnt. He said I got to turn it on when I go to sleep. I said your kidding why shud I turn it on when Im going to sleep. Who ever herd of a thing like that. But he said if I want to get smart I got to do what he says. I told him I dint think I was going to get smart and he puts his hand on my sholder and said Charlie you dont know it yet but your getting smarter all the time. You wont notice for a while. I think he was just being nice to make me feel good because I dont look any smarter.

Oh yes I almost forgot. I asked him when I can go back to the class at Miss Kinnians school. He said I wont go their. He said that soon Miss Kinnian will come to the hospitil to start and teach me speshul.

MAR 29   That crazy TV kept up all night. How can I sleep with something yelling crazy things all night in my ears. And the nutty pictures. Wow. I don't know what it says when Im up so how am I going to know when Im sleeping.

Dr Strauss says its ok. He says my brains are lerning when I sleep and that will help me when Miss Kinnian starts my lessons in the hospitl (only I found out it isn't a hospitil its a labatory.) I think its all crazy. If you can get smart when your sleeping why do people go to school. That thing I don't think will work. I use to watch the late show and the late late show on TV all the time and it never made me smart. Maybe you have to sleep while you watch it.

Dr Strauss showed me how to keep the TV turned low so now I can sleep. I don't hear a thing. And I still dont understand what it says. A few times I play it over in the morning to find out what I lerned when I was sleeping and I don't think so. Miss Kinnian says Maybe its another langwidge. But most times it sounds american. It talks faster than even Miss Gold who was my teacher in 6 grade.

I told Dr. Strauss what good is it to get smart in my sleep. I want to be smart when Im awake. He says its the same thing and I have two minds. Theres the *subconscious* and the *conscious* (thats how you spell it). And one dont tell the other one what its doing. They dont even talk to each other. Thats why I dream. And boy have I been having crazy dreams. Wow. Ever since that night TV. The late late late show.

I forgot to ask him if it was only me or if everybody had those two minds.

(I just looked up the word in the dictionary Dr Strauss gave me. The word is *subconscious. adj. Of the nature of mental operations yet not present in consciousness; as, subconscious conflict of desires.*) There's more but I still dont know what it means. This isnt a very good dictionary for dumb people like me.

Anyway the headache is from the party. My friends from the factery Joe Carp and Frank Reilly invited me to go to Muggsys Saloon for some drinks. I don't like to drink but they said we will have lots of fun. I had a good time.

Joe Carp said I shoud show the girls how I mop out the toilet in the factory and he got me a mop. I showed them and everyone laffed when I told that Mr. Donnegan said I was the best janiter he ever had because I like my job and do it good and never miss a day except for my operashun.

I said Miss Kinnian always said Charlie be proud of your job because you do it good.

Everybody laffed and we had a good time and they gave me lots of drinks and Joe said Charlie is a card when hes potted. I dont know what that means but everybody likes me and we have fun. I cant wait to be smart like my best friends Joe Carp and Frank Reilly.

I dont remember how the party was over but I think I went out to buy a newspaper and coffe for Joe and Frank and when I came back there was no one their. I looked for them all over till late. Then I dont remember so good but I think I got sleepy or sick. A nice cop brot me back home Thats what my landlady Mrs Flynn says.

But I got a headache and a big lump on my head. I think maybe I fell but Joe Carp says it was the cop they beat up drunks some times. I don't think so. Miss Kinnian says cops are to help people. Anyway I got a bad headache and Im sick and hurt all over. I dont think Ill drink anymore.

APRIL 6   I beat Algernon! I dint even know I beat him until Burt the tester told me. Then the second time I lost because I got so exited I fell off the chair before I finished. But after that I beat him 8 more times. I must be getting smart to beat a smart mouse like Algernon. But I don't *feel* smarter.

I wanted to race Algernon some more but Burt said thats enough for one day. They let me hold him for a minit. Hes not so bad. Hes soft like a ball of cotton. He blinks and when he opens his eyes their black and pink on the eges.

I said can I feed him because I felt bad to beat him and I wanted to be nice and make friends. Burt said no Algernon is a very specshul mouse with an operashun like mine, and he was the first of all the animals to stay smart so long. He told me Algernon is so smart that every day he has to solve a test to get his food. Its a thing like a lock on a door that changes every time Algernon goes in to eat so he has to lern something new to get his food. That made me sad because if he couldn't lern he woud be hungry.

I don't think its right to make you pass a test to eat. How would Dr Nemur like it to have to pass a test every time he wants to eat. I think Ill be friends with Algernon.

APRIL 9   Tonight after work Miss Kinnian was at the laboratory. She looked like she was glad to see me but scared. I told her dont worry Miss Kinnian Im not smart yet and she laffed. She said I have confidence in you Charlie the way you struggled so hard to read and right better than all the others. At werst you will have it for a littel wile and your doing somthing for science.

We are reading a very hard book. Its called *Robinson Crusoe* about a man who gets merooned on a dessert Iland. Hes smart and figers out all kinds of things so he can have a house and food and hes a good swimmer. Only I feel sorry because hes all alone and has no frends. But I think their must be somebody else on the iland because theres a picture with his funny umbrella looking at footprints. I hope he gets a frend and not be lonly.

APRIL 10   Miss Kinnian teaches me to spell better. She says look at a word and close your eyes and say it over and over until you remember. I have lots of truble with *through* that you say *threw* and *enough* and *tough* that you dont say *enew* and *tew*. You got to say *enuff* and *tuff*. Thats how I use to write it before I started to get smart. I'm confused but Miss Kinnian says theres no reason in spelling.

APR 14   Finished *Robinson Crusoe*. I want to find out more about what happens to him but Miss Kinnian says thats all there is. *Why*.

APR 15   Miss Kinnian says Im lerning fast. She read some of the Progress Reports and she looked at me kind of funny. She says Im a fine person and Ill show them all. I asked her why. She said never mind but I shouldnt feel bad if I find out everybody isnt nice like I think. She said for a person who god gave so little to you done more then a lot of people with brains they never even used. I said all my friends are smart people but there good. They like me and they never did anything that wasnt nice. Then she got something in her eye and she had to run out to the ladys room.

APR 16   Today, I lerned, the *comma,* this is a comma (,) a period, with a tail, Miss Kinnian, says its importent, because, it makes writing, better, she said, somebody, coud lose, a lot of money, if a comma, isnt, in the, right place, I dont have, any money, and I dont see, how a comma, keeps you, from losing it,

APR 17   I used the comma wrong. Its punctuation. Miss Kinnian told me to look up long words in the dictionary to lern to spell them. I said whats the difference if you can read it anyway. She said its part of your education so now on Ill look up all the words Im not sure how to spell. It takes a long time to write that way but I only have to look up once and after that I get it right.
You got to mix them up, she showed? me" how. to mix! them (and now; I can! mix up all kinds" of punctuation, in! my

writing? There, are lots! of rules? to lern; but Im gettin'g them in my head.

One thing I like about, Dear Miss Kinnian: (thats the way it goes in a business letter if I ever go into business) is she, always gives me' a reason" when—I ask. She's a gen'ius! I wish I cou'd be smart" like, her;

(Punctuation, is; fun!)

APRIL 18   What a dope I am! I didn't even understand what she was talking about. I read the grammar book last night and it explanes the whole thing. Then I saw it was the same way as Miss Kinnian was trying to tell me, but I didn't get it.

Miss Kinnian said that the TV working in my sleep helped out. She and I reached a plateau. Thats a flat hill.

After I figured out how puncuation worked, I read over all my old Progress Reports from the beginning. Boy, did I have crazy spelling and punctuation! I told Miss Kinnian I ought to go over the pages and fix all the mistakes but she said, "No, Charlie, Dr. Nemur wants them just as they are. That's why he let you keep them after they were photostated, to see your own progress. You're coming along fast, Charlie."

That made me feel good. After the lesson I went down and played with Algernon. We don't race any more.

APRIL 20   I feel sick inside. Not sick like for a doctor, but inside my chest it feels empty like getting punched and a heartburn at the same time. I wasn't going to write about it, but I guess I got to, because its important. Today was the first time I ever stayed home from work.

Last night Joe Carp and Frank Reilly invited me to a party. There were lots of girls and some men from the factory. I remembered how sick I got last time I drank too much, so I told Joe I didn't want anything to drink. He gave me a plain coke instead.

We had a lot of fun for a while. Joe said I should dance with Ellen and she would teach me the steps. I fell a few times and I couldn't understand why because no one else was dancing besides Ellen and me. And all the time I was tripping because somebody's foot was always sticking out.

Then when I got up I saw the look on Joe's face and it gave me a funny feeling in my stomach. "He's a scream," one of the girls said. Everybody was laughing.

"Look at him. He's blushing. Charlie is blushing."

"Hey, Ellen, what'd you do to Charlie? I never saw him act like that before."

I didn't know what to do or where to turn. Everyone was looking at me and laughing and I felt naked. I wanted to hide. I ran outside and I threw up. Then I walked home. It's a funny thing I never knew that Joe and Frank and the others liked to have me around all the time to make fun of me.

Now I know what it means when they say "to pull a Charlie Gordon."

I'm ashamed.

PROGRESS REPORT 11

APRIL 21 Still didn't go into the factory. I told Mrs. Flynn my landlady to call and tell Mr. Donnegan I was sick. Mrs. Flynn looks at me very funny lately like she's scared.

I think it's a good thing about finding out how everybody laughs at me. I thought about it a lot. It's because I'm so dumb and I don't even know when I'm doing something dumb. People think it's funny when a dumb person can't do things the same way they can.

Anyway, now I know I'm getting smarter every day. I know punctuation and I can spell good. I like to look up all the hard words in the dictionary and I remember them. I'm reading a lot now, and Miss Kinnian says I read very fast. Sometimes I even understand what I'm reading about, and it stays in my mind. There are times when I can close my eyes and think of a page and it all comes back like a picture.

Besides history, geography and arithmetic, Miss Kinnian said I should start to learn foreign languages. Dr. Strauss gave me some more tapes to play while I sleep. I still don't understand how that conscious and unconscious mind works, but Dr. Strauss says not to worry yet. He asked me to promise that when I start learning college subjects next week I wouldn't read any books on psychology—that is, until he gives me permission.

I feel a lot better today, but I guess I'm still a little angry that all the time people were laughing and making fun of me because I wasn't so smart. When I become intelligent like Dr. Strauss says, with three times my I.Q. of 68, then maybe I'll be like everyone else and people will like me.

I'm not sure what an I.Q. is. Dr. Nemur said it was something that measured how intelligent you were—like a scale in the drugstore weighs pounds. But Dr. Strauss had a big argument with him and said an I.Q. didn't weigh intelligence at all. He said an I.Q. showed how much intelligence you could get, like the numbers on the outside of a measuring cup. You still had to fill the cup up with stuff.

Then when I asked Burt, who gives me my intelligence tests and works with Algernon, he said that both of them were wrong (only I had to promise not to tell them he said so). Burt says that the I.Q. measures a lot of different things including some of the things you learned already, and it really isn't any good at all.

So I still don't know what I.Q. is except that mine is going to be over 200 soon. I didn't want to say anything, but I don't see how if they don't know *what* it is, or *where* it is—I don't see how they know *how much* of it you've got.

Dr. Nemur says I have to take a *Rorschach Test* tomorrow. I wonder what *that* is.

APRIL 22   I found out what a Rorschach is. It's the test I took before the operation—the one with the inkblots on the pieces of cardboard.

I was scared to death of those inkblots. I knew the man was going to ask me to find the pictures and I knew I couldn't. I was thinking to myself, if only there was some way of knowing what kind of pictures were hidden there. Maybe there weren't any pictures at all. Maybe it was just a trick to see if I was dumb enough to look for something that wasn't there. Just thinking about that made me sore at him.

"All right, Charlie," he said, "you've seen these cards before, remember?"

"Of course I remember."

The way I said it, he knew I was angry, and he looked surprised. "Yes, of course. Now I want you to look at this. What might this be? What do you see on this card? People see all sorts of things in these inkblots. Tell me what it might be for you—what it makes you think of."

I was shocked. That wasn't what I had expected him to say. "You mean there are no pictures hidden in those inkblots?"

He frowned and took off his glasses. "What?"

"Pictures. Hidden in the inkblots. Last time you told me everyone could see them and you wanted me to find them too."

He explained to me that the last time he had used almost the exact same words he was using now. I didn't believe it, and I still have the suspicion that he misled me at the time just for the fun of it. Unless—I don't know any more—could I have been *that* feeble-minded?

We went through the cards slowly. One looked like a pair of bats tugging at something. Another one looked like two men fencing with swords. I imagined all sorts of things. I guess I got carried away. But I didn't trust him any more, and I kept turning them around, even looking on the back to see if there was anything there I was supposed to catch. While he was making his notes, I peeked out of the corner of my eye to read it. But it was all in code that looked like this:

$$WF + A \qquad DdF—Ad \text{ orig.} \qquad WF—A$$
$$SF + obj$$

The test still doesn't make sense to me. It seems to me that anyone could make up lies about things that they didn't really imagine? Maybe I'll understand it when Dr. Strauss lets me read up on psychology.

APRIL 25   I figured out a new way to line up the machines in the factory, and Mr. Donnegan says it will save him ten thousand dollars a year in labor and increased production. He gave me a $25 bonus.

I wanted to take Joe Carp and Frank Reilly out to lunch to celebrate, but Joe said he had to buy some things for his wife, and Frank said he was meeting his cousin for lunch. I guess it'll take a little time for them to get used to the changes in me. Everybody seems to be frightened of me. When I went over to Amos Borg and tapped him, he jumped up in the air.

People don't talk to me much any more or kid around the way they used to. It makes the job kind of lonely.

APRIL 27   I got up the nerve today to ask Miss Kinnian to have dinner with me tomorrow night to celebrate my bonus.

At first she wasn't sure it was right, but I asked Dr. Strauss and he said it was okay. Dr. Strauss and Dr. Nemur don't seem to be getting along so well. They're arguing all the time. This evening I heard them shouting. Dr. Nemur was saying that it was *his* experiment and *his* research, and Dr. Strauss shouted back that he contributed just as much, because he found me through Miss Kinnian and he performed the operation. Dr. Strauss said that someday thousands of neuro-surgeons might be using his technique all over the world.

Dr. Nemur wanted to publish the results of the experiment at the end of this month. Dr. Strauss wanted to wait a while to be sure. Dr. Strauss said Dr. Nemur was more interested in the Chair of Psychology at Princeton than he was in the experiment. Dr. Nemur said Dr. Strauss was nothing but an opportunist trying to ride to glory on *his* coattails.

When I left afterwards, I found myself trembling. I don't know why for sure, but it was as if I'd seen both men clearly for the first time. I remember hearing Burt say Dr. Nemur had a shrew of a wife who was pushing him all the time to get things published so he could become famous. Burt said that the dream of her life was to have a big shot husband.

APRIL 28 I don't understand why I never noticed how beautiful Miss Kinnian really is. She has brown eyes and feathery brown hair that comes to the top of her neck. She's only thirty-four! I think from the beginning I had the feeling that she was an unreachable genius—and very, very old. Now, every time I see her she grows younger and more lovely.

We had dinner and a long talk. When she said I was coming along so fast I'd be leaving her behind, I laughed.

"It's true, Charlie. You're already a better reader than I am. You can read a whole page at a glance while I can take in only a few lines at a time. And you remember every single thing you read. I'm lucky if I can recall the main thoughts and the general meaning."

"I don't feel intelligent. There are so many things I don't understand."

She took out a cigarette and I lit it for her. "You've got to be a *little* patient. You're accomplishing in days and weeks what it takes normal people to do in a lifetime. That's what makes it so amazing. You're like a giant sponge now, soaking things in. Facts, figures, general knowledge. And soon you'll begin to connect them, too. You'll see how different branches of learning are related. There are many levels, Charlie, like steps on a giant ladder that take you up higher and higher to see more and more of the world around you.

"I can see only a little bit of that, Charlie, and I won't go much higher than I am now, but you'll keep climbing up and up, and see more and more, and each step will open new worlds that you never even knew existed." She frowned. "I hope . . . I just hope to God—"

"What?"

"Never mind, Charles. I just hope I wasn't wrong to advise you to go into this in the first place."

I laughed. "How could that be? It worked, didn't it? Even Algernon is still smart."

We sat there silently for a while and I knew what she was thinking about as she watched me toying with the chain of my rabbit's foot and my keys. I didn't want to think of that possibility any more than elderly people want to think of death. I *knew* that this was only the beginning. I knew what she meant about levels because I'd seen some of them already. The thought of leaving her behind made me sad.

I'm in love with Miss Kinnian.

PROGRESS REPORT 12

APRIL 30   I've quit my job with Donnegan's Plastic Box Company. Mr. Donnegan insisted it would be better for all concerned if I left. What did I do to make them hate me so?

The first I knew of it was when Mr. Donnegan showed me the petition. Eight hundred names, everyone in the factory, except Fanny Girden. Scanning the list quickly, I saw at once that hers was the only missing name. All the rest demanded that I be fired.

Joe Carp and Frank Reilly wouldn't talk to me about it. No one else would either, except Fanny. She was one of the few people I'd known who set her mind to something and believed it no matter what the rest of the world proved, said or did—and Fanny did not believe that I should have been fired. She had been against the petition on principle and despite the pressure and threats she'd held out.

"Which don't mean to say," she remarked, "that I don't think there's something mighty strange about you, Charlie. Them changes. I don't know. You used to be a good, dependable, ordinary man—not too bright maybe, but honest. Who knows what you done to yourself to get so smart all of a sudden. Like everybody around here's been saying, Charlie, it's not right."

"But how can you say that, Fanny? What's wrong with a

man becoming intelligent and wanting to acquire knowledge and understanding of the world around him?"

She stared down at her work and I turned to leave. Without looking at me, she said: "It was evil when Eve listened to the snake and ate from the tree of knowledge. It was evil when she saw that she was naked. If not for that none of us would ever have to grow old and sick, and die."

Once again, now, I have the feeling of shame burning inside me. This intelligence has driven a wedge between me and all the people I once knew and loved. Before, they laughed at me and despised me for my ignorance and dullness; now, they hate me for my knowledge and understanding. What in God's name do they want of me?

They've driven me out of the factory. Now I'm more alone than ever before. . . .

MAY 15   Dr. Strauss is very angry at me for not having written any progress reports in two weeks. He's justified because the lab is now paying me a regular salary. I told him I was too busy thinking and reading. When I pointed out that writing was such a slow process that it made me impatient with my poor handwriting, he suggested I learn to type. It's much easier to write now because I can type seventy-five words a minute. Dr. Strauss continually reminds me of the need to speak and write simply so people will be able to understand me.

I'll try to review all the things that happened to me during the last two weeks. Algernon and I were presented to the *American Psychological Association* sitting in convention with the *World Psychological Association*. We created quite a sensation. Dr. Nemur and Dr. Strauss were proud of us.

I suspect that Dr. Nemur, who is sixty—ten years older than Dr. Strauss—finds it necessary to see tangible results of his work. Undoubtedly the result of pressure by Mrs. Nemur.

Contrary to my earlier impressions of him, I realize that Dr. Nemur is not at all a genius. He has a very good mind, but it struggles under the spectre[5] of self-doubt. He wants people to take him for a genius. Therefore it is important for him to feel that his work is accepted by the world. I believe that Dr. Nemur was afraid of further delay because he worried that someone else might make a discovery along these lines and take the credit from him.

5. **spectre** (spĕk′tər): something that arouses fear or dread, such as a ghost.

Dr. Strauss on the other hand might be called a genius, although I feel his areas of knowledge are too limited. He was educated in the tradition of narrow specialization; the broader aspects of background were neglected far more than necessary—even for a neuro-surgeon.

I was shocked to learn the only ancient languages he could read were Latin, Greek and Hebrew, and that he knows almost nothing of mathematics beyond the elementary levels of the calculus of variations.[6] When he admitted this to me, I found myself almost annoyed. It was as if he'd hidden this part of himself in order to deceive me, pretending—as do many people I've discovered—to be what he is not. No one I've ever known is what he appears to be on the surface.

Dr. Nemur appears to be uncomfortable around me. Sometimes when I try to talk to him, he just looks at me strangely and turns away. I was angry at first when Dr. Strauss told me I was giving Dr. Nemur an inferiority complex. I thought he was mocking me and I'm oversensitive at being made fun of.

How was I to know that a highly respected psycho-experimentalist like Nemur was unacquainted with Hindustani and Chinese? It's absurd when you consider the work that is being done in India and China today in the very field of his study.

I asked Dr. Strauss how Nemur could refute Rahajamati's attack on his method if Nemur couldn't even read them in the first place. That strange look on Strauss' face can mean only one of two things. Either he doesn't want to tell Nemur what they're saying in India, or else—and this worries me—Dr. Strauss doesn't know either. I must be careful to speak and write clearly and simply so people won't laugh.

MAY 18   I am very disturbed. I saw Miss Kinnian last night for the first time in over a week. I tried to avoid all discussions of intellectual concepts and to keep the conversation on a simple, everyday level, but she just stared at me blankly and asked me what I meant about the mathematical variance equivalent in Dorbermann's *Fifth Concerto*.[7]

When I tried to explain she stopped me and laughed. I guess I

6. **calculus of variations:** a branch of higher mathematics developed by Jakob and Johann Bernoulli in the seventeenth century.
7. **Dorbermann's *Fifth Concerto*:** fictional music composer, and fictional composition.

got angry, but I suspect I'm approaching her on the wrong level. No matter what I try to discuss with her, I am unable to communicate. I must review Vrostadt's equations on *Levels of Semantic Progression.*[8] I find I don't communicate with people much any more. Thank God for books and music and things I can think about. I am alone at Mrs. Flynn's boarding house most of the time and seldom speak to anyone.

MAY 20   I would not have noticed the new dishwasher, a boy of about sixteen, at the corner diner where I take my evening meals if not for the incident of the broken dishes.

They crashed to the floor, sending bits of white china under the tables. The boy stood there, dazed and frightened, holding the empty tray in his hand. The catcalls from the customers (the cries of "hey, there go the profits!" . . . *"Mazeltov!"*[9] . . . and "well, *he* didn't work here very long . . ." which invariably seem to follow the breaking of glass or dishware in a public restaurant) all seemed to confuse him.

When the owner came to see what the excitement was about, the boy cowered as if he expected to be struck. "All right! All right, you dope," shouted the owner, "don't just stand there! Get the broom and sweep that mess up. A broom . . . a broom, you idiot! It's in the kitchen!"

The boy saw he was not going to be punished. His frightened expression disappeared and he smiled as he came back with the broom to sweep the floor. A few of the rowdier customers kept up the remarks, amusing themselves at his expense.

"Here, sonny, over here there's a nice piece behind you . . ."

"He's not so dumb. It's easier to break 'em than wash em!"

As his vacant eyes moved across the crowd of onlookers, he slowly mirrored their smiles and finally broke into an uncertain grin at the joke he obviously did not understand.

I felt sick inside as I looked at his dull, vacuous smile, the wide, bright eyes of a child, uncertain but eager to please. They were laughing at him because he was mentally retarded.

And I had been laughing at him too.

8. Vrostadt's equations on *Levels of Semantic Progression*: fictional semanticist. Semantics is the study of the development of speech forms, signs, and symbols.

9. Mazeltov (mäz'əl · tôv): expression of best wishes, used by Jews on fortunate occasions. It is a corruption of two Hebrew words, *Mazal tov*.

Suddenly I was furious at myself and all those who were smirking at him. I jumped up and shouted, "Shut up! Leave him alone! It's not his fault he can't understand! He can't help what he is! But he's still a human being!"

The room grew silent. I cursed myself for losing control. I tried not to look at the boy as I walked out without touching my food. I felt ashamed for both of us.

How strange that people of honest feelings and sensibility, who would not take advantage of a man born without arms or eyes—how such people think nothing of abusing a man born with low intelligence. It infuriated me to think that not too long ago I had foolishly played the clown.

And I had almost forgotten.

I'd hidden the picture of the old Charlie Gordon from myself because now that I was intelligent it was something that had to be pushed out of my mind. But today in looking at that boy, for the first time I saw what I had been. *I was just like him!*

Only a short time ago, I learned that people laughed at me. Now I can see that unknowingly I joined with them in laughing at myself. That hurts most of all.

I have often reread my progress reports and seen the illiteracy, the childish naiveté,[10] the mind of low intelligence peering from a dark room, through the keyhole at the dazzling light outside. I see that even in my dullness I knew I was inferior, and that other people had something I lacked—something denied me. In my mental blindness, I thought it was somehow connected with the ability to read and write, and I was sure that if I could get those skills I would automatically have intelligence too.

Even a feeble-minded man wants to be like other men.

A child may not know how to feed itself, or what to eat, yet it knows of hunger.

This then is what I was like. I never knew. Even with my gift of intellectual awareness, I never really knew.

This day was good for me. Seeing the past more clearly, I've decided to use my knowledge and skills to work in the field of increasing human intelligence levels. Who is better equipped for this work? Who else has lived in both worlds? These are my people. Let me use my gift to do something for them.

Tomorrow, I will discuss with Dr. Strauss how I can work in

10. **naiveté** (nä·ēv'tā'): innocence, simplicity.

this area. I may be able to help him work out the problems of widespread use of the technique which was used on me. I have several good ideas of my own.

There is so much that might be done with this technique. If I could be made into a genius, what about thousands of others like myself? What fantastic levels might be achieved by using this technique on normal people? On *geniuses?*

There are so many doors to open. I am impatient to begin.

PROGRESS REPORT 13

MAY 23   It happened today. Algernon bit me. I visited the lab to see him as I do occasionally, and when I took him out of his cage, he snapped at my hand. I put him back and watched him for a while. He was unusually disturbed and vicious.

MAY 24   Burt, who is in charge of the experimental animals, tells me that Algernon is changing. He is less co-operative; he refuses to run the maze any more; general motivation has decreased. And he hasn't been eating. Everyone is upset about what this may mean.

MAY 25   They've been feeding Algernon, who now refuses to work the shifting-lock problem. Everyone identifies me with Algernon. In a way we're both the first of our kind. They're all pretending that Algernon's behavior is not necessarily significant for me. But it's hard to hide the fact that some of the other animals who were used in this experiment are showing strange behavior.

Dr. Strauss and Dr. Nemur have asked me not to come to the lab any more. I know what they're thinking but I can't accept it. I am going ahead with my plans to carry their research forward. With all due respect to both these fine scientists, I am well aware of their limitations. If there is an answer, I'll have to find it out for myself. Suddenly, time has become very important to me.

MAY 29   I have been given a lab of my own and permission to go ahead with the research. I'm onto something. Working day and night. I've had a cot moved into the lab. Most of my writing time is spent on the notes which I keep in a separate folder, but from time to time I feel it necessary to put down my moods and thoughts from sheer habit.

I find the *calculus of intelligence* to be a fascinating study. Here is the place for the application of all the knowledge I have acquired.

MAY 31 Dr. Strauss thinks I'm working too hard. Dr. Nemur says I'm trying to cram a lifetime of research and thought into a few weeks. I know I should rest, but I'm driven on by something inside that won't let me stop. I've got to find the reason for the sharp regression in Algernon. I've got to know *if* and *when* it will happen to me.

June 4

LETTER TO DR. STRAUSS (*copy*)

Dear Dr. Strauss:

Under separate cover I am sending you a copy of my report entitled, "The Algernon-Gordon Effect: A Study of Structure and Function of Increased Intelligence," which I would like to have published.

As you see, my experiments are completed. I have included in my report all of my formulae, as well as mathematical analysis in the appendix. Of course, these should be verified.

Because of its importance to both you and Dr. Nemur (and need I say to myself, too?) I have checked and rechecked my results a dozen times in the hope of finding an error. I am sorry to say the results must stand. Yet for the sake of science, I am grateful for the little bit that I here add to the knowledge of the function of the human mind and of the laws governing the artificial increase of human intelligence.

I recall your once saying to me that an experimental *failure* or the *disproving* of a theory was as important to the advancement of learning as a success would be. I know now that this is true. I am sorry, however, that my own contribution to the field must rest upon the ashes of the work of two men I regard so highly.

Yours truly,
Charles Gordon

JUNE 5 I must not become emotional. The facts and the results of my experiments are clear, and the more sensational aspects of my own rapid climb cannot obscure the fact that the tripling of intelligence by the surgical technique developed by Drs. Strauss and Nemur must be viewed as having little or no practical applicability (at the present time) to the increase of human intelligence.

As I review the records and data on Algernon, I see that although he is still in his physical infancy, he has regressed mentally. Motor activity is impaired; there is a general reduction of glandular activity; there is an accelerated loss of coordination.

There are also strong indications of progressive amnesia.[11]

As will be seen by my report, these and other physical and mental deterioration[12] syndromes[13] can be predicted with significant results by the application of my formula.

The surgical stimulus to which we were both subjected has resulted in an intensification and acceleration of all mental processes. The unforeseen development, which I have taken the liberty of calling the *Algernon-Gordon Effect,* is the logical extension of the entire intelligence speed-up. The hypothesis here proven may be described simply in the following terms: Artificially increased intelligence deteriorates at a rate of time directly proportional to the quantity of the increase.

I feel that this, in itself, is an important discovery.

As long as I am able to write, I will continue to record my thoughts in these progress reports. It is one of my few pleasures. However, by all indications, my own mental deterioration will be very rapid.

I have already begun to notice signs of emotional instability and forgetfulness, the first symptoms of the burnout.

JUNE 10 Deterioration progressing. I have become absent-minded. Algernon died two days ago. Dissection[14] shows my predictions were right. His brain had decreased in weight and there

11. **amnesia** (ăm·nē'zhə): partial or total loss of memory, especially through shock, injury, psychological disturbance or illness.
12. **deterioration** (dĭ·tîr'ē·ə·rā'shən): loss or decay.
13. **syndromes** (sĭn'drōms'): combinations of signs indicating disease.
14. **dissection** (dĭ·sĕk'shən): dividing a dead animal into its parts in order to study structure or cause of death.

was a general smoothing out of cerebral convolutions,[15] as well as a deepening and broadening of brain fissures.[16]

I guess the same thing is or will soon be happening to me. Now that it's definite, I don't want it to happen.

I put Algernon's body in a cheese box and buried him in the back yard. I cried.

JUNE 15 Dr. Strauss came to see me again. I wouldn't open the door and I told him to go away. I want to be left to myself. I am touchy and irritable. I feel the darkness closing in. It's hard to throw off thoughts of suicide. I keep telling myself how important this journal will be.

It's a strange sensation to pick up a book you enjoyed just a few months ago and discover you don't remember it. I remembered how great I thought John Milton[17] was, but when I picked up *Paradise Lost* I couldn't understand it at all. I got so angry I threw the book across the room.

I've got to try to hold on to some of it. Some of the things I've learned. Oh, God, please don't take it all away.

JUNE 19 Sometimes, at night, I go out for a walk. Last night, I couldn't remember where I lived. A policeman took me home. I have the strange feeling that this has all happened to me before—a long time ago. I keep telling myself I'm the only person in the world who can describe what's happening to me.

JUNE 21 Why can't I remember? I've got to fight. I lie in bed for days and I don't know who or where I am. Then it all comes back to me in a flash. Fugues[18] of amnesia. Symptoms of senility—second childhood. I can watch them coming on. It's so cruelly logical. I learned so much and so fast. Now my mind is deteriorating rapidly. I won't let it happen. I'll fight it. I can't help

---

15. **cerebral convolutions** (kŏn'və·loo'shəns): ridges or folds in the surface of the brain.
16. **fissures** (fĭsh'ərs): cracks.
17. **John Milton**: English poet and writer (1608–1674) in behalf of political and religious liberty. He wrote the long, richly allusive poem *Paradise Lost* (1665) after he had· become blind.
18. **fugues** (fūgs): usually, music based on short themes which are repeated with slight variations; here, temporary flights from the real world.

thinking of the boy in the restaurant, the blank expression, the silly smile, the people laughing at him. No—please—not that again. . . .

JUNE 22   I'm forgetting things that I learned recently. It seems to be following the classic pattern—the last things learned are the first things forgotten. Or is that the pattern? I'd better look it up again. . . .

I re-read my paper on the *Algernon-Gordon Effect* and I get the strange feeling that it was written by someone else. There are parts I don't even understand.

Motor activity impaired. I keep tripping over things, and it becomes increasingly difficult to type.

JUNE 23   I've given up using the typewriter. My coordination is bad. I feel I'm moving slower and slower. Had a terrible shock today. I picked up a copy of an article I used in my research, Krueger's *Uber psychische Ganzheit,*[19] to see if it would help me understand what I had done. First I thought there was something wrong with my eyes. Then I realized I could no longer read German. I tested myself in other languages. All gone.

JUNE 30   A week since I dared to write again. It's slipping away like sand through my fingers. Most of the books I have are too hard for me now. I get angry with them because I know that I read and understood them just a few weeks ago.

I keep telling myself I must keep writing these reports so that somebody will know what is happening to me. But it gets harder to form the words and remember spellings. I have to look up even simple words in the dictionary now and it makes me impatient with myself.

Dr. Strauss comes around almost every day, but I told him I wouldn't see or speak to anybody. He feels guilty. They all do. But I don't blame anyone. I knew what might happen. But how it hurts.

JULY 7   I don't know where the week went. Todays Sunday I know because I can see through my window people going to church. I think I stayed in bed all week but I remember Mrs.

19. Krueger's *Uber psychische Ganzheit:* fictional scientist's work in German (translation: *Concerning a Psychic Totality*).

Flynn bringing food to me a few times. I keep saying over and over I've got to do something but then I forget or maybe its just easier not to do what I say I'm going to do.

I think of my mother and father a lot these days. I found a picture of them with me taken at a beach. My father has a big ball under his arm and my mother is holding me by the hand. I dont remember them the way they are in the picture. All I remember is my father drunk most of the time and arguing with mom about money.

He never shaved much and he used to scratch my face when he hugged me. My Mother said he died but Cousin Miltie said he heard his dad say that my father ran away with another woman. When I asked my mother she slapped me and said my father was dead. I dont think I ever found out the truth but I dont care much. (He said he was going to take me to see cows on a farm once but he never did. He never kept his promises. . . .)

JULY 10 My landlady Mrs. Flynn is very worried about me. She says the way I lay around all day and dont do anything I remind her of her son before she threw him out of the house. She said she doesn't like loafers. If Im sick its one thing, but if Im a loafer thats another thing and she won't have it. I told her I think Im sick.

I try to read a little bit every day, mostly stories, but sometimes I have to read the same thing over and over again because I don't know what it means. And its hard to write. I know I should look up all the words in the dictionary but its so hard and Im so tired all the time.

Then I got the idea that I would only use the easy words instead of the long hard ones. That saves time. I put flowers on Algernons grave about once a week. Mrs. Flynn thinks Im crazy to put flowers on a mouses grave but I told her that Algernon was special.

JULY 14 Its sunday again. I dont have anything to do to keep me busy now because my television set is broke and I dont have any money to get it fixed. (I think I lost this months check from the lab. I dont remember)

I get awful headaches and asperin doesnt help me much. Mrs. Flynn knows Im really sick and she feels very sorry for me. Shes a wonderful woman whenever someone is sick.

JULY 22   Mrs. Flynn called a strange doctor to see me. She was afraid I was going to die. I told the doctor I wasnt too sick and I only forget sometimes. He asked me did I have any friends or relatives and I said no I dont have any. I told him I had a friend called Algernon once but he was a mouse and we used to run races together. He looked at me kind of funny like he thought I was crazy. He smiled when I told him I used to be a genius. He talked to me like I was a baby and he winked at Mrs. Flynn. I got mad and chased him out because he was making fun of me the way they all used to.

JULY 24   I have no more money and Mrs Flynn says I got to go to work somewhere and pay the rent because I havent paid for two months. I dont know any work but the job I used to have at Donnegans Box Company. I dont want to go back because they all knew me when I was smart and maybe they'll laugh at me. But I dont know what else to do to get money.

JULY 25   I was looking at some of my old progress reports and its very funny but I cant read what I wrote. I can make out some of the words but they dont make sense.

Miss Kinnian came to the door but I said go away I don't want to see you. She cried and I cried too but I wouldnt let her in because I didn't want her to laugh at me. I told her I didnt like her any more. I told her I didnt want to be smart any more. Thats not true. I still love her and I still want to be smart but I had to say that so shed go away. She gave Mrs. Flynn money to pay the rent. I dont want that. I got to get a job.

Please . . . please let me not forget how to read and write. . . .

JULY 27   Mr. Donnegan was very nice when I came back and asked him for my old job of janitor. First he was very suspicious but I told him what happened to me then he looked very sad and put his hand on my shoulder and said Charlie Gordon you got guts.

Everybody looked at me when I came downstairs and started working in the toilet sweeping it out like I used to. I told myself Charlie if they make fun of you dont get sore because you remember their not so smart as you once thot they were. And besides they were once your friends and if they laughted at you that doesnt meant anything because they liked you too.

One of the new men who came to work there after I went away made a nasty crack he said hey Charlie I hear your a very smart fella a real quiz kid. Say something intelligent. I felt bad but Joe Carp came over and grabbed him by the shirt and said leave him alone you lousy cracker or I'll break your neck. I didn't expect Joe to take my part so I guess hes really my friend.

Later Frank Reilly came over and said Charlie if anybody bothers you or trys to take advantage you call me or Joe and we will set em straight. I said thanks Frank and I got choked up so I had to turn around and go into the supply room so he wouldnt see me cry. Its good to have friends.

JULY 28   I did a dumb thing today I forgot I wasn't in Miss Kinnians class at the adult center any more like I use to be. I went in and sat down in my old seat in the back of the room and she looked at me funny and she said Charles. I dint remember she ever called me that before only Charlie so I said hello Miss Kinnian Im redy for my lesin today only I lost my reader that we was using. She startid to cry and run out of the room and everybody looked at me and I saw they wasnt the same pepul who use to be in my class.

Then all of a suddin I remembered some things about the operashun and me getting smart and I said holy smoke I reely pulled a Charlie Gordon that time. I went away before she come back to the room.

Thats why Im going away from New York for good. I dont want to do nothing like that agen. I dont want Miss Kinnian to feel sorry for me. Evry body feels sorry at the factery and I dont want that eather so Im going someplace where nobody knows that Charlie Gordon was once a genus and now he cant even reed a book or rite good.

Im taking a cuple of books along and even if I cant reed them Ill practise hard and maybe I wont forget every thing I lerned. If I try reel hard maybe Ill be a littel bit smarter then I was before the operashun. I got my rabits foot and my luky penny and maybe they will help me.

If you ever reed this Miss Kinnian dont be sorry for me Im glad I got a second chanse to be smart becaus I lerned a lot of things that I never even new were in this world and Im grateful that I saw it all for a littel bit. I dont know why Im dumb agen or what I did wrong maybe its because I dint try hard enuff. But if I try and practis very hard maybe Ill get a littl smarter and know what all the words are. I remember a littel bit how nice I had a feeling with the blue book that has the torn cover when I red it. Thats why Im gonna keep trying to get smart so I can have that feeling agen. Its a good feeling to know things and be smart. I wish I had it rite now if I did I would sit down and reed all the time. Anyway I bet Im the first dumb person in the world who ever found out something importent for science. I remember I did something but I dont remember what. So I gess its like I did it for all the dumb pepul like me.

Goodbye Miss Kinnian and Dr. Strauss and evreybody. And P.S. please tell Dr Nemur not to be such a grouch when pepul laff at him and he would have more frends. Its easy to make frends if you let pepul laff at you. Im going to have lots of frends where I go.

P.P.S. Please if you get a chanse put some flowrs on Algernons grave in the bak yard. . . .

Meaning

1. Why was Charlie chosen for the test?
2. How did Charlie's character and personality change as he grew more intelligent? How did his feelings about himself change?
3. Why did the factory workers demand that Charlie be fired?
4. What was the *Algernon-Gordon Effect?*
5. The *theme* of a story is the idea that underlies the plot. What is the theme of "Flowers for Algernon"? How does the ending contribute to the presentation of the theme?

Method

1. Why do you think Keyes chose the title "Flowers for Algernon"?
2. How does the author's use of progress reports to tell his story help to develop sympathy for Charlie?
3. A *motif* is an element (a character, idea, or phrase) that recurs several times in a story. How is the Algernon motif used to

foreshadow events as well as to unify the story and heighten the dramatic effect?

4. Which progress report provides the climax or turning point of the story?

5. What do you think of the *resolution* or dénouement of the story? Consider some alternative solutions. Would any of them fit the story better than the resolution that the author chose?

Language: Style

One of the best clues to the changes in Charlie's intelligence is the way his *style* in writing progress reports changes. Style is the way a writer uses language to express ideas. Consciously or unconsciously, a writer chooses and arranges words in sentences that can be simple or complicated. A sequence of several sentences can be varied or about the same in length and in structure.

Read the following sentences from "Flowers for Algernon." Identify the simple, monotonous style that was appropriate to Charlie's lower intelligence at the beginning and end of the story. Notice the simple vocabulary and the subject-followed-by-verb construction. How does Charlie's style change as he becomes more intelligent?

1. "I hope they use me. Miss Kinnian says maybe they can make me smart. I want to be smart."

2. "When I left afterwards, I found myself trembling. I don't know why for sure, but it was as if I'd seen both men clearly for the first time."

3. "Once again, now, I have the feeling of shame burning inside me. This intelligence has driven a wedge between me and all the people I once knew and loved."

4. "The surgical stimulus to which we were both subjected has resulted in an intensification and acceleration of all mental processes."

5. "I told him I saw a inkblot. He said yes and it made me feel good."

Discussion and Composition

1. If Charlie had known beforehand that he would eventually lose the intelligence he gained, do you think he still would have undergone the operation? Why or why not?

2. What are some attitudes toward handicapped people that you have observed or read about? What might be done to change people's attitudes?

3. The journal entries or "progress reports" in this story reveal to the reader Charlie's thoughts, feelings, and perceptions. Continue the story by writing a journal entry from Miss Kinian's point of view, giving her reaction to the events Charlie describes on July 28. Try to convey Miss Kinian's feelings about Charlie and about what has happened to him.

DANIEL GARZA

(born 1938)

Daniel Garza's family emigrated from Mexico and settled in Texas in the early 1900s. Born and raised in an agricultural community near Hillsboro, Texas, Garza attended public schools before studying at Texas Christian University in Ft. Worth. He later served as an officer in the U.S. Army.

Like many contemporary Mexican American writers, Garza describes in his works the difficult economic and social conditions faced by Mexican Americans—conditions that Garza experienced firsthand while growing up. In 1962, he was recognized for his writings on Mexican Americans when he received the *Harper's Magazine* Southwest Literature Award for an article on seasonal cotton pickers. Several of Garza's works—including the story "Everybody Knows Tobie," which appears on the following pages—have been anthologized over the past twenty years.

EVERYBODY KNOWS TOBIE

When I was thirteen years old my older brother, Tobie, had the town newspaper route. Everyone in the town knew him well because he had been delivering their papers for a year and a half. Tobie used to tell me that he had the best route of all because his customers would pay promptly each month, and sometimes, he used to brag that the nice people of the town would tip him a quarter or maybe fifty cents at the end of the month because he would trudge up many stairs to deliver the paper personally.

The other newspaper boys were not as lucky as Tobie because sometimes their customers would not be at home when they went by to collect payment for that month's newspapers, or maybe at the end of the month the customers would just try to avoid the paper boys to keep from paying.

Yes, Tobie had it good. The biggest advantage, I thought, that Tobie had over all the newspaper boys was that he knew the Gringos[1] of the town so well that he could go into a Gringo barbershop and get a haircut without having the barber tell him to go to the Mexican barber in our town or maybe just embarrassing him in front of all the Gringo customers in the shop as they often did when Chicano[2] cotton pickers came into their places during the fall months.

The Gringo barbers of my town were careful whom they allowed in their shops during the cotton harvest season in the fall. September and October and cotton brought Chicanos from the south to the north of Texas where I lived, and where the cotton was sometimes plentiful and sometimes scarce. Chicanos is what we say in our language, and it is slang among our people. It means the Mexicans of Texas. These Chicano cotton pickers came from the Rio Grande Valley in South Texas, and sometimes, even people from Mexico made the trip to the north of Texas. All these Chicanos came to my little town in which many Gringos lived, and a few of us who spoke both English and Spanish.

When the Chicanos came to my town on Saturdays after working frightfully in the cotton fields all week, they would go to the town market for food, and the fathers would buy candy and ice cream for their flocks of little black-headed ones. The younger ones, the *jóvenes*[3], would go to the local movie house. And then maybe those who had never been to the north of Texas before would go to the Gringos' barbershops for haircuts, not knowing that they would be refused. The Gringo barbers would be very careful not to let them come too close to their shops because the regular Gringo customers would get mad, and sometimes they would curse the Chicanos.

"Hell, it's them damn pepper bellies again. Can't seem to get rid of 'em in the fall," the prejudiced Gringos of my town would say. Some of the nicer people would only become uneasy at seeing so many Chicanos with long, black, greasy hair wanting haircuts.

The barbers of the town like Tobie, and they invited him to their shops for haircuts. Tobie said that the barbers told him that they

---

1. Gringos (green'gohs): foreigners who speak English, especially persons from the United States. It is sometimes used as a strongly negative term but not always; in this story it could be interchanged with the word *Anglo*.
2. Chicano (chee-kah'noh): Mexican American.
3. jóvenes (hoh'beh-nehs).

would cut his hair because he did not belong to that group of people who came from the south of Texas. Tobie understood. And he did not argue with the barbers because he knew how Chicanos from South Texas were, and how maybe Gringo scissors would get all greasy from cutting their hair.

During that fall Tobie encouraged me to go to the Gringo's place for a haircut. "Joey, when are you going to get rid of that mop of hair?" he asked.

"I guess I'll get rid of it when Mr. López learns how to cut flat-tops."

"Golly, Joey, Mr. López is a good ole guy and all that, but if he doesn't know how to give flat-tops then you should go to some other barber for flat-tops. Really, kid-brother, that hair looks awful."

"Yeah, but I'm afraid."

"Afraid of what?" Tobie asked.

"I'm afraid the barber will mistake me for one of those guys from South Texas and run me out of his shop."

"Oh, piddle," Tobie said. "Mr. Brewer . . . you know, the barber who cuts my hair . . . is a nice man, and he'll cut your hair. Just tell him you're my kid-brother."

I thought about this new adventure for several days, and then on a Saturday, when there was no school, I decided on the haircut at Mr. Brewer's. I hurriedly rode my bike to town and parked it in the alley close to the barbershop. As I walked into the shop, I noticed that all of a sudden the Gringos inside stopped their conversation and looked at me. The shop was silent for a moment. I thought then that maybe this was not too good and that I should leave. I remembered what Tobie had told me about being his brother, and about Mr. Brewer being a nice man. I was convinced that I belonged in the Gringo barbershop.

I found an empty chair and sat down to wait my turn for a haircut. One Gringo customer sitting next to me rose and explained to the barber that he had to go to the courthouse for something. Another customer left without saying anything. And then one, who was dressed in dirty coveralls and a faded khaki shirt, got up from Mr. Brewer's chair and said to him, "Say, Tom, looks like you got yourself a little tamale to clip."

Mr. Brewer smiled only.

My turn was next, and I was afraid. But I remembered again that this was all right because I was Tobie's brother, and everybody liked Tobie. I went to Mr. Brewer's chair. As I started to sit down, he looked at me and smiled a nice smile.

He said, "I'm sorry, sonny, but I can't cut your hair. You go to Mr. López's. He'll cut your hair."

Mr. Brewer took me to the door and pointed the way to López's barbershop. He pointed with his finger and said, "See, over there behind that service station. That's his place. You go there. He'll clip your hair."

Tears were welling in my eyes. I felt a lump in my throat. I was too choked up to tell him I was Tobie's brother, and that it was all right to cut my hair. I only looked at him as he finished giving directions. He smiled again and patted me on the back. As I left, Mr. Brewer said, "Say hello to Mr. López for me, will you, sonny?"

I did not turn back to look at Mr. Brewer. I kept my head bowed as I walked to Mr. López's because tears filled my eyes, and these tears were tears of hurt to the pride and confidence which I had slowly gained in my Gringo town.

I thought of many things as I walked slowly. Maybe this was a foolish thing which I had done. There were too many Gringos in the town, and too few of us who lived there all the year long. This was a bad thing because the Gringos had the right to say yes or no, and we could only follow what they said. It was useless to go against them. It was foolish. But I was different from the Chicanos who came from the south, not much different. I did live in the town the ten months of the year when the other Chicanos were in the south or in Mexico. Then I remembered what the barber had told my brother about the South Texas people, and why the Gringo customers had left while I was in Mr. Brewer's shop. I began to understand. But it was very hard for me to realize that even though I had lived among Gringos all of my life I still had to go to my own people for such things as haircuts. Why wouldn't Gringos cut my hair? I was clean. My hair was not long and greasy.

I walked into Mr. López's shop. There were many Chicanos sitting in the chairs and even on the floor waiting their turn for a haircut. Mr. López paused from his work as he saw me enter and said, "Sorry, Joey, full up. Come back in a couple of hours."

I shrugged my shoulders and said O.K. As I started to leave I remembered what Mr. Brewer had told me to say to Mr. López. "Mr. López," I said, and all the Chicanos, the ones who were waiting, turned and looked at me with curious eyes. "Mr. Brewer told me to tell you hello."

Mr. López shook his head approvingly, not digesting the content of my statement. The Chicanos looked at me again and began to whisper among themselves. I did not hear, but I understood.

I told Mr. López that I would return later in the day, but I did not because there would be other Chicanos wanting haircuts on Saturday. I could come during the week when he had more time, and when all the Chicanos would be in the fields working.

I went away feeling rejected both by the Gringos and even my people, the entire world I knew.

Back in the alley where my bike was parked I sat on the curb for a long while thinking how maybe I did not fit into this town. Maybe my place was in the south of Texas where there were many of my kind of people, and where there were more Chicano barbershops and less Gringo barbers. Yes, I thought, I needed a land where I could belong to one race. I was so concerned with myself that I did not notice a Chicano, a middle-aged man dressed in a new chambray shirt and faded denim pants, studying me.

He asked, "*Qué pasó, Chamaco?*"[4]

"*Nada,*"[5] I answered.

"Maybe the cotton has not been good for you this year."

"No, *señor*[6]. I live here in the town."

And then the Chicano said, "Chico, I mistook you for one of us."

Suddenly the Chicano became less interested in me and walked away unconcerned.

I could not have told him that I had tried for a haircut at the Gringo's because he would have laughed at me, and called me a *pocho*,[7] a Chicano who prefers Gringo ways. These experienced Chicanos knew the ways of the Gringos in the north of Texas.

After the Chicano had left me, I thought that maybe these things which were happening to me in the town would all pass in a short time. The entire cotton crop would soon be harvested, and the farmers around my town would have it baled and sold. Then the Chicanos would leave the north of Texas and journey back to their homes in the valley in the south and to Mexico.

---

4. **Qué pasó, Chamaco?** (keh pah-soh´, chah-mah´koh?): What happened, boy?
5. **Nada** (nah´thah): nothing.
6. **señor** (seh-nyohr´): sir; mister.
7. **pocho** (poh´choh).

My town would be left alone for ten more months of the year, and in this time everything and everybody would be all right again. The Gringo barbers would maybe think twice before sending me to Mr. López's.

Early in November the last of the cotton around my town had been harvested. The people of South Texas climbed aboard their big trucks with tall sideboards and canvas on the top to shield the sun, and they began their long journey to their homes in the border country.

The streets of the little town were now empty on Saturday. A few farmers came to town on Saturday and brought their families to do their shopping; still the streets were quiet and empty.

In my home there was new excitement for me. Tobie considered leaving his newspaper route for another job, one that would pay more money. And I thought that maybe he would let me take over his route. This was something very good. By taking his route I would know all the Gringos of the town, and maybe . . . maybe then the barbers would invite me to their shops as they had invited Tobie.

At supper that night I asked Tobie if he would take me on his delivery for a few days, and then let me deliver the newspaper on my own.

Tobie said, "No, Joey. You're too young to handle money. Besides, the newspaper bag would be too heavy for you to carry on your shoulder all over town. No, I think I'll turn the route over to Red."

My father was quiet during this time, but soon he spoke, "Tobie, you give the route to Joey. He knows about money. And he needs to put a little muscle on his shoulders."

The issue was settled.

The next day Tobie took me to the newspaper office. Tobie's boss, a nice elderly man wearing glasses, studied me carefully, scratched his white head, and then asked Tobie, "Well, what do you think?"

"Oh," Tobie said, "I told him he was too young to handle this job, but he says he can do it."

"Yes, sir," I butted enthusiastically.

Tobie's boss looked at me and chuckled, "Well, he's got enough spunk."

He thought some more.

Tobie spoke, "I think he'll make you a good delivery boy, sir."

A short silence followed while Tobie's boss put his thoughts down on a scratch pad on his desk.

Finally, the boss said, "We'll give him a try, Tobie." He looked at me. "But, young 'un, you'd better be careful with that money. It's your responsibility."

"Yes, sir," I gulped.

"O.K., that's settled," the boss said.

Tobie smiled and said, "Sir, I'm taking him on my delivery for a few days so he can get the hang of it, and then I'll let him take it over."

The boss agreed. I took his hand and shook it and promised him that I would do my extra best. Then Tobie left, and I followed behind.

In a few days I was delivering the *Daily News* to all the Gringos of the town, and also to Mr. Brewer.

Each afternoon, during my delivery, I was careful not to go into Mr. Brewer's with the newspaper. I would carefully open the door and drop the paper in. I did this because I thought that maybe Mr. Brewer would remember me, and this might cause an embarrassing incident. But I did this a very few times because one afternoon Mr. Brewer was standing at the door. He saw me. I opened the door and quickly handed him the newspaper, but before I could shut the door he said, "Say, sonny, aren't you the one I sent to Mr. López's a while back?"

"Yes, sir," I said.

"Why'd you stay around here? Didn't your people go back home last week? You do belong to 'em, don't you?"

"No, sir," I said. "I live here in the town."

"You mean to say you're not one of those . . . ?"

"No, sir."

"Well, I'll be durned." He paused and thought. "You know, sonny, I have a young Meskin boy who lives here in town come to this here shop for haircuts every other Saturday. His name is . . . durn, can't think of his name to save my soul . . ."

"Tobie?"

"Yeah, yeah, that's his name. Fine boy. You know him?"

"Yes, sir. He's my older brother."

Then Mr. Brewer's eyes got bigger in astonishment, "Well, I'll be doubly durned." He paused and shook his head unbelievingly. "And I told you to go to Mr. López's. Why didn't you speak up and tell me you was Tobie's brother? I woulda put you in that there chair and clipped you a pretty head of hair."

"Oh, I guess I forgot to tell you," I said.

"Well, from now on, sonny, you come to this here shop, and I'll cut your hair."

"But what about your customers? Won't they get mad?"

"Naw. I'll tell 'em you're Tobie's brother, and everything will be all right. Everybody in town knows Tobie, and everybody likes him."

Then a customer walked into the barbershop. He looked at Mr. Brewer, and then at me, and then at my newspaper bag. And then the Gringo customer smiled a nice smile at me.

"Well, excuse me, sonny, got a customer waitin'. Remember now, come Saturday, and I'll clip your hair."

"O.K., Mr. Brewer. Bye."

Mr. Brewer turned and said good-bye.

As I continued my delivery I began to chuckle small bits of contentment to myself because Mr. Brewer had invited me to his shop for haircuts, and because the Gringo customer had smiled at me, and because now all the Gringos of the town would know me and maybe accept me.

Those incidents which had happened to me during the cotton harvest in my town: Mr. Brewer sending me to Mr. López's for the haircut, and the Chicano cotton picker avoiding me after discovering that I was not one of his people, and the Gringo customers leaving Mr. Brewer's barbershop because of me; all seemed so insignificant. And now I felt that delivering the *Daily News* to the businessmen had given me a place among them, and all because of the fact that everybody in my town knew Tobie.

Meaning

1. Why does Joey feel "different from" the migrant workers? In what ways is he like them?
2. Why does Joey want to take over Tobie's newspaper route? How do his feelings about himself change when he takes over his brother's job?

3. At the end of the story, how does Joey feel about the discrimination he has experienced? Do you think Joey's feelings are consistent with his values? Why or why not?
4. What do you think is the *theme,* or underlying message, of this story?

Method

1. Explain the significance of the title. Who is "everybody" and in what sense do they "know" Tobie?
2. "Everybody Knows Tobie" is narrated from the first-person point of view. Why do you think the author chose to tell the story from Joey's viewpoint?
3. How does the use of dialogue help reveal the prejudiced attitudes of the characters in the story?
4. A *symbol* is something that has meaning in itself but also suggests something further, such as an attitude or a value. In what ways does a haircut serve as a symbol in this story?

Discussion and Composition

1. Describe the relationship between the two brothers, Joey and Tobie. Tell how you think they feel about each other, and give details from the story to support your opinion.
2. Do you think people sometimes hold prejudices without realizing it? If so, why? How might people become more thoughtful about their perceptions and treatment of those who are different from them?
3. Write a character sketch of Joey as he might be in ten years. Describe Joey's good traits and bad traits, and evaluate his overall character. As you plan your sketch, think about how Joey will change as he grows older. How will he feel about himself? Do you think he will have the same attitudes and values? Provide examples from the story to support your speculations.

TONI CADE BAMBARA
(born 1939)

Drama, dance, and linguistics are some of the fields that Toni Cade Bambara has studied intensively. She was born in New York City and graduated from Queens College in New York. She received her master's degree from the City University of New York, and has also studied in France and in Italy.

Her career has included work as a community organizer, health and youth worker, program director at settlement houses and hospitals, freelance writer, editor, and college teacher. She has written and had published articles, book and film reviews, and several volumes of short stories. She has also written one novel, *The Salt Eaters*.

BLUES AIN'T NO
MOCKIN BIRD

The puddle had frozen over, and me and Cathy went stompin in it. The twins from next door, Tyrone and Terry, were swingin so high out of sight we forgot we were waitin our turn on the tire. Cathy jumped up and came down hard on her heels and started tap-dancin. And the frozen patch splinterin every which way underneath kinda spooky. "Looks like a plastic spider web," she said. "A sort of weird spider, I guess, with many mental problems." But really it looked like the crystal paperweight Granny kept in the parlor. She was on the back porch, Granny was, making the cakes drunk. The old ladle dripping rum into the Christmas tins, like it used to drip maple syrup into the pails when we lived in the Judson's woods, like it poured cider into the vats when we were on the Cooper place, like it used to scoop buttermilk and soft cheese when we lived at the dairy.

"Go tell that man we ain't a bunch of trees."

"Ma'am?"

"I said to tell that man to get away from here with that

camera." Me and Cathy look over toward the meadow where the men with the station wagon'd been roamin around all mornin. The tall man with a huge camera lassoed to his shoulder was buzzin our way.

"They're makin movie pictures," yelled Tyrone, stiffenin his legs and twistin so the tire'd come down slow so they could see.

"They're makin movie pictures," sang out Terry.

"That boy don't never have anything original to say," say Cathy grown-up.

By the time the man with the camera had cut across our neighbor's yard, the twins were out of the trees swingin low and Granny was onto the steps, the screen door bammin soft and scratchy against her palms. "We thought we'd get a shot or two of the house and everything and then—"

"Good mornin," Granny cut him off. And smiled that smile.

"Good mornin," he said, head all down the way Bingo does when you yell at him about the bones on the kitchen floor. "Nice place you got here, aunty. We thought we'd take a—"

"Did you?" said Granny with her eyebrows. Cathy pulled up her socks and giggled.

"Nice things here," said the man, buzzin his camera over the yard. The pecan barrels, the sled, me and Cathy, the flowers, the printed stones along the driveway, the trees, the twins, the toolshed.

"I don't know about the thing, the it, and the stuff," said Granny, still talkin with her eyebrows. "Just people here is what I tend to consider."

Camera man stopped buzzin. Cathy giggled into her collar.

"Mornin, ladies," a new man said. He had come up behind us when we weren't looking. "And gents," discovering the twins givin him a nasty look. "We're filmin for the county," he said with a smile. "Mind if we shoot a bit around here?"

"I do indeed," said Granny with no smile. Smilin man was smiling up a storm. So was Cathy. But he didn't seem to have another word to say, so he and the camera man backed on out the yard, but you could hear the camera buzzin still. "Suppose you just shut that machine off," said Granny real low through her teeth, and took a step down off the porch and then another.

"Now, aunty," Camera said, pointin the thing straight at her.

"Your mama and I are not related."

Smilin man got his notebook out and a chewed-up pencil.

"Listen," he said movin back into our yard, "we'd like to have a statement from you . . . for the film. We're filmin for the county, see. Part of the food stamp campaign. You know about the food stamps?"

Granny said nuthin.

"Maybe there's somethin you want to say for the film. I see you grow your own vegetables," he smiled real nice. "If more folks did that, see, there'd be no need—"

Granny wasn't sayin nuthin. So they backed on out, buzzin at our clothesline and the twins' bicycles, then back on down to the meadow. The twins were danglin in the tire, lookin at Granny. Me and Cathy were waitin, too, cause Granny always got somethin to say. She teaches steady with no let-up. "I was on this bridge one time," she started off. "Was a crowd cause this man was goin to jump, you understand. And a minister was there and the police and some other folks. His woman was there, too."

"What was they doin?" asked Tyrone.

"Trying to talk him out of it was what they was doin. The minister talkin about how it was a mortal sin, suicide. His woman takin bites out of her own hand and not even knowin it, so nervous and cryin and talkin fast."

"So what happened?" asked Tyrone.

"So here comes . . . this person . . . with a camera, takin pictures of the man and the minister and the woman. Takin pictures of the man in his misery about to jump, cause life so bad and people been messin with him so bad. This person takin up the whole roll of film practically. But savin a few, of course."

"Of course," said Cathy, hatin the person. Me standin there wonderin how Cathy knew it was "of course" when I didn't and it was *my* grandmother.

After a while Tyrone say, "Did he jump?"

"Yeh, did he jump?" say Terry all eager.

And Granny just stared at the twins till their faces swallow up the eager and they don't even care any more about the man jumpin. Then she goes back onto the porch and lets the screen door go for itself. I'm lookin to Cathy to finish the story cause she knows Granny's whole story before me even. Like she knew how come we move so much and Cathy ain't but a third cousin we picked up on the way last Thanksgivin visitin. But she knew it was on account of people drivin Granny crazy till she'd get up in the night and start packin. Mumblin and packin and wakin everybody

up sayin, "Let's get on away from here before I kill me somebody."
Like people wouldn't pay her for things like they said they would.
Or Mr. Judson bringin us boxes of old clothes and raggedy maga-
zines. Or Mrs. Cooper comin in our kitchen and touchin every-
thing and sayin how clean it all was. Granny goin crazy, and
Granddaddy Cain pullin her off the people, sayin, "Now, now,
Cora." But next day loadin up the truck, with rocks all in his jaw,
madder than Granny in the first place.

"I read a story once," said Cathy soundin like Granny
teacher. "About this lady Goldilocks who barged into a house that
wasn't even hers. And not invited, you understand. Messed over
the people's groceries and broke up the people's furniture. Had the
nerve to sleep in the folks' bed."

"Then what happened?" asked Tyrone. "What they do, the
folks, when they come in to all this mess?"

"Did they make her pay for it?" asked Terry, makin a fist.
"I'd've made her pay me."

I didn't even ask. I could see Cathy actress was very likely to
just walk away and leave us in mystery about this story which I
heard was about some bears.

"Did they throw her out?" asked Tyrone, like his father
sounds when he's bein extra nasty-plus to the washin-machine
man.

"Woulda," said Terry. "I woulda gone upside[1] her head with
my fist and—"

"You woulda done whatcha always do—go cry to Mama,
you big baby," said Tyrone. So naturally Terry starts hittin on
Tyrone, and next thing you know they tumblin out the tire and
rollin on the ground. But Granny didn't say a thing or send the
twins home or step out on the steps to tell us about how we can't
afford to be fightin amongst ourselves. She didn't say nuthin. So I
get into the tire to take my turn. And I could see her leanin up
against the pantry table, starin at the cakes she was puttin up for
the Christmas sale, mumblin real low and grumpy and holding her
forehead like it wanted to fall off and mess up the rum cakes.

Behind me I hear before I can see Granddaddy Cain comin
through the woods in his field boots. Then I twist around to see
the shiny black oilskin cuttin through what little left there was of
yellows, reds, and oranges. His great white head not quite round

1. **upside:** *dialect,* to hit on the side.

cause of this bloody thing high on his shoulder, like he was wearin a cap on sideways. He takes the shortcut through the pecan grove, and the sound of twigs snapping overhead and underfoot travels clear and cold all the way up to us. And here comes Smilin and Camera up behind him like they was goin to do somethin. Folks like to go for him sometimes. Cathy say it's because he's so tall and quiet and like a king. And people just can't stand it. But Smilin and Camera don't hit him in the head or nuthin. They just buzz on him as he stalks by with the chicken hawk slung over his shoulder, squawkin, drippin red down the back of the oilskin. He passes the porch and stops a second for Granny to see he's caught the hawk at last, but she's just starin and mumblin, and not at the hawk. So he nails the bird to the toolshed door, the hammerin crackin through the eardrums. And the bird flappin himself to death and droolin down the door to paint the gravel in the drive- way red, then brown, then black. And the two men movin up on tiptoe like they was invisible or we were blind, one.

"Get them persons out of my flower bed, Mister Cain," say Granny moanin real low like at a funeral.

"How come your grandmother calls her husband 'Mister Cain' all the time?" Tyrone whispers all loud and noisy and from the city and don't know no better. Like his mama, Miss Myrtle, tell us never mind the formality as if we had no better breeding than to call her Myrtle, plain. And then this awful thing—a giant hawk—come wailin up over the meadow, flyin low and tilted and screamin, zigzaggin through the pecan grove, breakin branches and hollerin, snappin past the clothesline, flyin every which way, flying into things reckless with crazy.

"He's come to claim his mate," say Cathy fast, and ducks down. We all fall quick and flat into the gravel driveway, stones scraping my face. I squinch my eyes open again at the hawk on the door, tryin to fly up out of her death like it was just a sack flown into by mistake. Her body holdin her there on that nail, though. The mate beatin the air overhead and clutchin for hair, for heads, for landin space.

The camera man duckin and bendin and runnin and fallin, jigglin the camera and scared. And Smilin jumpin up and down swipin at the huge bird, tryin to bring the hawk down with just his raggedy ole cap. Granddaddy Cain straight up and silent, watchin the circles of the hawk, then aimin the hammer off his wrist. The giant bird fallin, silent and slow. Then here comes

Camera and Smilin all big and bad now that the awful screechin thing is on its back and broken, here they come. And Granddaddy Cain looks up at them like it was the first time noticin, but not payin them too much mind cause he's listenin, we all listenin, to that low groanin music comin from the porch. And we figure any minute, somethin in my back tells me any minute now, Granny gonna bust through that screen with somethin in her hand and murder on her mind. So Granddaddy say above the buzzin, but quiet, "Good day, gentlemen." Just like that. Like he'd invited them in to play cards and they'd stayed too long and all the sand-wiches were gone and Reverend Webb was droppin by and it was time to go.

They didn't know what to do. But like Cathy say, folks can't stand Granddaddy tall and silent and like a king. They can't nei-ther. The smile the men smilin is pullin the mouth back and showin the teeth. Lookin like the wolf man, both of them. Then Grandaddy holds his hand out—this huge hand I used to sit in when I was a baby and he'd carry me through the house to my mother like I was a gift on a tray. Like he used to on the trains. They called the other men just waiters. But they spoke of Granddaddy separate and said, The Waiter. And said he had en-gines in his feet and motors in his hands and couldn't no train throw him off and couldn't nobody turn him round. They were big enough for motors, his hands were. He held that one hand out all still and it gettin to be not at all a hand but a person in itself.

"He wants you to hand him the camera," Smilin whispers to Camera, tiltin his head to talk secret like they was in the jungle or somethin and come upon a native that don't speak the language. The men start untyin the straps, and they put the camera into that great hand speckled with the hawk's blood all black and crackly now. And the hand don't even drop with the weight, just the fingers move, curl up around the machine. But Granddaddy lookin straight at the men. They lookin at each other and every-where but at Granddaddy's face.

"We filmin for the county, see," say Smilin. "We puttin together a movie for the food stamp program . . . filmin all around these parts. Uhh, filmin for the county.

"Can I have my camera back?" say the tall man with no machine on his shoulder, but still keepin it high like the camera was still there or needed to be. "Please, sir."

Then Grandaddy's other hand flies up like a sudden and gentle bird, slaps down fast on top of the camera and lifts off half like it was a calabash cut for sharing.

"Hey," Camera jumps forward. He gathers up the parts into his chest and everything unrollin and fallin all over. "Whatcha tryin to do? You'll ruin the film." He looks down into his chest of metal reels and things like he's protectin a kitten from the cold.

"You standin in the misses' flower bed," say Grandaddy. "This is our own place."

The two men look at him, then at each other, then back at the mess in the camera man's chest, and they just back off. One sayin over and over all the way down to the meadow, "Watch it, Bruno. Keep ya fingers off the film." Then Grandaddy picks up the hammer and jams it into the oilskin pocket, scrapes his boots, and goes into the house. And you can hear the squish of his boots headin through the house. And you can see the funny shadow he throws from the parlor window onto the ground by the string-bean patch. The hammer draggin the pocket of the oilskin out so Granddaddy looked even wider. Granny was hummin now—high, not low and grumbly. And she was doin the cakes again, you could smell the molasses from the rum.

"There's this story I'm goin to write one day," say Cathy dreamer. "About the proper use of the hammer."

"Can I be in it?" Tyrone say with his hand up like it was a matter of first come, first served.

"Perhaps," say Cathy, climbin onto the tire to pump us up. "If you there and ready."

Meaning

1. Why was Granny angry at the cameraman? Do you think it was unfair of Granddaddy Cain to expose the film? Why or why not?

2. Explain the title, "Blues Ain't No Mockin Bird." What bird represents the "blues" in this story?

3. A *contrast* is a striking difference between two things. An author uses contrast for dramatic effect. How are Smilin and Camera a contrast to the Cains?

4. A *symbol* is an object, person, or place that suggests and stands for something else, usually an idea or an attitude. For example, the lion stands for courage, the lamb for meekness. What do the camera and the hammer symbolize in this story?

Method

1. This story is told from the first person point of view. What do you find out about the narrator? Why do you think the author chose this narrator and not any of the other characters in the story?
2. Are Smilin, Granny, and Cathy clearly drawn characters? Identify specific techniques of characterization in the story to support your answer.
3. What is the climax of the story? How does the author build towards this turning point?
4. How would you describe the *tone* of this story—the author's attitude toward her subject and her characters?

Language: Nonstandard English

Standard English is the kind of English that educated people consider to be correct and acceptable. It is the English you learn in school. Millions of Americans, however, speak *nonstandard* English—in special situations if they are educated enough to make the choice between standard and nonstandard, or all the time.

Nonstandard English includes slang, the vernacular, and dialect. *Slang* is made up of words and expressions that have been given a new meaning, sometimes popular only for a short time (for example, "dig" for "understand," "laid back" for "relaxed.") The *vernacular* may include slang, but it refers specifically to the everyday, informal language that is commonly spoken by people in an area (for example, "I could have sunk through the floor," instead of "I was very embarrassed.") A *dialect* is the spoken language of a particular group whose pronunciation, grammar, vocabulary, and intonation may differ from the standard language.

The author's use of dialect in "Blues Ain't No Mockin Bird" makes her dialogue vivid and realistic. Reread the following sentences from "Blues Ain't No Mockin Bird." Decide how each one would be written in standard English. Notice how the use of standard English changes the flavor of the original and makes it less interesting.

1. "Then she goes back onto the porch and lets the screen door go for itself."
2. "'You woulda done whatcha always do—go cry to Mama, you big baby,' said Tyrone."
3. "Me and Cathy look over toward the meadow where the men with the station wagon'd been roamin around all mornin."
4. "'That boy don't never have anything original to say,' say Cathy grown-up."
5. "Like she knew how come we move so much and Cathy ain't but a third cousin we picked up on the way last Thanksgivin visitin."

Discussion and Composition

1. Suppose that you saw television news footage of the family and setting described in the story. Would you consider the filming an invasion of privacy, or would you consider it realistic reporting of a social condition? To what extent would your attitude depend on how the footage was presented?

2. The two elderly people in this story are strong, independent characters who take charge of their lives and defend their personal rights. Write about an older person—perhaps a relative or a family friend—who has been an inspiration to you. In your composition, first give a description of the person, and then tell how he or she has influenced your life.

FRANK R. STOCKTON
(1834–1902)

Known primarily as an author of humorous fiction during his lifetime, Frank R. Stockton began writing only as a hobby. Born in Philadelphia, Stockton graduated from high school but did not go to college. Instead, he began to earn his living as a wood-engraver and was quite successful; his work appeared in national magazines. In his spare time, Stockton began writing fairy tales for children. He enjoyed this pastime so much that he left his engraving business to begin a second career as a journalist, editor, and freelance writer.

For many years he was an editor of *St. Nicholas,* a magazine for children. In addition to fantasies, he wrote amusing, sometimes satirical stories and novels for adults. "The Lady, or the Tiger?," his most famous short story, was written to be read before a literary society. It stirred up so much discussion that Stockton published the story in a magazine. He was flooded with letters demanding a solution to the riddle, which he never gave.

THE LADY, OR THE TIGER?

In the very olden time, there lived a semibarbaric king who was a man of exuberant fancy and of an authority so irresistible that, at his will, he turned his varied fancies into facts. He was greatly given to self-communing, and when he and himself agreed upon anything, the thing was done. When everything moved smoothly, his nature was bland and genial; but whenever there was a little hitch, he was blander and more genial still, for nothing pleased him so much as to make the crooked straight, and crush down uneven places.

Among his borrowed notions was that of the public arena, in which, by exhibitions of manly and beastly valor, the minds of his subjects were refined and cultured.

But even here the exuberant and barbaric fancy asserted itself. This vast amphitheater[1] with its encircling galleries, its mysterious vault, and its unseen passages, was an agent of poetic justice, in which crime was punished, or virtue rewarded, by the decrees of an impartial and incorruptible chance.

When a subject was accused of a crime of sufficient importance to interest the king, public notice was given that on an appointed day the fate of the accused person would be decided in the king's arena.

When all the people had assembled in the galleries, and the king, surrounded by his court, sat high up on his throne of royal state on one side of the arena, he gave a signal, a door beneath him opened, and the accused subject stepped out into the amphitheater. Directly opposite him, on the other side of the enclosed space, were two doors, exactly alike and side by side. It was the duty and the privilege of the person on trial to walk directly to these doors and open one of them. He could open either door he pleased. He was subject to no guidance or influence but that of the aforementioned impartial and incorruptible chance. If he opened the one, there came out of it a hungry tiger, the fiercest and most cruel that could be procured, which immediately sprang upon him and tore him to pieces as a punishment for his guilt. The moment that the case of the criminal was thus decided, doleful iron bells were clanged, great wails went up from the hired mourners posted on the outer rim of the arena, and the vast audience, with bowed heads and downcast hearts, wended slowly their homeward way, mourning greatly that one so young and fair, or so old and respected, should have merited so dire a fate.

But if the accused person opened the other door, there came forth from it a lady, the most suitable to his years and station that His Majesty could select among his fair subjects; and to this lady he was immediately married as a reward of his innocence. It mattered not that he might already possess a wife and family or that his affections might be engaged upon an object of his own selection. The king allowed no such arrangements to interfere with his great scheme of punishment and reward. The exercises, as in the other instance, took place immediately, and in the arena. Another door opened beneath the king, and a priest, followed by a band of choristers, and dancing maidens blowing joyous airs on golden

1. **amphitheater** (ăm′fə·thē′ ə·tər): an oval or round area enclosed by rising tiers of seats.

horns, advanced to where the pair stood side by side, and the wedding was promptly and cheerily solemnized. Then the gay brass bells rang forth their merry peals, and the people shouted glad hurrahs, and the innocent man, preceded by children strewing flowers on his path, led his bride to his home.

This was the king's semibarbaric method of administering justice. Its perfect fairness is obvious. The criminal could not know out of which door would come the lady. He opened either he pleased, without having the slightest idea whether, in the next instant, he was to be devoured or married. On some occasions the tiger came out of one door, and on some, out of the other. The decisions were not only fair—they were positively decisive. The accused person was instantly punished if he found himself guilty, and if innocent, he was rewarded on the spot, whether he liked it or not. There was no escape from the judgments of the king's arena.

The institution was a very popular one. When the people gathered together on one of the great trial days, they never knew whether they were to witness a bloody slaughter or a hilarious wedding. This element of uncertainty lent an interest to the occasion which it could not otherwise have attained. Thus the masses were entertained and pleased, and the thinking part of the community could bring no charge of unfairness against this plan; for did not the accused person have the whole matter in his own hands?

This semibarbaric king had a daughter as blooming as his most rosy fancies, and with a soul as fervent and imperious[2] as his own. As is usual in such cases, she was the apple of his eye, and was loved by him above all humanity. Among his courtiers was a young man of that fineness of blood and lowness of station common to the heroes of romance who love royal maidens. This royal maiden was well satisfied with her lover, for he was handsome and brave to a degree unsurpassed in all this kingdom, and she loved him with an ardor that had enough of barbarism in it to make it exceedingly warm and strong. This love affair moved on happily for many months until, one day, the king happened to discover its existence. He did not hesitate nor waver in regard to his duty. The youth was immediately cast into prison, and a day was appointed for his trial in the king's arena. This, of course, was an especially

---

2. imperious (ĭm·pêr'ē·əs): arrogant, overbearing.

important occasion, and His Majesty, as well as all the people, was greatly interested in the workings and development of this trial. Never before had such a case occurred—never before had a subject dared to love the daughter of a king. In after years such things became commonplace enough, but then they were, in no slight degree, novel and startling.

The tiger cages of the kingdom were searched for the most savage and relentless beasts, from which the fiercest monster might be selected for the arena, and the ranks of maiden youth and beauty throughout the land were carefully surveyed by competent judges, in order that the young man might have a fitting bride in case fate did not determine for him a different destiny. Of course, everybody knew that the deed with which the accused was charged had been done. He had loved the princess, and neither he, she, nor anyone else thought of denying the fact. But the king would not think of allowing any fact of this kind to interfere with the workings of the court of judgment, in which he took such great delight and satisfaction. No matter how the affair turned out, the youth would be disposed of, and the king would take pleasure in watching the course of events which would determine whether or not the young man had done wrong in allowing himself to love the princess.

The appointed day arrived. From far and near the people gathered and thronged the great galleries of the arena, while crowds, unable to gain admittance, massed themselves against its outside walls. The king and his court were in their places, opposite the twin doors—those fateful portals, so terrible in their similarity!

All was ready. The signal was given. A door beneath the royal party opened, and the lover of the princess walked into the arena. Tall, beautiful, fair, his appearance was greeted with a low hum of admiration and anxiety. Half the audience had not known so grand a youth had lived among them. No wonder the princess loved him! What a terrible thing for him to be there!

As the youth advanced into the arena, he turned, as the custom was, to bow to the king. But he did not think at all of that royal personage; his eyes were fixed upon the princess, who sat to the right of her father. Had it not been for the barbarism in her nature, it is probable that lady would not have been there. But her intense and fervid soul would not allow her to be absent on an occasion in which she was so terribly interested. From the moment that the decree had gone forth that her lover should decide his fate in the king's arena, she had thought of nothing, night or day, but this great event and the various subjects connected with it. Possessed of more power, influence, and force of character than anyone who had ever before been interested in such a case, she had done what no other person had done—she had possessed herself of the secret of the doors. She knew in which of the two rooms behind those doors stood the cage of the tiger, with its open front, and in which waited the lady. Through these thick doors, heavily curtained with skins on the inside, it was impossible that any noise or suggestion should come from within to the person who should approach to raise the latch of one of them. But gold, and the power of a woman's will, had brought the secret to the princess.

Not only did she know in which room stood the lady, ready to emerge, all blushing and radiant, should her door be opened, but she knew who the lady was. It was one of the fairest and loveliest of the damsels of the court who had been selected as the reward of the accused youth, should he be proved innocent of the crime of aspiring to one so far above him; and the princess hated her. Often had she seen, or imagined that she had seen, this fair creature throwing glances of admiration upon the person of her lover, and sometimes she thought these glances were perceived and even returned. Now and then she had seen them talking together. It was but for a moment or two, but much can be said in a brief space. It may have been on most unimportant topics, but how could she know that? The girl was lovely, but she had dared to raise her eyes to the loved one of the princess, and, with all the intensity of the savage blood transmitted to her through long lines of wholly barbaric ancestors, she hated the woman who blushed and trembled behind that silent door.

When her lover turned and looked at her, and his eye met hers as she sat there paler and whiter than anyone in the vast ocean of anxious faces about her, he saw, by that power of quick perception which is given to those whose souls are one, that she knew behind which door crouched the tiger, and behind which stood the lady. He had expected her to know it. He understood her nature, and his soul was assured that she would never rest until she had made plain to herself this thing, hidden to all other lookers-on, even to the king. The only hope for the youth in which there was any element of certainty was based upon the success of the princess in discovering this mystery, and the moment he looked upon her, he saw she had succeeded.

Then it was that his quick and anxious glance asked the question, "Which?" It was as plain to her as if he shouted it from where he stood. There was not an instant to be lost. The question was asked in a flash; it must be answered in another.

Her right arm lay on the cushioned parapet before her. She raised her hand, and made a slight, quick movement toward the right. No one but her lover saw her. Every eye but his was fixed on the man in the arena.

He turned, and with a firm and rapid step he walked across the empty space. Every heart stopped beating, every breath was held, every eye was fixed immovably upon that man. Without the slightest hesitation, he went to the door on the right and opened it.

Now, the point of the story is this: Did the tiger come out of that door, or did the lady?

The more we reflect upon this question, the harder it is to answer. It involves a study of the human heart which leads us through roundabout pathways of passion, out of which it is difficult to find our way. Think of it, fair reader, not as if the decision of the question depended upon yourself, but upon that hot-blooded, semibarbaric princess, her soul at a white heat beneath the combined fires of despair and jealousy. She had lost him, but who should have him?

How often, in her waking hours and in her dreams, had she started in wild horror and covered her face with her hands as she thought of her lover opening the door on the other side of which waited the cruel fangs of the tiger!

But how much oftener had she seen him at the other door! How in her grievous reveries[3] had she gnashed her teeth and torn her hair when she saw his start of rapturous delight as he opened the door of the lady! How her soul had burned in agony when she had seen him rush to meet that woman, with her flushing cheek and sparkling eye of triumph; when she had seen him lead her forth, his whole frame kindled with the joy of recovered life; when she had heard the glad shouts from the multitude, and the wild ringing of the happy bells; when she had seen the priest, with his joyous followers, advance to the couple, and make them man and wife before her very eyes; and when she had seen them walk away together upon their path of flowers, followed by the tremen-

3. reveries (rĕv'ər·ēs): dreams.

dous shouts of the hilarious multitude, in which her one despairing shriek was lost and drowned!

Would it not be better for him to die at once, and go to wait for her in the blessed regions of semibarbaric futurity?

And yet, that awful tiger, those shrieks, that blood!

Her decision had been indicated in an instant, but it had been made after days and nights of anguished deliberation. She had known she would be asked, she had decided what she would answer, and without the slightest hesitation, she had moved her hand to the right.

The question of her decision is one not to be lightly considered, and it is not for me to presume to set up myself as the one person able to answer it. So I leave it with all of you: Which came out of the opened door—the lady or the tiger?

Meaning

1. How did the king determine his subjects' innocence or guilt? Why was his system of justice *ironic,* that is, quite the opposite of justice?
2. Why did the king want to dispose of the hero of this story?
3. What is the *theme* of "The Lady, or the Tiger?" What double meaning can you read into the title of this story?
4. To what extent does the author attempt to arouse the reader's sympathy for his characters? Give evidence for your answer by citing examples from the story.

Method

1. Why do you think the author decided not to include dialogue in his story? Would you have liked some dialogue? Tell where you would have included it and why.
2. This story is told from the third-person point of view. What is the author's attitude toward the king? How soon is his attitude evident?
3. Do you wish the author had *not* told you which door the hero opened? Give reasons for your answer.
4. Instead of using one adjective, noun, verb, or adverb, the author of "The Lady, or the Tiger?" often uses two to strengthen the dramatic effect. Here are some examples of this technique: ". . . his nature was bland and genial. . . ."

"It mattered not that he might already possess a wife and family. . . ."

". . . the wedding was promptly and cheerily solemnized."

"From far and near the people gathered and thronged. . . ."

Find other examples of this technique in the story.

Language: Latin Roots for English Words

Many English words are built on Latin roots. The words *opposite* and *disposed*, for example, use the Latin root *-pos* or *pon-* (to put or place). *Opposite* begins with the Latin prefix *op-*, which means against, while *dispose* includes the Latin prefix *dis-*, which means opposite or away. How does knowing these Latin meanings help you understand the definitions of *opposite* and *dispose?*

The following words have been taken from "The Lady, or the Tiger?" Find the Latin root of each word and its meaning in your dictionary.

1. justice
2. virtue
3. audience
4. transmitted
5. barbaric
6. incorruptible
7. deliberation
8. imagined

Composition

1. Which door do you think the princess chose—the one concealing the lady, or the tiger? Write your version of how the story might have ended, beginning after the sentence, "Without the slightest hesitation, he went to the door on the right and opened it." Describe not only what happens when the door opens but also how each of the main characters reacts to the consequences.

2. The author explains in clear and specific detail how the king's system of justice worked. Write an explanation of a procedure or process that you know well. Here are some points to keep in mind: **a.** make sure you know exactly how to perform the procedure; **b.** begin by explaining the purpose of the procedure; **c.** divide the process into stages and present the steps in chronological order; **d.** use transitional words and expressions such as *first, on the average, next,* and *finally;* and **e.** conclude by stating the results that follow when the stages are followed carefully.

EUDORA WELTY
(born 1909)

The small towns of Mississippi have been the setting for Eudora Welty's fiction and for her life. Born in Jackson, Mississippi, she was the oldest child in a well-to-do family. As a young girl, she considered both writing and painting as future careers. She attended the Mississippi College for Women and completed her education at the University of Wisconsin and Columbia University Graduate School of Business.

Because of the Depression, she was unable to get a job in advertising, her field at Columbia. Working instead for the Works Progress Administration, she traveled throughout Mississippi, combining her two interests of making visual and verbal pictures by photographing people and writing articles about them. In 1936, her first short story was published, and her photographs were exhibited in a New York gallery.

Clear but metaphorical language is typical of Welty's style. In her use of first-person narration and dialogue she displays an excellent grasp of the rhythms of Southern speech. Much of her work focuses on such human problems as the conflicting needs for independence and for love. In 1973, her short novel *The Optimist's Daughter*, which contains some autobiographical information, was awarded the Pulitzer Prize.

A WORN PATH

It was December—a bright frozen day in the early morning. Far out in the country there was an old Negro woman with her head tied in a red rag, coming along a path through the pinewoods. Her name was Phoenix[1] Jackson. She was very old and small and she walked slowly in the dark pine shadows, moving a

---

1. **Phoenix:** in Egyptian mythology, a bird of great beauty said to live for 500 years in the desert, to burn and destroy itself by fire, to rise again from its ashes youthful and beautiful, and to live through another life cycle. The phoenix was supposedly the size of an eagle with partly red and partly golden plumage. It is often used as a symbol of immortality.

little from side to side in her steps, with the balanced heaviness and lightness of a pendulum in a grandfather clock. She carried a thin, small cane made from an umbrella, and with this she kept tapping the frozen earth in front of her. This made a grave and persistent noise in the still air, that seemed meditative like the chirping of a solitary little bird.

She wore a dark striped dress reaching down to her shoe tops, and an equally long apron of bleached sugar sacks, with a full pocket: all neat and tidy, but every time she took a step she might have fallen over her shoelaces, which dragged from her unlaced shoes. She looked straight ahead. Her eyes were blue with age. Her skin had a pattern all of its own of numberless branching wrinkles and as though a whole little tree stood in the middle of her forehead, but a golden color ran underneath, and the two knobs of her cheeks were illumined by a yellow burning under the dark. Under the red rag her hair came down on her neck in the frailest of ringlets, still black, and with an odor like copper.

Now and then there was a quivering in the thicket. Old Phoenix said, "Out of my way, all you foxes, owls, beetles, jack rabbits, coons, and wild animals! . . . Keep out from under these feet, little bobwhites. . . . Keep the big wild hogs out of my path. Don't let none of those come running my direction. I got a long way." Under her small black-freckled hand her cane, limber as a buggy whip, would switch at the brush as if to rouse up any hiding things.

On she went. The woods were deep and still. The sun made the pine needles almost too bright to look at, up where the wind rocked. The cones dropped as light as feathers. Down in the hollow was the mourning dove[2]—it was not too late for him.

The path ran up a hill. "Seem like there is chains about my feet, time I get this far," she said, in the voice of argument old people keep to use with themselves. "Something always take a hold of me on this hill—pleads I should stay."

After she got to the top, she turned and gave a full, severe look behind her where she had come. "Up through pines," she said at length. "Now down through oaks."

Her eyes opened their widest and she started down gently. But before she got to the bottom of the hill a bush caught her dress.

---

2. **mourning dove:** the wild dove, which is known for its mournful cry.

Her fingers were busy and intent, but her skirts were full and long, so that before she could pull them free in one place they were caught in another. It was not possible to allow the dress to tear. "I in the thorny bush," she said. "Thorns, you doing your appointed work. Never want to let folks pass, no sir. Old eyes thought you was a pretty little *green* bush."

Finally, trembling all over, she stood free, and after a moment dared to stoop for her cane.

"Sun so high!" she cried, leaning back and looking, while the thick tears went over her eyes. "The time getting all gone here."

At the foot of this hill was a place where a log was laid across the creek.

"Now comes the trial," said Phoenix.

Putting her right foot out, she mounted the log and shut her eyes. Lifting her skirt, leveling her cane fiercely before her, like a festival figure in some parade, she began to march across. Then she opened her eyes and she was safe on the other side.

"I wasn't as old as I thought," she said.

But she sat down to rest. She spread her skirts on the bank around her and folded her hands over her knees. Up above her was a tree in a pearly cloud of mistletoe.[3] She did not dare to close her eyes, and when a little boy brought her a plate with a slice of marble cake on it she spoke to him. "That would be acceptable," she said. But when she went to take it there was just her own hand in the air.

So she left that tree, and had to go through a barbed-wire fence. There she had to creep and crawl, spreading her knees and stretching her fingers like a baby trying to climb the steps. But she talked loudly to herself: she could not let her dress be torn now, so late in the day, and she could not pay for having her arm or her leg sawed off if she got caught fast where she was.

At last she was safe through the fence and risen up out in the clearing. Big dead trees, like black men with one arm, were standing in the purple stalks of the withered cotton field. There sat a buzzard.

"Who you watching?"

In the furrow she made her way along.

---

3. **mistletoe:** semiparasitic green plant with yellow flowers and white berries. Druids, priests of the ancient Celtic religion, believed that mistletoe had magic powers, especially when it grew on an oak, which they considered a sacred tree.

"Glad this not the season for bulls," she said, looking sideways, "and the good Lord made his snakes to curl up and sleep in the winter. A pleasure I don't see no two-headed snake coming around that tree, where it come once. It took a while to get by him, back in the summer."

She passed through the old cotton and went into a field of dead corn. It whispered and shook and was taller than her head. "Through the maze now," she said, for there was no path.

Then there was something tall, black, and skinny there, moving before her.

At first she took it for a man. It could have been a man dancing in the field. But she stood still and listened, and it did not make a sound. It was as silent as a ghost.

"Ghost," she said sharply, "who be you the ghost of? For I have heard of nary[4] death close by."

But there was no answer, only the ragged dancing in the wind.

She shut her eyes, reached out her hand, and touched a sleeve. She found a coat and inside that an emptiness, cold as ice.

"You scarecrow," she said. Her face lighted. "I ought to be shut up for good," she said with laughter. "My senses is gone. I too old. I the oldest people I ever know. Dance, old scarecrow," she said, "while I dancing with you."

She kicked her foot over the furrow, and with mouth drawn down, shook her head once or twice in a little strutting way. Some husks blew down and whirled in streamers about her skirts.

Then she went on, parting her way from side to side with the cane, through the whispering field. At last she came to the end, to a wagon track where the silver grass blew between the red ruts. The quail were walking around like pullets,[5] seeming all dainty and unseen.

"Walk pretty," she said. "This the easy place. This the easy going."

She followed the track, swaying through the quiet bare fields, through the little strings of trees silver in their dead leaves, past cabins silver from weather, with the doors and windows boarded shut, all like old women under a spell sitting there. "I walking in their sleep," she said, nodding her head vigorously.

4. **nary:** *dialect,* not one.
5. **pullets:** young hens.

In a ravine she went where a spring was silently flowing through a hollow log. Old Phoenix bent and drank. "Sweet gum[6] makes the water sweet," she said, and drank more. "Nobody know who made this well, for it was here when I was born."

The track crossed a swampy part where the moss hung as white as lace from every limb. "Sleep on, alligators, and blow your bubbles." Then the track went into the road.

Deep, deep the road went down between the high green-colored banks. Overhead the live-oaks met, and it was as dark as a cave.

A black dog with a lolling[7] tongue came up out of the weeds by the ditch. She was meditating, and not ready, and when he came at her she only hit him a little with her cane. Over she went in the ditch, like a little puff of milkweed.

Down there, her senses drifted away. A dream visited her, and she reached her hand up, but nothing reached down and gave her a pull. So she lay there and presently went to talking. "Old woman," she said to herself, "that black dog come up out of the weeds to stall you off, and now there he sitting on his fine tail, smiling at you."

A white man finally came along and found her—a hunter, a young man, with his dog on a chain.

"Well, Granny!" he laughed. "What are you doing there?"

"Lying on my back like a June bug waiting to be turned over, mister," she said, reaching up her hand.

He lifted her up, gave her a swing in the air, and set her down. "Anything broken, Granny?"

"No sir, them old dead weeds is springy enough," said Phoenix, when she had got her breath. "I thank you for your trouble."

"Where do you live, Granny?" he asked, while the two dogs were growling at each other.

"Away back yonder, sir, behind the ridge. You can't even see it from here."

"On your way home?"

"No sir, I going to town."

"Why, that's too far! That's as far as I walk when I come out myself, and I get something for my trouble." He patted the stuffed bag he carried, and there hung down a little closed claw. It was

6. **sweet gum:** a tree that yields a sweet, gummy substance.
7. **lolling:** drooping.

one of the bobwhites, with its beak hooked bitterly to show it was dead. "Now you go on home, Granny!"

"I bound to go to town, mister," said Phoenix. "The time come around."

He gave another laugh, filling the whole landscape. "I know you old colored people! Wouldn't miss going to town to see Santa Claus!"

But something held old Phoenix very still. The deep lines in her face went into a fierce and different radiation. Without warning, she had seen with her own eyes a flashing nickel fall out of the man's pocket onto the ground.

"How old are you, Granny?" he was saying.

"There is no tellin, mister," she said, "no telling."

Then she gave a little cry and clapped her hands and said, "Git on away from here, dog! Look! Look at that dog!" She laughed as if in admiration. "He ain't scared of nobody. He a big black dog." She whispered, "Sic him!"

"Watch me get rid of that cur," said the man. "Sic him, Pete! Sic him!"

Phoenix heard the dogs fighting, and heard the man running and throwing sticks. She even heard a gunshot. But she was slowly bending forward by that time, further and further forward, the lids stretched down over her eyes, as if she were doing this in her sleep. Her chin was lowered almost to her knees. The yellow palm of her hand came out from the fold of her apron. Her fingers slid down and along the ground under the piece of money with the grace and care they would have in lifting an egg from under a setting hen. Then she slowly straightened up, she stood erect, and the nickel was in her apron pocket. A bird flew by. Her lips moved. "God watching me the whole time. I come to stealing."

The man came back, and his own dog panted about them. "Well, I scared him off that time," he said, and then he laughed and lifted his gun and pointed it at Phoenix.

She stood straight and faced him.

"Doesn't the gun scare you?" he said, still pointing it.

"No, sir, I seen plenty go off closer by, in my day, and for less than what I done," she said, holding utterly still.

He smiled, and shouldered the gun. "Well, Granny," he said, "you must be a hundred years old, and scared of nothing. I'd give you a dime if I had any money with me. But you take my advice and stay home, and nothing will happen to you."

"I bound to go on my way, mister," said Phoenix. She inclined her head in the red rag. Then they went in different directions, but she could hear the gun shooting again and again over the hill.

She walked on. The shadows hung from the oak trees to the road like curtains. Then she smelled wood smoke, and smelled the river, and she saw a steeple and the cabins on their steep steps. Dozens of little black children whirled around her. There ahead was Natchez[8] shining. Bells were ringing. She walked on.

In the paved city it was Christmas time. There were red and green electric lights strung and crisscrossed everywhere, and all turned on in the daytime. Old Phoenix would have been lost if she had not distrusted her eyesight and depended on her feet to know where to take her.

She paused quietly on the sidewalk where people were passing by. A lady came along in the crowd, carrying an armful of red-, green- and silver-wrapped presents; she gave off perfume like the red roses in hot summer, and Phoenix stopped her.

"Please, missy, will you lace up my shoe?" She held up her foot.

"What do you want, Grandma?"

"See my shoe," said Phoenix. "Do all right for out in the country, but wouldn't look right to go in a big building."

"Stand still then, Grandma," said the lady. She put her packages down on the sidewalk beside her and laced and tied both shoes tightly.

"Can't lace 'em with a cane," said Phoenix. "Thank you, missy. I doesn't mind asking a nice lady to tie up my shoe, when I gets out on the street."

Moving slowly and from side to side, she went into the big building, and into a tower of steps, where she walked up and around and around until her feet knew to stop.

She entered a door, and there she saw nailed up on the wall the document that had been stamped with the gold seal and framed in the gold frame, which matched the dream that was hung up in her head.

"Here I be," she said. There was a fixed and ceremonial stiffness over her body.

---

8. **Natchez** (năch′ĭz): a port city in southwest Mississippi located on the Mississippi River.

"A charity case, I suppose," said an attendant who sat at the desk before her.

But Phoenix only looked above her head. There was sweat on her face, the wrinkles in her skin shone like a bright net.

"Speak up, Grandma," the woman said. "What's your name? We must have your history, you know. Have you been here before? What seems to be the trouble with you?"

Old Phoenix only gave a twitch to her face as if a fly were bothering her.

"Are you deaf?" cried the attendant.

But then the nurse came in.

"Oh, that's just old Aunt Phoenix," she said. "She doesn't come for herself—she has a little grandson. She makes these trips just as regular as clockwork. She lives away back off the Old Natchez Trace."[9] She bent down. "Well, Aunt Phoenix, why don't you take a seat? We won't keep you standing after your long trip." She pointed.

The old woman sat down, bolt upright in the chair.

"Now, how is the boy?" asked the nurse.

Old Phoenix did not speak.

"I said, how is the boy?"

But Phoenix only waited and stared straight ahead, her face very solemn and withdrawn into rigidity.

"Is his throat any better?" asked the nurse. "Aunt Phoenix, don't you hear me? Is your grandson's throat any better since the last time you came for the medicine?"

With her hands on her knees, the old woman waited, silent, erect and motionless, just as if she were in armor.

"You mustn't take up our time this way, Aunt Phoenix," the nurse said. "Tell us quickly about your grandson, and get it over. He isn't dead, is he?"

At last there came a flicker and then a flame of comprehension across her face, and she spoke.

"My grandson. It was my memory had left me. There I sat and forgot why I made my long trip."

"Forgot?" The nurse frowned. "After you came so far?"

Then Phoenix was like an old woman begging a dignified

---

9. **Old Natchez Trace:** an old road, over 500 miles long, which runs from Nashville, Tennessee, to Natchez. *Trace* means a path or trail through the woods.

forgiveness for waking up frightened in the night. "I never did go to school, I was too old at the Surrender,"[10] she said in a soft voice. "I'm an old woman without an education. It was my memory fail me. My little grandson, he is just the same, and I forgot it in the coming."

"Throat never heals, does it?" said the nurse, speaking in a loud, sure voice to Old Phoenix. By now she had a card with something written on it, a little list. "Yes. Swallowed lye. When was it?—January—two-three years ago—"

Phoenix spoke unasked now. "No, missy, he not dead, he just the same. Every little while his throat begin to close up again, and he not able to swallow. He not get his breath. He not able to help himself. So the time come around, and I go on another trip for the soothing medicine."

"All right. The doctor said as long as you came to get it, you could have it," said the nurse. "But it's an obstinate case."

"My little grandson, he sit up there in the house all wrapped up, waiting by himself," Phoenix went on. "We is the only two left in the world. He suffer and it don't seem to put him back at all. He got a sweet look. He going to last. He wear a little patch quilt and peep out holding his mouth open like a little bird. I remembers so plain now. I not going to forget him again, no, the whole enduring time. I could tell him from all the others in creation."

"All right." The nurse was trying to hush her now. She brought her a bottle of medicine. "Charity," she said, making a check mark in a book.

Old Phoenix held the bottle close to her eyes, and then carefully put it into her pocket.

"I thank you," she said.

"It's Christmas time, Grandma," said the attendant. "Could I give you a few pennies out of my purse?"

"Five pennies is a nickel," said Phoenix stiffly.

"Here's a nickel," said the attendant.

Phoenix rose carefully and held out her hand. She received the nickel and then fished the other nickel out of her pocket and laid it beside the new one. She stared at her palm closely, with her head on one side.

---

10. Surrender: that is, of the Confederate forces under General Lee on April 9, 1865, at Appomattox Courthouse, which virtually ended the Civil War.

Then she gave a tap with her cane on the floor.

"This is what come to me to do," she said. "I going to the store and buy my child a little windmill they sells, made out of paper. He going to find it hard to believe there such a thing in the world. I'll march myself back where he waiting, holding it straight up in this hand."

She lifted her free hand, gave a little nod, turned around, and walked out of the doctor's office. Then her slow step began on the stairs, going down.

Meaning

1. Why was Phoenix Jackson going to Natchez? At what time of the year was she making the trip?
2. The title of a story often has symbolic meaning. What does the worn path into Natchez represent? What takes hold of Phoenix at one point and "pleads I should stay"?
3. The nurse noted that the medicine was given to Phoenix out of "charity." How charitable were the people Phoenix met in the city? Who in the story do you think exemplifies the true spirit of charity?
4. Which of the following words do you think best describes Phoenix: pathetic, clever, enduring, suffering, worried? Cite examples from the story to support your answer.

Method

1. What information does the author give you about Phoenix Jackson in the first paragraph? At what point in the story do you realize that she has difficulty in seeing?
2. What do we learn about Phoenix during her meeting with the hunter?
3. Find some examples of the use of dialect in the story. How does the dialect help to characterize Phoenix?
4. Why do you think the author does not reveal the purpose of Phoenix's trip until the end of the story?

Language: Figures of Speech

Writers often use figurative rather than literal language. An expression is *literal* when it is factual. "Rain poured down as they walked to school," is an example of literal language. Language is *figurative* when it appeals to your imagination by using figures of speech. "They walked to school under a curtain of rain," is an example of figurative language.

The two most common figures of speech are *simile* and *metaphor*. Both figures of speech compare two things that are essentially unlike. The writer's imagination sees one way in which the two things are strikingly like one another. When the writer tells the reader of the likeness that he or she sees, a vivid impression of the object is conveyed.

If the author says that the first thing compared is like the second, this direct comparison is called a *simile*. In describing Phoenix's hair, Eudora Welty says it had "an odor like copper."

If the writer does not use *like* or *as* in the comparison but still compares two objects, the implied comparison is called a *metaphor*. For example, Phoenix moved "with the balanced heaviness and lightness of a pendulum in a grandfather clock."

Identify which figure of speech is used in each of the following examples from "A Worn Path." Identify the two things that are compared in each figure of speech.

1. "This made a grave and persistent noise in the still air, that seemed meditative like the chirping of a solitary little bird."
2. ". . . her cane, limber as a buggy whip, would switch at the brush. . . ."
3. "The cones dropped as light as feathers."
4. "Over she went in the ditch, like a little puff of milk-weed."
5. "Moving slowly and from side to side, she went into the big building, and into a tower of steps. . . ."

Discussion and Composition

1. Phoenix possesses exceptional qualities that help her to survive in spite of her infirmities. Have you known people like

Phoenix who have lived dignified, courageous lives despite physical handicaps or other adversity? How are such people inspirations to others?

2. Eudora Welty has said that she was inspired to write "A Worn Path" after seeing a solitary old woman walking in the country. Write a story about a stranger you have seen on the street or in a photograph. Invent a "path" for your character—a journey, a destination, and a purpose—and describe the adventures he or she encounters along the way. Use specific sensory details to make your character and the events of the journey come alive for the reader.

LESLIE NORRIS

(born 1921)

Leslie Norris was born in Wales near Merthyr Tydfil, an industrial city that suffered greatly from the effects of the Depression.
While he was growing up, Norris often escaped the harsh environment of the city by exploring the surrounding Welsh countryside.
This contrast between urban poverty and natural beauty forms the
setting for many of his stories and poems.

After high school, Norris worked for a time in Merthyr
Tydfil. He then moved to England, where he attended college,
received degrees in Education and Philosophy, and worked as a
teacher and school administrator. He now lives in Utah and teaches
English at Brigham Young University.

Norris began publishing books of poetry in the 1940s, but he
has only recently begun to receive widespread recognition for his
work. In the 1970s, he began publishing stories in magazines such
as the *New Yorker* and the *Atlantic* and began to earn a reputation in
the United States as a gifted and skillful short-story writer. He has
published two short-story collections, *Sliding* (1976) and *The Girl
from Cardigan* (1988), which poignantly capture the flavor of his
early life in Wales.

THE WIND, THE COLD WIND

I was almost at the top of Victoria Road, under the big
maroon boarding advertising Camp Coffee, when I heard Jimmy
James shouting.

"Hey Ginger!" he shouted. "Hold on a minute, Ginger!"

He couldn't wait to reach me. He ran across the road in front
of the Cardiff bus as if it didn't exist. There he was, large, red-
faced, rolling urgently along like a boy with huge, slow springs in
his knees, like a boy heaving himself through heavy, invisible
water. Jimmy couldn't read very well. Once I'd written a letter
for him, to his sister who lived in Birmingham and worked in a
chocolate factory; once he'd let me walk to school with him and

other large, important boys. He stopped in front of me, weighty, impassable.

"I heard you were dead," he said. "The boys told me you were dead."

His large brown eyes looked down at me accusingly.

"Not me, Jim," I said. "Never felt fitter, Jim."

He thought that too sprightly by half. His fat cheeks reddened and he wagged a finger at me. It looked as thick as a club.

"Watch it, Ginge," he said.

He was fifteen years old, five years older than I, and big. He was a boy to be feared. I slowed it.

"No, Jim," I said smiling soberly, "I'm not dead."

"The boys told me you were," he said.

He was looking at me with the utmost care, his whole attitude reproachful and disappointed. I was immediately guilty. I had let Jimmy James down, I could see that. And then, in an instant, I understood, for something very like this had happened to me before.

The previous winter, in January, a boy called Tony Plumley had drowned in a pond on the mountain. I'd spent a lot of time worrying about Tony Plumley. The unready ice had split beneath him and tumbled him into the darkness. For weeks afterwards, lying in my bed at night, I'd followed him down, hearing him choke, feeling the stiffening chill of the water. I had watched his skin turn blue as ice, I had felt his lungs fill to the throat with suffocating water, known the moment when at last his legs had gone limp and boneless. I had given Tony Plumley all the pity and fear I possessed. And later, in irresistible terror, I had gone with him into his very grave. Then, one day when I had forgotten all about him and was running carefree along a dappled path in the summer woods, there he was, in front of me, Tony Plumley, alive. I thought of all that sympathetic terror spent and wasted and I was wildly angry. I charged him with being drowned.

"It wasn't me," Tony Plumley said, backing off fast.

"It was you," I said. "Put up your fists."

But Tony Plumley stood still and cautious outside the range of my eager jabs. Taking the greatest care, speaking slowly, he explained that he was not drowned at all, that he had never been sliding on the pond, that his mother would not have let him. It was another boy, Tony Powell, who had dropped through the cheating ice and died. I had been confused by the similarity of their names. I stood there trying to reconcile myself to a world in which the firm certainty of death had proved unfaithful, a world in which Tony Powell, a boy unknown to me, was suddenly dead. Perplexed, I dropped my avenging hands.

"Get moving, Plumley," I said.

He slid tactfully past me and thumped away down the path.

So I knew exactly how Jimmy James felt. I'd used a lot of emotion on Plumley and Jim must have been imagining my death with much the same intensity. I understood his disappointment, deserved his reproach, stood resignedly under his just anger. I knew, too, how the confusion had come about.

"It's not me, Jim," I said, "it's Maldwyn Farraday. It's because we've both got red hair."

This completely baffled Jim. He looked at me in despair.

"What's red hair got to do with it?" he said loudly.

"We've both got red hair," I explained, "Maldwyn Farraday and I. And we live in the same street and we're friends. It's Maldwyn's dead. People mix us up."

Jim didn't say anything.

"I'm going to the funeral tomorrow," I said.

Jimmy James curled his lip in contempt and turned away, his heavy shoulders outraged, his scuffed shoes slapping the pavement. I waited until he had turned the corner by the delicatessen and then I ran. I ran past the shops still ablaze for the Christmas which was already gone, I ran past Davies' where unsold decorated cakes still held their blue and pink rosettes, their tiny edible skaters and Father Christmasses, their stale, festive messages in scarlet piping; I ran past Mr. Roberts' shop without looking once at his sumptuous boxes of confectionery, at the cottonwool snowflakes falling in ranks regular as guardsmen down the glass of his window; past the symmetrical pyramids of fruit and vegetables in Mr. Leyshon's, the small, thin-skinned tangerines wrapped in silver foil, the boxes of dates from North Africa. I ran so that I did not have to think of Maldwyn.

Maldwyn had been my friend as long as I could remember. There was not a time when Maldwyn had not been around. He had great advantages as a friend. Not only could he laugh more loudly than anyone else, he was so awkward that with him the simplest exercise, just walking up the street, was hilarious chaos. And his house too, his house was big and gloriously untidy. In the basement was the workshop in which his father repaired all the machines in the neighborhood, all the lawn-mowers, the electric kettles and irons, the clocks and watches. He also repaired them in the kitchen, in the garden, in the hall, wherever he happened to be. Our fathers' ancient pistons to another paroxysm of irregular combustion. Mr. Farraday's hands held always a bundle of incomprehensible metal parts he was patiently arranging into efficiency. He'd let us watch him tease into place the cogs and rivets of some damaged artifact, telling us in his quiet voice what he was doing. Sometimes, when we were watching Mr. Farraday, Maldwyn's two sisters, long, thin and malevolent, would come round and enrage us. Then Mr. Farraday would turn us out of doors and the sisters would giggle away to play the piano in another room. Maldwyn could roar like a bull. When he did this, his sisters would put their hands to their ears and run screaming, but Mr. Farraday just smiled gently.

Maldwyn's parents had come from a village many miles away, in the west of Wales. Their house was often full of cousins from this village, smiling, talking in their open country voices. They drank a lot of tea, these cousins, and then they all went off to visit Enoch Quinell. Everybody knew Enoch Quinell, because he was a police-man and enormously fat. My father said Enoch weighed more than two hundred and eighty pounds. But Maldwyn's family knew Enoch particularly well because he, too, had come from their village and always went back there for his holidays.

We knew a lot of jokes about Enoch, about how he'd cracked the weigh bridge where the coal trucks were weighed, how he was supposed to have broken both ankles trying to stand on tip-toe. I used to think they were pretty funny jokes, but Maldwyn would be very angry if he heard one of them and offer to fight the boy who said it. He was a hopeless fighter, anybody could have picked him off with one hand, but we all liked him. On Saturday mornings he went shopping for Enoch, for food, for shaving soap, cigarettes, things like that. Sometimes I went with him.

Enoch lived in rooms above the police station, and we'd climb there, past the fire engine on the ground floor, its brass glittering, its hoses white and spotless, past the billiard room, then up the stairs to Enoch's place. Once I saw Enoch eat. He cooked for himself a steak so huge that I could find no way to describe it to my mother. And then he covered it in fried onions. Maldwyn used to get six-pence for doing Enoch's shopping.

He had been working for Enoch on Christmas Eve. I hadn't known that. All afternoon I'd been searching for him, around the back of the garages where we had a den, in the market; I couldn't find him anywhere. Just as I thought of going home, I saw Maldwyn at the top of the street. He was singing, but when I called him he stopped and waved. The lights were coming on in the houses and shops. Some children were singing carols outside Benny Everson's door. I could have told them it was a waste of time.

"Look what Enoch gave me," Maldwyn said. Enoch had given him ten shillings. We had never known such wealth.

"What are you going to do with it?" I asked, touching the silver with an envious finger.

"I'm going to buy Enoch a cigar," he said, "for Christmas. Coming over?"

We walked toward the High Street. Mr. Turner, the tobacconist, was a tall, pale man, exquisitely dressed. He had a silver snuffbox and was immaculately polite to everyone who entered his shop. I knew that he and Maldwyn would be hours choosing a cigar for Enoch. I could already hear Mr. Turner asking Maldwyn's opinion.

"Perhaps something Cuban?" Mr. Turner would say. "No? Something a little smaller, perhaps, a little milder?"

"Ugh?" Maldwyn would say, smiling, not understanding any of it, enjoying it all.

I couldn't stand it. When we got to the Market I told Maldwyn that I'd wait for him there. I told him I'd wait outside Marlow's where I could look at the brilliant windows of the sporting world, the rows of fishing rods and the racks of guns, the beautiful feathery hooks of salmon-flies in their perspex boxes, the soccer balls, the marvellous boxing shorts, glittering and colored like the peacock, the blood-red boxing gloves. Each week I spent hours at these windows and I was a long time there on Christmas Eve. Maldwyn didn't come back. At last I went home. My mother was crying and everybody in our house was quiet. Then they told me that Maldwyn was dead. He had rushed out of Mr. Turner's shop, carrying in his hand two cigars in a paper bag, and run straight under a truck.

"I've been watching for him," I said. "Outside Marlow's. He went to buy a cigar for Enoch."

I went early to bed and slept well. It didn't feel as if Maldwyn was dead. I thought of him as if he were in his house a few doors down the street, but when I walked past on Christmas morning the blinds were drawn across all the Farradays' windows and in some of the other houses too. The whole street was silent. And all that day

I was lost, alone. We didn't enjoy Christmas in our house. The next day Mr. Farraday came over to say that they were going to bury Maldwyn in their village, taking him away to the little church where his grandparents were buried. He asked me to walk with the funeral to the edge of town, with five other boys.

"You were his best friend," Mr. Farraday said.

Mr. Farraday looked exactly the same as he always did, his face pink and clean, his bony hands slow. I told him that I'd like to walk in Maldwyn's funeral. I had never been to a funeral.

The day they took Maldwyn away was cold. When I got up a hard frost covered the ground and the sky was gray. At ten o'clock I went down to Maldwyn's. The other boys were already there, standing around: Danny Simpson, Urias Ward, Reggie Evans, Georgie and Bobby Rowlands. We wore our best suits, our overcoats, our scarves, our gleaming shoes. The hearse and the black cars were waiting at the curb and little knots of men stood along the pavement, talking quietly. In a little while Maldwyn's door opened and three tall men carried out the coffin. I was astonished by its length; it looked long enough to hold a man, yet Maldwyn was shorter than I. He was younger too. I hadn't expected that there would be any noise, but there was. Gentle though the bearers were, the coffin bumped softly, with blunt wooden sounds, and grated when they slid it along the chromium tracks inside the hearse. I knew that little Georgie Rowlands was scared. His eyes were pale and large and he couldn't look away. The wreaths were carried from the house and placed in a careful pile on the coffin and inside the hearse. I could see mine, made of early daffodils and other flowers I couldn't name. My card was wired to it. I had written on it, "Goodbye Maldwyn, from all at Number 24."

"You boys will march at the side of the hearse," said Mr. Jewell, the undertaker, "three on each side, you understand?"

We nodded.

"And no playing about," Mr. Jewell said. "Just walk firmly along. And when we get to the park gates we'll stop for a second so that you can all get safely to the side of the road. We don't want accidents. Be careful, remember that."

"Yes," Reggie Evans said.

Danny Simpson and Georgie Rowlands were on my side of the hearse. As we walked up the street I could see my mother and brother, but I didn't even nod to them. They were with a gathering of neighbors, all looking cold and sad. We turned and marched towards the edge of town, perhaps a mile away. The wind, gusting and hard, blew at our legs and the edges of our coats. There were few people to see us go. At the park gates the whole procession stopped and we stood in a line at the side of the road. We saw the car in which Mr. and Mrs. Farraday sat, with their daughters. I didn't recognize them in their unaccustomed black, but Urias Ward did. I saw Enoch Quinell in one of the following cars, and he saw me. He looked me full in the face and he was completely unsmiling and serious. Picking up speed, the hearse and the other cars sped up the road, over the river bridge, out of sight. Left without a purpose, we waited until we knew they were far away.

"Let's go home through the park," Danny Simpson said.

We walked in single file along the stone parapet of the lake, looking at the grey water. The wind, blowing without hindrance over its surface, had cut it into choppy waves, restless, without pattern. Everything was cold. Out in the middle, riding the water as indifferently as if it had been a smooth summer day, were the two mute swans which lived there all year round. They were indescribably sad and beautiful, like swans out of some cruel story from the far north, like birds in some cold elegy I had but dimly heard and understood only its sorrow. I remembered that these swans were said to sing only as they died, and I resented then their patient mastery of the water, their manifest living. And then there came unbidden into my mind the images of all the death I knew. I saw my grandfather in his bed, when I had been taken to see him, but that was all right because his nose was high and sharp and his teeth were too big and he hadn't looked like my grandfather. He hadn't looked like a person at all. I saw again the dead puppy I had found on the river bank, his skin peeling smoothly away from his poor flesh, and this was frightening, for he came often to terrify me in nightmares, and I also wept in pity for him when I was sick or tired. And I saw the dead butterfly I had found behind the bookshelves where it had hidden from the approach of winter. It had been a Red Admiral, my favorite butterfly, and it had died there, spread so that I could marvel at the red and white markings on its dusky wings, their powder still undisturbed. I held it on the palm of my hand and it was dry and light, so light that when I closed my eyes I could not tell that I held it, as light as dust. And thinking of the unbroken butterfly, I knew that I would never again see Maldwyn Farraday, nor hear his voice, nor wake in the morning to the certainty that we would spend the day together. He was gone forever. A great and painful emptiness was in my chest and my throat. I stopped walking and took from my overcoat pocket the last of my Christmas chocolate, a half-pound block. I called the boys around me and, breaking the chocolate into sections, I divided it among us. There were two sections over, and I gave them to little Georgie Rowlands because he was the youngest. Tears were pouring down Reggie Evans' cheeks and the wind blew them across his nose and onto the collar of his overcoat.

"It's the wind," he said. "The bloody wind makes your eyes water."

He could scarcely speak and we stood near him, patting his shoulders, our mouths filled with chocolate, saying yes yes, the wind, the cold wind. But we were all crying, we were all bitterly weeping, our cheeks were wet and stinging with the harsh salt of our tears, we were overwhelmed by the recognition of our unique and common knowledge, and we had nowhere to turn for comfort but to ourselves.

Meaning

1. How would you characterize Jim's reaction to his realization that Ginger is alive? Why does Ginger understand his reaction?
2. What words or phrases would you use to describe Maldwyn's personality? Why?
3. Reread the last two paragraphs of the story and then think about the title of the story. What is the meaning of the title?
4. Why do you think the narrator makes a point of letting the reader know that people frequently confused him with Maldwyn?

Method

1. What is the purpose of including Ginger's reaction to Tony Plumley's supposed death?
2. How can the reader tell that the narrator is looking back on events that occurred when he was much younger?
3. What effect is achieved by setting the story during the Christmas season?

Language: Synonyms

Synonyms are words that have similar meanings. To find a list of synonyms for a given word, you would consult a reference book such as a thesaurus—a collection of synonyms and antonyms (words that have opposite meanings)—or a dictionary that lists synonyms. *Roget's International Thesaurus* lists the following words as synonyms for the word *person*: *human, mortal, individual,* and *creature.*

As this list shows, synonyms are not always interchangeable; each word brings a different shade of meaning to its context. For example, consider the following sentence: That person is a friend of mine. From the list of synonyms, *individual* would be the most appropriate replacement for *person* in this context, while the other three synonyms would be both inappropriate and misleading.

The following sentences are taken from "The Wind, The Cold Wind." Look up the meanings of the words in parentheses, and decide which of the two choices for each sentence is the the most appropriate replacement for the italicized word.

1. "He thought that too *sprightly* by half." (agile, lively)
2. "He was a *hopeless* fighter. . . ." (impossible, unhopeful)
3. "I stood there trying to *reconcile* myself to a world. . . ." (accept, adapt)
4. "I ran . . . past the *symmetrical* pyramids of fruits and vegetables. . . ." (equal, well-balanced)

Discussion and Composition

1. Many of the short stories and novels that are favorites of young people have characters, either human or animal, who die. Why do you think such works appeal to people? Have you read such works? If so, list the titles of works that come to mind, and discuss your reactions to them.

2. Do you find Ginger's reaction to discovering that Tony Plumley was still alive believable? Explain.

3. Write a brief essay in which you explain how the title of a work can be a key to its theme and meaning. Begin your essay with an introductory paragraph explaining why it is important to pay careful attention to a story's title. Develop your essay by explaining the significance of the titles of two short stories you have read. Show how each title adds to an understanding of the story's theme.

EDGAR ALLAN POE
(1809–1849)

No other American up to Edgar Allan Poe's time had excelled in the three major writing fields of poetry, fiction, and criticism. No other American up to his time so profoundly influenced European writers. Poe's short, tragic life was filled with personal failure. Yet he set the pattern for modern mystery and detective fiction, created masterpieces of supernatural horror, and set down original theories on how to write poetry and short stories.

Poe was born in Boston to a Southern family of traveling actors. His mother died when he was two, and he was taken in by the Allans of Richmond, Virginia, a wealthy family. They gave him their name as his middle name and supported him through school in Virginia and in England, where they lived for five years.

After short periods of time at the University of Virginia, where he ran up heavy gambling debts; in the Army, where he rose in two years to the rank of sergeant-major; and at West Point, where he forced his own dismissal, Poe decided to earn his living by writing. Over the next eighteen years, he wrote and edited for several different magazines and newspapers, but he was unable to hold a job for long. Even a small amount of alcohol affected him greatly, and he could not control his need for it. He suffered extreme poverty and could not support his young wife, who died of tuberculosis when she was twenty-five. Two years later, after a party where he had drunk heavily, he died.

Many of Poe's tales of the supernatural were written originally for newspapers and magazines. His first detective story, "The Murders in the Rue Morgue," was published in 1841. His creative genius was recognized in Europe long before he was famous in America. It was not until publication of his poem "The Raven" in 1845 that he became nationally known.

Poe's stories and poems usually deal with love, beauty, and death. He felt that a story or poem should produce a single emotional effect, and that every word, even every sound, should contribute to that effect. His work shows clearly that he followed his own rules.

THE MASQUE* OF
THE RED DEATH

The "Red Death" had long devastated the country. No pestilence had ever been so fatal, or so hideous. Blood was its Avatar[1] and its seal—the redness and the horror of blood. There were sharp pains, and sudden dizziness, and then profuse bleeding at the pores, with dissolution.[2] The scarlet stains upon the body and especially upon the face of the victim were the pest ban[3] which shut him out from the aid and from the sympathy of his fellow men. And the whole seizure, progress, and termination of the disease were the incidents of half an hour.

But the Prince Prospero was happy and dauntless and sagacious. When his dominions were half depopulated, he summoned to his presence a thousand hale and light-hearted friends from among the knights and dames of his court, and with these retired to the deep seclusion of one of his castellated abbeys.[4] This was an extensive and magnificent structure, the creation of the prince's own eccentric yet august taste. A strong and lofty wall girdled it in. This wall had gates of iron. The courtiers, having entered, brought furnaces and massy hammers, and welded the bolts. They resolved to leave means neither of ingress nor egress[5] to the sudden impulses of despair or frenzy from within. The abbey was amply provisioned. With such precautions the courtiers might bid defiance to contagion. The external world could take care of itself. In the meantime, it was folly to grieve or to think. The prince had provided all the appliances of pleasure. There were buffoons, there

---

* **masque:** an elaborately staged dramatic performance popular in the sixteenth and seventeenth centuries. The actors wore masks and usually represented mythological or symbolic figures. The acting consisted mostly of dancing and pantomime. Masque also means a masquerade, or a mask.

1. **Avatar** (ăv'ə·tär'): in Hindu theology, the bodily form taken by a god; the visible sign or indication of something; here, blood is the sign of the "Red Death."

2. **dissolution:** disintegration; decay; hence, death.

3. **pest ban:** the sign by which the disease (*pest*) was recognized and which resulted in the *banning* of the afflicted person.

4. **castellated** (kăs'tə·lā'tĭd) **abbeys:** castle-like monasteries.

5. **ingress** (ĭn'grĕs) **nor egress** (ē'grĕs): entrance nor exit.

were improvisatori,[6] there were ballet dancers, there were musicians, there was Beauty, there was wine. All these and security were within. Without was the Red Death.

It was toward the close of the fifth or sixth month of his seclusion, and while the pestilence raged most furiously abroad, that the Prince Prospero entertained his thousand friends at a masked ball of the most unusual magnificence.

It was a voluptuous[7] scene, that masquerade. But first let me tell of the rooms in which it was held. There were seven—an imperial suite. In many palaces, however, such suites form a long and straight vista, while the folding doors slide back nearly to the walls on either hand, so that the view of the whole extent is scarcely impeded. Here the case was very different, as might have been expected from the prince's love of the bizarre. The apartments were so irregularly disposed that the vision embraced but little more than one at a time. There was a sharp turn at every twenty or thirty yards, and at each turn a novel effect. To the right and left, in the middle of each wall, a tall and narrow Gothic window looked out upon a closed corridor which pursued the windings of the suite. These windows were of stained glass, whose color varied in accordance with the prevailing hue of the decorations of the chamber into which it opened. That at the eastern extremity was hung, for example, in blue—and vividly blue were its windows. The second chamber was purple in its ornaments and tapestries, and here the panes were purple. The third was green throughout, and so were the casements.[8] The fourth was furnished and lighted with orange, the fifth was white, the sixth with violet. The seventh apartment was closely shrouded in black velvet tapestries that hung all over the ceiling and down the walls, falling in heavy folds upon a carpet of the same material and hue. But, in this chamber only, the color of the windows failed to correspond with the decorations. The panes here were scarlet—a deep blood color. Now in no one of the seven apartments was there any lamp or candelabrum,[9] amid the profusion of golden ornaments that lay

---

6. improvisatori (ĕm′prŏv·ē·za·tō′rē): *Italian,* entertainers who improvise or make up songs, poems, or drama as they perform.

7. voluptuous (və·lŭp′choo·əs): delightful to the senses; yielding enjoyment through pleasures or luxuries.

8. casements: windows having sashes which open on hinges at the side.

9. candelabrum (kăn′də·lä′brəm): a large, ornamental, branched holder for candles.

scattered to and fro or depended[10] from the roof. There was no light of any kind emanating from lamp or candle within the suite of chambers. But in the corridors that followed the suite there stood, opposite each window, a heavy tripod, bearing a brazier[11] of fire, that projected its rays through the tinted glass and so glaringly illumined the room. And thus were produced a multitude of gaudy and fantastic appearances. But in the western or black chamber the effect of the firelight that streamed upon the dark hangings through the blood-tinted panes was ghastly in the extreme, and produced so wild a look upon the countenances of those who entered that there were few of the company bold enough to set foot within its precincts at all.

It was in this apartment, also, that there stood against the western wall a gigantic clock of ebony.[12] Its pendulum swung to and fro with a dull, heavy, monotonous clang; and when the minute hand made the circuit of the face, and the hour was to be stricken, there came from the brazen lungs of the clock a sound which was clear and loud and deep and exceedingly musical, but of so peculiar a note and emphasis that, at each lapse of an hour, the musicians of the orchestra were constrained to pause, momentarily, in their performance, to hearken to the sound; and thus the waltzers perforce[13] ceased their evolutions; and there was a brief disconcert[14] of the whole gay company; and, while the chimes of the clock yet rang, it was observed that the giddiest grew pale, and the more aged and sedate passed their hands over their brows as if in confused revery or meditation. But when the echoes had fully ceased, a light laughter at once pervaded the assembly; the musicians looked at each other and smiled as if at their own nervousness and folly, and made whispering vows, each to the other, that the next chiming of the clock should produce in them no similar emotion; and then, after the lapse of sixty minutes (which embrace three thousand and six hundred seconds of the Time that flies), there came yet another chiming of the clock, and then were the same disconcert and tremulousness and meditation as before.

But, in spite of these things, it was a gay and magnificent

10. **depended:** hung.
11. **brazier** (brā′zhər): a metal pan for holding burning coals.
12. **ebony** (ĕb′ə·nē): a rare black wood.
13. **perforce** (pĕr·fôrs′): by force of circumstances; of necessity.
14. **disconcert** (dĭs′kən·sûrt′): confusion. Explain this word by checking the meaning of its prefix and root.

revel. The tastes of the prince were peculiar. He had a fine eye for colors and effects. He disregarded the *decora*[15] of mere fashion. His plans were bold and fiery, and his conceptions glowed with barbaric luster. There are some who would have thought him mad. His followers felt that he was not. It was necessary to hear and see and touch him to be *sure* that he was not.

He had directed, in great part, the movable embellishments of the seven chambers, upon occasion of this great fete;[16] and it was his own guiding taste which had given character to the masqueraders. Be sure they were grotesque. There were much glare and glitter and piquancy and phantasm[17]—much of what has been seen in *Hernani*.[18] There were arabesque[19] figures with unsuited[20] limbs and appointments. There were delirious fancies such as the madman fashions. There were much of the beautiful, much of the wanton,[21] much of the bizarre, something of the terrible, and not a little of that which might have excited disgust. To and fro in the seven chambers there stalked, in fact, a multitude of dreams. And these—the dreams—writhed in and about, taking hue from the rooms, and causing the wild music of the orchestra to seem as the echo of their steps. And, anon, there strikes the ebony clock which stands in the hall of the velvet. And then, for a moment, all is still, and all is silent save the voice of the clock. The dreams are stiff-frozen as they stand. But the echoes of the chime die away—they have endured but an instant—and a light, half-subdued laughter floats after them as they depart. And now again the music swells, and the dreams live, and writhe to and fro more merrily than ever, taking hue from the many-tinted windows through which stream the rays from the tripods. But to the chamber which lies most westwardly of the seven, there are now none of the maskers who venture; for the night is waning away, and there flows a ruddier light through the blood-colored panes, and the blackness of the sable drapery appalls; and to him whose foot falls upon the sable carpet, there comes from the near clock of

15. **decora:** *Latin,* plural of *decorum;* that is, observances; proprieties.
16. **fete** (fāt): a lavish entertainment or festival.
17. **piquancy** (pē′kən·sē) **and phantasm** (făn′tăz·əm): liveliness and fantasy.
18. **Hernani:** a play by the French author Victor Hugo (1802–85).
19. **arabesque** (ăr′ə·bĕsk′): a design with an intricate pattern of angular and curved lines. Check your dictionary to find what position this refers to in ballet.
20. **unsuited:** unmatched.
21. **wanton** (wŏn′tən): unrestrained; unchaste.

ebony a muffled peal more solemnly emphatic than any which reaches *their* ears who indulge in the more remote gaieties of the other apartments.

But these other apartments were densely crowded, and in them beat feverishly the heart of life. And the revel went whirlingly on, until at length there commenced the sounding of midnight upon the clock. And then the music ceased; as I have told, and the evolutions of the waltzers were quieted, and there was an uneasy cessation of all things as before. But now there were twelve strokes to be sounded by the bell of the clock; and thus it happened, perhaps, that more of thought crept, with more of time, into the meditations of the thoughtful among those who reveled. And thus, too, it happened, perhaps, that before the last echoes of the last chime had utterly sunk into silence, there were many individuals in the crowd who had found leisure to become aware of the presence of a masked figure which had arrested the attention of no single individual before. And the rumor of this new presence having spread itself whisperingly around, there arose at length from the whole company a buzz, or murmur, expressive of disapprobation[22] and surprise—then, finally, of terror, of horror, and of disgust.

In an assembly of phantasms such as I have painted, it may well be supposed that no ordinary appearance could have excited such sensation. In truth the masquerade license[23] of the night was nearly unlimited; but the figure in question had out-Heroded Herod,[24] and gone beyond the bounds of even the prince's indefinite decorum. There are chords in the hearts of the most reckless which cannot be touched without emotion. The whole company, indeed, seemed now deeply to feel that in the costume and bearing of the stranger neither wit nor propriety existed. The figure was tall and gaunt, and shrouded from head to foot in the habiliments of the grave. The mask which concealed the visage was made so nearly to resemble the countenance of a stiffened corpse that the closest scrutiny must have had difficulty in detecting the cheat. And yet all

22. **disapprobation** (dĭs'ăp·rə·bā'shən): disapproval.
23. **masquerade license:** freedom to act irresponsibly without fear of being recognized.
24. **out-Heroded Herod:** had outdone Herod in violence, outrage, or extravagance. Herod was the king of Judea who is reported to have ordered the slaughter of all the male infants under two years of age in Bethlehem in an attempt to kill the newly born Jesus.

this might have been endured, if not approved, by the mad revelers around. But the mummer[25] had gone so far as to assume the type of the Red Death. His vesture was dabbled in *blood*—and his broad brow, with all the features of the face, was besprinkled with the scarlet horror.

When the eyes of Prince Prospero fell upon this spectral image (which with a slow and solemn movement, as if more fully to sustain its role, stalked to and fro among the waltzers) he was seen to be convulsed, in the first moment, with a strong shudder either of terror or distaste; but, in the next, his brow reddened with rage.

"Who dares?" he demanded hoarsely of the courtiers who stood near him—"who dares insult us with this blasphemous mockery? Seize him and unmask him—that we may know whom we have to hang at sunrise, from the battlements!"

It was in the eastern or blue chamber in which stood the Prince Prospero as he uttered these words. They rang throughout the seven rooms loudly and clearly—for the prince was a bold and robust man, and the music had become hushed at the waving of his hand.

It was in the blue room where stood the prince, with a group of pale courtiers by his side. At first, as he spoke, there was a slight rushing movement of this group in the direction of the intruder, who at the moment was also near at hand, and now, with deliberate and stately step, made closer approach to the speaker. But from a certain nameless awe with which the mad assumptions of the mummer had inspired the whole party, there were found none who put forth hand to seize him, so that unimpeded, he passed within a yard of the prince's person; and while the vast assembly, as if with one impulse, shrank from the centers of the rooms to the walls, he made his way uninterruptedly, but with the same solemn and measured step which had distinguished him from the first, through the blue chamber to the purple—through the purple to the green—through the green to the orange—through this again to the white—and even thence to the violet, ere a decided movement had been made to arrest him. It was then, however, that the Prince Prospero, maddening with rage and the shame of his own momentary cowardice, rushed hurriedly through the six chambers, while none followed him on account of a deadly terror

25. **mummer:** one who acts in a disguise or mask, expecially during festivals.

that had seized upon all. He bore aloft a drawn dagger, and had approached, in rapid impetuosity, to within three or four feet of the retreating figure, when the latter, having attained the extremity of the velvet apartment, turned suddenly and confronted his pursuer. There was a sharp cry—and the dagger dropped gleaming upon the sable carpet, upon which, instantly afterward, fell prostrate in death the Prince Prospero. Then, summoning the wild courage of despair, a throng of the revelers at once threw themselves into the black apartment, and seizing the mummer, whose tall figure stood erect and motionless within the shadow of the ebony clock, gasped in unutterable horror at finding the grave-cerements[26] and corpse-like mask which they handled with so violent a rudeness, untenanted[27] by any tangible form.

And now was acknowledged the presence of the Red Death. He had come like a thief in the night.[28] And one by one dropped the revelers in the blood-bedewed halls of their revel, and died each in the despairing posture of his fall. And the life of the ebony clock went out with that of the last of the gay. And the flames of the tripods expired. And Darkness and Decay and the Red Death held illimitable dominion over all.

26. **cerements** (sîr′məntz): cloth which is treated with wax and used as wrappings for the dead.
27. **untenanted:** Figure out the meaning by breaking this word into its prefix and root.
28. **thief in the night:** a biblical reference (1 Thessalonians 5:2), ". . . the day of the Lord so cometh as a thief in the night."

Meaning

1. Why do you think Poe chose the name Prospero for the prince?
2. Why do all the guests fear the strange "mummer"? What happens when they seize him?
3. What are the conflicts in the story? Explain your answer.
4. What would you say is the theme of "The Masque of the Red Death"? What does Poe emphasize: plot, character, atmosphere, or theme?

Method

1. The setting of the story, a masked ball, appears in paragraph three. What purposes, then, are served by paragraphs one and two?
2. To sustain the mood or atmosphere of horror, Poe makes a strong appeal to the senses, especially to sight and hearing. Find three passages that are visual images of horror. List three of the sounds that contribute to the same effect.
3. Notice that Poe sometimes uses very long sentences. Compare some of the sentences that go on for several lines. What do they seem to have in common? Why do you think Poe used such long, complicated sentences?
4. Poe's prose style has many of the characteristics of his poetry. Notice, for example, Poe's use of *alliteration,* that is, the repetition of the same sound at the beginning of words close together in a sentence. For example, "There were much glare and glitter and piquancy and phantasm. . . ."

   Notice also the *repetition* of words and phrases, as in "There were much of the beautiful, much of the wanton, much of the bizarre. . . ." List other examples of Poe's uses of alliteration and repetition.

Language: The Use of Adjectives

Notice, in the following sentences, the use of adjectives, sometimes three, even four, to achieve a *cumulative,* that is, a steadily increasing or mounting, effect.

1. "Its pendulum swung to and fro with a dull, heavy, monotonous clang. . . ."
2. ". . . a sound which was clear and loud and deep and exceedingly musical. . . ."
3. "His plans were bold and fiery, and his conceptions glowed with barbaric luster."

Notice that the *rhythm* of each sentence suits the idea that Poe wants to express. In the first sentence, Poe wants the reader to *hear* the clang of the pendulum, so he chooses to have adjectives in a series, with the number of syllables increasing with each word.

In the second sentence, what is the effect of Poe's use of *and* to separate the adjectives?

In the third sentence, Poe repeats the same idea twice, but *plans* and *conceptions* have quite different connotations. How does the second part of the sentence differ from the first part?

Discussion and Composition

1. Poe believed that a short story approached perfection only when every word, even every sound contributed to a single emotional effect. Of the short story writers other than Poe that you have read so far, who best follows Poe's ideas about writing? Which writer would you say Poe would like least? Discuss your choices with the class, giving specific examples.

2. Think of an event that would produce a feeling of fear, joy, horror, suspense, pity, or calm. Then write a paragraph in which you set the mood and atmosphere for the telling of such an event. For an example of this technique, you might re-read the description of the Red Death that sets the mood of horror for Poe's tale. As you write, try to choose words that are rich in their power of suggestion. Construct every sentence with care. Remember that everything must contribute to the single effect you wish to create.

RICHARD CONNELL

(1893–1949)

Richard Connell was born in Dutchess County, New York. He began writing at the age of ten, when he covered baseball games for the newspaper his father edited. By the time he was sixteen, he was editing the paper. At Harvard College, Connell edited the *Daily Crimson* and the *Lampoon,* Harvard's humor magazine. After graduating from college, he worked for a newspaper in New York for a time and later served in World War I. In 1919, he began his career as a freelance writer.

Of the several hundred stories that Connell published during his lifetime, "The Most Dangerous Game" is his best-known. Since the story's publication in 1912, its gripping, suspenseful plot has continued to fascinate readers. It has appeared in numerous anthologies and has been adapted for the movies and television.

THE MOST DANGEROUS GAME

"Off there to the right—somewhere—is a large island," said Whitney. "It's rather a mystery—"

"What island is it?" Rainsford asked.

"The old charts call it 'Ship-Trap Island,'" Whitney replied. "A suggestive name, isn't it? Sailors have a curious dread of the place. I don't know why. Some superstition—"

"Can't see it," remarked Rainsford, trying to peer through the dank tropical night that was palpable as it pressed its thick warm blackness in upon the yacht.

"You've good eyes," said Whitney, with a laugh, "and I've seen you pick off a moose moving in the brown fall bush at four hundred yards, but even you can't see four miles or so through a moonless Caribbean night."

"Nor four yards," admitted Rainsford. "Ugh! It's like moist black velvet."

"It will be light in Rio," promised Whitney. "We should make it in a few days. I hope the jaguar guns have come from Purdey's[1]. We should have some good hunting up the Amazon. Great sport, hunting."

"The best sport in the world," agreed Rainsford.

"For the hunter," amended Whitney. "Not for the jaguar."

"Don't talk rot, Whitney," said Rainsford. "You're a big-game hunter, not a philosopher. Who cares how a jaguar feels?"

"Perhaps the jaguar does," observed Whitney.

"Bah! They've no understanding."

"Even so, I rather think they understand one thing—fear. The fear of pain and the fear of death."

"Nonsense," laughed Rainsford. "This hot weather is making you soft, Whitney. Be a realist. The world is made up of two classes—the hunters and the huntees. Luckily, you and I are hunters. Do you think we've passed that island yet?"

"I can't tell in the dark. I hope so."

"Why?" asked Rainsford.

"The place has a reputation—a bad one."

"Cannibals?" suggested Rainsford.

"Hardly. Even cannibals wouldn't live in such a Godforsaken place. But it's gotten into sailor lore, somehow. Didn't you notice that the crew's nerves seemed a bit jumpy today?"

"They were a bit strange, now you mention it. Even Captain Nielsen—"

"Yes, even that tough-minded old Swede, who'd go up to the devil himself and ask him for a light. Those fishy blue eyes held a look I never saw there before. All I could get out of him was: 'This place has an evil name among seafaring men, sir.' Then he said to me, very gravely: 'Don't you feel anything?'—as if the air about us was actually poisonous. Now, you mustn't laugh when I tell you this—I did feel something like a sudden chill.

"There was no breeze. The sea was as flat as a plate-glass window. We were drawing near the island then. What I felt was a— a mental chill; a sort of sudden dread."

"Pure imagination," said Rainsford. "One superstitious sailor can taint the whole ship's company with his fear."

"Maybe. But sometimes I think sailors have an extra sense that tells them when they are in danger. Sometimes I think evil is a

1. **Purdey's:** a famous English manufacturer of hunting rifles and shotguns.

tangible thing—with wavelengths, just as sound and light have. An evil place can, so to speak, broadcast vibrations of evil. Anyhow, I'm glad we're getting out of this zone. Well, I think I'll turn in now, Rainsford."

"I'm not sleepy," said Rainsford. "I'm going to smoke another pipe up on the afterdeck."

"Good night, then, Rainsford. See you at breakfast."

"Right. Good night, Whitney."

There was no sound in the night as Rainsford sat there, but the muffled throb of the engine that drove the yacht swiftly through the darkness, and the swish and ripple of the wash of the propeller.

Rainsford, reclining in a steamer chair, indolently puffed on his favorite brier. The sensuous drowsiness of the night was on him. "It's so dark," he thought, "that I could sleep without closing my eyes; the night would be my eyelids—"

An abrupt sound startled him. Off to the right he heard it, and his ears, expert in such matters, could not be mistaken. Again he heard the sound, and again. Somewhere, off in the blackness, someone had fired a gun three times.

Rainsford sprang up and moved quickly to the rail, mystified. He strained his eyes in the direction from which the reports had come, but it was like trying to see through a blanket. He leaped upon the rail and balanced himself there, to get greater elevation; his pipe, striking a rope, was knocked from his mouth. He lunged for it; a short, hoarse cry came from his lips as he realized he had reached too far and had lost his balance. The cry was pinched off short as the blood-warm waters of the Caribbean Sea closed over his head.

He struggled up to the surface and tried to cry out, but the wash from the speeding yacht slapped him in the face and the salt water in his open mouth made him gag and strangle. Desperately he struck out with strong strokes after the receding lights of the yacht, but he stopped before he had swum fifty feet. A certain coolheadedness had come to him; it was not the first time he had been in a tight place. There was a chance that his cries could be heard by someone aboard the yacht, but that chance was slender, and grew more slender as the yacht raced on. He wrestled himself out of his clothes, and shouted with all his power. The lights of the yacht became faint and ever-vanishing fireflies; then they were blotted out entirely by the night.

Rainsford remembered the shots. They had come from the right, and doggedly he swam in that direction swimming with slow, deliberate strokes, conserving his strength. For a seemingly endless time he fought the sea. He began to count his strokes; he could do possibly a hundred more and then—

Rainsford heard a sound. It came out of the darkness, a high screaming sound, the sound of an animal in an extremity of anguish and terror.

He did not recognize the animal that made the sound; he did not try to; with fresh vitality he swam toward the sound. He heard it again; then it was cut short by another noise, crisp, staccato.

"Pistol shot," muttered Rainsford, swimming on.

Ten minutes of determined effort brought another sound to his ears—the most welcome he had ever heard—the muttering and growling of the sea breaking on a rocky shore. He was almost on the rocks before he saw them; on a night less calm he would have been shattered against them. With his remaining strength he dragged himself from the swirling waters. Jagged crags appeared to jut up into the opaqueness; he forced himself upward, hand over hand. Gasping, his hands raw, he reached a flat place at the top. Dense jungle came down to the very edge of the cliffs. What perils that tangle of trees and underbrush might hold for him did not concern Rainsford just then. All he knew was that he was safe from his enemy, the sea, and that utter weariness was on him. He flung himself down at the jungle edge and tumbled headlong into the deepest sleep of his life.

When he opened his eyes he knew from the position of the sun that it was late in the afternoon. Sleep had given him new vigor; a sharp hunger was picking at him. He looked about him, almost cheerfully.

"Where there are pistol shots, there are men. Where there are men, there is food," he thought. But what kind of men, he wondered, in so forbidding a place? An unbroken front of snarled and ragged jungle fringed the shore.

He saw no sign of a trail through the closely knit web of weeds and trees; it was easier to go along the shore, and Rainsford floundered along by the water. Not far from where he had landed, he stopped.

Some wounded thing, by the evidence a large animal, had thrashed about in the underbrush; the jungle weeds were crushed down and the moss was lacerated; one patch of weeds was stained crimson. A small, glittering object not far away caught Rainsford's eye and he picked it up. It was an empty cartridge.

"A twenty-two," he remarked. "That's odd. It must have

been a fairly large animal too. The hunter had his nerve to tackle it with a light gun. It's clear that the brute put up a fight. I suppose the first three shots I heard was when the hunter flushed his quarry[2] and wounded it. The last shot was when he trailed it here and finished it."

He examined the ground closely and found what he had hoped to find—the print of hunting boots. They pointed along the cliff in the direction he had been going. Eagerly he hurried along, now slipping on a rotten log or a loose stone, but making headway; night was beginning to settle down on the island.

Bleak darkness was blacking out the sea and jungle when Rainsford sighted the lights. He came upon them as he turned a crook in the coastline, and his first thought was that he had come upon a village, for there were many lights. But as he forged along he saw to his great astonishment that all the lights were in one enormous building—a lofty structure with pointed towers plunging upward into the gloom. His eyes made out the shadowy outlines of a palatial château[3]; it was set on a high bluff, and on three sides of it cliffs dived down to where the sea licked greedy lips in the shadows.

"Mirage," thought Rainsford. But it was no mirage, he found, when he opened the tall spiked iron gate. The stone steps were real enough; the massive door with a leering gargoyle[4] for a knocker was real enough; yet about it all hung an air of unreality.

He lifted the knocker, and it creaked up stiffly, as if it had never before been used. He let it fall, and it startled him with its booming loudness. He thought he heard steps within; the door remained closed. Again Rainsford lifted the heavy knocker, and let it fall. The door opened then, opened as suddenly as if it were on a spring, and Rainsford stood blinking in the river of glaring gold light that poured out. The first thing Rainsford's eyes discerned was the largest man Rainsford had ever seen—a gigantic creature, solidly made and black-bearded to the waist. In his hand the man held a long-barreled revolver, and he was pointing it straight at Rainsford's heart.

Out of the snarl of beard two small eyes regarded Rainsford.

"Don't be alarmed," said Rainsford, with a smile which he

2. **flushed his quarry:** forced the game that was being hunted into the open.
3. **château** (shă-tō'): castle or large country house.
4. **gargoyle** (gär'goil'): a grotesque carved figure, usually of an animal or mythical creature.

hoped was disarming. "I'm no robber. I fell off a yacht. My name is Sanger Rainsford of New York City."

The menacing look in his eyes did not change. The revolver pointed as rigidly as if the giant were a statue. He gave no sign that he understood Rainsford's words, or that he had even heard them. He was dressed in uniform, a black uniform trimmed with gray astrakhan[5].

"I'm Sanger Rainsford of New York," Rainsford began again. "I fell off a yacht. I am hungry."

The man's only answer was to raise with his thumb the hammer of his revolver. Then Rainsford saw the man's free hand go to his forehead in a military salute, and he saw him click his heels together and stand at attention. Another man was coming down the broad marble steps, an erect, slender man in evening clothes. He advanced to Rainsford and held out his hand.

In a cultivated voice marked by a slight accent that gave it added precision and deliberateness, he said: "It is a very great pleasure and honor to welcome Mr. Sanger Rainsford, the celebrated hunter, to my home."

Automatically Rainsford shook the man's hand.

"I've read your book about hunting snow leopards in Tibet, you see," explained the man. "I am General Zaroff."

Rainsford's first impression was that the man was singularly handsome; his second was that there was an original, almost bizarre quality about the general's face. He was a tall man past middle age, for his hair was a vivid white; but his thick eyebrows and pointed military mustache were as black as the night from which Rainsford had come. His eyes, too, were black and very bright. He had high cheekbones, a sharp-cut nose, a spare, dark face, the face of a man used to giving orders, the face of an aristocrat. Turning to the giant in uniform, the general made a sign. The giant put away his pistol, saluted, withdrew.

"Ivan is an incredibly strong fellow," remarked the general, "but he has the misfortune to be deaf and dumb. A simple fellow, but, I'm afraid, like all his race, a bit of a savage."

"Is he Russian?"

"He is a Cossack[6]," said the general, and his smile showed red lips and pointed teeth. "So am I."

5. **astrakhan** (ăs′trǝ-kăn′): the curled fur of young lambs.
6. **Cossack:** Cossacks are a people of the southern Soviet Union noted for their horsemanship and their courage and fierceness in battle.

"Come," he said, "we shouldn't be chatting here. We can talk later. Now you want clothes, food, rest. You shall have them. This is a most restful spot."

Ivan had reappeared, and the general spoke to him with lips that moved but gave forth no sound.

"Follow Ivan, if you please, Mr. Rainsford," said the general. "I was about to have my dinner when you came. I'll wait for you. You'll find that my clothes will fit you, I think."

It was to a huge, beam-ceilinged bedroom with a canopied bed big enough for six men that Rainsford followed the silent giant. Ivan laid out an evening suit, and Rainsford, as he put it on, noticed that it came from a London tailor who ordinarily cut and sewed for none below the rank of duke.

The dining room to which Ivan conducted him was in many ways remarkable. There was a medieval magnificence about it; it suggested a baronial hall of feudal times with its oaken panels, its high ceiling, its vast refectory table where twoscore men could sit down to eat. About the hall were the mounted heads of many animals—lions, tigers, elephants, moose, bears; larger or more perfect specimens Rainsford had never seen. At the great table the general was sitting, alone.

"You'll have a cocktail, Mr. Rainsford," he suggested. The cocktail was surpassingly good; and, Rainsford noted, the table appointments were of the finest—the linen, the crystal, the silver, the china.

They were eating borsch, the rich, red soup with sour cream so dear to Russian palates. Half apologetically General Zaroff said: "We do our best to preserve the amenities of civilization here. Please forgive any lapses. We are well off the beaten track, you know. Do you think the champagne has suffered from its long ocean trip?"

"Not in the least," declared Rainsford. He was finding the general a most thoughtful and affable host, a true cosmopolite. But there was one small trait of the general's that made Rainsford uncomfortable. Whenever he looked up from his plate he found the general studying him, appraising him narrowly.

"Perhaps," said General Zaroff, "you were surprised that I recognized your name. You see, I read all books on hunting published in English, French, and Russian. I have but one passion in my life, Mr. Rainsford, and it is the hunt."

"You have some wonderful heads here," said Rainsford as he ate a particularly well-cooked filet mignon. "That Cape buffalo is the largest I ever saw."

"Oh, that fellow. Yes, he was a monster."

"Did he charge you?"

"Hurled me against a tree," said the general. "Fractured my skull. But I got the brute."

"I've always thought," said Rainsford, "that the Cape buffalo is the most dangerous of all big game."

For a moment the general did not reply; he was smiling his curious red-lipped smile. Then he said slowly: "No. You are wrong, sir. The Cape buffalo is not the most dangerous big game." He sipped his wine. "Here in my preserve on this island," he said in the same slow tone, "I hunt more dangerous game."

Rainsford expressed his surprise. "Is there big game on this island?"

The general nodded. "The biggest."

"Really?"

"Oh, it isn't here naturally, of course. I have to stock the island."

"What have you imported, general?" Rainsford asked. "Tigers?"

The general smiled. "No," he said. "Hunting tigers ceased to interest me some years ago. I exhausted their possibilities, you see. No thrill left in tigers, no real danger. I live for danger, Mr. Rainsford."

The general took from his pocket a gold cigarette case and offered his guest a long black cigarette with a silver tip; it was perfumed and gave off a smell like incense.

"We will have some capital hunting, you and I," said the general. "I shall be most glad to have your society."

"But what game—" began Rainsford.

"I'll tell you," said the general. "You will be amused, I know. I think I may say, in all modesty, that I have done a rare thing. I have invented a new sensation. May I pour you another glass of port, Mr. Rainsford?"

"Thank you, general."

The general filled both glasses, and said: "God makes some men poets. Some He makes kings, some beggars. Me He made a hunter. My hand was made for the trigger, my father said. He was a very rich man with a quarter of a million acres in the Crimea, and he was an ardent sportsman. When I was only five years old he gave me a little gun, specially made in Moscow for me, to shoot sparrows with. When I shot some of his prize turkeys with it, he did not punish me; he complimented me on my marksmanship. I killed my first bear in the Caucasus when I was ten. My whole life has been one prolonged hunt. I went into the army—it was expected of noblemen's sons—and for a time commanded a division of Cossack cavalry, but my real interest was always the hunt. I have hunted every kind of game in every land. It would be impossible for me to tell you how many animals I have killed."

The general puffed at his cigarette.

"After the debacle[7] in Russia I left the country, for it was imprudent for an officer of the Czar to stay there. Many noble Russians lost everything. I, luckily, had invested heavily in American securities, so I shall never have to open a tearoom in Monte Carlo or drive a taxi in Paris. Naturally, I continued to hunt—grizzlies in your Rockies, crocodiles in the Ganges, rhinoceroses in East Africa. It was in Africa that the Cape buffalo hit me and laid me up for six months. As soon as I recovered I started for the Amazon to hunt jaguars, for I had heard they were unusually cunning. They weren't." The Cossack sighed. "They were no match at all for a hunter with his wits about him, and a high-powered rifle. I was bitterly disappointed. I was lying in my tent with a splitting headache one night when a terrible thought pushed its way into my mind. Hunting was beginning to bore me! And hunting, remember, had been my life. I have heard that in America businessmen often go to pieces when they give up the business that has been their life."

"Yes, that's so," said Rainsford.

The general smiled. "I had no wish to go to pieces," he said. "I must do something. Now, mine is an analytical mind, Mr. Rainsford. Doubtless that is why I enjoy the problems of the chase."

"No doubt, General Zaroff."

"So," continued the general, "I asked myself why the hunt no longer fascinated me. You are much younger than I am, Mr. Rainsford, and have not hunted as much, but you perhaps can guess the answer."

"What was it?"

"Simply this: hunting had ceased to be what you call 'a sporting proposition.' It had become too easy. I always got my quarry. Always. There is no greater bore than perfection."

---

7. **debacle** (dĭ-bä′kəl): collapse; here, referring to the overthrow of the empire of the czars in 1917.

The general lit a fresh cigarette.

"No animal had a chance with me any more. That is no boast; it is a mathematical certainty. The animal had nothing but his legs and his instinct. Instinct is no match for reason. When I thought of this it was a tragic moment for me, I can tell you."

Rainsford leaned across the table, absorbed in what his host was saying.

"It came to me as an inspiration what I must do," the general went on.

"And that was?"

The general smiled the quiet smile of one who has faced an obstacle and surmounted it with success. "I had to invent a new animal to hunt," he said.

"A new animal? You're joking."

"Not at all," said the general. "I never joke about hunting. I needed a new animal. I found one. So I bought this island, built this house, and here I do my hunting. The island is perfect for my purposes—there are jungles with a maze of trails in them, hills, swamps—"

"But the animal, General Zaroff?"

"Oh," said the general, "it supplies me with the most exciting hunting in the world. No other hunting compares with it for an instant. Every day I hunt, and I never grow bored now, for I have a quarry with which I can match my wits."

Rainsford's bewilderment showed in his face.

"I wanted the ideal animal to hunt," explained the general. "So, I said: 'What are the attributes of an ideal quarry?' And the answer was, of course: 'It must have courage, cunning, and, above all, it must be able to reason.'"

"But no animal can reason," objected Rainsford.

"My dear fellow," said the general, "there is one that can."

"But you can't mean—" gasped Rainsford.

"And why not?"

"I can't believe you are serious, General Zaroff. This is a grisly joke."

"Why should I not be serious? I am speaking of hunting."

"Hunting? General Zaroff, what you speak of is murder."

The general laughed with entire good nature. He regarded Rainsford quizzically. "I refuse to believe that so modern and civilized a young man as you seem to be harbors romantic ideas about the value of human life. Surely your experiences in the war—"

"Did not make me condone cold-blooded murder," finished Rainsford stiffly.

Laughter shook the general. "How extraordinarily droll you are!" he said. "One does not expect nowadays to find a young man of the educated class, even in America, with such a naive, and, if I may say so, mid-Victorian point of view. It's like finding a snuffbox in a limousine. Ah, well, doubtless you had Puritan ancestors. So many Americans appear to have had. I'll wager you'll forget your notions when you go hunting with me. You've a genuine new thrill in store for you, Mr. Rainsford."

"Thank you, I'm a hunter, not a murderer."

"Dear me," said the general, quite unruffled. "Again that unpleasant word. But I think I can show you that your scruples are quite ill-founded."

"Yes?"

"Life is for the strong, to be lived by the strong, and, if need be, taken by the strong. The weak of the world were put here to give the strong pleasure. I am strong. Why should I not use my gift? If I wish to hunt, why should I not? I hunt the scum of the earth—sailors from tramp ships—lascars, blacks, Chinese, whites, mongrels—a thoroughbred horse or hound is worth more than a score of them."

"But they are men," said Rainsford hotly.

"Precisely," said the general. "That is why I use them. It gives me pleasure. They can reason, after a fashion. So they are dangerous."

"But where do you get them?"

The general's left eyelid fluttered down in a wink. "This island is called Ship-Trap," he answered. "Sometimes an angry god of the high seas sends them to me. Sometimes, when Providence is not so kind, I help Providence a bit. Come to the window with me."

Rainsford went to the window and looked out toward the sea.

"Watch! Out there!" exclaimed the general, pointing into the night. Rainsford's eyes saw only blackness, and then, as the general pressed a button, far out to sea Rainsford saw the flash of lights.

The general chuckled. "They indicate a channel," he said, "where there's none: giant rocks with razor edges crouch like a sea monster with wide-open jaws. They can crush a ship as easily as I crush this nut." He dropped a walnut on the hardwood floor and brought his heel grinding down on it. "Oh, yes," he said, casually, as if in answer to a question, "I have electricity. We try to be civilized here."

"Civilized? And you shoot down men?"

A trace of anger was in the general's black eyes, but it was there for but a second, and he said, in his most pleasant manner: "Dear me, what a righteous young man you are! I assure you I do not do the thing you suggest. That would be barbarous. I treat these visitors with every consideration. They get plenty of good food and exercise. They get into splendid physical condition. You shall see for yourself tomorrow."

"What do you mean?"

"We'll visit my training school," smiled the general. "It's in the cellar. I have about a dozen pupils down there now. They're from the Spanish bark *San Lucar* that had the bad luck to go on the rocks out there. A very inferior lot, I regret to say. Poor specimens and more accustomed to the deck than to the jungle."

He raised his hand, and Ivan, who served as waiter, brought thick Turkish coffee. Rainsford, with an effort, held his tongue in check.

"It's a game, you see," pursued the general blandly. "I suggest to one of them that we go hunting. I give him a supply of food and an excellent hunting knife. I give him three hours' start. I am to follow, armed only with a pistol of the smallest caliber and range. If my quarry eludes me for three whole days, he wins the game. If I find him"—the general smiled—"he loses."

"Suppose he refuses to be hunted?"

"Oh," said the general, "I give him his option, of course. He need not play that game if he doesn't wish to. If he does not wish to hunt, I turn him over to Ivan. Ivan once had the honor of serving as official knouter[8] to the Great White Czar, and he has his own ideas of sport. Invariably, Mr. Rainsford, invariably they choose the hunt."

"And if they win?"

The smile on the general's face widened. "To date I have not lost," he said.

Then he added, hastily: "I don't wish you to think me a braggart, Mr. Rainsford. Many of them afford only the most elementary sort of problem. Occasionally I strike a tartar. One almost did win. I eventually had to use the dogs."

---

8. **knouter** (nout'ər): A knout is a leather whip that was used in Russia to punish criminals.

"The dogs?"

"This way, please. I'll show you."

The general steered Rainsford to a window. The lights from the windows sent a flickering illumination that made grotesque patterns on the courtyard below, and Rainsford could see moving about there a dozen or so huge black shapes; as they turned toward him, their eyes glittered greenly.

"A rather good lot, I think," observed the general. "They are let out at seven every night. If anyone should try to get into my house—or out of it—something extremely regrettable would occur to him." He hummed a snatch of song from the Folies Bergère.

"And now," said the general, "I want to show you my new collection of heads. Will you come with me to the library?"

"I hope," said Rainsford, "that you will excuse me tonight, General Zaroff. I'm really not feeling at all well."

"Ah, indeed?" the general inquired solicitously. "Well, I suppose that's only natural, after your long swim. You need a good, restful night's sleep. Tomorrow you'll feel like a new man, I'll wager. Then we'll hunt, eh? I've one rather promising prospect—"

Rainsford was hurrying from the room.

"Sorry you can't go with me tonight," called the general. "I expect rather fair sport—a big, strong fellow. He looks resourceful—Well, good night, Mr. Rainsford; I hope you have a good night's rest."

The bed was good, and the pajamas of the softest silk, and he was tired in every fiber of his being, but nevertheless Rainsford could not quiet his brain with the opiate of sleep. He lay, eyes wide open. Once he thought he heard stealthy steps in the corridor outside his room. He sought to throw open the door; it would not open. He went to the window and looked out. His room was high up in one of the towers. The lights of the château were out now, and it was dark and silent, but there was a fragment of sallow moon, and by its wan light he could see, dimly, the courtyard; there, weaving in and out in the pattern of shadow, were black, noiseless forms; the hounds heard him at the window and looked up, expectantly, with their green eyes. Rainsford went back to the bed and lay down. By many methods he tried to put himself to sleep. He had achieved a doze when, just as morning began to come, he heard, far off in the jungle, the faint report of a pistol.

General Zaroff did not appear until luncheon. He was dressed faultlessly in the tweeds of a country squire. He was solicitous about the state of Rainsford's health.

"As for me," sighed the general, "I do not feel so well. I am worried, Mr. Rainsford. Last night I detected traces of my old complaint."

To Rainsford's questioning glance the general said: "Ennui. Boredom."

Then, taking a second helping of crepes suzette, the general explained: "The hunting was not good last night. The fellow lost his head. He made a straight trail that offered no problems at all. That's the trouble with these sailors; they have dull brains to begin with, and they do not know how to get about in the woods. They do excessively stupid and obvious things. It's most annoying. Will you have another glass of Chablis, Mr. Rainsford?"

"General," said Rainsford firmly, "I wish to leave this island at once."

The general raised his thickets of eyebrows; he seemed hurt. "But, my dear fellow," the general protested, "you've only just come. You've had no hunting—"

"I wish to go today," said Rainsford. He saw the dead black eyes of the general on him, studying him. General Zaroff's face suddenly brightened.

He filled Rainsford's glass with venerable Chablis from a dusty bottle.

"Tonight," said the general, "we will hunt—you and I."

Rainsford shook his head. "No, general," he said. "I will not hunt."

The general shrugged his shoulders and delicately ate a hot-house grape. "As you wish, my friend," he said. "The choice rests entirely with you. But may I not venture to suggest that you will find my idea of sport more diverting than Ivan's?"

He nodded toward the corner to where the giant stood, scowling, his thick arms crossed on his hogshead of chest.

"You don't mean—" cried Rainsford.

"My dear fellow," said the general, "have I not told you I always mean what I say about hunting? This is really an inspiration. I drink to a foeman worthy of my steel—at last."

The general raised his glass, but Rainsford sat staring at him.

"You'll find this game worth playing," the general said enthusiastically. "Your brain against mine. Your woodcraft against mine. Your strength and stamina against mine. Outdoor chess! And the stake is not without value, eh?"

"And if I win—" began Rainsford huskily.

"I'll cheerfully acknowledge myself defeated if I do not find you by midnight of the third day," said General Zaroff. "My sloop will place you on the mainland near a town."

The general read what Rainsford was thinking.

"Oh, you can trust me," said the Cossack. "I will give you my word as a gentleman and a sportsman. Of course you, in turn, must agree to say nothing of your visit here."

"I'll agree to nothing of the kind," said Rainsford.

"Oh," said the general, "in that case—But why discuss that now? Three days hence we can discuss it over a bottle of Veuve Cliquot, unless—"

The general sipped his wine.

Then a businesslike air animated him. "Ivan," he said to Rainsford, "will supply you with hunting clothes, food, a knife. I suggest you wear moccasins; they leave a poorer trail. I suggest too that you avoid a big swamp in the southeast corner of the island. We call it Death Swamp. There's quicksand there. One foolish fellow tried it. The deplorable part of it was that Lazarus followed him. You can imagine my feelings, Mr. Rainsford. I loved Lazarus; he was the finest hound in my pack. Well, I must beg you to excuse me now. I always take a siesta after lunch. You'll hardly have time for a nap, I fear. You'll want to start, no doubt. I shall not follow till dusk. Hunting at night is so much more exciting than by day, don't you think? Au revoir[9], Mr. Rainsford, au revoir."

General Zaroff, with a deep, courtly bow, strolled from the room.

From another door came Ivan. Under one arm he carried khaki hunting clothes, a haversack of food, a leather sheath containing a long-bladed hunting knife; his right hand rested on a cocked revolver thrust in the crimson sash about his waist. . . .

Rainsford had fought his way through the bush for two hours. "I must keep my nerve. I must keep my nerve," he said through tight teeth.

He had not been entirely clearheaded when the château gates snapped shut behind him. His whole idea at first was to put distance between himself and General Zaroff, and, to this end, he had plunged along, spurred on by the sharp rowels of something very like panic. Now he had got a grip on himself, had stopped, and was

---

9. **Au revoir** (ō rə-vwar′): French for "until we meet again."

taking stock of himself and the situation.

He saw that straight flight was futile; inevitably it would bring him face to face with the sea. He was in a picture with a frame of water, and his operations, clearly, must take place within that frame.

"I'll give him a trail to follow," muttered Rainsford, and he struck off from the rude paths he had been following into the trackless wilderness. He executed a series of intricate loops; he doubled on his trail again and again, recalling all the lore of the fox hunt, and all the dodges of the fox. Night found him leg-weary, with hands and face lashed by the branches, on a thickly wooded ridge. He knew it would be insane to blunder on through the dark, even if he had the strength. His need for rest was imperative and he thought: "I have played the fox, now I must play the cat of the fable." A big tree with a thick trunk and outspread branches was nearby, and, taking care to leave not the slightest mark, he climbed up into the crotch, and stretching out on one of the broad limbs, after a fashion, rested. Rest brought him new confidence and almost a feeling of security. Even so zealous a hunter as General Zaroff could not trace him there, he told himself; only the devil himself could follow that complicated trail through the jungle after dark. But, perhaps, the general was a devil—

An apprehensive night crawled slowly by like a wounded snake, and sleep did not visit Rainsford, although the silence of a dead world was on the jungle. Toward morning when a dingy gray was varnishing the sky, the cry of some startled bird focused Rainsford's attention in that direction. Something was coming through the bush, coming slowly, carefully, coming by the same winding way Rainsford had come. He flattened himself down on the limb, and through a screen of leaves almost as thick as tapestry, he watched. The thing that was approaching was a man.

It was General Zaroff. He made his way along with his eyes fixed in utmost concentration on the ground before him. He paused, almost beneath the tree, dropped to his knees and studied the ground. Rainsford's impulse was to hurl himself down like a panther, but he saw that the general's right hand held something metallic—a small automatic pistol.

The hunter shook his head several times, as if he were puzzled. Then he straightened up and took from his case one of his black cigarettes; its pungent incenselike smoke floated up to Rainsford's nostrils.

Rainsford held his breath. The general's eyes had left the

ground and were traveling inch by inch up the tree. Rainsford froze there, every muscle tensed for a spring. But the sharp eyes of the hunter stopped before they reached the limb where Rainsford lay; a smile spread over his brown face. Very deliberately he blew a smoke ring into the air; then he turned his back on the tree and walked carelessly away, back along the trail he had come. The swish of the underbush against his hunting boots grew fainter and fainter.

The pent-up air burst hotly from Rainsford's lungs. His first thought made him feel sick and numb. The general could follow a trail through the woods at night; he could follow an extremely difficult trail; he must have uncanny powers; only by the merest chance had the Cossack failed to see his quarry.

Rainsford's second thought was even more terrible. It sent a shudder of cold horror through his whole being. Why had the general smiled? Why had he turned back?

Rainsford did not want to believe what his reason told him was true, but the truth was as evident as the sun that had by now pushed through the morning mists. The general was playing with him! The general was saving him for another day's sport! The Cossack was the cat; he was the mouse. Then it was that Rainsford knew the full meaning of terror.

"I will not lose my nerve. I will not."

He slid down from the tree, and struck off again into the woods. His face was set and he forced the machinery of his mind to function. Three hundred yards from his hiding place he stopped where a huge dead tree leaned precariously on a smaller, living one. Throwing off his sack of food. Rainsford took his knife from its sheath and began to work with all his energy.

The job was finished at last, and he threw himself down behind a fallen log a hundred feet away. He did not have to wait long. The cat was coming again to play with the mouse.

Following the trail with the sureness of a bloodhound came General Zaroff. Nothing escaped those searching black eyes, no crushed blade of grass, no bent twig, no mark, no matter how faint, in the moss. So intent was the Cossack on his stalking that he was upon the thing Rainsford had made before he saw it. His foot touched the protruding bough that was the trigger. Even as he touched it, the general sensed his danger and leaped back with the agility of an ape. But he was not quite quick enough; the dead tree, delicately adjusted to rest on the cut living one, crashed down and struck the general a glancing blow on the shoulder as it fell; but for his alertness, he must have been smashed beneath it. He staggered, but he did not fall; nor did he drop his revolver. He stood there, rubbing his injured shoulder, and Rainsford, with fear again gripping his heart, heard the general's mocking laugh ring through the jungle.

"Rainsford," called the general, "if you are within sound of my voice, as I suppose you are, let me congratulate you. Not many men know how to make a Malay man-catcher. Luckily, for me, I too have hunted in Malacca. You are proving interesting, Mr. Rainsford. I am going now to have my wound dressed; it's only a slight one. But I shall be back. I shall be back."

When the general, nursing his bruised shoulder, had gone, Rainsford took up his flight again. It was flight now, a desperate, hopeless flight, that carried him on for some hours. Dusk came, then darkness, and still he pressed on. The ground grew softer under his moccasins; the vegetation grew ranker, denser; insects bit him savagely. Then, as he stepped forward, his foot sank into the ooze. He tried to wrench it back, but the muck sucked viciously at his foot as if it were a giant leech. With a violent effort, he tore his foot loose. He knew where he was now. Death Swamp and its quicksand.

His hands were tight closed as if his nerve were something tangible that someone in the darkness was trying to tear from his grip. The softness of the earth had given him an idea. He stepped back from the quicksand a dozen feet or so and, like some huge prehistoric beaver, he began to dig.

Rainsford had dug himself in in France when a second's delay meant death. That had been a placid pastime compared to his digging now. The pit grew deeper; when it was above his shoulders, he climbed out and from some hard saplings cut stakes and sharpened them to a fine point. These stakes he planted in the bottom of the pit with the points sticking up. With flying fingers he wove a rough carpet of weeds and branches and with it he covered the mouth of the pit. Then, wet with sweat and aching with tiredness, he crouched behind the stump of a lightning-charred tree.

He knew his pursuer was coming; he heard the padding sound of feet on the soft earth, and the night breeze brought him the perfume of the general's cigarette. It seemed to Rainsford that the general was coming with unusual swiftness; he was not feeling his way along, foot by foot. Rainsford, crouching there, could not see the general, nor could he see the pit. He lived a year in a minute. Then he felt an impulse to cry aloud with joy, for he heard the sharp crackle of the breaking branches as the cover of the pit gave way; he heard the sharp scream of pain as the pointed stakes found their mark. He leaped up from his place of concealment. Then he cowered back. Three feet from the pit a man was standing, with an electric torch in his hand.

"You've done well, Rainsford," the voice of the general called. "Your Burmese tiger pit has claimed one of my best dogs. Again you score. I think, Mr. Rainsford, I'll see what you can do against my whole pack. I'm going home for a rest now. Thank you for a most amusing evening."

At daybreak Rainsford, lying near the swamp, was awakened by a sound that made him know that he had new things to learn about fear. It was a distant sound, faint and wavering, but he knew it. It was the baying of a pack of hounds.

Rainsford knew he could do one of two things. He could stay where he was and wait. That was suicide. He could flee. That was postponing the inevitable. For a moment he stood there, thinking. An idea that held a wild chance came to him, and tightening his belt, he headed away from the swamp.

The baying of the hounds drew nearer, then still nearer, nearer, ever nearer. On a ridge Rainsford climbed a tree. Down a watercourse, not a quarter of a mile away, he could see the bush moving. Straining his eyes, he saw the lean figure of General Zaroff; just ahead of him Rainsford made out another figure whose wide shoulders surged through the tall jungle weeds; it was the giant Ivan, and he seemed pulled forward by some unseen force; Rainsford knew that Ivan must be holding the pack in leash.

They would be on him any minute now. His mind worked frantically. He thought of a native trick he had learned in Uganda. He slid down the tree. He caught hold of a springy young sapling and to it he fastened his hunting knife, with the blade pointing down the trail; with a bit of wild grapevine he tied back the sapling. Then he ran for his life. The hounds raised their voices as they hit the fresh scent. Rainsford knew now how an animal at bay feels.

He had to stop to get his breath. The baying of the hounds stopped abruptly, and Rainsford's heart stopped too. They must have reached the knife.

He shinnied excitedly up a tree and looked back. His pursuers had stopped. But the hope that was in Rainsford's brain when he climbed died, for he saw in the shallow valley that General Zaroff was still on his feet. But Ivan was not. The knife, driven by the recoil of the springing tree, had not wholly failed.

Rainsford had hardly tumbled to the ground when the pack took up the cry again.

"Nerve, nerve, nerve!" he panted, as he dashed along. A blue gap showed between the trees dead ahead. Ever nearer drew the hounds. Rainsford forced himself on toward that gap. He reached it. It was the shore of the sea. Across a cove he could see the gloomy gray stone of the château. Twenty feet below him the sea rumbled and hissed. Rainsford hesitated. He heard the hounds. Then he leaped far out into the sea. . . .

When the general and his pack reached the place by the sea, the Cossack stopped. For some minutes he stood regarding the blue-green expanse of water. He shrugged his shoulders. Then he sat down, took a drink of brandy from a silver flask, lit a perfumed cigarette, and hummed a bit from *Madame Butterfly*[10].

General Zaroff had an exceedingly good dinner in his great paneled dining hall that evening. With it he had a bottle of Pol Roger and half a bottle of Chambertin. Two slight annoyances kept him from perfect enjoyment. One was the thought that it would be difficult to replace Ivan; the other was that his quarry had escaped him; of course the American hadn't played the game—so thought the general as he tasted his after-dinner liqueur. In his library he read, to soothe himself, from the works of Marcus Aurelius[11]. At ten he went up to his bedroom. He was deliciously tired, he said to himself, as he locked himself in. There was a little moonlight, so, before turning on his light, he went to the window and looked down at the courtyard. He could see the great hounds, and he called: "Better luck another time," to them. Then he switched on the light.

A man, who had been hiding in the curtains of the bed, was standing there.

"Rainsford!" screamed the general. "How did you get here?"

"Swam," said Rainsford. "I found it quicker than walking through the jungle."

The general sucked in his breath and smiled. "I congratulate you," he said. "You have won the game."

Rainsford did not smile. "I am still a beast at bay," he said, in a low, hoarse voice. "Get ready, General Zaroff."

10. *Madame Butterfly:* an opera by Giacomo Puccini.
11. **Marcus Aurelius:** Roman emperor (161–180), whose book, *Meditations,* is considered a classic of philosophy.

The general made one of his deepest bows. "I see," he said. "Splendid! One of us is to furnish a repast for the hounds. The other will sleep in this very excellent bed. On guard, Rainsford. . . ."

He had never slept in a better bed, Rainsford decided.

Meaning

1. What is the background of each of the main characters? How are these men similar? How are they different?
2. What methods does Rainsford use to outwit Zaroff?
3. What is Rainsford's attitude toward animals at the beginning of the story? What evidence can you find to indicate his attitude changes during the course of the story?
4. What is "the most dangerous game"? What alternate meanings might the word *game* have in the title?

Method

1. Authors often hint at, or *foreshadow,* what is to come later in a story. How does the discussion on the ship between Rainsford and Whitney foreshadow the events to come? How do Rainsford's swim and his walk to the château provide further foreshadowing?
2. What external conflicts are there in this story? What are the internal conflicts? Which conflict do you think is most important?
3. What incidents are designed to make the reader anxious for Rainsford's safety? In other words, how does the author create suspense?
4. After Rainsford jumps into the sea, the author begins to tell the story through Zaroff's eyes. Why do you think he does this?

Language: Context Clues to Meaning

While reading "The Most Dangerous Game," you may have encountered words that were not familiar to you. Often, it is possible to determine the meaning of a word from its context—from the words or sentences that come before and after it.

Using context clues, determine what you think each of the italicized words may mean. Consult a dictionary to find out whether you are correct.

1. ". . . the dank tropical night . . . was *palpable* as it pressed its thick warm blackness in upon the yacht."
2. ". . . the jungle weeds were crushed down and the moss was *lacerated*."
3. ". . . the table *appointments* were made of the finest—the linen, the crystal, the silver, the china."
4. "Whenever he looked up from his plate he found the general studying him, *appraising* him narrowly."
5. "He was *solicitous* about the state of Rainsford's health."

Discussion and Composition

1. Consider the following words from Zaroff: "Life is for the strong, to be lived by the strong, and, if need be, taken by the strong. The weak were put here to give the strong pleasure." How do you react to this statement? Do you think many people agree with Zaroff? Explain.

2. What other stories have you read and what films have you seen that contain evil characters like Zaroff? Were the evil characters defeated? Why do you think people enjoy stories and films in which good triumphs over evil?

3. How do you feel about Rainsford's reasons for hunting animals? Write a persuasive essay in which you argue for or against hunting for sport. First, form a clear position statement. Then freewrite for about ten minutes, listing reasons and examples that support and illustrate your point. Review your list, and decide which reasons and examples are the most appropriate and convincing. You might then devote a paragraph of your essay to each reason. Include a final paragraph that sums up your argument and re-emphasizes your position.

LANGSTON HUGHES
(1902–1967)

One of the first to portray realistically the black experience in America was Langston Hughes, who wrote poetry, short stories, songs, movies, plays, and nonfiction.

Hughes began writing poetry early. He was selected as class poet of his grammar school. A year after he graduated from high school in Cleveland, he wrote perhaps his most famous poem, "The Negro Speaks of Rivers." He taught at a school in Mexico for a year, and then he spent a year at Columbia University. He left Columbia to live in Harlem, where black artists, writers, and musicians were beginning to gather, providing the mutual encouragement and inspiration that would culminate in the Harlem Renaissance of the late 1920s.

Although Hughes was writing steadily at this time, he received little payment for his work. After several bare-subsistence jobs in New York, he shipped aboard a freighter bound for Africa. He continued to write poetry while working as a seaman and a cook; later, working as a busboy and a waiter in European nightclubs, he became familiar with blues and jazz played by the great musicians of his time.

Returning to the United States, Hughes found work as a busboy in a Washington, D.C., hotel. In 1925, when the poet Vachel Lindsay visited the hotel, Hughes left three of his poems beside Lindsay's plate. Lindsay immediately recognized Hughes's abilities; the favorable publicity resulting from this incident helped Hughes get a scholarship to Lincoln University. Before he graduated in 1929, two books of his poetry had been published to critical acclaim.

Although Hughes traveled to many countries lecturing and writing, his works traveled further. He is one of the most frequently translated twentieth-century American writers. He edited several collections of writing by black authors, especially young unknown poets in the United States and in Africa. Although he is best known for his poems, which capture the essence of gospel and jazz rhythms, he produced every form of writing with one central purpose, in his words, "to explain and illuminate the Negro condition in America."

THANK YOU, M'AM

She was a large woman with a large purse that had everything in it but hammer and nails. It had a long strap and she carried it slung across her shoulder. It was about eleven o'clock at night, and she was walking alone, when a boy ran up behind her and tried to snatch her purse. The strap broke with the single tug the boy gave it from behind. But the boy's weight, and the weight of the purse combined caused him to lose his balance so, instead of taking off full blast as he had hoped, the boy fell on his back on the sidewalk, and his legs flew up. The large woman simply turned around and kicked him right square in his blue jeaned sitter. Then she reached down, picked the boy up by his shirt front, and shook him until his teeth rattled.

After that the woman said, "Pick up my pocketbook, boy, and give it here."

She still held him. But she bent down enough to permit him to stoop and pick up her purse. Then she said, "Now ain't you ashamed of yourself?"

Firmly gripped by his shirt front, the boy said, "Yes'm."

The woman said, "What did you want to do it for?"

The boy said, "I didn't aim to."

She said, "You a lie!"

By that time two or three people passed, stopped, turned to look, and some stood watching.

"If I turn you loose, will you run?" asked the woman.

"Yes'm," said the boy.

"Then I won't turn you loose," said the woman. She did not release him.

"I'm very sorry lady, I'm sorry," whispered the boy.

"Um-hum! And your face is dirty. I got a great mind to wash your face for you. Ain't you got nobody home to tell you to wash your face?"

"No'm," said the boy.

"Then it will get washed this evening," said the large woman starting up the street, dragging the frightened boy behind her.

He looked as if he were fourteen or fifteen, frail and willow-wild, in tennis shoes and blue jeans.

The woman said, "You ought to be my son. I would teach

you right from wrong. Least I can do right now is to wash your face. Are you hungry?"

"No'm," said the being-dragged boy. "I just want you to turn me loose."

"Was I bothering *you* when I turned that corner?" asked the woman.

"No'm."

"But you put yourself in contact with *me*," said the woman. "If you think that that contact is not going to last awhile, you got another thought coming. When I get through with you, sir, you are going to remember Mrs. Luella Bates Washington Jones."

Sweat popped out on the boy's face and he began to struggle. Mrs. Jones stopped, jerked him around in front of her, put a half-nelson[1] about his neck, and continued to drag him up the street. When she got to her door, she dragged the boy inside, down a hall, and into a large kitchenette-furnished room at the rear of the house. She switched on the light and left the door open. The boy could hear other roomers laughing and talking in the large house. Some of their doors were open, too, so he knew he and the woman were not alone. The woman still had him by the neck in the middle of her room.

She said, "What is your name?"

"Roger," answered the boy.

"Then, Roger, you go to that sink and wash your face," said the woman, whereupon she turned him loose—at last. Roger looked at the door—looked at the woman—looked at the door—*and went to the sink.*

"Let the water run until it gets warm," she said. "Here's a clean towel."

"You gonna take me to jail?" asked the boy, bending over the sink.

"Not with that face, I would not take you nowhere," said the woman. "Here I am trying to get home to cook me a bite to eat and you snatch my pocketbook! Maybe you ain't been to your supper either, late as it be. Have you?"

"There's nobody home at my house," said the boy.

"Then we'll eat," said the woman. "I believe you're hungry—or been hungry—to try to snatch my pocketbook."

---

1. **half-nelson:** wrestling hold; from behind, one arm is placed under the opponent's corresponding arm, with the hand placed against the back of the neck.

"I wanted a pair of blue suede shoes," said the boy.

"Well, you didn't have to snatch *my* pocketbook to get some suede shoes," said Mrs. Luella Bates Washington Jones. "You could of asked me."

"M'am?"

The water dripping from his face, the boy looked at her. There was a long pause. A very long pause. After he had dried his face and not knowing what else to do dried it again, the boy turned around, wondering what next. The door was open. He could make a dash for it down the hall. He could run, run, run, run, *run!*

The woman was sitting on the day-bed. After awhile she said, "I were young once and I wanted things I could not get."

There was another long pause. The boy's mouth opened. Then he frowned, but not knowing he frowned.

The woman said, "Um-hum! You thought I was going to say *but,* didn't you? You thought I was going to say, *but I didn't snatch people's pocketbooks.* Well, I wasn't going to say that." Pause. Silence. "I have done things, too, which I would not tell you, son— neither tell God, if he didn't already know. So you set down while I fix us something to eat. You might run that comb through your hair so you will look presentable."

In another corner of the room behind a screen was a gas plate and an icebox. Mrs. Jones got up and went behind the screen. The woman did not watch the boy to see if he was going to run now, nor did she watch her purse which she left behind her on the day-bed. But the boy took care to sit on the far side of the room where he thought she could easily see him out of the corner of her eye, if she wanted to. He did not trust the woman *not* to trust him. And he did not want to be mistrusted now.

"Do you need somebody to go the store," asked the boy, "maybe to get some milk or something?"

"Don't believe I do," said the woman, "unless you just want sweet milk yourself. I was going to make cocoa out of this canned milk I got here."

"That will be fine," said the boy.

She heated some lima beans and ham she had in the icebox, made the cocoa, and set the table. The woman did not ask the boy anything about where he lived, or his folks, or anything else that would embarrass him. Instead, as they ate, she told him about her job in a hotel beauty-shop that stayed open late, what the work was like, and how all kinds of women came in and out, blondes, red-heads, and Spanish. Then she cut him a half of her ten-cent cake.

"Eat some more, son," she said.

When they were finished eating she got up and said, "Now, here, take this ten dollars and buy yourself some blue suede shoes. And next time, do not make the mistake of latching onto *my* pocketbook *nor nobody else's*—because shoes come by devilish like that will burn your feet. I got to get my rest now. But I wish you would behave yourself, son, from here on in."

She led him down the hall to the front door and opened it. "Goodnight! Behave yourself, boy!" she said, looking out into the street.

The boy wanted to say something else other than, "Thank you, m'am," to Mrs. Luella Bates Washington Jones, but he couldn't do so as he turned at the barren stoop and looked back at the large woman in the door. He barely managed to say "Thank you," before she shut the door. And he never saw her again.

Meaning

1. Do you think that Roger is used to stealing? Why or why not?
2. How does Roger's attitude toward Mrs. Jones change? How does he feel about her at the end of the story?
3. What word does the author use several times to describe Mrs. Jones' physical appearance? Describe Mrs. Jones' character and personality.

Method

1. This story begins with a physical conflict in the first paragraph. What more important conflicts are there later on in the story?
2. Instead of telling what Roger is thinking, Langston Hughes writes, "There was a long pause." Why do you think he chose not to reveal the boy's thoughts?
3. "Thank You, Ma'am" is told primarily in dialogue. What effect does this use of dialogue have on the reader?
4. What is the writer's attitude toward his subject and his characters? How do you know?

Language: Dialogue

Well-written dialogue reproduces the way the characters in a story would actually talk. Good dialogue makes a story lively and interesting. It reveals character as well as advancing the plot. Reread the following dialogue between Roger and Mrs. Jones. Notice how the language differs from standard English. Try rewriting the conversation in standard English. What advantage does the original language have over standard English?

1. "The woman said, 'What did you want to do it for?' The boy said, 'I didn't aim to.' She said, 'You a lie!'"

2. "'You gonna take me to jail?' asked the boy. . . . 'Not with that face, I would not take you nowhere,' said the woman. 'Here I am trying to get home to cook me a bite to eat and you snatch my pocketbook! Maybe you ain't been to your supper either, late as it be. Have you?'"

Composition

1. Write a dialogue between two people. Show some aspect of the personality and character of at least one of the people in the dialogue through his or her use of language. Before you begin writing, form a clear idea of who your characters are, what their relationship is to one another, and what their dialogue is about. Here are some ideas:

    A storeclerk and a teenager
    A young person and a grandparent
    A student and a teacher
    A highway-patrol officer and a driver

2. Imagine that you are Roger, about ten years later, at twenty-five. Write a letter to Mrs. Jones telling her where you are and what you are doing. Before you begin, think about what might have happened to Roger in those ten years and what he might want to tell Mrs. Jones. Next, decide what tone Roger's letter will take. For example, will he be serious, respectful, happy, grateful? Choose your words carefully to create the desired tone and effect.

SAKI (H. H. MUNRO)
(1870-1916)

The British humorist and satirist, Hector Hugh Munro, took the pen name Saki early in his writing career. Saki, the "bringer of drink," was a character in *The Rubáiyát*,[1] a book of Persian poetry that Munro greatly admired.

Munro was born in Burma, where his English father was a police officer. After the death of his mother when he was two, he was brought up in England by two tyrannical aunts. He later avenged himself on their strictness by portraying them in his writing.

At the age of twenty-five, Munro began his writing career as a political satirist for a newspaper. He then worked and traveled for six years as a foreign correspondent. In 1908, Munro settled near London and began to earn his living as a professional writer of often whimsical, sometimes bitterly satirical short stories. At the outbreak of World War I, he enlisted in the British army. He was killed in action in 1916.

Like O. Henry, with whom he is often compared, Munro is considered a master of the well-contrived plot and the surprise ending.

THE STORY-TELLER

It was a hot afternoon, and the railway carriage was correspondingly sultry, and the next stop was at Templecombe, nearly an hour ahead. The occupants of the carriage were a small girl, and a smaller girl, and a small boy. An aunt belonging to the children

---

[1] **The Rubáiyát** (roo'bī·yät) **of Omar Khayyám** (kī·äm'): a book of verses written in the eleventh century by Omar Khayyám, a Persian poet and astronomer. It contains the poet's meditations on life and his counsel to eat, drink, and be merry while life lasts. A translation by Edward FitzGerald (1809-1883) appeared in England in 1859. *Rubáiyát* is the Arabic word for quatrains, or four-lined stanzas.

occupied one corner seat, and the further corner seat on the opposite side was occupied by a bachelor who was a stranger to their party, but the small girls and the small boy emphatically occupied the compartment. Both the aunt and the children were conversational in a limited, persistent way, reminding one of the attentions of a housefly that refused to be discouraged. Most of the aunt's remarks seemed to begin with "Don't," and nearly all of the children's remarks began with "Why?" The bachelor said nothing out loud.

"Don't, Cyril, don't," exclaimed the aunt, as the small boy began smacking the cushions of the seat, producing a cloud of dust at each blow.

"Come and look out of the window," she added.

The child moved reluctantly to the window. "Why are those sheep being driven out of that field?" he asked.

"I expect they are being driven to another field where there is more grass," said the aunt weakly.

"But there is lots of grass in that field," protested the boy; "there's nothing else but grass there. Aunt, there's lots of grass in that field."

"Perhaps the grass in the other field is better," suggested the aunt fatuously.[2]

"Why is it better?" came the swift, inevitable question.

"Oh, look at those cows!" exclaimed the aunt. Nearly every field along the line had contained cows or bullocks, but she spoke as though she were drawing attention to a rarity.

"Why is the grass in the other field better?" persisted Cyril.

The frown on the bachelor's face was deepening to a scowl. He was a hard, unsympathetic man, the aunt decided in her mind. She was utterly unable to come to any satisfactory decision about the grass in the other field.

The smaller girl created a diversion by beginning to recite "On the Road to Mandalay."[3] She only knew the first line, but she put her limited knowledge to the fullest possible use. She repeated the line over and over again in a dreamy but resolute and very audible voice; it seemed to the bachelor as though someone

2. fatuously: foolishly, stupidly.
3. "On the Road to Mandalay": a poem by the English author and poet, Rudyard Kipling (1865–1936).

had had a bet with her that she could not repeat the line aloud two thousand times without stopping. Whoever it was who had made the wager was likely to lose his bet.

"Come over here and listen to a story," said the aunt, when the bachelor had looked twice at her and once at the communication cord.[4]

The children moved listlessly toward the aunt's end of the carriage. Evidently her reputation as a storyteller did not rank high in their estimation.

In a low, confidential voice, interrupted at frequent intervals by loud, petulant questions from her listeners, she began an unenterprising and deplorably uninteresting story about a little girl who was good, and made friends with every one on account of her goodness, and was finally saved from a mad bull by a number of rescuers who admired her moral character.

"Wouldn't they have saved her if she hadn't been good?" demanded the bigger of the small girls. It was exactly the question that the bachelor had wanted to ask.

"Well, yes," admitted the aunt lamely, "but I don't think they would have run quite so fast to her help if they had not liked her so much."

"It's the stupidest story I've ever heard," said the bigger of the small girls, with immense conviction.

"I didn't listen after the first bit, it was so stupid," said Cyril.

The smaller girl made no actual comment on the story, but she had long ago recommenced a murmured repetition of her favorite line.

"You don't seem to be a success as a storyteller," said the bachelor suddenly from his corner.

The aunt bristled in instant defense at this unexpected attack.

"It's a very difficult thing to tell stories that children can both understand and appreciate," she said stiffly.

"I don't agree with you," said the bachelor.

"Perhaps *you* would like to tell them a story," was the aunt's retort.

"Tell us a story," demanded the bigger of the small girls.

"Once upon a time," began the bachelor, "there was a little girl called Bertha, who was extraordinarily good."

The children's momentarily aroused interest began at once to

4. **communication cord:** emergency cord.

flicker; all stories seemed dreadfully alike, no matter who told them.

"She did all that she was told, she was always truthful, she kept her clothes clean, ate milk puddings as though they were jam tarts, learned her lessons perfectly, and was polite in her manners."

"Was she pretty?" asked the bigger of the small girls.

"Not as pretty as any of you," said the bachelor, "but she was horribly good."

There was a wave of reaction in favor of the story; the word *horrible* in connection with goodness was a novelty that commended itself. It seemed to introduce a ring of truth that was absent from the aunt's tales of infant life.

"She was so good," continued the bachelor, "that she won several medals for goodness, which she always wore, pinned on to her dress. There was a medal for obedience, another medal for punctuality, and a third for good behavior. They were large metal medals and they clinked against one another as she walked. No other child in the town where she lived had as many as three medals, so everybody knew that she must be an extra good child."

"Horribly good," quoted Cyril.

"Everybody talked about her goodness, and the Prince of the country got to hear about it, and he said that as she was so very good she might be allowed once a week to walk in his park, which was just outside the town. It was a beautiful park, and no children were ever allowed in it, so it was a great honor for Bertha to be allowed to go there."

"Were there any sheep in the park?" demanded Cyril.

"No," said the bachelor, "there were no sheep."

"Why weren't there any sheep?" came the inevitable question arising out of that answer.

The aunt permitted herself a smile, which might almost have been described as a grin.

"There were no sheep in the park," said the bachelor, "because the Prince's mother had once had a dream that her son would either be killed by a sheep or else by a clock falling on him. For that reason the Prince never kept a sheep in his park or a clock in his palace."

The aunt suppressed a gasp of admiration.

"Was the Prince killed by a sheep or by a clock?" asked Cyril.

"He is still alive so we can't tell whether the dream will come true," said the bachelor unconcernedly; "anyway, there were no sheep in the park, but there were lots of little pigs running all over the place."

"What color were they?"

"Black with white faces, white with black spots, black all over, gray with white patches, and some were white all over."

The storyteller paused to let a full idea of the park's treasures sink into the children's imaginations; then he resumed:

"Bertha was rather sorry to find that there were no flowers in the park. She had promised her aunts, with tears in her eyes, that she would not pick any of the kind Prince's flowers, and she had meant to keep her promise, so of course it made her feel silly to find that there were no flowers to pick."

"Why weren't there any flowers?"

"Because the pigs had eaten them all," said the bachelor promptly. "The gardeners had told the Prince that you couldn't have pigs and flowers, so he decided to have pigs and no flowers."

There was a murmur of approval at the excellence of the Prince's decision; so many people would have decided the other way.

"There were lots of other delightful things in the park. There were ponds with gold and blue and green fish in them, and trees with beautiful parrots that said clever things at a moment's notice, and humming birds that hummed all the popular tunes of the day. Bertha walked up and down and enjoyed herself immensely, and thought to herself: 'If I were not so extraordinarily good I should not have been allowed to come into this beautiful park and enjoy all that there is to be seen in it,' and her three medals clinked against one another as she walked and helped to remind her how very good she really was. Just then an enormous wolf came prowling into the park to see if it could catch a fat little pig for its supper."

"What color was it?" asked the children, amid an immediate quickening of interest.

"Mud-color all over, with a black tongue and pale gray eyes that gleamed with unspeakable ferocity. The first thing that it saw in the park was Bertha; her pinafore was so spotlessly white and clean that it could be seen from a great distance. Bertha saw the wolf and saw that it was stealing toward her, and she began to wish that she had never been allowed to come into the park. She ran as hard as she could, and the wolf came after her with huge leaps and bounds. She managed to reach a shrubbery of myrtle bushes and she hid herself in one of the thickest of the bushes. The wolf came sniffing among the branches, its black tongue lolling out of its mouth and its pale gray eyes glaring with rage. Bertha was terribly frightened, and thought to herself: 'If I had not been so extraordinarily good, I should have been safe in the town at this moment.' However, the scent of the myrtle was so strong that the wolf could not sniff out where Bertha was hiding, and the bushes were so thick that he might have hunted about in them for a long time without catching sight of her, so he thought he might as well go off and catch a little pig instead. Bertha was trembling very much at having the wolf prowling and sniffing so near her, and as she trembled the medal for obedience clinked against the medals for good conduct and punctuality. The wolf was just moving away when he heard the sound of the medals clinking and stopped to listen; they clinked again in a bush quite near him. He dashed into the bush, his pale gray eyes gleaming with ferocity and triumph, and dragged Bertha out and devoured her to the last morsel. All that was left of her were her shoes, bits of clothing, and the three medals for goodness."

"Were any of the little pigs killed?"

"No, they all escaped."

"The story began badly," said the smaller of the small girls, "but it had a beautiful ending."

"It is the most beautiful story that I ever heard," said the bigger of the small girls, with immense decision.

"It is the *only* beautiful story I have ever heard," said Cyril.

A dissentient[5] opinion came from the aunt.

"A most improper story to tell to young children! You have undermined the effect of years of careful teaching."

"At any rate," said the bachelor, collecting his belongings preparatory to leaving the carriage, "I kept them quiet for ten minutes, which was more than you were able to do."

"Unhappy woman!" he observed to himself as he walked down the platform of Templecombe station; "for the next six months or so those children will assail her in public with demands for an improper story!"

5. **dissentient** (dĭ·sĕn'shənt): dissenting; expressing disagreement.

Meaning

1. What makes the theme of the bachelor's story unconventional?
2. Which do you think is more annoying to the bachelor—the children's behavior or the aunt's? Give reasons for your answer.
3. What is ironic about the way the "horribly good girl" met her end?
4. Compare and contrast the aunt's story and the bachelor's story. How are they alike? How do they differ?

Method

1. How does the bachelor's story appeal to the children's senses of sight and sound?
2. Why is the railway car setting essential to the plot of this story? What is the function of setting in the bachelor's story?
3. Sometimes to create a humorous or dramatic effect a writer will deliberately exaggerate or overstate a fact. An extravagantly exaggerated statement is called *hyberbole* (hī·pûr′bə·lē). Saki uses hyberbole in "The Story-Teller" when he writes, "She was so good that she won several medals for goodness."

   Saki also achieves humorous effects by the use of *irony*, which is typical of his style. In *verbal irony* or irony of statement, the author or speaker says the opposite of what he really means, or the opposite of what the listener or reader expects. In *irony of situation*, what happens is the opposite of what is expected.

   Another way Saki creates humor is by using words that are *ambiguous*, that is, words that have multiple meanings.

   Explain which of the above methods each of the following quotations from "The Story-Teller" involves:

   a. "The gardeners had told the Prince that you couldn't have pigs and flowers, so he decided to have pigs and no flowers."
   b. "She had promised her aunts, with tears in her eyes, that she would not pick any of the kind Prince's flowers, . . . so of course it made her feel silly to find that there were no flowers to pick."
   c. ". . . and humming birds that hummed all the popular tunes of the day."

d. "The wolf was just moving away when he heard the sound of the medals clinking and stopped to listen; they clinked again in a bush quite near him."

e. ". . . for the next six months or so those children will assail her in public with demands for an improper story!"

Language: Adverbs

In "The Story-Teller," carefully chosen adverbs often serve to suggest the actions, appearances, and personalities of the characters. For example, the bachelor says several times that Bertha was "horribly" good. Through the use of the adverb "horribly," Saki exaggerates Bertha's goodness and suggests that it is an unpleasant trait.

For each of the following examples, explain how the italicized adverb helps to capture a character or scene. What does it tell you about the character or characters? How does it describe the action taking place?

1. ". . . the small girls and the small boy *emphatically* occupied the compartment."

2. " 'Perhaps the grass in the other field is better,' suggested the aunt *fatuously*."

3. "The children moved *listlessly* toward the aunt's end of the carriage."

Discussion and Composition

1. Saki, through the storyteller, is satirizing the stories adults usually tell to children. What aspects of such stories does he ridicule? What techniques does he use to create this satirical effect?

2. Write a satire attacking some aspect of modern society that seems foolish to you. Use exaggeration and ironic praise to poke fun at your subject. For example, you might satirize television commercials by writing an exaggerated script for a commercial advertising a "revolutionary" new product. Choose a subject that you are familiar with and that you have strong opinions about.

3. A *moral* is a practical lesson, usually stated in a sentence or two, that sums up the theme of a fable. Write a moral for the bachelor's tale that you think captures the storyteller's intended message.

GUY DE MAUPASSANT*
(1850–1893)

France's most famous short story writer was Guy de Maupassant. He lived the greater part of his short life in Paris, and was one of the first fiction writers to be financially successful; it is estimated that for several years before his death, his earnings amounted to more than $70,000 a year.

De Maupassant's parents were unhappily married and separated when he was eleven. At seventeen, he met Gustave Flaubert, the great French novelist, who became his friend, foster father, and writing teacher. De Maupassant began law studies in Paris, but enlisted in the French army when war broke out. After the war, he became a government clerk and began writing under Flaubert's guidance. In 1880, a month before Flaubert's death, de Maupassant became famous with the publication of his story *"Boule de Suif"* ("Ball of Fat").

Despite a serious nervous disorder, which ended in insanity and death in his early forties, de Maupassant wrote more than three hundred short stories and six novels.

A shrewd observer of people, de Maupassant fashioned his characters with sharp, clean lines—like photographs taken with a well-focused camera. He used a minimum of details and wrote with unusual objectivity. His style has served as a model for many writers.

THE NECKLACE

She was one of those pretty and charming girls, born, as if by an accident of fate, into a family of clerks. With no dowry,[1] no prospects, no way of any kind of being met, understood, loved, and married by a man both prosperous and famous, she was finally married to a minor clerk in the Ministry of Education.

---

* **Guy de Maupassant** (gē də mō·pȧ·sän').
1. **dowry** (dour′ē): money or property that a woman brings to her husband at marriage.

She dressed plainly because she could not afford fine clothes, but was as unhappy as a woman who has come down in the world; for women have no family rank or social class. With them, beauty, grace, and charm take the place of birth and breeding. Their natural poise, their instinctive good taste, and their mental cleverness are the sole guiding principles which make daughters of the common people the equals of ladies in high society.

She grieved incessantly, feeling that she had been born for all the little niceties and luxuries of living. She grieved over the shabbiness of her apartment, the dinginess of the walls, the worn-out appearance of the chairs, the ugliness of the draperies. All these things, which another woman of her class would not even have noticed, gnawed at her and made her furious. The sight of the little Breton[2] girl who did her humble housework roused in her disconsolate[3] regrets and wild daydreams. She would dream of silent chambers, draped with Oriental tapestries and lighted by tall bronze floor lamps, and of two handsome butlers in knee breeches, who, drowsy from the heavy warmth cast by the central stove,[4] dozed in large overstuffed armchairs.

She would dream of great reception halls hung with old silks, of fine furniture filled with priceless curios, and of small, stylish, scented sitting rooms just right for the four o'clock chat with intimate friends, with distinguished and sought-after men whose attention every woman envies and longs to attract.

When dining at the round table, covered for the third day with the same cloth, opposite her husband who would raise the cover of the soup tureen, declaring delightedly, "Ah! a good stew! There's nothing I like better. . . ." she would dream of fashionable dinner parties, of gleaming silverware, of tapestries making the walls alive with characters out of history and strange birds in a fairyland forest; she would dream of delicious dishes served on wonderful china, of gallant compliments whispered and listened to with a sphinxlike smile as one eats the rosy flesh of a trout or nibbles at the wings of a grouse.

She had no evening clothes, no jewels, nothing. But those were the things she wanted; she felt that was the kind of life for

---

2. **Breton** (brĕt′n): a native of Brittany, a province in northwestern France; servants were frequently recruited from outlying districts for service in Paris.

3. **disconsolate** (dĭs·kŏn′sə·lĭt): inconsolable; hopelessly depressing.

4. **central stove:** a large stove for heating placed in the center of a room, used in France at the time this story takes place.

her. She so much longed to please, be envied, be fascinating and sought after.

She had a well-to-do friend, a classmate of convent school days, whom she would no longer go to see, simply because she would feel so distressed on returning home. And she would weep for days on end from vexation, regret, despair, and anguish.

Then one evening, her husband came home proudly holding out a large envelope.

"Look," he said, "I've got something for you."

She excitedly tore open the envelope and pulled out a printed card bearing these words:

"The Minister of Education and Mme Georges Ramponneau[5] beg M. and Mme Loisel[6] to do them the honor of attending an evening reception at the ministerial mansion on Friday, January 18."

Instead of being delighted, as her husband had hoped, she scornfully tossed the invitation on the table, murmuring, "What good is that to me?"

"But, my dear, I thought you'd be thrilled to death. You never get a chance to go out, and this is a real affair, a wonderful one! I had an awful time getting a card. Everybody wants one; it's much sought after, and not many clerks have a chance at one. You'll see all the most important people there."

She gave him an irritated glance, and burst out impatiently, "What do you think I have to go in?"

He hadn't given that a thought. He stammered, "Why, the dress you wear when we go to the theater. That looks quite nice, I think."

He stopped talking, dazed and distracted to see his wife burst out weeping. Two large tears slowly rolled from the corners of her eyes to the corners of her mouth. He gasped, "Why, what's the matter? What's the trouble?"

By sheer will power she overcame her outburst and answered in a calm voice while wiping the tears from her wet cheeks:

"Oh, nothing. Only I don't have an evening dress and therefore I can't go to that affair. Give the card to some friend at the office whose wife can dress better than I can."

5. **Mme Georges Ramponneau** (mà·dàm′ zhôrzh ràm′pə·nō).
6. **M. . . . Loisel** (mə·syûr′. . . . lwà·zĕl′).

He was stunned. He resumed, "Let's see, Mathilde.[7] How much would a suitable outfit cost—one you could wear for other affairs too—something very simple?"

She thought it over for several seconds, going over her allowance and thinking also of the amount she could ask for without bringing an immediate refusal and an exclamation of dismay from the thrifty clerk.

Finally, she answered hesitatingly, "I'm not sure exactly, but I think with four hundred francs[8] I could manage it."

He turned a bit pale, for he had set aside just that amount to buy a rifle so that, the following summer, he could join some friends who were getting up a group to shoot larks on the plain near Nanterre.[9]

However, he said, "All right. I'll give you four hundred francs. But try to get a nice dress."

As the day of the party approached, Mme Loisel seemed sad, moody, and ill at ease. Her outfit was ready, however. Her husband said to her one evening, "What's the matter? You've been all out of sorts for three days."

And she answered, "It's embarrassing not to have a jewel or a gem—nothing to wear on my dress. I'll look like a pauper: I'd almost rather not go to that party."

He answered, "Why not wear some flowers? They're very fashionable this season. For ten francs you can get two or three gorgeous roses."

She wasn't at all convinced. "No . . . There's nothing more humiliating than to look poor among a lot of rich women."

But her husband exclaimed, "My, but you're silly! Go see you friend Mme Forestier[10] and ask her to lend you some jewelry. You and she know each other well enough for you to do that."

She gave a cry of joy, "Why, that's so! I hadn't thought of it."

The next day she paid her friend a visit and told her of her predicament.

Mme Forestier went toward a large closet with mirrored

7. **Mathilde** (mà·tēld′).
8. **four hundred francs:** at that time, about eighty dollars.
9. **Nanterre** (nän·târ′): a French town near Paris.
10. **Forestier** (fô·rə·styā′).

doors, took out a large jewel box, brought it over, opened it, and said to Mme Loisel: "Pick something out, my dear."

At first her eyes noted some bracelets, then a pearl necklace, then a Venetian cross, gold and gems, of marvelous workmanship. She tried on these adornments in front of the mirror, but hesitated, unable to decide which to part with and put back. She kept on asking, "Haven't you something else?"

"Oh, yes, keep on looking. I don't know just what you'd like."

All at once she found, in a black satin box, a superb diamond necklace: and her pulse beat faster with longing. Her hands trembled as she took it up. Clasping it around her throat, outside her high-necked dress, she stood in ecstasy looking at her reflection.

Then she asked, hesitatingly, pleading, "Could I borrow that, just that and nothing else?"

"Why, of course."

She threw her arms around her friend, kissed her warmly, and fled with her treasure.

The day of the party arrived. Mme Loisel was a sensation. She was the prettiest one there, fashionable, gracious, smiling, and wild with joy. All the men turned to look at her, asked who she was, begged to be introduced. All the cabinet officials wanted to waltz with her. The minister took notice of her.

She danced madly, wildly, drunk with pleasure, giving no thought to anything in the triumph of her beauty, the pride of her success, in a kind of happy cloud composed of all the adulation,[11] of all the admiring glances, of all the awakened longings, of a sense of complete victory that is so sweet to a woman's heart.

She left around four o'clock in the morning. Her husband, since midnight, had been dozing in a small empty sitting room with three other gentlemen whose wives were having too good a time.

He threw over her shoulders the wraps he had brought for going home, modest garments of everyday life whose shabbiness clashed with the stylishness of her evening clothes. She felt this and longed to escape, unseen by the other women who were draped in expensive furs.

Loisel held her back.

"Hold on! You'll catch cold outside. I'll call a cab."

11. **adulation** (ăj'oo·lā'shən): excessive flattery or admiration.

But she wouldn't listen to him and went rapidly down the stairs. When they were on the street, they didn't find a carriage; and they set out to hunt for one, hailing drivers whom they saw going by at a distance.

They walked toward the Seine,[12] disconsolate and shivering. Finally on the docks they found one of those carriages that one sees in Paris only after nightfall, as if they were ashamed to show their drabness during daylight hours.

It dropped them at their door in the Rue des Martyrs,[13] and they climbed wearily up to their apartment. For her, it was all over. For him, there was the thought that he would have to be at the ministry at ten o'clock.

Before the mirror, she let the wraps fall from her shoulders to see herself once again in all her glory. Suddenly she gave a cry. The necklace was gone.

Her husband, already half-undressed, said, "What's the trouble?"

She turned toward him despairingly, "I . . . I . . . I don't have Mme Forestier's necklace."

"What! You can't mean it! It's impossible!"

They hunted everywhere, through the folds of the dress, through the folds of the coat, in the pockets. They found nothing.

He asked, "Are you sure you had it when leaving the dance?"

"Yes, I felt it when I was in the hall of the ministry."

"But, if you had lost it on the street we'd have heard it drop. It must be in the cab."

"Yes. Quite likely. Did you get its number?"

"No. Didn't you notice it either?"

"No."

They looked at each other aghast. Finally Loisel got dressed again.

"I'll retrace our steps on foot," he said, "to see if I can find it."

And he went out. She remained in her evening clothes, without the strength to go to bed, slumped in a chair in the unheated room, her mind a blank.

---

12. **Seine** (sān): a river which runs through Paris.
13. **Rue des Martyrs:** Street of the Martyrs in Montmartre, a working class section near Place Pigalle, named for St. Dennis and companions.

Her husband came in about seven o'clock. He had had no luck.

He went to the police station, to the newspapers to post a reward, to the cab companies, everywhere the slightest hope drove him.

That evening Loisel returned, pale, his face lined; still he had learned nothing.

"We'll have to write your friend," he said, "to tell her you have broken the catch and are having it repaired. That will give us a little time to turn around."

She wrote to his dictation.

At the end of a week, they had given up all hope.

And Loisel, looking five years older, declared, "We must take steps to replace that piece of jewelry."

The next day they took the case to the jeweler whose name they found inside. He consulted his records. "I didn't sell that necklace, madame," he said. "I only supplied the case."

Then they went from one jeweler to another hunting for a similar necklace, going over their recollections, both sick with despair and anxiety.

They found, in a shop in Palais Royal,[14] a string of diamonds which seemed exactly like the one they were seeking. It was priced at forty thousand francs. They could get it for thirty-six.[15]

They asked the jeweler to hold it for them for three days. And they reached an agreement that he would take it back for thirty-four thousand if the lost one was found before the end of February.

Loisel had eighteen thousand francs he had inherited from his father. He would borrow the rest.

He went about raising the money, asking a thousand francs from one, four hundred from another, a hundred here, sixty there. He signed notes, made ruinous deals, did business with loan sharks, ran the whole gamut[16] of moneylenders. He compromised the rest of his life, risked his signature without knowing if he'd be able to honor it, and then, terrified by the outlook for the future, by the blackness of despair about to close around him, by the

---

14. **Palais Royal** (pà·lā′ rwà·yàl′): or Royal Palace. A very fashionable set of buildings and gardens in Paris well known for its exclusive shops.
15. **thirty-six [thousand francs]:** in 1884, the year of "The Necklace," about seven thousand two hundred dollars.
16. **gamut** (găm′ət): the whole range of something.

prospect of all the privations[17] of the body and tortures of the spirit, he went to claim the new necklace with the thirty-six thousand francs which he placed on the counter of the shopkeeper.

When Mme Loisel took the necklace back, Mme Forestier said to her frostily, "You should have brought it back sooner; I might have needed it."

She didn't open the case, an action her friend was afraid of. If she had noticed the substitution, what would she have thought? What would she have said? Would she have thought her a thief?

Mme Loisel experienced the horrible life the needy live. She played her part, however, with sudden heroism. That frightful debt had to be paid. She would pay it. She dismissed her maid; they rented a garret under the eaves.

She learned to do the heavy housework, to perform the hateful duties of cooking. She washed dishes, wearing down her shell-pink nails scouring the grease from pots and pans; she scrubbed dirty linen, shirts, and cleaning rags, which she hung on a line to dry; she took the garbage down to the street each morning and brought up water, stopping on each landing to get her breath. And, clad like a peasant woman, basket on arm, guarding sou[18] by sou her scanty allowance, she bargained with the fruit dealers, the grocer, the butcher, and was insulted by them.

Each month notes had to be paid, and others renewed to give more time.

Her husband labored evenings to balance a tradesman's accounts, and at night, often, he copied documents at five sous a page.

And this went on for ten years.

Finally, all was paid back, everything including the exorbitant[19] rates of the loan sharks and accumulated compound interest.

Mme Loisel appeared an old woman, now. She became heavy, rough, harsh, like one of the poor. Her hair untended, her skirts askew, her hands red, her voice shrill, she even slopped water on her floors and scrubbed them herself. But, sometimes, while her husband was at work, she would sit near the window and think of that long-ago evening when, at the dance, she had been so beautiful and admired.

17. **privations** (prī·vā′shəns): the lack of what is essential for existence.
18. **sou** (sōō): a coin at that time worth about a penny.
19. **exorbitant** (ĭg·zôr′bə·tənt): excessive.

What would have happened if she had not lost that necklace? Who knows? Who can say? How strange and unpredictable life is! How little there is between happiness and misery!

Then one Sunday when she had gone for a walk on the Champs Élysées[20] to relax a bit from the week's labors, she suddenly noticed a woman strolling with a child. It was Mme Forestier, still young-looking, still beautiful, still charming.

Mme Loisel felt a rush of emotion. Should she speak to her? Of course. And now that everything was paid off, she would tell her the whole story. Why not?

She went toward her. "Hello, Jeanne."

The other, not recognizing her, showed astonishment at being spoken to so familiarly by this common person. She stammered, "But . . . madame . . . I don't recognize . . . You must be mistaken."

"No, I'm Mathilde Loisel."

Her friend gave a cry, "Oh, my poor Mathilde, how you've changed!"

"Yes, I've had a hard time since last seeing you. And plenty of misfortunes—and all on account of you!"

"Of me . . . How do you mean?"

"Do you remember that diamond necklace you lent me to wear to the dance at the ministry?"

"Yes, but what about it?"

"Well, I lost it."

"You lost it! But you returned it."

"I brought you another just like it. And we've been paying for it for ten years now. You can imagine that wasn't easy for us who had nothing. Well, it's over now, and I am glad of it."

Mme Forestier stopped short. "You mean to say you bought a diamond necklace to replace mine?"

"Yes. You never noticed, then? They were quite alike."

And she smiled with proud and simple joy.

Mme Forestier, quite overcome, clasped her by the hands, "Oh, my poor Mathilde. But mine was only paste.[21] Why, at most it was worth only five hundred francs!"[22]

---

20. **Champs Élysées** (shän zā·lē·zā'): a fashionable avenue in Paris.
21. **paste:** a brilliant glass used in making imitation diamonds.
22. **five hundred francs:** about one hundred dollars then.

Meaning

1. What kind of people are Mathilde and her husband at the beginning of the story? How do they change after the necklace is lost? Are their actions consistent with their characteristics and values? Why or why not?
2. Why did it never occur to the Loisels that the necklace might be paste?
3. The things we value are the things by which we set our goals and make our decisions. What comment on values does this story make?
4. What is the theme of the story?

Method

1. A *symbol* is something that has meaning in itself but also suggests a further meaning. How is the necklace used as a symbol in this story?
2. Do you think that "The Necklace" has a *trick* ending—a conclusion that comes as a surprise to the reader? Or has the reader been prepared for the ironic ending? Give reasons for your answer.
3. De Maupassant and O. Henry have often been compared as storytellers. They both usually take the author omniscient (third-person narrator) point of view. Compared with O. Henry in "The Ransom of Red Chief," does de Maupassant write more or less *objectively?* (An author is said to write objectively when he or she does not give opinions about the characters.) Give some examples from both of these authors' stories in this book to support your answer.
4. Why doesn't de Maupassant end the story by telling how Mathilde felt when she learned the necklace was false? How would this have changed the story?

Language: Forming Adjectives and Adverbs

A suffix added to a word can change the word to an adjective or adverb. The sample adjectives and adverbs on the following page are taken from "The Necklace":

Adjectives

Suffix	Meaning	Adjective
1. *–able, –ible*	able, fit, likely	suitable
2. *–ful*	full of, marked by	wonderful
3. *–like*	like, similar	sphinxlike
4. *–ous*	marked by, given to	prosperous
5. *–y*	showing, suggesting, apt to	drowsy, moody

Adverbs

Suffix	Meaning	Adverb
–ly	like, of, nature of, in the manner of	finally, plainly

Add a suffix to each of the following words to form an adjective or an adverb. Write a sentence for each new word you form.

1. marvel		6. soul
2. simple		7. courage
3. play		8. war
4. joy		9. hope
5. peace		10. prosper

Discussion and Composition

1. The author writes, "What would have happened if she had not lost that necklace? Who knows? Who can say? How strange and unpredictable life is! How little there is between happiness and misery!"

Discuss what you think Mathilde's chances for happiness would have been had she *not* lost the necklace. Be sure to give reasons.

2. With a group of your classmates, write and perform an "after" scene to the story in which Mathilde tells her husband that the necklace was paste. First brainstorm some ideas for the scene. Discuss how Mathilde will break the news to her husband and how he will react. Then work together to create dialogue for the two characters. Finally, read the final version of your scene to the class, with two members of your group taking the parts of Mathilde and her husband.

FENG JICAI

(born 1942)

Born into a wealthy family in Tianjin, China, Feng Jicai began to write and paint at an early age. He intended to study art after graduating from high school, but his exceptional height attracted the attention of the coach of a professional basketball team, who persuaded Feng to become a basketball player. Although Feng enjoyed the sport, he missed his artistic pursuits and finally resigned from the team.

Feng's efforts as a writer and painter were frowned upon by the Chinese Communist government. The leader of the Communists at this time, Mao Zedong, had begun what he called the Great Proletarian Cultural Revolution (1965-1968), a nationwide program designed to instil Mao's philosophies and ideals into the populace. Any activities that could be seen as anti-communist, anti-Mao, or anti-Chinese were not tolerated by the government. Feng, whose writings tended toward political satire, was assaulted in the street by the Red Guards, and his collection of books and art was destroyed. To avoid further persecution, Feng began to hide his works: discovery of them by people loyal to Mao could have led to his imprisonment or even execution.

Ironically, the Cultural Revolution that led to Feng's persecution also motivated much of his writing. He has said that the brutalities of this period provided him with the insights into human nature that his works express.

After Mao's death in 1976, Feng's work began to appear in print. He has published several novels as well as numerous short stories and essays. In contrast to the pro-communist themes adopted by many contemporary Chinese writers, Feng's writings explore broader, more universal themes that appeal to a wide readership.

THE MAO BUTTON

He vowed to get himself a stupendous Mao button[1] tonight after work.

Actually, the one he had worn to the office today was big and novel enough to arouse a good deal of envy.

His brother-in-law had gotten it specially for him from a certain unit in the navy and had brought it to his place just last night. Everyone in his family had wanted it. After squabbling over it for about half an hour, they had agreed to take turns: each would have it for a day until it had circulated once, then each would keep it for a week at a time. He had gotten it first, not because he was head of the house, but because he had wanted so desperately to show it off at work. He had insisted, and he had won.

He was delighted with himself all morning at the office. He created a real sensation. "You've outdone us all today, Mr. Kong!" said everyone who saw him, as they bent down to pore over the button as if it were some kind of jewel.

Their envious looks went straight to his head. He was certain that his Mao button was the best at the office today. At lunch he paraded around the cafeteria to make sure everyone noticed him. But then Mr. Chen, from the production department, approached him sporting an even bigger, newer, more eye-catching button on his neatly pressed jacket. An embossed portrait of the Leader was centered in a great red enamel sun, below which a giant golden steamship forged through the waves[2]. The Leader was depicted from the front instead of the usual profile. He was wearing an army cap, and his cap and collar bore insignia. The gilding was superb: the flash of gold against red dazzled the eye. The button was a collector's item. Kong felt his own button darken like a light that had gone out. And it was so small by comparison—his whole button was no bigger than the portrait on Mr. Chen's, whose entire button must have been more than three inches across: about as big as a sesame cake[3].

1. **Mao button:** a pin-on badge depicting Mao Zedong, former Chairman of the People's Republic of China.
2. **embossed portrait...through the waves:** the red sun represents the Communist revolution, which forges onward (the steamship) under Mao's rule.
3. **sesame cake:** a round, bread-like cake made of sesame seeds.

Mr. Chen was extremely coolheaded and always kept a straight face. As they walked by each other, Mr. Chen just eyed Kong's chest and passed him like some champion athlete meeting a young amateur. Hurt, jealous, and angry, Kong made up his mind to go right out and get an enormous Mao button, even if it cost him his life's savings. He just had to bring Mr. Chen down a peg or two.

When he got home in the evening he told his family about his failure. After a quick dinner he found all the Mao buttons in the house, wrapped them in a handkerchief, and stuffed them into his pocket. He even snatched up the buttons his wife and son were wearing. Then he dashed out to The East Is Red[4] Avenue, the busiest shopping street in town. He had heard that the open space beyond the parking lot of the big department store was the place to go to trade Mao buttons. People said you could get all the latest styles there. He had never been before.

By the time he got there the sky was dark and all the lights were on, but shoppers still crowded the street. Practically everyone was wearing Mao buttons; they seemed to have become another part of the human body. Some people wore four or five across their chests, the way European generals used to wear their medals a hundred years ago. It seemed to Kong that people with unusual Mao buttons held their heads higher than the rest, while those with ordinary little outmoded buttons moved drearily through the crowd. No matter how much status, income, or power you had, the quality of your Mao button was all-determining at this particular moment. Had the Mao button become the acid test[5] of the wearer's political stance and loyalty to the Leader? A touchstone? A monitor of the heart?

As he walked he paid no attention to the people coming toward him; he had eyes only for their Mao buttons. Colorful, glittering buttons of all sizes were rushing at him like stars shooting by a rocket ship in outer space. Then he spotted a button exactly like Mr. Chen's. He reached out and grabbed its wearer by the arm.

"Just what do you think you're doing?" the man demanded, obviously startled.

---

4. **The East Is Red:** a slogan popular in China; it celebrates the fact that China has adopted a communist government.
5. **acid test:** ultimate proof; derived from practice of testing coins with acid to detect phony materials.

Kong took a closer look at him: a short, fat, paunchy old soldier. Perhaps he was an officer.

"Excuse me, uh—" Kong asked with an ingratiating laugh, "could you spare your Mao button? I have all kinds—you could have your pick. Do you think we could make a deal?"

The soldier sneered as if to say that his button was a priceless family heirloom. He looked annoyed at Kong's effrontery. Kong was still clutching his sleeve. "No way," he snapped, shoving Kong aside, and waddled away.

Kong was angry, but he comforted himself with the thought that even if he had gotten the button, it would merely have put him on an equal footing with Mr. Chen. What he wanted was to outdo him. Then he caught sight of the swarm of button traders beyond the parking lot. His heart began to pound like that of a fisherman who spots a shimmering school of fish, and he broke into a run.

Once in the crowd, Kong felt hot and flushed, but the sight was mind-boggling: an endless variety of Mao buttons and an assortment of hawkers to match.

Some wore the buttons they hoped to trade and called out what kinds they were looking for:

"Who has a Wuhan Steelworks[6] 'two-and-a-half'?"—a button two-and-a-half inches in diameter—"I'll swap you for it!"

Some displayed their buttons on hand towels; others, who mistook flashy colors for beauty, had their wares in flat glass cases lined with colored paper on the sides and green satin on the bottom. Still others pinned their buttons to their caps so that people had to crane their necks to see them. The crowd thronged the south and east edges of the parking lot. Some people had even spilled over into the lot and squeezed their way in between the cars. With their haggling, shouts, and laughter, the place was noisier than an open-air market at the busiest hour of the morning.

Someone tapped him on the shoulder. "What kind are you looking for?"

The speaker was a big, tall middle-aged man with the unctuous manner of a practiced salesman. But he was wearing a baggy blue jacket with only a single bottlecap-sized Mao button on the chest. He did not look as though he had any special goods.

---

6. **Wuhan Steelworks:** Wuhan (woo'han) is an industrial city in central China where workers organized in support of Mao's revolution.

"I want a big one. At least a 'three-and-a-half.' Do you have any?"

"Oh-ho—no little trinkets for you, eh! Do you mind if the workmanship is a bit rough?" the man asked. He seemed to have what Kong wanted.

"Let me see it."

"First tell me what you have," the man replied without batting an eyelid. He was as haughty as a Mao-button millionaire.

"I've got dozens of different kinds," said Kong, reaching for his pocket.

The man touched Kong's wrist. "Don't take them out in this mob. Somebody'll swipe them. Come with me!"

They elbowed their way out of the crowd, crossed the street, and entered the dark alley beside the Revolution Hat and Shoe Store. The man led him to the second lamppost.

"Let me see your goods," he ordered.

Kong handed the man his handkerchief of Mao buttons. The man inspected them, shaking his head and clucking in disapproval, and gave them back.

"You got any better ones?" he asked after a moment's thought.

"No, these are all I have."

The man paused again. "You're going to have a hard time trading that bunch of buttons for a 'three-and-a-half,'" he said, pointing at Kong's handkerchief of buttons. "Don't forget—the big ones are hot items now."

"Well, I should have a look at yours, whether you're going to trade or not. Then we'll see what's what," Kong retorted scornfully. After all, he had not even seen the man's wares.

Instead of answering, the man unfastened his outer jacket and whisked it open. Kong's eyes nearly popped out of his head: at least a hundred different Mao buttons were pinned to the man's inner jacket. He was a walking Mao-button treasure house. Kong had never seen any of the styles before.

"You haven't seen anything yet," the man said before Kong could look his fill. "Take a peek inside—that's where the big ones are." And he opened the button-covered jacket to reveal yet another garment laden with row upon row of shiny buttons. They were huge: all were at least as big as a fist, and one, the size of the lid of a mug, caught the eye like a crane among chickens.

"That's the one I want!" cried Kong in delight, his heart thumping.

"What? This one?" the man asked with a chuckle. "Do you know how big it is? It's a 'four.' You see where it says 'Loyalty' three times in gold along here? This is a 'Triple Loyalty'[7] button from Xianjiang[8]. Nobody around here has seen these yet. I guess you don't know the market: even four times the buttons you've got here wouldn't buy you one of these. All your buttons put together are worth at most a 'three-and-a-half.' And that's only if you trade with me—nobody else would give you such a good deal. Your buttons are too little and too ordinary."

"Why don't you just let me have this 'four'? I've got forty or fifty buttons here, and—" Kong pleaded. He was madly in love with the button. If only he could just wear it tomorrow, Mr. Chen and everyone else at the office would be green with envy.

Just then a swarthy little man appeared on the left and approached to look at the Mao buttons on the tall man's chest.

The tall man glanced at the newcomer and yanked his outer jacket shut. "No deal!" he announced rudely, and stalked away, jingling like a horse in bell harness.

Kong thought, "I can't let him get away—at least I've got to trade him for a 'three-and-a-half.'" He was about to run after the tall man when the swarthy little man put out an arm to stop him. With his chin of bristly black stubble and his dark clothes, he looked as if he were carved in jet. His round gleaming eyes seemed to cast a black luster over his entire person.

"Don't trade with him—gypping beginners is his racket," he said in a rasping voice. "Those 'Triple Loyalty' buttons from Xianjiang are a dime a dozen; they're considered passé. Now tell me what you've got—I'll make you a deal. *I've* got a Mao button like nothing you've ever seen before."

"Is it big?"

"Big! Well, it's bigger than that 'Triple Loyalty' button of his. But it's not just big—it's a real novelty. But let me see yours first."

Kong produced his package of buttons again and let the man examine them like a customs inspector. Then the man led him deeper into the alley. The streetlights were burned out, and it was pitch-dark. Kong was afraid that the stranger was going to mug him. The farther they went, the darker it got, until the man's murky

7. **Triple Loyalty:** a slogan meaning loyalty to the thought (or philosophies) of Chairman Mao, loyalty to Chairman Mao's revolutionary road, and loyalty to Chairman Mao himself.
8. **Xianjiang** (zhian'jiang).

silhouette almost blended into the gloomy black shadows.

"Couldn't I take a look at it here?" he asked, making a supreme effort to be brave.

"All right," agreed the swarthy little man, and like the tall man before him he unfastened his jacket, but his chest was a dark blur without a single Mao button. Before Kong could ask any questions he heard a click, and a round, glowing, moonlike object magically appeared on the man's left breast. It seemed to Kong that a luminous hole had opened up in the man's chest or that his heart had lit up. And inside was a picture: a color portrait of Chairman Mao waving from the Tian Anmen Rostrum[9]!

When he recovered from his momentary stupefaction, Kong understood: the man was wearing a round glass case lit by a flashlight bulb. In the case a color photo of the Leader waving a giant hand was mounted behind a red cardboard railing. The light bulb was probably between the photo and the cardboard. The battery was concealed on the man's person; the wiring hung down from the back of the case; and the switch was in his hand. A flip of the switch and presto! The Mao button would light up like a color television. A truly great invention!

The man clicked the light off. "Well, how do you like it?" came his smug, wheedling voice in the dark. "Isn't it incredible? What'll you give me for it? But don't forget that the batteries and switch alone are worth a lot of money!"

Kong had to agree that the button was a real novelty. But his interest quickly faded. This was some homemade contraption, not a proper button. And you had to carry around a complete set of electrical equipment—wiring, batteries, a switch—as if you were an electric fan. Besides, it might be eye-catching at night, but it would be totally lackluster by day.

"It's very nice," he said politely after a moment's thought, "but I think I won't take it, since it's not a proper button. What I'd like is a regular button, at least a 'three-and-a-half,' if you have any."

The man launched into a sales pitch, but Kong would not change his mind. Then the man grabbed him eagerly by the wrist. Kong, who had been afraid to start with, thought the man was going to rob him of his Mao buttons. Jerking his arm free, he ran for the brightly lit entrance to the alley.

9. **Tian Anmen Rostrum:** speaker's platform in Tian Anmen Square, the large central plaza in Beijing, China's capital.

"Stop him!" he heard the man shout behind him.

It occurred to Kong that some of the man's cronies might be lurking nearby. He shot out of the alley and into the street, where he almost collided with an approaching bicycle. Skittish as a hare, he jumped over the front wheel and darted back into the crowd of button traders by the parking lot. For fear that the swarthy little man might spot him, he stooped over, hiding his face, and stole through the crowd. Luckily he escaped without further mishap and ran all the way home.

When his wife saw how pale and breathless he was, she thought he was ill. She scolded him, once she found out what had happened, and poured him a hot cup of tea to calm him down.

"You've got Mao buttons on the brain!" she said. "You never do what you're supposed to when you get home from work—and tonight, of all things, you run out onto the streets to swap buttons. Don't you know what kind of riffraff you could have run into out there? And you took the kid's and my buttons too! If they'd been stolen, what would we have worn tomorrow? People would say I'd gone without my button because I didn't love Chairman Mao. They'd arrest me as a counterrevolutionary[10], and there wouldn't be anybody here to cook for you when you got home from work every day. It takes finesse to get good Mao buttons. Look at Mr. Wang—now there's a real operator. He may be unassuming, but he's got more buttons than anybody."

"Which Mr. Wang?"

"The one who lives on the third floor of the front building. You still don't know who I mean? Of course you do—Mrs. Wang's husband. What's the matter with you? Did they scare you silly out there?"

"Oh—yes—I see. So where does he get so many buttons?"

"He's on the staff of a badge factory where they make nothing but Mao buttons. His boss gives him hundreds of them to take along on every business trip. You have to grease palms with them nowadays to get a hotel room, buy train tickets, or ask anyone a favor. They're worth more than cash. A little while ago Mrs. Wang told me that her husband paid for a new truck for his factory with nothing but Mao buttons."

10. **counterrevolutionary:** one who opposes a revolution.

"How many buttons did that cost?"

"The man's clever—he may not have parted with all that many. My guess is that a shrewd fellow like him lines his own pocket on the sly whenever he has the chance. Why else would Mrs. Wang have a new Mao button every time I see her? When I ask her about them she just laughs it off instead of answering, but I'm sure she gets them all from her husband. Just now I went over there to collect their water bill and found them gloating over their buttons. I burst in without knocking and really got an eyeful."

"Did you get a good look at them? What kinds did they have?"

"I couldn't begin to tell you. There were at least a thousand— the bed and table were both covered with them."

"Were there any big ones?"

"Big ones? I swear one of them was as big as a saucepan lid."

So the object of his far-flung search had been right next door all along. Leaving his tea untouched on the table, he ran to the front building as fast as his legs could carry him. "Mr. Wang!" he began to shout, even before he got to the third floor. Like some invisible hand, joy clutched at his vocal cords and made his voice tremble.

Once inside Mr. Wang's apartment, he begged him to show his treasures. Mr. Wang grudgingly obliged, since Kong was an old neighbor. Now here was a great Mao-button collection! Mr. Wang was a Mao-button millionaire if there ever was one. Kong was developing an inferiority complex[11].

Then he spotted the enormous button that his wife had mentioned. Mr. Wang said that it was a "five-and-a-half." Kong weighed it in his palm. It was surprisingly heavy: at least half a pound. But the picture was commonplace: a big red sun with a profile of the Leader in the middle and a chain of nine sunflowers across the bottom. The flowers looked more like coarse sieves. The buffing, painting, and gilding were shoddy. However, it was definitely the biggest in the world—Mr. Chen's would look tiny by comparison. Kong wanted a big one: they were the best—they stood out and really made a statement. He begged Mr. Wang for it and showed his buttons one more time. Luckily he had one with a picture of the

---

11. **inferiority complex:** a persistent feeling that one is unimportant or of little worth in comparison to others.

globe and the caption: "The People of the World Yearn for the Red Sun."[12] Mr. Wang happened to need this one to complete a set of four, so Kong gave it to him, along with two others, in exchange for the biggest button in history. He arrived home cradling his treasure in trembling hands.

"Wow!" his wife and son exclaimed when they saw it.

The next morning he rose early, shaved, washed his face and neck, and put on clean clothes, as carefully as if he were going to be awarded a medal. Next, ignoring his wife's protests, he used one of her soft new handkerchiefs to polish the huge button with petroleum jelly. He had some trouble pinning it on. It covered half of his narrow chest when he wore it on the side, but placed in the middle it looked frivolous, like the breastplate of an ancient general. And his jacket sagged under its tremendous weight. Worst of all, since the pin was right in the center of the back, the button tilted outward like a picture frame instead of lying flat. Kong was at a loss until his wife suggested that he change into his denim jacket; although the weather was still too warm for denim, the stiff material allowed the button to lie flat the way it was supposed to.

With the button on, he struck a few poses and admired himself in the mirror.

"Hooray!" his son cheered, clapping his hands. "My dad is tops! My dad is number one!"

The child was adorable—his compliments were the icing on the cake.

Yes, he really was the sensation of the day! People ogled him as he rode his bicycle down the street. Some pointed him out to their companions, but he sped past them before they could get a good look at him. He was on cloud nine. To prolong the gratification, he took the long way to work. People on a passing bus pressed their noses flat against the windows to stare. As he approached the gate of his office building he tensed up like an actor about to take his first plunge through a brightly lit stage door. He was headed for the limelight.

He entered the gate and locked his bicycle in the yard.

"Hey, everybody," someone shouted, "come see Mr. Kong's Mao button!" In no time flat he was surrounded by a crowd. People

---

12. **"The People of the World Yearn for the Red Sun"**: slogan expressing the belief that everyone wants to become communist like China.

were jostling each other and craning their necks to see. They were looking at his button with amazement and envy, and at him with a new respect. Everyone was yelling, which attracted more people.

"Now that's a big button. Where did you get it?"

"Mr. Kong, you're a real go-getter!"

"Of course! I'm loyal to Chairman Mao," he said with a smug laugh, keeping one hand on the button in case anyone tried to snatch it.

Some people tried to move his fingers out of the way so that they could get a better look at the button; others tried to peek at the back to find out where it was made.

"It doesn't say anything on the back," he cried, clutching the button. "It was produced by a classified military factory. Please quit yanking on it, the pin is too small—" He seemed anxious, but in fact he was jubilant. The excitement he was causing was a sign that his button was without compare not only at the office, but probably in the whole city. Unless someone made a button as big as a crock lid, which only a giant could wear. Then he remembered Mr. Chen: where was yesterday's victor now?

The crowd had swelled to thirty or forty people. Everyone was babbling at once. He could not hear anything. His heavy denim jacket had brought the sweat out on his forehead. Unable to stand it any longer, he began to wriggle his way out of the unbearable crush, away from the hands that were pulling on him.

"Let me out, you're squashing me!"

He was tickled pink.

Finally he squeezed his way out like a noodle out of a noodle machine. He was exhilarated. But just then he heard a clank, as though a heavy metal platter had fallen to the ground. Then he heard it rolling around. He did not realize what the sound was until he reached up and found that his Mao button was gone.

"Oh, no! My button fell off!" he cried. Everyone froze and he began a frantic search. It was not on the ground in front of him, so he stepped back to turn around and look behind him. He felt something hard and slippery underfoot.

"Oh, no! You're standing on a button with a portrait of Chairman Mao!" he heard a woman say, before he could grasp what had happened.

In terror he looked down and saw the Mao button under his heel. He should have been able to lift his foot quickly, but it was as unresponsive as a piece of wood. His body went limp and his weight sank into the offending leg. With all eyes riveted upon him, he stood rooted to the spot.

This blunder was a heinous crime that brought him to the brink of destruction. There is no need to recount the details here. Suffice it to say that he recovered from his Mao-button mania and came to look upon these former objects of his affection with fear and trembling. These events are all behind him now. But there is one question that puzzles him to this day. Perhaps the only clue to its answer lies in the following "natural phenomenon"[13]: you can travel the entire three million seven hundred and seven thousand square miles of our country today and see hardly a single Mao button. . . .

13. **"natural phenomenon":** an occurrence, like a rainbow, that appears because of natural laws.

Meaning

1. What beliefs and values do the Mao buttons represent for the people who wear them?
2. Why is Mr. Kong determined to have the biggest and best Mao button? What sacrifices is he willing to make to acquire it?
3. What is ironic about the success of Mr. Kong's search?
4. Reread the last paragraph of the story. What do you think is the "question" that puzzles Mr. Kong?

Method

1. How does the author prepare the reader for the final turn of events? What events and details foreshadow the story's outcome?
2. What do you think of the resolution of the story? Do you find the ending satisfying and believable? Why or why not?
3. *Satire* is a kind of writing that ridicules the follies and weaknesses of human beings. The satirist uses humor and irony to show the absurdity of something, such as a lifestyle or a value, and to persuade the reader to examine the subject in a critical way. In what ways is "The Mao Button" a satire? What or whom does the author ridicule, and what is his message?

Language: Prefixes

A *prefix* is an element that is placed before the root of a word to change its use or meaning. Three of the most common prefixes are *un-*, *dis-*, and *in-*, all of which mean "not." The prefix *in-* can also mean "in, on, or without." The following words are from "The Mao Button." Write a new sentence for each word. Be sure you understand the meaning of each root word before you write your sentence.

1. invisible	**7.** unassuming
2. instead	**8.** unfastened
3. ingratiating	**9.** untouched
4. incredible	**10.** unbearable
5. insignia	**11.** unresponsive
6. disapproval	**12.** unusual

Discussion and Composition

1. What objects are the "Mao buttons" of today? In other words, what kinds of status symbols do some people feel they must have? Discuss the differences between the significance of status symbols to the people you know and the significance of the Mao buttons to the people in the story.

2. Imagine a situation similar to the one in the story, in which a certain object becomes a fad. Write a satire about a person who is determined to own one of these items at any cost. Tell why the person wants the item, what course the person pursues to acquire it, and what obstacles he or she must overcome to achieve this end. You might then conclude your story by describing the consequences of the person's obsession and telling how the person feels about the object once he or she actually has it.

3. The final paragraph of this story hints that Mr. Kong suffered as a result of his accident with the Mao button. In a short narrative, continue the story. Describe the reaction of the crowd to Mr. Kong's actions, and tell what you think happened to bring Mr. Kong to "the brink of destruction."

BORDEN DEAL
(1922–1985)

Like T. J., the boy hero of his short story "Antaeus,"
Borden Deal knew the joys and difficulties of farm life. He was
born in Pontotoc, Mississippi, to a family of cotton farmers. In
his youth, growing up in the lean years of the Great Depression,
he worked at various jobs around the country—for a circus, the
Civilian Conservation Corps, and the Labor Department in
Washington, D.C.

After serving in the Navy during World War II, he attended
the University of Alabama, graduating in 1949. He published his
first short story, "Exodus," in 1948, while he was still in college.
He went on to write more than a hundred short stories and several
novels. *Walk Through the Valley* (1956), *Dunbar's Cove* (1957), *The
Insolent Breed* (1959), and *The Least One* (1962) are regional novels
about farm communities.

ANTAEUS*

This was during the wartime, when lots of people were coming North for jobs in factories and war industries, when people
moved around a lot more than they do now, and sometimes kids
were thrown into new groups and new lives that were completely
different from anything they had ever known before. I remember
this one kid, T. J. his name was, from somewhere down South,
whose family moved into our building during that time. They'd
come North with everything they owned piled into the back seat
of an old-model sedan that you wouldn't expect could make the
trip, with T. J. and his three younger sisters riding shakily on top
of the load of junk.

---

*__Antaeus__ (ăn·tē′əs): in Greek mythology, a giant who challenged his enemies
to wrestling matches, with the odds always in his favor because each fall to earth
renewed his tremendous strength and led to his victory. Antaeus was killed by
Hercules, who held him aloft, detached from mother Earth, and strangled him.

Our building was just like all the others there, with families crowded into a few rooms, and I guess there were twenty-five or thirty kids about my age in that one building. Of course, there were a few of us who formed a gang and ran together all the time after school, and I was the one who brought T. J. in and started the whole thing.

The building right next door to us was a factory where they made walking dolls. It was a low building with a flat, tarred roof that had a parapet[1] all around it about head-high, and we'd found out a long time before that no one, not even the watchman, paid any attention to the roof because it was higher than any of the other buildings around. So my gang used the roof as a headquarters. We could get up there by crossing over to the fire escape from our own roof on a plank and then going on up. It was a secret place for us, where nobody else could go without our permission.

I remember the day I first took T. J. up there to meet the gang. He was a stocky, robust kid with a shock[2] of white hair, nothing sissy about him except his voice; he talked in this slow, gentle voice like you never heard before. He talked different from any of us and you noticed it right away. But I liked him anyway, so I told him to come on up.

We climbed up over the parapet and dropped down on the roof. The rest of the gang were already there.

"Hi," I said. I jerked my thumb at T. J. "He just moved into the building yesterday."

He just stood there, not scared or anything, just looking, like the first time you see somebody you're not sure you're going to like.

"Hi," Blackie said. "Where are you from?"

"Marion County," T. J. said.

We laughed. "Marion County?" I said. "Where's that?"

He looked at me for a moment like I was a stranger, too. "It's in Alabama," he said, like I ought to know where it was.

"What's your name?" Charley said.

"T. J.," he said, looking back at him. He had pale blue eyes that looked washed-out, but he looked directly at Charley, waiting for his reaction. He'll be all right, I thought. No sissy in him, except that voice. Who ever talked like that?

1. **parapet** (păr′ə·pĭt): a low wall or protecting railing on the edge of a platform, roof, or bridge.
2. **shock:** a thick bushy mass.

"T. J.," Blackie said. "That's just initials. What's your real name? Nobody in the world has just initials."

"I do," he said. "And they're T. J. That's all the name I got."

His voice was resolute with the knowledge of his rightness, and for a moment no one had anything to say. T. J. looked around at the rooftop and down at the black tar under his feet. "Down yonder where I come from," he said, "we played out in the woods. Don't you-all have no woods around here?"

"Naw," Blackie said. "There's the park a few blocks over, but it's full of kids and cops and old women. You can't do a thing."

T. J. kept looking at the tar under his feet. "You mean you ain't got no fields to raise nothing in?—no watermelons or nothing?"

"Naw," I said scornfully. "What do you want to grow something for? The folks can buy everything they need at the store."

He looked at me again with that strange, unknowing look. "In Marion County," he said, "I had my own acre of cotton and my own acre of corn. It was mine to plant and make ever' year."

He sounded like it was something to be proud of, and in some obscure way it made the rest of us angry. Blackie said, "Who'd want to have their own acre of cotton and corn? That's just work. What can you do with an acre of cotton and corn?"

T. J. looked at him. "Well, you get part of the bale offen your acre," he said seriously. "And I fed my acre of corn to my calf."

We didn't really know what he was talking about, so we were more puzzled than angry; otherwise, I guess we'd have chased him off the roof and wouldn't let him be part of our gang. But he was strange and different, and we were all attracted by his stolid[3] sense of rightness and belonging, maybe by the strange softness of his voice contrasting our own tones of speech into harshness.

He moved his foot against the black tar. "We could make our own field right here," he said softly, thoughtfully. "Come spring we could raise us what we want to—watermelons and garden truck and no telling what all."

"You'd have to be a good farmer to make these tar roofs grow any watermelons," I said. We all laughed.

But T. J. looked serious. "We could haul us some dirt up

3. **stolid** (stŏl′ĭd): unemotional; calm.

here," he said. "And spread it out even and water it, and before you know it, we'd have us a crop in here." He looked at us intently. "Wouldn't that be fun?"

"They wouldn't let us," Blackie said quickly.

"I thought you said this was you-all's roof," T. J. said to me. "That you-all could do anything you wanted to up here."

"They've never bothered us," I said. I felt the idea beginning to catch fire in me. It was a big idea, and it took a while for it to sink in; but the more I thought about it, the better I liked it. "Say," I said to the gang. "He might have something there. Just make us a regular roof garden, with flowers and grass and trees and everything. And all ours, too," I said. "We wouldn't let anybody up here except the ones we wanted to."

"It'd take a while to grow trees," T. J. said quickly, but we weren't paying any attention to him. They were all talking about it suddenly, all excited with the idea after I'd put it in a way they could catch hold of it. Only rich people had roof gardens, we knew, and the idea of our own private domain excited them.

"We could bring it up in sacks and boxes," Blackie said. "We'd have to do it while the folks weren't paying any attention to us, for we'd have to come up to the roof of our building and then cross over with it."

"Where could we get the dirt?" somebody said worriedly.

"Out of those vacant lots over close to school," Blackie said. "Nobody'd notice if we scraped it up."

I slapped T. J. on the shoulder. "Man, you had a wonderful idea," I said, and everybody grinned at him, remembering that he had started it. "Our own private roof garden."

He grinned back. "It'll be ourn," he said. "All ourn." Then he looked thoughtful again. "Maybe I can lay my hands on some cotton seed, too. You think we could raise us some cotton?"

We'd started big projects before at one time or another, like any gang of kids, but they'd always petered out for lack of organization and direction. But this one didn't; somehow or other T. J. kept it going all through the winter months. He kept talking about the watermelons and the cotton we'd raise, come spring, and when even that wouldn't work, he'd switch around to my idea of flowers and grass and trees, though he was always honest enough to add that it'd take a while to get any trees started. He always had it on his mind and he'd mention it in school, getting them lined up to carry dirt that afternoon, saying in a casual way that he reckoned a few more weeks ought to see the job through.

Our little area of private earth grew slowly. T. J. was smart enough to start in one corner of the building, heaping up the carried earth two or three feet thick so that we had an immediate result to look at, to comtemplate with awe. Some of the evenings T. J. alone was carrying earth up to the building, the rest of the gang distracted by other enterprises or interests, but T. J. kept plugging along on his own, and eventually we'd all come back to him again and then our own little acre would grow more rapidly.

He was careful about the kind of dirt he'd let us carry up there, and more than once he dumped a sandy load over the parapet into the areaway below because it wasn't good enough. He found out the kinds of earth in all the vacant lots for blocks around. He'd pick it up and feel it and smell it, frozen though it was sometimes, and then he'd say it was good growing soil or it wasn't worth anything, and we'd have to go on somewhere else.

Thinking about it now, I don't see how he kept us at it. It was hard work, lugging paper sacks and boxes of dirt all the way up the stairs of our own building, keeping out of the way of the grownups so they wouldn't catch on to what we were doing. They probably wouldn't have cared, for they didn't pay much attention to us, but we wanted to keep it secret anyway. Then we had to go through the trap door to our roof, teeter over a plank to the fire escape, then climb two or three stories to the parapet and drop down onto the roof. All that for a small pile of earth that sometimes didn't seem worth the effort. But T. J. kept the vision bright within us, his words shrewd and calculated toward the fulfillment of his dream; and he worked harder than any of us. He seemed driven toward a goal that we couldn't see, a particular point in time that would be definitely marked by signs and wonders that only he could see.

The laborious earth just lay there during the cold months, inert and lifeless, the clods lumpy and cold under our feet when we walked over it. But one day it rained, and afterward there was a softness in the air, and the earth was live and giving again with moisture and warmth.

That evening T. J. smelled the air, his nostrils dilating with the odor of the earth under his feet. "It's spring," he said, and there was a gladness rising in his voice that filled us all with the same feeling. "It's mighty late for it, but it's spring. I'd just about decided it wasn't never gonna get here at all."

We were all sniffing at the air, too, trying to smell it the way that T. J. did, and I can still remember the sweet odor of the earth under our feet. It was the first time in my life that spring and spring earth had meant anything to me. I looked at T. J. then, knowing in a faint way the hunger within him through the toilsome winter months, knowing the dream that lay behind his plan. He was a new Antaeus, preparing his own bed of strength.

"Planting time," he said. "We'll have to find us some seed."

"What do we do?" Blackie said. "How do we do it?"

"First we'll have to break up the clods," T. J. said. "That won't be hard to do. Then we plant the seeds, and after a while they come up. Then you got you a crop." He frowned. "But you ain't got it raised yet. You got to tend it and hoe it and take care of it, and all the time it's growing and growing, while you're awake and while you're asleep. Then you lay it by when it's growed and let it ripen, and then you got you a crop."

"There's those wholesale seed houses over on Sixth," I said. "We could probably swipe some grass seed over there."

T. J. looked at the earth. "You-all seem mighty set on raising some grass," he said. "I ain't never put no effort into that. I spent all my life trying not to raise grass."

"But it's pretty," Blackie said. "We could play on it and take sunbaths on it. Like having our own lawn. Lots of people got lawns."

"Well," T. J. said. He looked at the rest of us, hesitant for the first time. He kept on looking at us for a moment. "I did have it in mind to raise some corn and vegetables. But we'll plant grass."

He was smart. He knew where to give in. And I don't suppose it made any difference to him, really. He just wanted to grow something, even if it was grass.

"Of course," he said, "I do think we ought to plant a row of watermelons. They'd be mighty nice to eat while we was a-laying on that grass."

We all laughed. "All right," I said. "We'll plant us a row of watermelons."

Things went very quickly then. Perhaps half the roof was covered with the earth, the half that wasn't broken by ventilators, and we swiped pocketfuls of grass seed from the open bins in the wholesale seed house, mingling among the buyers on Saturdays and during the school lunch hour. T. J. showed us how to prepare the earth, breaking up the clods and smoothing it and sowing the grass seed. It looked rich and black now with moisture, receiving of the seed, and it seemed that the grass sprang up overnight, pale green in the early spring.

We couldn't keep from looking at it, unable to believe that we had created this delicate growth. We looked at T. J. with understanding now, knowing the fulfillment of the plan he had carried along within his mind. We had worked without full understanding of the task, but he had known all the time.

We found that we couldn't walk or play on the delicate blades, as we had expected to, but we didn't mind. It was enough just to look at it, to realize that it was the work of our own hands, and each evening the whole gang was there, trying to measure the growth that had been achieved that day.

One time a foot was placed on the plot of ground, one time only, Blackie stepping onto it with sudden bravado.[4] Then he looked at the crushed blades and there was shame in his face. He did not do it again. This was his grass, too, and not to be desecrated.[5] No one said anything, for it was not necessary.

T. J. had reserved a small section for watermelons, and he was still trying to find some seed for it. The wholesale house didn't have any watermelon seeds, and we didn't know where we could lay our hands on them. T. J. shaped the earth into mounds, ready to receive them, three mounds lying in a straight line along the edge of the grass plot.

We had just about decided that we'd have to buy the seeds if we were to get them. It was a violation of our principles, but we were anxious to get the watermelons started. Somewhere or other, T. J. got his hands on a seed catalog and brought it one evening to our roof garden.

"We can order them now," he said, showing us the catalog. "Look!"

We all crowded around, looking at the fat, green watermelons pictured in full color on the pages. Some of them were split open, showing the red, tempting meat, making our mouths water.

---

4. **bravado** (brə·vä′dō): pretense of bravery.
5. **desecrated** (dĕs′ə·krāt·ĕd): treated irreverently.

"Now we got to scrape up some seed money," T. J. said, looking at us. "I got a quarter. How much you-all got?"

We made up a couple of dollars among us and T. J. nodded his head. "That'll be more than enough. Now we got to decide what kind to get. I think them Kleckley Sweets. What do you-all think?"

He was going into esoteric[6] matters beyond our reach. We hadn't even known there were different kinds of melons. So we just nodded our heads and agreed that yes, we thought the Kleckley Sweets too.

"I'll order them tonight," T. J. said. "We ought to have them in a few days."

"What are you boys doing up here?" an adult voice said behind us.

It startled us, for no one had ever come up here before in all the time we had been using the roof of the factory. We jerked around and saw three men standing near the trap door at the other end of the roof. They weren't policemen or night watchmen, but three men in plump business suits, looking at us. They walked toward us.

"What are you boys doing up here?" the one in the middle said again.

We stood still, guilt heavy among us, levied[7] by the tone of voice, and looked at the three strangers.

The men stared at the grass flourishing behind us. "What's this?" the man said. "How did this get up here?"

"Sure is growing good, ain't it?" T. J. said conversationally. "We planted it."

The men kept looking at the grass as if they didn't believe it. It was a thick carpet over the earth now, a patch of deep greenness startling in the sterile industrial surroundings.

'Yes, sir," T. J. said proudly. "We toted that earth up here and planted that grass." He fluttered the seed catalog. "And we're just fixing to plant us some watermelon."

The man looked at him then, his eyes strange and faraway. "What do you mean, putting this on the roof of my building?" he said. "Do you want to go to jail?"

6. **esoteric** (ĕs′ə·tĕr′ĭk): mysterious; understood only by a small group possessing special knowledge.

7. **levied** (lĕv′ēd): To levy is to impose or collect a tax or a fine by authority or force; here, guilt is established or levied by the man's tone of voice.

T. J. looked shaken. The rest of us were silent, frightened by the authority of his voice. We had grown up aware of adult authority, of policemen and night watchmen and teachers, and this man sounded like all the others. But it was a new thing to T. J.

"Well, you wasn't using the roof," T. J. said. He paused a moment and added shrewdly, "So we just thought to pretty it up a little bit."

"And sag it so I'd have to rebuild it," the man said sharply. He started turning away, saying to another man beside him, "See that all that junk is shoveled off by tomorrow."

"Yes, sir," the man said.

T. J. started forward. "You can't do that," he said. "We toted it up here, and it's our earth. We planted it and raised it and toted it up here."

The man stared at him coldly. "But it's my building," he said. "It's to be shoveled off tomorrow."

"It's our earth," T. J. said desperately. "You ain't got no right!"

The men walked on without listening and descended clumsily through the trapdoor. T. J. stood looking after them, his body tense with anger, until they had disappeared. They wouldn't even argue with him, wouldn't let him defend his earth-rights.

He turned to us. "We won't let 'em do it," he said fiercely. "We'll stay up here all day tomorrow and the day after that, and we won't let 'em do it."

We just looked at him. We knew there was no stopping it.

He saw it in our faces, and his face wavered for a moment before he gripped it into'determination. "They ain't got no right," he said. "It's our earth. It's our land. Can't nobody touch a man's own land."

We kept looking at him, listening to the words but knowing that it was no use. The adult world had descended on us even in our richest dream, and we knew there was no calculating the adult world, no fighting it, no winning against it.

We started moving slowly toward the parapet and the fire escape, avoiding a last look at the green beauty of the earth that T. J. had planted for us, had planted deeply in our minds as well as in our experience. We filed slowly over the edge and down the steps to the plank, T. J. coming last, and all of us could feel the weight of his grief behind us.

"Wait a minute," he said suddenly, his voice harsh with the effort of calling.

We stopped and turned, held by the tone of his voice, and looked at him standing above us on the fire escape.

"We can't stop them?" he said, looking down at us, his face strange in the dusky light. "There ain't no way to stop em?"

"No," Blackie said with finality. "They own the building."

We stood still for a moment, looking up at T. J., caught into inaction by the decision working in his face. He stared back at us, and his face was pale and mean in the poor light, with a bald nakedness in his skin like cripples have sometimes.

"They ain't gonna touch my earth," he said fiercely. "They ain't gonna lay a hand on it! Come on."

He turned around and started up the fire escape again, almost running against the effort of climbing. We followed more slowly, not knowing what he intended. By the time we reached him, he had seized a board and thrust it into the soil, scooping it up and flinging it over the parapet into the areaway below. He straightened and looked at us.

"They can't touch it," he said. "I won't let 'em lay a dirty hand on it!"

We saw it then. He stooped to his labor again and we followed, the gusts of his anger moving in frenzied labor among us as we scattered along the edge of earth, scooping it and throwing it over the parapet, destroying with anger the growth we had nurtured with such tender care. The soil carried so laboriously upward to the light and the sun cascaded swiftly into the dark areaway, the green blades of grass crumpled and twisted in the falling.

It took less time than you would think; the task of destruction is infinitely easier than that of creation. We stopped at the end, leaving only a scattering of loose soil, and when it was finally over, a stillness stood among the group and over the factory building. We looked down at the bare sterility of black tar, felt the harsh texture of it under the soles of our shoes, and the anger had gone out of us, leaving only a sore aching in our minds like overstretched muscles.

T. J. stood for a moment, his breathing slowing from anger and effort, caught into the same contemplation of destruction as all of us. He stooped slowly, finally, and picked up a lonely blade of grass left trampled under our feet and put it between his teeth, tasting it, sucking the greenness out of it into his mouth. Then he started walking toward the fire escape, moving before any of us were ready to move, and disappeared over the edge.

We followed him, but he was already halfway down to the ground, going on past the board where we crossed over, climbing down into the areaway. We saw the last section swing down with his weight, and then he stood on the concrete below us, looking at the small pile of anonymous earth scattered by our throwing. Then he walked across the place where we could see him and disappeared toward the street without glancing back, without looking up to see us watching him.

They did not find him for two weeks.

Then the Nashville police caught him just outside the Nashville freight yards. He was walking along the railroad track, still heading south, still heading home.

As for us, who had no remembered home to call us, none of us ever again climbed the escapeway to the roof.

Meaning

1. The city children want to plant grass, flowers, and trees, whereas T. J. wants cotton and watermelon. How do these preferences reflect their lives up to this point?
2. To the narrator, the garden represents a new concept of spring. For T. J., the garden is a "bed of strength." Explain the difference in light of what you know of T. J.'s background and the myth of Antaeus, who needed contact with the earth in order to survive.
3. Only a person with leadership ability could accomplish the seemingly impossible task of creating a garden on a tar roof. List what you think are the qualities of an ideal leader, and show how T. J. measures up to them.
4. What two reactions to the adult world are shown by T. J. and the other boys when they are ordered off the roof?
5. What is the *theme*, or main idea, of this story?

Method

1. Why does the author have a city boy narrate the story?
2. One of the most dramatic scenes in the story takes place when

T. J. confronts the three men. How does the author make this a tense encounter?

3. Until the three men appear, there is little conflict in this story. What do you think is the author's purpose in introducing the conflict at that point?

4. What do you think of the story's conclusion? Give reasons for your answer.

Language: Antonyms

An antonym (from Greek *anti*, against, and *onyma*, name) is a word that is opposite in meaning to another word. For example, *dark* is an antonym for *light*. However, note that *light* can also be an antonym for *heavy*. Some antonyms are formed by using a prefix, as in *active-inactive*, or *natural-unnatural*. For what word is each of the following an antonym?

1. delicate
2. different
3. started
4. gentle
5. unknowing
6. gladness

Discussion and Composition

1. If you were T. J., how would you answer someone who asked you, "What do you want to grow something for? The folks can buy everything they need at the store." Give some good reasons to support your position. Skim through the story to get a basis for your ideas.

2. The country-born T. J. finds it hard to believe that the "gang" has no woods to play in. Imagine the reverse situation in which a city-born child moves to the country. Write an essay explaining the difficulties he or she might encounter in adjusting to country life. For example, you might discuss what he or she would miss about the city and what aspects of country life would seem strange and puzzling.

GINA BERRIAULT
(born 1926)

Born to immigrant parents, Gina Berriault had no formal education beyond high school. While she trained herself to be a writer, she worked at various times as a waitress, store clerk, news reporter, and librarian. In 1963, she received a fellowship from *Centro Mexicano de Escritores* in Mexico City. In 1966, she was appointed a scholar to the Radcliffe Institute for Independent Study in Cambridge. Massachusetts. Her stories have been awarded two *Paris Review* fiction prizes and have appeared in major collections.

The setting for most of Gina Berriault's stories is northern California, where she now lives. Her writing deals primarily with isolated people whose loneliness she portrays with vividly realistic details.

THE STONE BOY

Arnold drew his overalls and raveling gray sweater over his naked body. In the other narrow bed his brother Eugene went on sleeping, undisturbed by the alarm clock's rusty ring. Arnold, watching his brother sleeping, felt a peculiar dismay; he was nine, six years younger than Eugie, and in their waking hours it was he who was subordinate. To dispel emphatically his uneasy advantage over his sleeping brother, he threw himself on the hump of Eugie's body.

"Get up! Get up!" he cried.

Arnold felt his brother twist away and saw the blankets lifted in a great wing, and, all in an instant, he was lying on his back under the covers with only his face showing like a baby, and Eugie was sprawled on top of him.

"Whassa matter with you?" asked Eugie in sleepy anger, his face hanging close.

"Get up," Arnold repeated. "You said you'd pick peas with me."

Stupidly, Eugie gazed around the room as if to see if morning had come into it yet. Arnold began to laugh derisively, making soft, snorting noises, and was thrown off the bed. He got up from the floor and went down the stairs, the laughter continuing, like hiccups, against his will. But when he opened the staircase door and entered the parlor, he hunched up his shoulders and was quiet because his parents slept in the bedroom downstairs.

Arnold lifted his .22-caliber rifle from the rack on the kitchen wall. It was an old lever-action Winchester that his father had given him because nobody else used it any more. On their way down to the garden he and Eugie would go by the lake, and if there were any ducks on it he'd take a shot at them. Standing on the stool before the cupboard, he searched on the top shelf in the confusion of medicines and ointments for man and beast and found a small yellow box of .22 cartridges. Then he sat down on the stool and began to load his gun.

It was cold in the kitchen so early, but later in the day, when his mother canned the peas, the heat from the wood stove would be almost unbearable. Yesterday she had finished preserving the huckleberries that the family had picked along the mountain, and before that she had canned all the cherries his father had brought from the warehouse in Corinth. Sometimes, on these summer days, Arnold would deliberately come out from the shade where he was playing and make himself as uncomfortable as his mother was in the kitchen by standing in the sun until the sweat ran down his body.

Eugie came clomping down the stairs and into the kitchen, his head drooping with sleepiness. From his perch on the stool Arnold watched Eugie slip on his green knit cap. Eugie didn't really need a cap; he hadn't had a haircut in a long time and his brown curls grew thick and matted, close around his ears and down his neck, tapering there to a small whorl.[1] Eugie passed his left hand through his hair before he set his cap down with his right. The very way he slipped his cap on was an announcement of his status; almost everything he did was a reminder that he was eldest—first he, then Nora, then Arnold—and called attention to how tall he was (almost as tall as his father), how long his legs were, and how small he was in the hips, and what a neat dip above his buttocks his thick-soled logger's boots gave him. Arnold never

---

1. **whorl** (hwêrl or hwôrl): spiral or curl.

tired of watching Eugie offer silent praise unto himself. He wondered, as he sat enthralled, if when he got to be Eugie's age he would still be undersized and his hair still straight.

Eugie eyed the gun. "Don't you know this ain't duck season?" he asked gruffly, as if he were the sheriff.

"No, I don't know," Arnold said with a snigger.

Eugie picked up the tin washtub for the peas, unbolted the door with his free hand and kicked it open. Then, lifting the tub to his head, he went clomping down the back steps. Arnold followed, closing the door behind him.

The sky was faintly gray, almost white. The mountains behind the farm made the sun climb a long way to show itself. Several miles to the south, where the range opened up, hung an orange mist, but the valley in which the farm lay was still cold and colorless.

Eugie opened the gate to the yard and the boys passed between the barn and the row of chicken houses, their feet stirring up the carpet of brown feathers dropped by the molting chickens. They paused before going down the slope to the lake. A fluky morning wind ran among the shocks of wheat that covered the slope. It sent a shimmer northward across the lake, gently moving the rushes that formed an island in the center. Killdeer,[2] their white markings flashing, skimmed the water, crying their shrill, sweet cry. And there at the south end of the lake were four wild ducks, swimming out from the willows into open water.

Arnold followed Eugie down the slope, stealing, as his brother did, from one shock of wheat to another. Eugie paused before climbing through the wire fence that divided the wheatfield from the marshy pasture around the lake. They were screened from the ducks by the willows along the lake's edge.

"If you hit your duck, you want me to go in after it?" Eugie said.

"If you want," Arnold said.

Eugie lowered his eyelids, leaving slits of mocking blue. "You'd drown 'fore you got to it, them legs of yours are so puny," he said.

He shoved the tub under the fence and, pressing down the center wire, climbed through into the pasture.

Arnold pressed down the bottom wire, thrust a leg through

2. **killdeer:** a bird that lives in shore areas.

and leaned forward to bring the other leg after. His rifle caught on the wire and he jerked at it. The air was rocked by the sound of the shot. Feeling foolish, he lifted his face, baring it to an expected shower of derision from his brother. But Eugie did not turn around. Instead, from his crouching position, he fell to his knees and then pitched forward onto his face. The ducks rose up crying from the lake, cleared the mountain background and beat away northward across the pale sky.

Arnold squatted beside his brother. Eugie seemed to be climbing the earth, as if the earth ran up and down, and when he found he couldn't scale it he lay still.

"Eugie?"

Then Arnold saw it, under the tendril of hair at the nape of the neck—a slow rising of bright blood. It had an obnoxious movement, like that of a parasite.

"Hey, Eugie," he said again. He was feeling the same discomfort he had felt when he had watched Eugie sleeping; his brother didn't know that he was lying face down in the pasture.

Again he said, "Hey, Eugie," an anxious nudge in his voice. But Eugie was as still as the morning about them.

Arnold set his rifle on the ground and stood up. He picked up the tub and, dragging it behind him, walking along by the willows to the garden fence and climbed through. He went down on his knees among the tangled vines. The pods were cold with the night, but his hands were strange to him, and not until some time had passed did he realize that the pods were numbing his fingers. He picked from the top of the vine first, then lifted the vine to look underneath for pods and then moved on to the next.

It was a warmth on his back, like a large hand laid firmly there, that made him raise his head. Way up on the slope the gray farmhouse was struck by the sun. While his head had been bent the land had grown bright around him.

When he got up his legs were so stiff that he had to go down on his knees again to ease the pain. Then, walking sideways, he dragged the tub, half full of peas, up the slope.

The kitchen was warm now; a fire was roaring in the stove with a close-up, rushing sound. His mother was spooning eggs from a pot of boiling water and putting them into a bowl. Her short brown hair was uncombed and fell forward across her eyes as she bent her head. Nora was lifting a frying pan full of trout from the stove, holding the handle with a dish towel. His father had just come in from bringing the cows from the north pasture to the barn, and was sitting on the stool, unbuttoning his red plaid Mackinaw.[3]

"Did you boys fill the tub?" his mother asked.

"They ought of by now," his father said. "They went out of the house an hour ago. Eugie woke me up comin' downstairs. I heard you shootin'—did you get a duck?"

"No," Arnold said. They would want to know why Eugie wasn't coming in for breakfast, he thought. "Eugie's dead," he told them.

They stared at him. The pitch crackled in the stove.

"You kids playin' a joke?" his father asked.

"Where's Eugene?" his mother asked scoldingly. She wanted, Arnold knew, to see his eyes, and when he glanced at her she put the bowl and spoon down on the stove and walked past him. His father stood up and went out the door after her. Nora followed them with little skipping steps, as if afraid to be left alone.

Arnold went into the barn, down along the foddering passage past the cows waiting to be milked, and climbed into the loft. After a few minutes he heard a terrifying sound coming toward the house. His parents and Nora were returning from the willows, and sounds sharp as knives were rising from his mother's breast and carrying over the sloping fields. In a short while he heard his father go down the back steps, slam the car door and drive away.

Arnold lay still as a fugitive, listening to the cows eating close by. If his parents never called him, he thought, he would stay up in the loft forever, out of the way. In the night he would sneak down for a drink of water from the faucet over the trough and for whatever food they left for him by the barn.

The rattle of his father's car as it turned down the lane recalled him to the present. He heard voices from his Uncle Andy and Aunt Alice as they and his father went past the barn to the lake. He could feel the morning growing heavier with sun. Someone, probably Nora, had let the chickens out of their coops and they were cackling in the yard.

3. **Mackinaw** (măk'ə·nô): a heavy woolen jacket, usually in a plaid design. The name comes from Mackinac, an island in Michigan which is the site of an Indian burial ground called *Michilemackinac* (which means green turtle). At one time, supplies such as Mackinaws were distributed to the Indians at Mackinac.

After a while another car turned down the road off the highway. The car drew to a stop and he heard the voices of strange men. The men also went past the barn and down to the lake. The undertakers, whom his father must have phoned from Uncle Andy's house, had arrived from Corinth. Then he heard everybody come back and heard the car turn around and leave.

"Arnold!" It was his father calling from the yard.

He climbed down the ladder and went out into the sun, picking wisps of hay from his overalls.

Corinth, nine miles away, was the county seat. Arnold sat in the front seat of the old Ford between his father, who was driving, and Uncle Andy; no one spoke. Uncle Andy was his mother's brother, and he had been fond of Eugie because Eugie had resembled him. Andy had taken Eugie hunting and had given him a knife and a lot of things, and now Andy, his eyes narrowed, sat tall and stiff beside Arnold.

Arnold's father parked the car before the courthouse. It was a two-story brick building with a lamp on each side of the bottom step. They went up the wide stone steps, Arnold and his father going first, and entered the darkly paneled hallway. The shirt-sleeved man in the sheriff's office said that the sheriff was at Carlson's Parlor examining the Curwing boy.

Andy went off to get the sheriff while Arnold and his father waited on a bench in the corridor. Arnold felt his father watching him, and he lifted his eyes with painful casualness to the announcement, on the opposite wall, of the Corinth County Annual Rodeo, and then to the clock with its loudly clucking pendulum. After he had come down from the loft his father and Uncle Andy had stood in the yard with him and asked him to tell them everything, and he had explained to them how the gun had caught on the wire. But when they had asked him why he hadn't run back to the house to tell his parents, he had had no answer—all he could say was that he had gone down into the garden to pick the peas. His father had stared at him in a pale, puzzled way, and it was then that he had felt his father and the others set their cold, turbulent silence against him. Arnold shifted on the bench, his only feeling a small one of compunction[4] imposed by his father's eyes.

At a quarter past nine Andy and the sheriff came in. They all

4. **compunction** (kəm·pŭngk′shən): uneasiness or regret coming from a sense of guilt.

went into the sheriff's private office, and Arnold was sent forward to sit in the chair by the sheriff's desk; his father and Andy sat down on the bench against the wall.

The sheriff lumped down into his swivel chair and swung toward Arnold. He was an old man with white hair like wheat stubble. His restless green eyes made him seem not to be in his office but to be hurrying and bobbing around somewhere else.

"What did you say your name was?" the sheriff asked.

"Arnold," he replied, but he could not remember telling the sheriff his name before.

"Curwing?"

"Yes."

"What were you doing with a .22, Arnold?"

"It's mine," he said.

"Okay. What were you going to shoot?"

"Some ducks," he replied.

"Out of season?"

He nodded.

"That's bad," said the sheriff. "Were you and your brother good friends?"

What did he mean—good friends? Eugie was his brother. That was different from a friend, Arnold thought. A best friend was your own age, but Eugie was almost a man. Eugie had had a way of looking at him, slyly and mockingly and yet confidentially, that had summed up how they both felt about being brothers. Arnold had wanted to be with Eugie more than with anybody else but he couldn't say they had been good friends.

"Did they ever quarrel?" the sheriff asked his father.

"Not that I know," his father replied. "It seemed to me that Arnold cared a lot for Eugie."

"Did you?" the sheriff asked Arnold.

If it seemed so to his father, then it was so. Arnold nodded.

"Were you mad at him this morning?"

"No."

"How did you happen to shoot him?"

"We was crawlin' through the fence."

"Yes?"

"An' the gun got caught on the wire."

"Seems the hammer must of caught," his father put in.

"All right, that's what happened," said the sheriff. "But what I want you to tell me is this. Why didn't you go back to the house and tell your father right away? Why did you go and pick peas for an hour?"

Arnold gazed over his shoulder at his father, expecting his father to have an answer for this also. But his father's eyes, larger and ever lighter blue than usual, were fixed upon him curiously. Arnold picked at a callus in his right palm. It seemed odd now that he had not run back to the house and wakened his father, but he could not remember why he had not. They were all waiting for him to answer.

"I come down to pick peas," he said.

"Didn't you think," asked the sheriff, stepping carefully from word to word, "that it was more important for you to go tell your parents what had happened?"

"The sun was gonna come up," Arnold said.

"What's that got to do with it?"

"It's better to pick peas while they're cool."

The sheriff swung away from him, laid both hands flat on his desk. "Well, all I can say is," he said across to Arnold's father and Uncle Andy, "he's either a moron or he's so reasonable that he's way ahead of us." He gave a challenging snort. "It's come to my notice that the most reasonable guys are mean ones. They don't feel nothing."

For a moment the three men sat still. Then the sheriff lifted his hand like a man taking an oath. "Take him home," he said.

Andy uncrossed his legs. "You don't want him?"

"Not now," replied the sheriff. "Maybe in a few years."

Arnold's father stood up. He held his hat against his chest. "The gun ain't his no more," he said wanly.

Arnold went first through the hallway, hearing behind him the heels of his father and Uncle Andy striking the floor boards. He went down the steps ahead of them and climbed into the back seat of the car. Andy paused as he was getting into the front seat and gazed back at Arnold, and Arnold saw that his uncle's eyes had absorbed the knowingness from the sheriff's eyes. Andy and his father and the sheriff had discovered what made him go down into the garden. It was because he was cruel, the sheriff had said, and didn't care about his brother. Was that the reason? Arnold lowered his eyelids meekly against his uncle's stare.

The rest of the day he did his tasks around the farm, keeping apart from the family. At evening, when he saw his father stomp tiredly into the house, Arnold did not put down his hammer and leave the chicken coop he was repairing. He was afraid that they did not want him to eat supper with them. But in a few minutes another fear that they would go to the trouble of calling him and that he would be made conspicuous by his tardiness made him follow his father into the house. As he went through the kitchen he saw the jars of peas standing in rows on the workbench, a reproach to him.

No one spoke at supper, and his mother, who sat next to him, leaned her head in her hand all through the meal, curving her fingers over her eyes so as not to see him. They were finishing their small, silent supper when the visitors began to arrive, knocking hard on the back door. The men were coming from their farms now that it was growing dark and they could not work any more.

Old Man Matthews, gray and stocky, came first, with his two sons, Orion, the elder, and Clint, who was Eugie's age. As the callers entered the parlor, where the family ate, Arnold sat down in a rocking chair. Even as he had been undecided before supper whether to remain outside or take his place at the table, he now thought that he should go upstairs, and yet he stayed to avoid being conspicuous by his absence. If he stayed, he thought, as he always stayed and listened when visitors came, they would see that he was only Arnold and not the person the sheriff thought he was. He sat with his arms crossed and his hands tucked into his armpits and did not lift his eyes.

The Matthews men had hardly settled down around the table, after Arnold's mother and Nora had cleared away the dishes, when another car rattled down the road and someone else rapped on the back door. This time it was Sullivan, a spare and sandy man, so nimble of gesture and expression that Arnold had never been able to catch more than a few of his meanings. Sullivan, in dusty jeans, sat down in the other rocker, shot out his skinny legs and began to talk in his fast way, recalling everything that Eugene had ever said to him. The other men interrupted to tell of occasions they remembered, and after a time Clint's young voice, hoarse like Eugene's had been, broke in to tell about the time Eugene had beat him in a wrestling match.

Out in the kitchen the voices of Orion's wife and of Mrs. Sullivan mingled with Nora's voice but not, Arnold noticed, his mother's. Then dry little Mr. Cram came, leaving large Mrs. Cram in the kitchen, and there was no chair left for Mr. Cram to sit in. No one asked Arnold to get up and he was unable to rise. He knew that the story had got around to them during the day about how he had gone and picked peas after he had shot his brother, and he knew that although they were talking only about Eugie they were thinking about him and if he got up, if he moved even his foot, they would all be alerted. Then Uncle Andy arrived and leaned his tall, lanky body against the doorjamb and there were two men standing.

Presently Arnold was aware that the talk had stopped. He knew without looking up that the men were watching him.

"Not a tear in his eye," said Andy, and Arnold knew that it was his uncle who had gestured the men to attention.

"He don't give a hoot, is that how it goes?" asked Sullivan, trippingly.

"He's a reasonable fellow," Andy explained. "That's what the sheriff said. It's us who ain't reasonable. If we'd of shot our brother, we'd of come runnin' back to the house, cryin' like a baby. Well, we'd of been unreasonable. What would of been the use of actin' like that? If your brother is shot dead, he's shot dead. What's the use of gettin' emotional about it? The thing to do is go down to the garden and pick peas. Am I right?"

The men around the room shifted their heavy, satisfying weight of unreasonableness.

Matthews' son Orion said: "If I'd of done what he done, Pa would've hung my pelt by the side of that big coyote's in the barn."

Arnold sat in the rocker until the last man had filed out. While his family was out in the kitchen bidding the callers good night and the cars were driving away down the dirt lane to the highway, he picked up one of the kerosene lamps and slipped quickly up the stairs. In his room he undressed by lamplight, although he and Eugie had always undressed in the dark, and not until he was lying in his bed did he blow out the flame. He felt nothing, not any grief. There was only the same immense silence and crawling inside of him; it was the way the house and fields felt under a merciless sun.

He awoke suddenly. He knew that his father was out in the yard, closing the doors of the chicken houses so that the chickens could not roam out too early and fall prey to the coyotes that came down from the mountains at daybreak. The sound that had wakened him was the step of his father as he got up from the rocker and went down the back steps. And he knew that his mother was awake in her bed.

Throwing off the covers, he rose swiftly, went down the stairs and across the dark parlor to his parents' room. He rapped on the door.

"Mother?"

From the closed room her voice rose to him, a seeking and retreating voice. "Yes?"

"Mother?" he asked insistently. He had expected her to realize that he wanted to go down on his knees by her bed and tell her that Eugie was dead. She did not know it yet, nobody knew it, and yet she was sitting up in bed, waiting to be told, waiting for him to confirm her dread. He had expected her to tell him to come in, to allow him to dig his head into her blankets and tell her about the terror he had felt when he had knelt beside Eugie. He had come to clasp her in his arms and, in his terror, to pommel[5] her breasts with his head. He put his hand upon the knob.

"Go back to bed, Arnold," she called sharply.

But he waited.

"Go back! Is night when you get afraid?"

At first he did not understand. Then, silently, he left the door and for a stricken moment stood by the rocker. Outside everything was still. The fences, the shocks of wheat seen through the window before him were so still it was as if they moved and breathed in the daytime and had fallen silent with the lateness of the hour. It was a silence that seemed to observe his father, a figure moving alone around the yard, his lantern casting a circle of light by his feet. In a few minutes his father would enter the dark house, the lantern still lighting his way.

Arnold was suddenly aware that he was naked. He had thrown off his blankets and come down the stairs to tell his mother how he felt about Eugie, but she had refused to listen to him and his nakedness had become upardonable. At once he went back up the stairs, fleeing from his father's lantern.

At breakfast he kept his eyelids lowered as if to deny the humiliating night. Nora, sitting at his left, did not pass the pitcher of milk to him and he did not ask for it. He would never again, he vowed, ask them for anything, and he ate his fried eggs and

5. **pommel:** beat

potatoes only because everybody ate meals—the cattle ate, and the cats; it was customary for everybody to eat.

"Nora, you gonna keep that pitcher for yourself?" his father asked.

Nora lowered her head unsurely.

"Pass it on to Arnold," his father said.

Nora put her hands in her lap.

His father picked up the metal pitcher and set it down at Arnold's plate.

Arnold, pretending to be deaf to the discord, did not glance up, but relief rained over his shoulders at the thought that his parents recognized him again. They must have lain awake after his father had come in from the yard: had they realized together why he had come down the stairs and knocked at their door?

"Bessie's missin' this morning," his father called out to his mother, who had gone into the kitchen. "She went up the mountain last night and had her calf, most likely. Somebody's got to go up and find her 'fore the coyotes get the calf."

That had been Eugie's job, Arnold thought. Eugie would climb the cattle trails in search of a newborn calf and come down the mountain carrying the calf across his back, with the cow running down along behind him, mooing in alarm.

Arnold ate the few more forkfuls of his breakfast, put his hands on the edge of the table and pushed back his chair. If he went for the calf he'd be away from the farm all morning. He could switch the cow down the mountain slowly, and the calf would run along at its mother's side.

When he passed through the kitchen his mother was setting a kettle of water on the stove. "Where you going?" she asked awkwardly.

"Up to get the calf," he replied, averting his face.

"Arnold?"

At the door he paused reluctantly, his back to her, knowing that she was seeking him out, as his father was doing, and he called upon his pride to protect him from them.

"Was you knocking at my door last night?"

He looked over his shoulder at her, his eyes narrow and dry.

"What'd you want?" she asked humbly.

"I didn't want nothing," he said flatly.

Then he went out the door and down the back steps, his legs trembling from the fright his answer gave him.

Meaning

1. Describe the relationship between Arnold and his mother. How has their relationship changed at the end of the story?
2. How did the accident happen? What foreshadowing is given in the first paragraph of the story?
3. Why did Arnold pick peas instead of telling his family immediately about the tragedy? Do you think that his reaction was realistic? Why or why not?
4. The night after the accident, Arnold tries to talk to his mother about Eugie's death. How does she respond, and what effect does her reaction have on Arnold?

Method

1. What purpose does the first paragraph of the story serve? What do you find out about the family, and especially about the relationship between the two brothers?
2. What is the climax of the story?
3. When do you find out how Arnold really feels about Eugene's death?
4. Arnold's father and mother both forgive Arnold and recognize that they have made a mistake. What is the evidence of their change of heart?
5. Gina Berriault has been called a pessimistic writer. Do you think "The Stone Boy" is a pessimistic story? Why or why not?

Language: Personification

You have learned that *simile* and *metaphor* are figures of speech used to compare two unlike objects. A *simile* is a comparison that includes the words *like* or *as*: "It had an obnoxious movement like that of a parasite." A metaphor is an implied comparison that does not use *like* or *as*: ". . . the blankets lifted in a great wing . . ." *Personification* in a figure of speech that gives human characteristics, such as human powers and feelings, to nonhuman or even lifeless ideas or objects. Identify which of these figures of speech is used in each of the following examples from "The Stone Boy."

1. ". . . feet stirring up the carpet of brown feathers. . . ."
2. "It was a warmth on his back, like a large hand laid firmly there. . . ."

3. "Arnold lay still as a fugitive. . . ."
4. "He could feel the morning growing heavier with sun."
5. ". . . the clock with its loudly clucking pendulum."
6. ". . . white hair like wheat stubble."

Discussion and Composition

1. Although Arnold does not react outwardly to his brother's death, by the end of the story the reader suspects that he mourns Eugie's loss deeply. Discuss why you think Arnold reacted as he did after Eugie was shot.

2. In a composition, explore the significance of the title "The Stone Boy." Explain how the title relates to Arnold and to the other characters' perceptions of him. Tell whether you think that Arnold has, in some way, become a "stone boy" by the end of the story.

JESSAMYN WEST
(1902–1984)

Born in Indiana, Jessamyn West moved with her family to Yorba Linda, California, when she was a child. Most of her writing is set in rural Indiana and California. She attended Whittier College and married shortly after graduation. She taught in a one-room schoolhouse for several years, and was studying for a doctorate in English literature at the University of California when she fell ill with tuberculosis. She tells of her mother's battle to save her life in *The Woman Said Yes* (1976).

A long recovery period from her illness gave Jessamyn West the opportunity to begin writing. As her mother nursed her back to health, she told Jessamyn about her ancestors and of their pioneer life. Working in a reclining position because she was too weak to sit at a desk, Jessamyn West wrote fictional stories based on her Quaker heritage. *The Friendly Persuasion* (1945) her first book, which was later made into a movie, is a collection of these stories.

Jessamyn West wrote novels, short stories, autobiographical books, and essays. She wrote for *The New York Times Book Review* and other critical media. She was a much sought-after lecturer and teacher in the literary community and was awarded five honorary doctorates in humane letters and literature. This story is from *Cress Delahanty* (1953), a collection of stories that originally appeared in the *New Yorker*, *The Ladies Home Journal*, *Harper's Magazine*, *Colliers*, *Woman's Day*, *The New Mexico Quarterly* and *The Colorado Quarterly*.

THEN HE GOES FREE

While her mother and father awaited the arrival of Mr. and Mrs. Kibbler who had called asking to speak to them "about Cress and Edwin Jr.," Mr. Delahanty reminded his wife how wrong she had been about Cress.

"Not two months ago," he said, "in this very room you told me you were worried because Cress wasn't as interested in the boys as a girl her age should be. In this very room. And now look what's happened."

Mrs. Delahanty, worried now by Mrs. Kibbler's message, spoke more sharply than she had intended. "Don't keep repeating, 'in this very room,'" she said, "as if it would have been different if I'd said it in the back porch or out of doors. Besides, what has happened?"

Mr. Delahanty took off his hat, which he'd had on when Mrs. Kibbler phoned, and sailed it out of the living room toward the hall table, which he missed. "Don't ask me what's happened," he said, "I'm not the girl's mother."

Mrs. Delahanty took off her own hat and jabbed the hat pins back into it. "What do you mean, you're not the girl's mother? Of course you're not. No one ever said you were."

Mr. Delahanty picked up his fallen hat, put it on the chair beside the hall table and came back into the living room. "A girl confides in her mother," he told his wife.

"A girl confides in her mother!" Mrs. Delahanty was very scornful. "Who tells you these things, John Delahanty? Not *your* mother. She didn't have any daughter. Not me. Cress doesn't confide in anyone. How do you know these things, anyway, about mothers and daughters?"

John Delahanty seated himself upon the sofa, legs extended, head back, as straight and unrelaxed as a plank.

"Don't catch me up that way, Gertrude," he said. "You know I don't know them." Without giving his wife any opportunity to crow over this victory he went on quickly: "What I'd like to know is why did the Kibblers have to pick a Saturday night for this call? Didn't they know we'd be going into town?"

Like most ranchers, John Delahanty stopped work early on Saturdays so that, after a quick clean-up and supper, he and his wife could drive into town. There they did nothing very important: bought groceries, saw a show, browsed around in hardware stores, visited friends. But after a week of seeing only themselves—the Delahanty ranch was off the main highway—it was pleasant simply to saunter along the sidewalks looking at the cars, the merchandise, the people in their town clothes. This Saturday trip to town was a jaunt they both looked forward to during the week, and tonight's trip, because of February's warmer air and suddenly, it seemed, longer twilight, would have been particularly pleasant.

"Five minutes more," said Mr. Delahanty, "and we'd have been on our way."

"Why didn't you tell Mrs. Kibbler we were just leaving?"

"I did. And she said for anything less important she wouldn't think of keeping us."

Mrs. Delahanty came over to the sofa and stood looking anxiously down at her husband. "John, exactly what did Mrs. Kibbler say?"

"The gist of it," said Mr. Delahanty, "was that . . ."

"I don't care about the gist of it. That's just what you think she said. I want to know what she really said."

Mr. Delahanty let his head fall forward, though he still kept his legs stiffly extended. "What she really said was, 'Is this Mr. John Delahanty?' And I said, 'Yes.' Then she said, 'This is Mrs. Edwin Kibbler, I guess you remember me.'"

"Remember her?" Mrs. Delahanty exclaimed. "I didn't know you even knew her."

"I don't," said Mr. Delahanty, "but I remember her all right. She came before the school board about a month ago to tell us we ought to take those two ollas[1] off the school grounds. She said it was old-fashioned to cool water that way, that the ollas looked messy and were unhygienic."

"Did you take them off?" Mrs. Delahanty asked, without thinking. As a private person John Delahanty was reasonable and untalkative. As clerk of the school board he inclined toward dogmatism[2] and long-windedness. Now he began a defense of the ollas and the school board's action in retaining them.

"Look, John," said Mrs. Delahanty, "I'm not interested in the school board or its water coolers. What I want to know is, what did Mrs. Kibbler say about Cress?"

"Well, she said she wanted to have a little talk with us about Cress—and Edwin Jr."

"I know that." Impatience made Mrs. Delahanty's voice sharp. "But what about them?"

Mr. Delahanty drew his feet up toward the sofa, then bent down and retied a shoelace. "About what Cress did to him— Edwin Jr."

1. **ollas** (ŏl′əs): wide-mouthed water jars.
2. **dogmatism** (dôg′mə·tĭz·əm): positive, authoritative statements of opinion.

"*Did* to him!" said Mrs. Delahanty aghast.

"That's what his mother said."

Mrs. Delahanty sat down on the hassock at her husband's feet. "Did to him," she repeated again. "Why, what could Cress do to him? He's two or three years older than Cress, fifteen or sixteen anyway. What could she do to him?"

Mr. Delahanty straightened up. "She could hit him, I guess." he ventured.

"Hit him? What would she want to hit him for?"

"I don't know," said Mr. Delahanty. "I don't know that she did hit him. Maybe she kicked him. Anyway, his mother seems to think the boy's been damaged in some way."

"Damaged," repeated Mrs. Delahanty angrily. "Damaged! Why, Cress is too tender-hearted to hurt a fly. She shoos them outside instead of killing them. And you sit there talking of hitting and kicking."

"Well," said Mr. Delahanty mildly, "Edwin's got teeth out. I don't know how else she could get them out, do you?"

"I'm going to call Cress," said Mrs. Delahanty, "and ask her about this. I don't believe it for a minute."

"I don't think calling her will do any good. She left while I was talking to Mrs. Kibbler."

"What do you mean, left?"

"Went for a walk, she said."

"Well, teeth out," repeated Mrs. Delahanty unbelievingly. "Teeth out! I didn't know you could get teeth out except with pliers or a chisel."

"Maybe Edwin's teeth are weak."

"Don't joke about this, John Delahanty. It isn't any joking matter. And I don't believe it. I don't believe Cress did it or that that boy's teeth are out. Anyway I'd have to see them to believe it."

"You're going to," Mr. Delahanty said. "Mrs. Kibbler's bringing Edwin especially so you can."

Mrs. Delahanty sat for some time without saying anything at all. Then she got up and walked back and forth in front of her husband, turning her hat, which she still held, round and round on one finger. "Well, what does Mrs. Kibbler expect us to do now?" she asked. "If they really are out, that is?"

"For one thing," replied Mr. Delahanty, "she expects us to

pay for some new ones. And for another . . ." Mr. Delahanty paused to listen. Faintly, in the distance a car could be heard. "Here she is now," he said.

Mrs. Delahanty stopped her pacing. "Do you think I should make some cocoa for them, John? And maybe some marguerites?"

"No, I don't," said Mr. Delahanty. "I don't think Mrs. Kibbler considers this a social visit."

As the car turned into the long driveway which led between the orange grove on one side and the lemon grove on the other to the Delahanty house, Mrs. Delahanty said, "I still don't see why you think this proves I'm wrong."

Mr. Delahanty had forgotten about his wife's wrongness. "How do you mean wrong?" he asked.

"About Cress's not being interested in the boys."

"Oh," he said. "Well, you've got to be pretty interested in a person—one way or another—before you hit him."

"That's a perfectly silly notion," began Mrs. Delahanty, but before she could finish, the Kibblers had arrived.

Mr. Delahanty went to the door while Mrs. Delahanty stood in the back of the room by the fireplace unwilling to take one step toward meeting her visitors.

Mrs. Kibbler was a small woman with a large, determined nose, prominent blue eyes and almost no chin. Her naturally curly hair—she didn't wear a hat—sprang away from her head in a great cage-shaped pompadour[3] which dwarfed her face.

Behind Mrs. Kibbler was Mr. Kibbler, short, dusty, soft-looking, bald, except for a fringe of hair about his ears so thick that the top of his head, by contrast, seemed more naked than mere lack of hair could make it.

Behind Mr. Kibbler was Edwin Jr. He was as thin as his mother, as mild and soft-looking as his father; and to these qualities he added an unhappiness all of his own. He gave one quick look at the room and the Delahantys through his thick-lensed spectacles, after which he kept his eyes on the floor.

Mr. Delahanty closed the door behind the callers, then introduced his wife to Mrs. Kibbler. Mrs. Kibbler in turn introduced her family to the Delahantys. While the Kibblers were seating

---

3. **pompadour** (p̆om'pə·dôr): hairstyle in which the hair is combed up and back from the forehead, often over a roll.

themselves—Mrs. Kibbler and Edwin Jr. on the sofa, Mr. Kibbler on a straight-backed chair in the room's darkest corner—Mrs. Delahanty, out of nervousness, bent and lit the fire, which was laid in the fireplace, though the evening was not cold enough for it. Then she and Mr. Delahanty seated themselves in the chairs on each side of the fireplace.

Mrs. Kibbler looked at the fire with some surprise. "Do you find it cold this evening, Mrs. Delahanty?" she asked.

"No," said Mrs. Delahanty, "I don't. I don't know why I lit the fire."

To this Mrs. Kibbler made no reply. Instead, without preliminaries, she turned to her son. "Edwin," she said, "show the Delahantys what their daughter did to your teeth."

Mrs. Delahanty wanted to close her eyes, look into the fire, or find, as Edwin Jr. had done, a spot of her own on the floor to examine. There was an almost imperceptible[4] ripple along the length of the boy's face as if he had tried to open his mouth but found he lacked the strength. He momentarily lifted his eyes from the floor to dart a glance into the dark corner where his father sat. But Mr. Kibbler continued to sit in expressionless silence.

"Edwin," said Mrs. Kibbler, "speak to your son."

"Do what your mother says, son," said Mr. Kibbler.

Very slowly, as if it hurt him, Edwin opened his mouth.

His teeth were white, and in his thin face they seemed very large, as well. The two middle teeth, above, had been broken across in a slanting line. The lower incisor[5] appeared to be missing entirely.

"Wider, Edwin," Mrs. Kibbler urged. "I want the Delahantys to see exactly what their daughter is responsible for."

But before Edwin could make any further effort Mrs. Delahanty cried, "No, that's enough."

"I didn't want you to take our word for anything," Mrs. Kibbler said reasonably. "I wanted you to see."

"Oh, we see, all right," said Mrs. Delahanty earnestly.

Mr. Delahanty leaned forward and spoke to Mrs. Kibbler. "While we see the teeth, Mrs. Kibbler, it just isn't a thing we think Crescent would do. Or in fact how she *could* do it. We think Edwin must be mistaken."

---

4. imperceptible (ĭm′pər·sĕp′·tə·bəl): too small or slight to be noticed.
5. incisor (ĭn·sī′zer): a cutting tooth at the front of the jaw.

"You mean lying?" asked Mrs. Kibbler flatly.

"Mistaken," repeated Mr. Delahanty.

"Tell them, Edwin," said Mrs. Kibbler.

"She knocked me down," said Edwin, very low.

Mrs. Delahanty, although she was already uncomfortably warm, held her hands nearer the fire, even rubbed them together a time or two.

"I simply can't believe that," she said.

"You mean hit you with her fist and knocked you down?" asked Mr. Delahanty.

"No," said Edwin even lower than before. "Ran into me."

"But not on purpose," said Mrs. Delahanty.

Edwin nodded. "Yes," he said. "On purpose."

"But why?" asked Mr. Delahanty. "Why? Cress wouldn't do such a thing, I know—without some cause. Why?"

"Tell them why, Edwin," said his mother.

Edwin's head went even nearer the floor—as if the spot he was watching had diminished or retreated.

"For fun," he said.

It was impossible not to believe the boy as he sat there hunched, head bent, one eyelid visibly twitching. "But Cress would never do such a thing," said Mrs. Delahanty.

Mrs. Kibbler disregarded this. "It would not have been so bad, Mr. Delahanty, except that Edwin was standing by one of those ollas. When your daughter shoved Edwin over she shoved the olla over, too. That's probably what broke his teeth. Heavy as cement and falling down on top of him and breaking up in a thousand pieces. To say nothing of his being doused with water on a cold day. And Providence[6] alone can explain why his glasses weren't broken."

"What had you done, Edwin?" asked Mrs. Delahanty again.

"Nothing," whispered Edwin.

"All we want," said Mrs. Kibbler, "is what's perfectly fair. Pay the dentist's bill. And have that girl of yours apologize to Edwin."

Mrs. Delahanty got up suddenly and walked over to Edwin. She put one hand on his thin shoulder and felt him twitch under her touch like a frightened colt.

---

6. **Providence** (prŏv′ ə dəns): the care and help of a supernatural being or force.

"Go on, Edwin," she said. "Tell me the truth. Tell me why."

Edwin slowly lifted his head. "Go on, Edwin," Mrs. Delahanty encouraged him.

"He told you once," said Mrs. Kibbler. "Fun. That girl of yours is a big, boisterous thing from all I hear. She owes my boy an apology."

Edwin's face continued to lift until he was looking directly at Mrs. Delahanty.

He started to speak—but had said only three words, "Nobody ever wants," when Cress walked in from the hall. She had evidently been there for some time, for she went directly to Edwin.

"I apologize for hurting you, Edwin," she said.

Then she turned to Mrs. Kibbler. "I've got twelve seventy-five saved for a bicycle. That can go to help pay for his teeth."

After the Kibblers left, the three Delahantys sat for some time without saying a word. The fire had about died down and outside an owl, hunting finished, flew back toward the hills, softly hooting.

"I guess if we hurried we could just about catch the second show," Mr. Delahanty said.

"I won't be going to shows for a while," said Cress.

The room was very quiet. Mrs. Delahanty traced the outline of one of the bricks in the fireplace.

"I can save twenty-five cents a week that way. Toward his teeth," she explained.

Mrs. Delahanty took the poker and stirred the coals so that for a second there was an upward drift of sparks; but the fire was too far gone to blaze. Because it had not yet been completely dark when the Kibblers came, only one lamp had been turned on. Now that night had arrived the room was only partially lighted; but no one seemed to care. Mr. Delahanty, in Mr. Kibbler's dark corner, was almost invisible. Mrs. Delahanty stood by the fireplace. Cress sat where Edwin had sat, looking downward, perhaps at the same spot at which he had looked.

"One day at school," she said, "Edwin went out in the fields at noon and gathered wild flower bouquets for everyone. A lupine, a poppy, two barley heads, four yellow violets. He tied them together with blades of grass. They were sweet little bouquets. He went without his lunch to get them fixed, and when we came back from eating there was a bouquet on every desk in the study hall. It looked like a flower field when we came in and Edwin did it to surprise us."

After a while Mr. Delahanty asked, "Did the kids like that?"

"Yes, they liked it. They tore their bouquets apart," said Cress, "and used the barley beards to tickle each other. Miss Ingols made Edwin gather up every single flower and throw it in the wastepaper basket."

After a while Cress said, "Edwin has a collection of bird feathers. The biggest is from a buzzard, the littlest from a hummingbird. They're all different colors. The brightest is from a woodpecker."

"Does he kill birds," Mr. Delahanty asked, "just to get a feather?"

"Oh, no!" said Cress. "He just keeps his eyes open to where a bird might drop a feather. It would spoil his collection to get a feather he didn't find that way."

Mr. Delahanty sighed and stirred in his wooden chair so that it creaked a little.

"Edwin would like to be a missionary to China," said Cress. Some particle in the fireplace as yet unburned, blazed up in a sudden spurt of blue flame. "Not a preaching missionary," she explained.

"A medical missionary?" asked Mr. Delahanty.

"Oh, no! Edwin says he's had to take too much medicine to ever be willing to make other people take it."

There was another long silence in the room. Mrs. Delahanty sat down in the chair her husband had vacated and once more held a hand toward the fire. There was just enough life left in the coals to make the tips of her fingers rosy. She didn't turn toward Cress at all or ask a single question. Back in the dusk Cress's voice went on.

"He would like to teach them how to play baseball."

Mr. Delahanty's voice was matter-of-fact. "Edwin doesn't look to me like he would be much of a baseball player."

"Oh he isn't," Cress agreed. "He isn't even any of a baseball player. But he could be a baseball authority. Know everything and teach by diagram. That's what he'd have to do. And learn from them how they paint. He says some of their pictures look like they had been painted with one kind of bird feather and some with another. He knows they don't really paint with bird feathers," she explained. "That's just a fancy of his."

The night wind moving in off the Pacific began to stir the eucalyptus[7] trees in the windbreak.[8] Whether the wind blew off sea or desert, didn't matter, the long eucalyptus leaves always lifted and fell with the same watery, surflike sound.

"I'm sorry Edwin happened to be standing by that olla," said Mr. Delahanty. "That's what did the damage, I suppose."

"Oh, he had to stand there," said Cress. "He didn't have any choice. That's the mush pot."

"Mush pot," repeated Mr. Delahanty.

"It's a circle round the box the olla stands on," said Crescent. "Edwin spends about his whole time there. While we're waiting for the bus anyway."

"Crescent," asked Mr. Delahanty, "what is this mush pot?"

"It's prison," said Cress, surprise in her voice. "It's where the prisoners are kept. Only at school we always call it the mush pot."

"Is this a game?" asked Mr. Delahanty.

"It's dare base," said Crescent. "Didn't you ever play it? You choose up sides. You draw two lines and one side stands in the middle and tries to catch the other side as they run by. Nobody ever chooses Edwin. The last captain to choose just gets him. Because he can't help himself. They call him the handicap. He gets caught first thing and spends the whole game in the mush pot because nobody will waste any time trying to rescue him. He'd just get caught again, they say, and the whole game would be nothing but rescue Edwin."

"How do you rescue anyone, Cress?" asked her father.

"Run from home base to the mush pot without being caught. Then take the prisoner's hand. Then he goes free."

"Were you trying to rescue Edwin, Cress?"

Cress didn't answer her father at once. Finally she said, "It was my duty. I chose him for our side. I chose him first of all and didn't wait just to get him. So it was my duty to rescue him. Only I ran too hard and couldn't stop. And the olla fell down on top of him and knocked his teeth out. And humiliated him. But he was free," she said. "I got there without being caught."

---

7. **eucalyptus** (yo͞o′kə lĭp′təs): a tall tree native to Australia.
8. **windbreak:** fence row of trees that protects from the wind.

Mrs. Delahanty spoke with a great surge of warmth and anger. "Humiliated him! When you were only trying to help him. Trying to rescue him. And you were black and blue for days yourself! What gratitude."

Cress said, "But he didn't want to be rescued, Mother. Not by me anyway. He said he liked being in the mush pot. He said . . . he got there on purpose . . . to observe. He gave me back the feathers I'd found for him. One was a road-runner feather. The only one he had."

"Well, you can start a feather collection of your own," said Mr. Delahanty with energy. "I often see feathers when I'm walking through the orchard. After this I'll save them for you."

"I'm not interested in feathers," said Cress. Then she added, "I can get two bits an hour any time suckering[9] trees for Mr. Hudson or cleaning blackboards at school. That would be two fifty a week at least. Plus the twelve seventy-five. How much do you suppose his teeth will be?"

"Cress," said her father, "you surely aren't going to let the Kibblers go on thinking you knocked their son down on purpose, are you? Do you want Edwin to think that?"

"Edwin doesn't really think that," Cress said. "He knows I was rescuing him. But now I've apologized—and if we pay for the new teeth and everything, maybe after a while he'll believe it."

She stood up and walked to the hall doorway. "I'm awfully tired," she said. "I guess I'll go to bed."

"But Cress," asked Mrs. Delahanty, "why do you want him to believe it? When it isn't true?"

Cress was already through the door, but she turned back to explain. "You don't knock people down you are sorry for," she said.

After Cress had gone upstairs Mrs. Delahanty said, "Well, John, you were right, of course."

"Right?" asked Mr. Delahanty, again forgetful.

"About Cress's being interested in the boys."

"Yes," said Mr. Delahanty. "Yes, I'm afraid I was."

9. **suckering**: removing shoots, pruning.

Meaning

1. Who seems to understand Cress better in this story—her mother or her father? Give reasons for your answer.
2. Contrast Mr. and Mrs. Kibbler with Mr. and Mrs. Delahanty. How do their relationships differ: husband to wife; parents to child?
3. What do you think Edwin started to say just before Cress walked in from the hall? Why do you think she came in at that moment?
4. How did Cress feel about Edwin before she knocked him down? Have her feelings changed at the end of the story? How do you know?

Method

1. The author reveals to you gradually why the Kibblers are coming over to visit the Delahantys. Why do you think she does not tell you at the beginning of the story?
2. How do the Kibblers' outward appearance and manner provide clues to their character and personality?
3. The main character, Cress, does not appear until the story is half over. Before you actually meet her in the story, how has the author prepared you to accept the kind of person she is?
4. What is the *mood*, or prevailing feeling, of the story? Is the mood the same at the end of the story? If not, how and why has it changed?

Language: Abstract and Concrete Words

An *abstract* word represents a generality, quality, or characteristic that may be difficult to define. An abstract word is a word such as *beauty* or *truth*—an idea that cannot be perceived by the senses.

A *concrete* word, on the other hand, stands for something that can be perceived by the senses, a word such as *chair* or *table*. Concrete words can be more or less specific. The word *rocker*, for example, is more specific than *chair*, but *chair* is more specific than *furniture*.

The following words have been taken from the story. Decide which words are abstract and which are concrete. Look again at each of the concrete words and decide which are the most specific.

1. victory	7. teeth	13. violets
2. birds	8. incisors	14. stores
3. hummingbird	9. flowers	15. bicycle
4. fun	10. notion	16. minutes
5. apology	11. plank	17. circle
6. Providence	12. impatience	18. handicap

Discussion and Composition

1. Although you may not have been familiar with "dare base," Cress' clear explanation probably helped you to visualize the game. In a paragraph or two, explain a game that you know well for someone who has never played it. Before you begin writing, you may find it helpful to make an outline listing the rules of the game step by step. Include all of the information your reader would need in order to play the game.

2. On page 264, each of the Kibblers is described vividly in two or three sentences. Describe someone you know or an imaginary character in fifty words or less. Be sure that all of your details convey a single main impression of the person you are describing. To help you in focusing on relevant details, you might begin by making a list of words and phrases that describe the person's appearance, personality, and actions. Then select details from your list that will contribute to the main impression you wish to create.

HELEN NORRIS

(born 1916)

Novelist and short-story writer Helen Norris was born in Miami, Florida, but has lived most of her life in Alabama. She graduated from the University of Alabama in Tuscaloosa, and she was a professor for many years at Huntingdon College in Montgomery. Although Norris's roots are in the South, her writing is not limited to regional concerns; instead, her stories span a variety of settings and themes.

In her fiction, Norris tries to avoid what she calls "bloodless writing"—stories and characters that fail to arouse strong feelings in the reader. Her colorful and vibrant characters live fully, and their struggles to understand themselves and their world capture the reader's sympathies.

Since the publication of her first novel in 1940, Norris has received numerous awards for her writing. Her most recent novel, *Walk with the Sickle Moon*, was published in 1989. She has published two collections of short stories, and the title story of her collection *The Christmas Wife* has been dramatized for television.

THE SINGING WELL

She was Emilu, named for two dead aunts, their names rammed together head-on like trains. And she thought as she lay on her back in the corn, racing her feet a toe at a time up the head-high stalks, letting one foot, then the other win: How you gonna handle these things that come up? Get around these grown-ups pushin' you into some kinda way you never wanted to be? But if you grew up so you could outsmart 'em, then you did what they wanted. You got yourself grown and no turnin' back. And maybe you couldn't stand it that way and waited around and hoped you would die, with cancer even, just to get it over. The way it seemed to her a lot of them did.

She was past eleven going on twelve and out of the torment of school for a while. The days of summer were long at first and then ran away like a rabbit flushed out of a blackberry bush. It scared her some, not just to be looking down the barrel of school. Eleven years old and going on twelve, she was staring right now both ways at once. She had got her feet planted plumb in the ground to keep from getting any older at all. But all the time she needed to get there. She had to know more, just to stay the same.

She knew that she was smarter than Melissa, her sister who grew up enough to get married. And smarter than Jo-Jo, who was off at their Uncle Joe's for the summer. But it wasn't sufficient. This thing coming at her was as big as a barn. Plowing her up into something else. Sometimes it was a freight train running her down. Sometimes she felt she was in there swimming and going under for the final time.

And then her grandfather came in July and she grabbed ahold of him to keep afloat.

How can you grow up when you have a grandfather like a Santa Claus with his beard cut off and he calls you little daughter and feeds you peanuts one at a time?

When he got out of the truck with her father, bigger almost than she had remembered, her mother said, "Emilu, run carry that box he's got in his hand. Lord knows what's in it." Emilu ran and dropped it hard coming up the steps. It flew apart, with an old uniform falling into the nandinas. And her mother said, "Well, I might've known. Well, bring it on in."

He was in his room when she got it together. The door was ajar. She waited in the hall. When she heard silence she edged in slowly with the box in her arms. He was sitting on the brass bed all hunched over, his chin down into the front of his shirt. His chest caved in and his face was like he was sorry he came.

She said to him then, "I folded it good." They looked at one another across the years between. Her mother had said he was seventy-seven. "It's got real pretty buttons sewed on."

He must have been, easy, six foot tall and big around. Like a football player with everything on, and shoulders big and round like a bear's. He had a great head of wavy white hair that curled around and under his ears. A sunned kind of face without many lines and blue-fire eyes that were almost hidden by the shelf of his brow and the white eyebrows that went so wild they must have been raked in the wrong direction. His hands were huge and brown from the sun, with white hairs matting on the backs of his fingers. His glance wavered, then returned to her. There was something in it different this visit from last.

"Are you Melissa?" he asked.

She was surprised and even shocked at his words. "No, Grandpa, I'm Emmy." He had called her that.

"Emmy?" He looked at the mirror above the green-painted dresser. "Not Melissa?"

"No, sir . . . Melissa got married and lives in Lafayette."

His glance swept her with such a lost look that she told him again, "I'm Emmy, sir."

He was very strange. But his blue eyes beheld her without a rejection. "Emmy . . . Emmy . . ." He moved a little inside his great frame and rubbed his arm. "I'll tell you how it is."

She waited for him to tell her but he seemed to have forgotten or thought better of it. "What, Grandpa?"

His eyes circled the room. "Is this the same room I stayed in before?"

"Sure, Grandpa."

"Same mirror and all?"

"Sure it is . . . You don't remember?"

He looked at her hard. "I'll tell you how it is: I don't recall you."

She was really amazed, but she tried not to show it. "We played euchre and all. You taught me, remember? Slapjack. Every day."

He shook his head slowly. "No. No, I don't recall." He spoke so sadly that she wanted to run away. "But it seems like whoever you are . . . it seems like a good thing, you standin' here now." He smiled at her almost. "We was good friends, you say?"

"We played euchre every day."

"What did I call you?"

"Emmy. You called me Emmy, like everybody does exceptin' Mama."

"You feel right. Somehow. How old would you be?"

"Eleven last month. I was nine before."

She couldn't wait to tell her mother.

"We shouldn't have him this summer. I said so to your father. He looks healthy. I will say that. I can't deny he's a downright specimen of health." Then she flattened her lips. "But his mind . . ."

"What's wrong with it?" said Emilu.

"Well, it's gone, that's all."

Emilu was defensive. "He talks all right."

"Talks!" her mother said and turned away to run water on the beans. "Just stay out of his way."

"Why?"

Her mother flung a sideways look at her. "Folks that get full of notions." And she left the room with the water still on.

Emilu sucked the knuckle of her finger. Her mother never came right out and answered a question. You thought you had her on the track and then she ducked into a side road.

Emilu ran out the back and circled the house. She could look through the window and see him on the bed. He hadn't moved. He seemed just the way he was two years ago. They stared at each other the way she had looked at a deer she met once that Jo-Jo had trapped and he looked at her knowing she wasn't the one did it but there he was in the fix he was in. She came in the front door and down the hall to him again.

He seemed glad she was there. She sat down at length on the chair by his bed. Then he opened his suitcase and rumpled around and came up with a bag of peanuts. He sat back on the bed and gave one to her and one to himself. They were very still while they looked at one another across their chewing.

That night before she went off to sleep she could hear him moving in the room across the hall, then a scraping sound, a sour wail of furniture being dragged across the floor. It went on for some time. She could hear her mother in the room next to hers. "My God, what's he doin'? I can't stand it, Ray." She heard her father's muffled voice . . .

And then it was daylight. The wind outside was rattling the shutters. She woke up thinking it was still the furniture being dragged around, then knowing it wasn't.

When she went to his room she saw the dresser standing slap across the corner. And now a square of dust marked the place it had been. He was sitting on the bed looking out of the window at the waving trees.

She was full of the morning. "How come you moved the dresser around in the night?"

He looked at her with haunted eyes.

"Grandpa . . . how come?"

He shook his head. "It ain't the same room," he said at last.

She started to tell him that it really was, but she stopped herself. She could hear the geese being chased by the dog. She could hear the bus passing, rounding the curve, and then taking the hill. She sat on the bed and swung her feet. "You wanta play euchre?"

He shook his head. "I don't recall it none."

"You taught me, Grandpa. I could teach you how. I remember it real good."

"Wouldn't serve. I'd fergit."

She said with pride, "I never forgot nothin' I ever knew."

He shook his head in wonder. "It goes," he said. "I can't figger where it goes, but it goes all right . . . I think when it all goes what'll I be then? What'll I be just a settin' somewhere? Sometimes it scares the livin' hell outa me."

She swung her feet. "I know ever dadblasted thing ever happen to me."

"You think so, little daughter. But there is things gittin' away from you in the night when you fergit to hold on."

She shook her head. "Not me. I got it all somewhere. In my head, I reckon."

"Course you ain't live long. There just ain't that much."

"There's a plenty, I guarantee. There is plenty done happen."

"Well, hold onto it, little daughter."

"I'm a holdin' on."

She got up and walked to the square of dust where the dresser had been. With her toe she scraped a circle and a zigzag line. "Slapjack is nothin' to it. How long you figger you can hold onto somethin'?"

"No way a tellin'. Hard to say, little daughter."

She swallowed twice. "You called me that before . . . when you were here before. You called me little daughter."

"Did I, now? I musta liked you mighty well."

"Oh, you did. You did. Better than the others. Sometimes we sung songs. On the porch. In the dark. We sung 'Old Black Joe' and 'Oh! Susannah, don't you cry for me . . .'" She was pleading now.

"I don't recall," he said.

A feeling of hopelessness swept over her. The two of them sat there locked in mourning.

"We got to start over," he told her gently. "You willin', little daughter?"

She was sad in a way she had never been before. He patted her hair. "You willin', little daughter?"

But she did not reply.

"Was you wearin' your hair a little different?" he said.

"Just the same," she said faintly and shook her brown mane. "Chopped off straight. I just can't stand it no other way."

"You willin', little daughter? It's hard," he acknowledged. "I know it ain't fair . . ."

Her voice was uncertain. "But it seems like you don't want to start over, Grandpa. I could help but it seems like you don't want to try."

He was silent for a while. "I got somethin' on my mind, little daughter, to 'tend to . . . I can't think of nothin' else. It's on me night and day."

"What is it?" she said.

"It's a misty thing now. But what's so strong is how good it was. Good. Good. If I could remember it. If I could get it back once and then tell somebody who wouldn't let go . . ."

He looked at her with something like a plea in his eyes. "That's where maybe you could come in."

"Where, Grandpa?"

"You gonna come in two ways, little mother. You gonna help me remember and then you take it from me and you don't let it go."

"So I can tell you again in case you forget?"

"No . . . no. I wouldn't need it again. Just need you to have it. Just to not let it go. Now, I gonna die. Someday not far away. Who cares?"

"I care, Grandpa." Then she said, disbelieving, "But someday I'm gonna die."

"Don't you think it. You gonna live forever. And if you felt yourself slippin' you could tell somebody . . . You could tell the best person you happen to know . . . like I'm tellin' you . . . when I git it back."

"Am I the best person you know?"

"You are the one best person left with any walkin'-about sense."

She swung her feet. "That ain't the general opinion around here."

"It's mine," he said.

"What about Grandma?"

"Best woman I ever knew. But she's gone, you know."

He stared out the window. "There was a thing that happen to me once. Best thing ever happen. I never told nobody, it was that good."

"You gonna tell me?"

"I'm gonna tell you if I can recall it. *If* I can recall it. If . . . if."

"If it was that good, how come you forgot it?" She was sorry she'd said it, for his face clouded over.

"I ain't entirely done that, little daughter. There's somethin' still there. But it don't come together. I hold onto one thing and somethin' else goes . . . It's gotta be the right kinda weather for holdin'. Today is no good. There's a wind a blowin'. We could work on it maybe we could tomorrow."

She listened to the sucking of wind in the eaves and beyond it the murmur of wind in the corn.

"When it blows I can't recollect one damn thing."

He did not seem to want to talk anymore. She studied a stain on the papered ceiling and decided it looked like a crow or a buzzard. After a while she got up. His eyes had gone into the cave of his brows.

"Grandpa," she said, "you gonna recollect it. I double-dog guarantee it you will."

She went outside and raced up the bank that surrounded the yard. The house was built in a wooded hollow that held a fall of rain like a bowl. She walked barefoot through the rim of corn her father had planted to hold the bank. The silk was bronzed and hung from the ears in tassels that seemed to beckon the wind. She pulled away some and stuffed it into her own two ears. She closed her eyes and between the rows wandered deaf and blind, groping for stalks, plunging, weaving one row with another. But still she could hear a bird mournfully chirping. She followed its cry. "I hear you, little bird . . . I'm comin', little bird . . . You need me, little bird." She stepped on a rock and opened her eyes. Standing on one foot, she spat on her toe and rubbed it up and down and sideways.

His door, when she passed it again, was still open and she looked inside. He was sitting in the chair. The box for the uniform was in his lap. He looked at her as if she had never left the room. "I see a well. . . . But it's blowin' too hard. Too hard to tell."

At last she said, "Grandpa? What happened had a well?"

He moved his head slowly from side to side. "Hold onto it," he said. That night before she slept she seemed to hear him singing in his room across the hall. It was a strange kind of tune. But not a tune at all, as if the notes got lost and he had to start again.

Her mother was a woman who put up food. When she was settled down into it somebody seemed to have started a war, and

Emilu said the next bus that came she was climbing on. Each day was closer to the end of the world till it felt like a yell coming out of her chest. You better clear out or you'd get yourself sliced and chopped and crushed and scorched and stirred, boiled over and mopped from the stove and the floor. Her mother pink-faced, with pale hair loose and hanging in strings that had got in the jam or the succotash. "Emilu, will you hand me the mop?" And her daddy saying, "Mavis, when are we eatin'?" "Well, Ray, you see me. I can't let go. Well, fix yourself somethin'. Emilu, fix your father somethin' to eat." And Emilu saying under her breath, "This family is nuts," and thinking that for a grown-up man her father was as helpless as Barrelhead, who had to have something dumped in his dish. How come you could call yourself fully growed-up, enough to have half of your hair done gone, and couldn't slide a piece of cheese into some bread?

"I ain't gonna never get married," she said. "I double-dog guarantee it I won't."

"Suit yourself," said her mother.

"I double-dog guarantee if I did I wouldn't put nothin' up in jars. It like to ruin ever summer there is."

"Watch your tongue, Emmy," her father said.

What with living through all the fury of canning, half the time she would go what somebody present would call too far and get sent from the table before dessert. Now that her grandfather was here for the summer, her mother cut her eyes to him as Emilu rose. "I hate to have your grandfather see you like this."

"He'll have to get used to it," Emilu said. "Ever'thing around here ends up I did it."

She went to her room and lay on her bed with her feet against the headboard. Without turning over she could reach underneath and ease out the box that held her secret things. On the lid she had written "Keep out or die." She opened it on her stomach and went through all its contents. A large dead June bug, a stick of teaberry gum, and a valentine that pictured a fluffy iced cake and was inscribed underneath: "You are the icing on my cake." On the back was printed "I could devour you" and below, "Guess who" with a series of question marks. She had thought it came from Alma, but Alma said no, it was probably a boy. She reviewed the possibility with horror and delight. She tore the gum in half and chewed out the sweet of it to make up for dessert.

Later on, she heard her grandfather moving the dresser around in his room. She got up and went to him. He had pushed it back into the place where it belonged.

He looked at her from where he stood by the window. "That woman muddies up my mind."

"You mean Mama?" she asked.

"I don't recall her," he said. "Was she here before?"

Emilu nodded.

"Well, she muddies my mind. Some women clear things. Your grandma . . . she did."

"What about me, Grandpa?"

"You clear things, little woman."

Her throat filled with pride.

"I been tryin' to get it straight."

She thought at first he meant who everyone was. But then she saw he meant the thing that had happened once. She heard her mother coming down the hall and slammed the door. She went and sat on the bed. "We gotta think about it harder."

He watched her in a kind of rich despair.

"Today is good," she said, coaxing him. "No rain. The sun is shinin'. The wind ain't blowin'."

He dropped into the chair before her. He hunched his head deep into the cave of his shoulders.

She sat and willed him to remember, holding her breath in as long as she could, plunging from one breathful into another.

"Little daughter . . ."

She sat stone-still and waited.

"There's a kinda mist . . . but I see a well . . ."

Still she waited. Then she said softly, as if she stroked a bird, "You already saw that, Grandpa." She waited again. "I got it for you."

He turned to look at her deeply. "You got it locked up tight? You won't fergit?"

She shook her head. "I got it."

She slung the hair from her eyes to see the things in his face. "Was it a real long time ago?"

"I reckon. It gits so it don't hardly matter when. It gits in your head and it don't hardly matter when it was. It's like it was in your blood," he said. "It's like it was always there."

There was pain in her chest from slowing her breath.

He began at last, "There comes a singin' in and outa my mind."

"I heard you singin' some in the night."

"It gits lost somewhere."

She smoothed his spread with a freckled hand. "It don't have to get lost with me to listen. I remember every tune I ever heard, I guarantee. Words too." She waited for him. "Is it got some words to it, Grandpa?"

"I can't hardly say. I hear the tune, the way it went . . ."

She swung her feet and then she made them stop. "Maybe if you was to shut your eyes like it was dark."

He stared at her fiercely from under his wild brows. She could see in his eyes how it was he sailed his mind like a kite on a string and the two of them watched it soar above the house. He was seeing her now as if she was the string that he wouldn't let go. "I hear a kinda beat like a heartbeat in the ground. I hear it but I feel it."

"What is it?" she said.

"It was turnin' red."

"And singin'?" she said.

His mind caught in the branches of the sycamore behind him.

"And singin', Grandpa?"

He was caught. He was lost.

She was waiting and wishing the tree frogs would shut up their racket for once. Barrelhead the dog began to bark at the squirrels. The bus in the distance had almost made the hill. At last she said, "Grandpa?"

His eyes had never left her face.

"Do you think you might of dreamed it?"

"No! No! It happened. Don't never say that again . . . Just hold onto what I give you. Are you doin' that, Mother?"

"I got it ever bit."

Sometimes he seemed to think that she was her grandmother whom she had never known. Sometimes she seemed to be his daughter, Aunt Lou, her father's sister whose name was part of her own. She was afraid to ask. She wanted him to have her whichever way he would.

Slowly, very slowly, his eyes lost light and seemed to recede beneath the crag of his brow. A dark, baffled look came over his face. "I lost it," he said.

They sat together, grieving, hearing the guineas gone to roost in the tree.

"I lost it," he said. Over the hill the train hit the bridge with a mournful cry and beat along the trestle and echoed in the hollow.

She went out and crossed the road and climbed the hill. If a bus came by beneath she liked to practice her aim and pitch a rock at its roof. There was no bus in sight. It was maybe too late. She slithered down the hill to the tracks and walked a rail. It was cold as winter ice. She had learned how to skip along the rail and never fall. She skipped to a killdeer sitting on the track and flipped a rock to make him fly. She used to put nails where the train would make them flat. Her father said it was illegal. Now she felt a mingling of yearning and defiance. In the failing light she found a lid from a snuff can tossed between the ties. She laid it on the rail and willed the train to change it into something shining that had never been before.

After supper was over she went to her room. She lay on her back with her head at the foot to keep from going to sleep, legs perfectly straight, staring into the dark. She listened to the silence in her grandfather's room. She probed her own mind for the memory he sought, thrusting to the darkness and beyond to where it lay. Then the night opened like a hole in a gunnysack and covered her head. In a moment she slept . . .

But she woke in the dark to the sound of his song. She lay still and listened. It was almost her dream. She got up and tiptoed to his door.

His singing was strange. It was not any song she had ever heard before. It had no words, just his voice, a little cracked, humming, calling the notes, as if he were lulling her back into sleep. She rubbed her eyes awake and listened intently with her ear to the door. She hummed beneath her breath until the tune was in her head. Then she slipped back to bed and sang it to herself till she had it for good. She sang it to the train and it answered her back as it skimmed the rails, making something shining for her in the dark.

The next day after lunch her mother called her to the kitchen to pick up the clean clothes and put them away.

"Emilu, I wish you'd stay away from those tracks. I knew a woman caught her foot in them once, and along came the train."

"What happened?"

"What happened! She got killed, that's what."

"Did she get it caught where the rails got hitched or under the rail or under the tie?"

"Now, how would I know? She didn't live to tell us."

"I bet she was wearin' shoes . . . I wouldn't have on shoes."

Her mother left the room with the towels. Emilu called out, "Was she kin to us?"

"No, she wasn't kin. Nobody kin to us would do a crazy thing like that."

"If she wasn't kin to us I bet it never happened. Somebody made it up to scare people off a trains."

Her mother appeared in the doorway. "Emilu, it's time you grew up to your age."

"I ain't got the slightest idea what that means." She looked at her toes and the bottoms of her feet.

She went out to the barn and stared a hen in the eye and shooed the red one off her nest. She took one of the three tan-colored eggs and put it in her pocket and whistled from the doorway. After a while she walked behind the sycamore tree and pulled a leaf and laid it on the ground and broke the egg into it neatly. She knelt and touched the sulfur half-moon with the tip of her tongue. Then she called to Barrelhead to come and get it.

She went looking for her grandfather and found him asleep beneath the sugarberry tree. She sat down beside him.

She watched him sleep, his white hair stirring in the breeze. Crickets were jumping from the grass to brush his great brown hand that hung from the arm of the wicker chair. He was the oldest person she had ever known, and at the same time he was like a little baby that needed a mother. Nobody but herself would pay him any mind. Her mother seemed to think he was too much trouble just to have at the table, and now she let Emilu take his breakfast to his room. And her father never talked to him hardly at all. They talked around him at the table like he wasn't there . . . She began to sing softly the song she had heard him making in the night. She sang it over and over again till after a while it seemed to be her song for singing him asleep. He woke up and listened with his eyes half closed. Then he shut them again and she thought he'd drifted off. But in a moment he said, "It was a woman done the singin'. It was like I was dreamin'. But when I come to she was singin' for real."

She listened in wonder. "Was it Grandma done the singin'?"

"No . . . no. But the moon was the brightest I ever seen."

He went to sleep again.

Her mother came to look at him and shake her head. "If it starts to rain I want that wicker chair inside."

"Mama," said Emilu, "can't you see he's asleep!"

"Well, I see that, Emilu. I don't need to be told. But if he's here for the summer we'll have to have things understood."

"I ain't got the slightest idea what that means."

"Never mind what it means. But I wish you wouldn't hang around him all the time."

"First it's the tracks and now it's Grandpa. There is more things around that I ain't got permission than there is I can do."

"Watch your tongue, Emilu."

Emilu stuck out her tongue and crossed her eyes to see it.

She had her supper and just before dark, while they sat around the table, she climbed the hill. The dark rails were now almost the color of the ground. They were like velvet ribbons you could hardly see. She skipped along on till she came to the shining round disc that caught the light from the sky. The lid from the snuff can was like silver money and thin as thin. She picked it up and kissed it again and again.

She heard a mewing sound and turned to see that Barrelhead had followed her. He could sound like a cat enough to fool a kitten. "Go back," she commanded. "Barrelhead, go back." He sat down at once, blinking his eyes into the risen moon. Finally he turned and slunk away up the hill. "And don't you go blabbin' on me," she called.

Then she was walking the rail in moonlight, treading its silver. To make her free, in her mouth she held the silver disc with its faint snuff taste of honey and spice. Free of growing up . . . whatever it was.

She heard in the distance the song of the train. It was calling to her like the bird in the corn. She was nearing the trestle. Deep in the iron her bare feet knew the yielding and tremor. The hollow below her was faintly in bloom. She walked straight on as she stepped to the bridge and boarded the trestle. The rails sang out. Around the curve toward her the great beast hurtled; she saw the trees ashen in its aureole of light. It sprang to the trestle. The white rails stammered. The churning of wheels. And then the glory of the shining rails.

Sucked into thunder, she turned and ran. Buried in thunder, running in terror, reaching the end, dropping to the gulley to dwell forever in the house of thunder. She was rolling over, naked to the storm. Her heart was drowned, her life dissolving in the roar of the wheels.

She came to rest at the bottom of the gulley. She floated over the world like foam. The frogs came back, tremulous, halting, then mounting a tenor of sad betrayal, then screaming as they remembered their song. She lay very still, and after a while she pitched her trembling voice to theirs. She could not tell if she made a sound. But beneath the moon she heard the singing in the well. She herself was in the well and heard the voice spilling down. For a moment she thought that she was dead, stone-cold train-dead.

The cry rose inside her: If I got myself killed nobody could help. I'm the onliest one there is knows about the well. Not even Grandpa remembers it now.

She got up slowly and clawed her way through vines and frogs. At the top she found the silver round still clamped in her teeth. She took it out and buried it beneath a rock . . .

Her father saw her in the hall. "What happened to you?"

"I fell down."

He looked her over and sighed. "You all right?"

"Sure."

He opened his bedroom door and went in.

She stopped outside her grandfather's room and listened for a time to his gentle snore. And through the door she whispered to him: "Grandpa, I outraced a train."

Then she undressed and lay down to sleep. And the thunder shook her and shook her bed. She lay on her back and crushed the pillow to her face and choked and sobbed. I almost died, God. You 'most let me die. And God said, What got into you, Emilu? And Emilu said, I wish I knew.

In the night a rising wind was raking the leaves, and she covered her head to shut it out. She knew that tomorrow he would be caved in with everything in him slipped off somewhere.

In the morning he was desolate, hollow-eyed.

She became after that a watcher of weather. Fearful, she would sniff the damp in the air. When the wind hunkered down in the hollow flinging the leaves, drumbeating the panes with fingers of rain, in another year she would have dashed through the trees, clarion with joy until they called her to shelter. Now she despaired, prowling in the hallway outside his room, gliding in to coax, "Don't worry, Grandpa. It won't last long."

But the rain ran down through the fissures in the bank to fill the bowl, and the house was a boat aground in the shallows. The pale moon floated its face in the yard for half the night. The geese honked curses from their dry retreat in a hollow oak. The watchdog guineas, gray and drenched, sat high on the branches above her window and warned of the wind in querulous tones. Below them, the tree frogs screeched their dominion of the sodden world—till daylight came.

She stole in softly with his plate of breakfast. He lay in bed. "Eat it hot, Grandpa. It will help you remember."

She sat brooding over him, warm with her tenderness, smoothing his cover. "Grandpa, there is a whole heap a little things I got locked in my mind. About the well and the singin' and the lady and all." She let her eyes stroke his bulky form. "Some other things too. All we got to do is get it together."

"I don't recollect a damn thing today."

"I could sing you the song."

"Give me the box, little woman." He pointed to it in the corner of the room.

She brought the box and took off the lid. He sat up and propped the pillow behind him. Then he drew from the box his uniform jacket and inched one arm into a sleeve. It was too small to cover more than half his chest.

"Did it shrink?" she asked.

He shook his head.

"You musta had it a long time ago."

He thought of it, frowning, with some surprise. "I don't recall."

"It's got real nice pretty buttons sewed on." Then she fed him some of the cereal. He ate it thoughtfully from her spoon.

"Little daughter," he said, "you got pretty ways."

"That ain't the general opinion around here."

"It's mine," he said.

He drank a little milk. "I think that woman out there wants me to leave."

"You mean Mama?"

"I don't recall her," he said.

"She ain't got such a crush on me neither, I guarantee."

They brooded together. He pulled the jacket a little more across his chest.

She swallowed on the words. "If you was to leave I wouldn't have nobody here."

He thought of it, his blue eyes circling the room. "You gonna help me, little mother. You gonna help me git it back."

She got up and closed the door and sat down again. She began to sing him softly the song of the well. He listened intently, then he hummed it to himself, breaking into a croon, his voice rising and sinking. His voice seemed to listen. And she listened with it, falling into its dream.

One day she brought his breakfast and he wasn't in his room. She put it down and waited. When he didn't return she tried the bathroom down the hall. The door was standing open. He was not inside. Her heart was in her throat. She closed the door to his room so her mother wouldn't see his breakfast on the tray. She searched for him among the trees in the hollow, with Barrelhead before her yipping at the squirrels. She looked into the corn and the wagon shed. She found him at last in the field beyond the corn on the back of a ditch looking into the stream. He was still in his brown cotton flannel robe, with the box for the uniform beneath his arm. His white hair was like something silver in the sun. She was so glad to find him that she almost cried.

He looked up bewildered when he saw her beside him. His face was flushed in the sun. "It ain't the well," he said.

It was not an easy thing to get him back inside the house when no one was around.

After that she knew she had to think of something more than just remembering what he gave her. He hadn't told her anything new for some time. She felt him growing empty, like he was hollowed out or something. She felt her mother just about to say he was crazy and maybe couldn't stay. And she felt herself sometimes like to break in two with holding off her mother and holding onto him.

Sometimes she almost got to wishing she was older, but then it scared her to look back and see how she was different at the first of the summer. Just with minding your own business, just treading water, things got dumped on you that you maybe couldn't handle any way but growing up. She thought it was enough to make you cuss out loud. And as soon as this was over she was backing up. But it was taking all she had and then some more to help him now. She had to get him what he wanted and then he could come back every summer of her life. Or they could live somewhere else, just the two of them together.

So she lay on her bed with her feet against the wallpaper, adding to the smudge she had already made. "I hate them rotten yellow roses," she said and stomped one with her heel.

She climbed the hill and dropped down to the rock where she had buried the snuff lid the train had flattened thin. She sat on the rock and crossed her freckled legs and held the lid in her mouth. She thought she would maybe chop her hair off at the roots and give her mother a fit. And then she was crying and didn't know why.

It was almost noon. She was getting hungry but she wouldn't go home. She sucked the lid in her mouth and thought of dipping snuff and spitting in a can, the way a black woman down the road would do, who took her spitting can with her wherever she went . . . Emilu spit into the weeds and cried.

And finally it came to her she knew about a well that used to be in a field a long way down the road. She had been there once when her daddy had bought a hound for himself. She had a drink from it then and the water had tasted like a mouth of ditch water with scum thrown in. Her father had said not to worry, it was good to drink. But Emilu had thought, You coulda sure fooled me.

And now it seemed to her a last desperate hope. She could find the place. She could head straight back to any place she'd ever been. Like a cat, her father said. "We could put Emilu in a sack and dump her off down the road. She'd turn up the next day. Melissa you can turn around once and she's lost. Not Emilu."

I got to use everything I got, which ain't all that much. She wiped her eyes on her shirt and hid the snuff lid again.

It was hard work telling him about the well. He didn't seem to listen to what she said. She seemed to be telling it all to herself. When she had finished he sat leaning over with his head in his hands.

"Grandpa, I guarantee it wouldn't hurt none to look."

He got up and went to the corner for the box and put it under his arm. "I'm ready, little daughter."

At first she was too surprised to speak. Then she said, "We gotta take that bus and we ain't got time to make it today. We gotta wait till tomorrow."

Tears sprang to his eyes.

She went to him and pulled him down into the chair. She smoothed and patted his hair like silk. "Grandpa, you got real pretty hair. It's real, real pretty, I'm tellin' you. It ain't no time at all till tomorrow gets here . . . Don't go mentionin' the bus. There is some folks around like to mess up your plans."

She found his peanuts on the dresser and they ate some together.

She had a little money for the bus. There was her grandmother on her mother's side who sent her a five-dollar bill every birthday came around. That way you could get it figured into your affairs. It had come in June and she hadn't busted into it yet. It would be enough for one way but not for coming back too. She slipped into her father's drawer and got some from the box in the corner at the back. She knew it would be the whole thing come down upon her if he found it out. Like she had robbed a train.

The bus would come by a little after two, but she got him ready early after lunch was over. She brushed and combed his hair and aimed his eyebrows in the right direction. He wanted to take along the box with his uniform, but she brought him around to taking just the jacket instead.

She put on her black leather sandals and her Easter dress that had the jacket with the braid. She thought to pack corn muffins left from lunch and stuff them into the pockets of her dress. And when her father left in the truck and her mother was sitting out in back in the swing the way she did after lunch, she took his hand and led him out to the road. She walked him down around the bend so that no one looking out could see them from the porch, and she pushed him into the shadow of an oak.

The air was empty, the way it is on summer afternoons when it's making up its mind if it intends to rain. It seemed to her the bus was a long time in coming. Then she heard it struggling with the hill. It was bearing down upon them. She stepped out to hail it and it came to a stop. She coaxed him up the steps. She had her money ready. She would not look around for fear of seeing someone who could know her. But when they were seated just behind the driver she did look down the aisle. The bus was almost empty. Three blacks, a woman and two men, were sitting in the rear. A white man halfway down appeared to be asleep.

She patted her grandfather's arm and smiled at him. His eyes were grave and trusting. She hooked her Sunday sandals on the driver's seat and stared at the back of his head and ears and tried to tell if he was kind and if he would stop where she said to stop.

He stopped the bus exactly where she pointed and never asked her a thing. But she saw him looking hard at the uniform.

There was a haze on the fields. She took her grandfather's hand and led him down a little dirt road between some burdock trees. Then the road ended and they were out in the open. She climbed through a fence and held the wire up for him. But he just stepped over with no trouble at all. There were cows ahead, mostly Jerseys. But a Guernsey bull raised his head as they passed and looked at her hard. She looked back hard and kept on going, though she was scared inside. Insects were chirring like crazy in the heat.

She found a spot beneath a tree and made him sit down. She folded his uniform and put it beside him. "I gotta find it, Grandpa. It might take a minute." She took off running.

She explored every hollow and behind every hillock. She almost panicked. She had been so sure it was there in the field . . . And then through a section of broken fence she found it. She went running back for him and coaxed him to it.

There it was in the weeds, a square of old boards greened over with moss. She tried to lift it. "It's under there, Grandpa. You lift it up. It's too heavy for me."

He stood looking down at it with deep concentration. His eyes were blue pinpoints back under his brows.

She wasn't sure that he understood. "It's a well, Grandpa. I found it. See. You take off the top and look down inside . . ." She scanned the sky for him. "It's a real good day. No wind or rainin'. It's a real good day for rememberin' things. I can remember even bein' a teeny baby. I can remember the farthest back I ever done."

He stood without moving.

Now she was pleading. "Take off the top, Grandpa. It'll be just fine." She knelt in the weeds and patted the boards.

Slowly he approached and stood looking down at her moving hands.

"Lift it up, Grandpa."

He stopped and grasped the edge of one board and threw the lid back with a crash. She fell over backward into the weeds. Then she got to her knees and peered into the well. A smell of decaying vegetation rose. She looked up at his face in the sky above her. He seemed bewildered. "Sit down with me, Grandpa."

He stared out across the field and stirred and half turned. She thought he would leave. She stood up and took his hand and pulled him down beside her. She was praying to herself: God, you gotta help me get it goin'. The hardest thing there is is to get somethin' goin' that ain't started yet.

She picked up a stone and dropped it into the well and heard it strike the ground. She turned to him a stricken face. "It used to be fulla water. I had a drink out it once . . . It's done dried up, I reckon . . . And it's got fulla dirt."

But his face was changing. She could not tell what it meant. He said to her, "Little daughter . . . you gonna give me what you got saved up. You hear?"

"It's a dried-up well."

"It don't matter about the water." He was impatient now. "Give me what all you got."

She held on to the muffins in each pocket of her dress. "I got a lady singin' and a well and a beatin' in the ground and somethin' red. I got the moon." She began to sing the well song but her voice was crying. She didn't want to cry, but her voice came out crying and she had to stop. "I got you said it was the best thing ever happen . . ."

"Not at first," he said.

"How come you told me it was?"

"Not at first," he said, shaking his head from side to side. Suddenly he grabbed the jacket and threw it on his back and drew it close around his throat. "It was some kinda . . . it musta been that war . . ."

"What war was it, Grandpa?" She tried to think of the wars she had heard about in school but they all ran together and she couldn't help.

He stroked his head.

"What was they fightin' about, Grandpa?" She had to keep him talking. The worst was when he stopped. "I wouldn't a fought 'less they give me a reason."

"They give one," he said. "I fergit what it was."

He pulled the uniform around his throat and put it to his lips and smelled of it.

"They was runnin' through trees and outa trees. I heard shootin' in the trees. I heard Jake gittin' hit, and I turn and saw blood comin' outa his throat. Like he was tryin' to tell me somethin', 'stead a words it was blood. Me and him kep' runnin' and then he warn't there. And then I fell down and I seen I had Jake's blood all over my side . . . It warn't his, it was mine. But I didn't know it. I thought it was his. I run further and I fell again. I fell into somethin' was a hole . . . was a well."

She heard thunder in the hills. He lifted his head. He heard it too. Now, she thought, he's gonna dry up like the well is done dried. But the words were still there. "I hear runnin'. I hear runnin'. Feet poundin' the ground. Like a heartbeat in the ground. And like all at once the sky goes away . . ."

He stopped.

"What was it Grandpa? Did you pass clean out?"

He put the jacket to his lips. "No . . . no. It was the top for the well." He reached out and stroked it with his fingers. "She covered me up."

"Who did, Grandpa?"

He shook his head.

"Who did it, Grandpa? You gotta think real hard."

"You recollect your mother used to cover you up? 'Fore you was good asleep?"

"It wasn't Grandma. It wasn't her. It was back in that war."

"She used to sing you asleep."

She stared at him in despair. "Not Grandma . . ." She lay back on the ground.

"That woman . . . in that war."

She heard him from where she lay and was afraid to move.

"Feet was poundin' all around me." He began to moan and tore the uniform away and threw it onto the ground. "I could hear the shoutin'. And she was settin' on top a me. On top a the well. Right on top a the well. And she was singin'. It was a song. I never heard nothin' like it." He began to sing the song, at first a whisper, then loud. She could hear it way down in the pit of her stomach. And she heard how the cows were listening to it in the field.

"Then she stopped," he said. He began to cry softly.

I'm a willin' to grow up some, God, if it takes it . . .

He grew calm and wiped his eyes on the back of his hand. "They was askin' did she see me. They was talkin' foreign words, but I knew what they said . . . When you is settin' hunched up underground in the dark . . . in the wet . . . in the blood . . . and they is huntin' you down like a rabbit . . . it don't matter what kinda words. I am sayin' it don't matter what kinda words."

Then she saw him lean across the well and fall in. But not fall. He climbed inside.

She got to her knees and looked down upon him where he sat with his head against the sides and his white hair all speckled with sticks and fern. She thought it might be that he was going to die. She had never seen somebody die before, and she was aching all over with wanting him to live.

She heard him saying, "She was singin' in the dark. I never heard nothin' like it. They come back a dozen times. They was huntin' me down. But she was singin' on the well and they never look inside."

She heard his voice growing into a song. "I was young to be dyin'. I ain't grew up, and I wanted it like a drink a cold water when your tongue is dry. I seen how it was I been wastin' the world. I ain't half look at things in the field or the road or sky. I ain't half smell the hay in the rain . . . I ain't love a woman. I seen 'em in doorways and walkin' pretty, but I ain't love one. I wanted a woman and the chil'ren she give. Lyin' with her at night, gittin' up at day . . . I wanted gittin' old."

She heard the cows lowing, coming close with their lowing. Bees sang in the trees.

Wanted getting old?

But it wasn't over. For he turned his face upward and into her own. His eyes were seeking something beyond her face, beyond her help. "Long time in the dark 'fore she open me up. I thought it was sun. It was moon shinin' on me the brightest I seen. It was like her face was up in the moon lookin' down at me. It was like I been given it all right there, the rest a my life poured into that hole in the ground where I was . . . I couldn't hardly bring myself to come up then, 'cause I had it all there. I reckon I was 'fraid if I lived it out it might not be that good."

"Was it?" she said, not knowing what he meant or what she asked or why.

But it seemed to be gone. All she could see was his head sunk down and the sticks and fern and the leaves in his hair.

He stirred. "Did you git it?" he cried.

She swallowed and nodded down into the well. "I got it, Grandpa."

"It's slippin', a'ready slippin'. You got it, little daughter?"

"I got it, Grandpa." Inside she was crying, not knowing what she had.

"That's good," he said. "It's yours. You keep it."

Keep what? Keep what?

Going back was hard. The sky was changing, going gray at the edges, then gray on top. By the time they were back at the road it was raining. She got him to sit on the side in the grass. She took off her jacket and put it over his head. The uniform she buttoned inside his shirt, but he didn't seem to care about it anymore. She felt it was raining down inside of her. Counting on her fingers, she guessed it would be a good five hours before the bus would return.

But long before that, her father's car lights picked them out through the mist.

"Emilu," said her mother in the front seat, turning, "I would expect from you a little more judgment."

"Shut up!" she cried, coming out of the rain. "I was helpin' Grandpa. I'll never tell what it was. Not if all my teeth rot out! Not if you lock me up forever!"

But he was the one they locked away . . .

Whatever it was he found in the well, sometimes she wished she could lock it up in the box she kept beneath her bed. A thing you have to keep in your mind, it gets shrunk up, or else it grows the way you do and blurs like a lantern held too close till, like it or not, you look away. But after a dozen summers were gone, it must have been when her child was born, she heard the cry of the thing they had found. She heard the singing inside of her.

Meaning

1. As the story opens, how does Emilu feel about growing up? What do these feelings reveal about her?
2. How does Emilu feel about her grandfather's arrival? How do her feelings change?
3. Why do you think Emilu's grandfather is determined to recall the incident at the well? Why does Emilu resolve to help him?
4. Why hasn't the grandfather told anyone about what happened at the well? Why does he want to tell Emilu about it?
5. When does Emilu become willing to grow up? Why?
6. What happened at the well? What did the incident mean to the grandfather at the time it occurred?
7. When does Emilu fully understand the significance of her grandfather's story? What does the story mean to her?

Method

1. What *conflicts* are present in this story? Which conflict is the most significant?
2. What indications does the author give that Emilu is in some ways childish? What actions reveal her more mature side?
3. What is the *climax* of the story, and how does the author build up to it?
4. How are Emilu's decision to race the train and Grandpa's experience at the well similar?

Language: Dialect

Dialect refers to the forms and patterns of speech used by the people in a specific area. Dialect often contains a rich variety of colorful expressions, slang words, and nonstandard usages.

The southern dialect that Emilu and her family speak is part of their everyday lives. If the characters spoke differently, their language would seem inconsistent with their background. However, a reader unfamiliar with this dialect might need to mentally translate some expressions into more familiar language as he or she encounters them. For example, *I don't recall it none* might be paraphrased as *I don't remember it at all*.

The following examples of dialect are taken from "The Singing Well." Rewrite each sentence using the language of your own everyday speech. Then rewrite each sentence in the formal, standard English that you might use in a composition. Be sure to keep the original meaning of each sentence.

1. "'Emilu, it's time you grew up to your age.'"
2. "'There is more things around that I ain't got permission than there is I can do.'"
3. "'I can remember the farthest back I ever done.'"

Discussion and Composition

1. Suppose that you lost your memories of the most important events of your life. Do you think that forgetting these things would cause you to lose your sense of yourself? Explain.

2. How would you describe the conflict between Emilu and her mother? Do you think that this type of conflict is typical of an eleven-year-old girl and her mother? Explain your answer.

3. The author uses a number of *similes*—figurative comparisons introduced by terms such as *like* or *as*. For example, instead of writing that the days passed quickly, she writes that they "ran away like a rabbit flushed out of a blackberry bush."

Find three other similes in the story, and think about the images they create in your mind. In what way are these similes more effective than nonfigurative language?

4. Write an essay in which you describe the behavior and physical appearance of an elderly person you know or have observed. Begin by freewriting for about ten minutes about that person. Review your freewriting, and think about the descriptive details that will need to be made more specific or concrete. You might begin your essay by stating your attitude toward the individual you are writing about. Devote at least one paragraph to a physical description of your subject and at least one paragraph to describing his or her actions.

RAY BRADBURY
(born 1920)

Although he has written seven novels, among them *Something Wicked This Way Comes* and *Fahrenheit 451*, Ray Bradbury is known mainly for his short stories. Most of these can be classified as *science fiction*, but they are not mere escape reading. There is a firm moral point of view behind all of his stories, and implicit in all of them is a rigorous social criticism. Bradbury neither praises nor condemns modern technology; rather, he observes it with a critical eye and calls upon the reader to be equally critical—to see its uses and its abuses.

Bradbury was born in Waukegan, Illinois, but was educated in Los Angeles, where he now lives. He has been a full-time author since he was twenty-three years old. He is a great admirer of Edgar Allan Poe, and one can see in his stories the single unified effect and the same sense of horror that Poe achieves in his stories.

Bradbury has also written many plays and film scripts. He has written a dramatic version of "The Pedestrian." Like "The Pedestrian," all of his writing stresses the value of the individual and the need for and power of the human imagination.

THE PEDESTRIAN

To enter out into that silence that was the city at eight o'clock of a misty evening in November, to put your feet upon that buckling concrete walk, to step over grassy seams and make your way, hands in pockets, through the silences, that was what Mr. Leonard Mead most dearly loved to do. He would stand upon the corner of an intersection and peer down long moonlit avenues of sidewalk in four directions, deciding which way to go, but it really made no difference; he was alone in this world of A.D. 2131, or as good as alone, and with a final decision made, a path selected, he would stride off sending patterns of frosty air before him like the smoke of a cigar.

Sometimes he would walk for hours and miles and return

only at midnight to his house. And on his way he would see the cottages and homes with their dark windows, and it was not unequal to walking through a graveyard, because only the faintest glimmers of firefly light appeared in flickers behind the windows. Sudden gray phantoms seemed to manifest[1] themselves upon inner room walls where a curtain was still undrawn against the night, or there were whisperings and murmurs where a window in a tomblike building was still open.

Mr. Leonard Mead would pause, cock his head, listen, look, and march on, his feet making no noise on the lumpy walk. For a long while now the sidewalks had been vanishing under flowers and grass. In ten years of walking by night or day, for thousands of miles, he had never met another person walking, not one in all that time.

He now wore sneakers when strolling at night, because the dogs in intermittent[2] squads would parallel his journey with barkings if he wore hard heels, and lights might click on and faces appear, and an entire street be startled by the passing of a lone figure, himself, in the early November evening.

On this particular evening he began his journey in a westerly direction, toward the hidden sea. There was a good crystal frost in the air; it cut the nose going in and made the lungs blaze like a Christmas tree inside; you could feel the cold light going on and off, all the branches filled with invisible snow. He listened to the faint push of his soft shoes through autumn leaves with satisfaction, and whistled a cold quiet whistle between his teeth, occasionally picking up a leaf as he passed, examining its skeletal pattern in the infrequent lamplights as he went on, smelling its rusty smell.

"Hello, in there," he whispered to every house on every side as he moved. "What's up tonight on Channel 4, Channel 7, Channel 9? Where are the cowboys rushing, and do I see the United States Cavalry over the next hill to the rescue?"

The street was silent and long and empty, with only his shadow moving like the shadow of a hawk in mid-country. If he closed his eyes and stood very still, frozen, he imagined himself upon the center of a plain, a wintry windless Arizona country with no house in a thousand miles, and only dry riverbeds, the streets, for company.

1. **manifest:** reveal.
2. **intermittent:** stopping and starting at intervals.

"What is it now?" he asked the houses, noticing his wrist watch. "Eight-thirty P.M. Time for a dozen assorted murders? A quiz? A revue? A comedian falling off the stage?"

Was that a murmur of laughter from within a moon-white house? He hesitated, but went on when nothing more happened. He stumbled over a particularly uneven section of walk as he came to a cloverleaf intersection which stood silent where two main highways crossed the town. During the day it was a thunderous surge of cars, the gas stations open, a great insect rustling and ceaseless jockeying for position[3] as the scarab beetles, a faint incense puttering from their exhausts, skimmed homeward to the far horizons. But now these highways too were like streams in a dry season, all stone and bed and moon radiance.

He turned back on a side street, circling around toward his home. He was within a block of his destination when the lone car turned a corner quite suddenly and flashed a fierce white cone of light upon him. He stood entranced, not unlike a night moth, stunned by the illumination and then drawn toward it.

A metallic voice called to him:

"Stand still. Stay where you are! Don't move!"

He halted.

"Put up your hands."

"But—" he said.

"Your hands up! Or we'll shoot!"

The police, of course, but what a rare, incredible thing; in a city of three million, there was only one police car left. Ever since a year ago, 2130, the election year, the force had been cut down from three cars to one. Crime was ebbing; there was no need now for the police, save for this one lone car wandering and wandering the empty streets.

"Your name?" said the police car in a metallic whisper. He couldn't see the men in it for the bright light in his eyes.

"Leonard Mead," he said.

"Speak up!"

"Leonard Mead!"

"Business or profession?"

"I guess you'd call me a writer."

"No profession," said the police car, as if talking to itself. The

---

3. jockeying for position: to maneuver for advantage; here, cars trying to get ahead of other cars, either on the highway or at the gas pumps.

light held him fixed like a museum specimen, needle thrust through chest.

"You might say that," said Mr. Mead. He hadn't written in years. Magazines and books didn't sell any more. Everything went on in the tomblike houses at night now, he thought, continuing his fancy. The tombs, ill-lit by television light, where the people sat like the dead, the gray or multi-colored lights touching their expressionless faces but never really touching *them*.

"No profession," said the phonograph voice, hissing. "What are you doing out?"

"Walking," said Leonard Mead.

"Walking!"

"Just walking," he said, simply, but his face felt cold.

"Walking, just walking, walking?"

"Yes, sir."

"Walking where? For what?"

"Walking for air. Walking to *see*."

"Your address!"

"Eleven South St. James Street."

"And there is air *in* your house, you have an air-*conditioner*, Mr. Mead?"

"Yes."

"And you have a viewing screen in your house to see with?"

"No."

"No?" There was a crackling quiet that in itself was an accusation.

"Are you married, Mr. Mead?"

"No."

"Not married," said the police voice behind the fiery beam. The moon was high and clear among the stars and the houses were gray and silent.

"Nobody wanted me," said Leonard Mead, with a smile.

"Don't speak unless you're spoken to!"

Leonard Mead waited in the cold night.

"Just walking, Mr. Mead?"

"Yes."

"But you haven't explained for what purpose."

"I explained: for air and to see, and just to walk."

"Have you done this often?"

"Every night for years."

The police car sat in the center of the street with its radio throat faintly humming.

"Well, Mr. Mead," it said.

"Is that all?" he asked politely.

"Yes," said the voice. "Here." There was a sigh, a pop. The back door of the police car sprang wide. "Get in."

"Wait a minute, I haven't done anything!"

"Get in."

"I protest!"

"Mr. Mead."

He walked like a man suddenly drunk. As he passed the front window of the car he looked in. As he had expected, there was no one in the front seat, no one in the car at all.

"Get in."

He put his hand to the door and peered into the back seat, which was a little cell, a little black jail with bars. It smelled of riveted steel. It smelled of harsh antiseptic; it smelled too clean and hard and metallic. There was nothing soft there.

"Now if you had a wife to give you an alibi," said the iron voice. "But—"

"Where are you taking me?"

The car hesitated, or rather gave a faint whirring click, as if information, somewhere, was dropping card by punch-slotted card under electric eyes. "To the Psychiatric Center for Research on Regressive Tendencies."

He got in. The door shut with a soft thud. The police car rolled through the night avenues, flashing its dim lights ahead.

They passed one house on one street a moment later, one house in an entire city of houses that were dark, but this one particular house had all its electric lights brightly lit, every window a loud yellow illumination, square and warm in the cool darkness."

"That's *my* house," said Leonard Mead.

No one answered him.

The car moved down the empty river bed streets and off away, leaving the empty streets with the empty sidewalks, and no sound and no motion all the rest of the chill November night.

Meaning

1. Leonard Mead's nightly walks would likely seem quite ordinary in a different setting. Why does his habit of walking seem odd in the story, and what comment does his behavior make on the rest of the population?
2. According to the narrator, the city in which Leonard Mead lives is practically free of crime. Why do you think this is so? What is ironic about Leonard Mead's arrest?

Method

1. Almost half of "The Pedestrian" consists of dialogue. How do the two speakers and their speeches differ? What is the effect of the repetition in the dialogue?
2. A *symbol* is something that has meaning in itself and also suggests something larger, such as an attitude or a value. How is Leonard Mead's house on St. James Street a symbol? What does it symbolize?

Discussion and Composition

1. The Psychiatric Center for Research on Regressive Tendencies sounds forbidding. What do you think will happen to Leonard Mead at the Center? Will they succeed in making him conform to the norms of society? Will he be strong enough to resist? Discuss the possible answers to these questions, and give reasons for your opinions.

2. Write a composition describing what you think the world will be like in the year 2131. You might give an overall picture of a future society or focus on a single aspect such as government, technology, environmental conditions, or a typical day in the life of an individual.

A GLOSSARY OF LITERARY TERMS

Alliteration: the repetition of a sound at the beginning, in the middle, or at the end of words. Although it is mainly a poetic device, alliteration is sometimes used in prose. For example:

> ". . . boys with their *eyes still squi*nted agains*t* the *shi*fting *wi*nds and the *shi*ny bra*ss* of the *w*aves, aw*k*w*ard* and heavy-foote*d* as *d*ucks on *d*ry lan*d.*"

Allusion: a reference to a person, a place, an event, or an artistic work that the author expects the reader to recognize. An allusion may be drawn from literature, history, geography, scripture, or mythology. A statement is enriched by an allusion because in a few words an author can evoke a particular atmosphere, story, or historical setting. For example, the title of Borden Deal's story "Antaeus" alludes to the Antaeus of Greek mythology, a giant who drew his strength from contact with the earth and who was defeated when Hercules held him aloft. This allusion foreshadows the fate of T. J., who also needs contact with the earth—with growing things—in order to survive.

Ambiguity: the possibility of more than one meaning. In literature, an author may deliberately use ambiguity to produce subtle or multiple variations in meaning. For example, the word *game* in the title of the story "The Most Dangerous Game" is deliberately ambiguous.

Analogy: a form of comparison that points out the likeness between two basically dissimilar things; it attempts to use a familiar object or idea to illustrate or to introduce a subject that is unfamiliar or complex.

Anecdote: a brief account, sometimes biographical, of an interesting or entertaining incident. A writer may use an anecdote to introduce or illustrate a topic.

Antagonist: the force or character opposing the main character or **protagonist**.

Atmosphere: the prevailing mental and emotional climate of a story; something the reader senses or feels. **Setting** and **tone** help to create and heighten atmosphere. Edgar Allan Poe is noted for creating stories of atmosphere. In "The Masque of the Red Death," for example, an atmosphere of death and terror prevails.

Autobiography and Biography: literature that presents an account of a person's life, usually in chronological order, using facts, events, and other information that is available. An *autobiography* is an account written by a person about himself or herself; a *biography* is an account written by another person.

Character: a person—or an animal, a thing, or a natural force presented as a person—appearing in a short story, novel, play, or narrative poem. Characters are sometimes described as *dynamic* or *static*. Dynamic characters experience some essential change in personality or attitude. Static characters remain the same throughout a narrative.

Characters are sometimes classified as *flat* or *round*. Flat characters have only one or two "sides," representing one or two traits. They are often stereotypes that can be summed up in a few words, for example, an "anxious miser" or a "strong, silent type." Round characters are complex and have many "sides" or traits. They are individuals, and their personalities are fully developed and require lengthy analysis.

Characterization: the techniques an author uses to develop the personalities of fictional characters so that they seem believable. These methods include:
a. direct analysis by the author of a character's thoughts, feelings, and actions;
b. physical description of a character;
c. description of a character's surroundings, such as the place in which he or she lives or works;
d. the speech or conversations of a character;
e. the behavior or actions of a character;
f. a character's reactions to events, situations, and other people;
g. the responses or reactions of other people in the story to a character's behavior, and in some cases, their remarks and conversations about the character.

Climax: the high point or turning point of a story. The author builds up to the climax through a series of complications.

Comparison and Contrast: a *comparison* shows the similarities between two things, while a *contrast* details the differences between things. In writing, this is a method used to clarify and illustrate a subject. Comparison and contrast are often used together. (See also **Contrast.**)

Complication: a series of difficulties forming the central action of a narrative. Complications in a story, for example, make a conflict difficult to resolve and add interest or suspense. In Frank R. Stockton's "The Lady, or the Tiger?" complications include the princess's discovery of "the secret of the doors" and her knowledge of the identity of the young woman.

Conflict: a struggle between opposing forces, people, or ideas in a story, novel, play, or narrative poem. Conflict can be *external* or *internal,* and it can take one of these forms: **a.** a person against another person, **b.** a person against society, **c.** a person against nature, **d.** two elements or ideas struggling for mastery within a person, or **e.** a combination of two or more of these types. For example, in "Top Man," there is a conflict between two people, Nace and Osborn, as well as a conflict between people and nature.

Connotation: the emotion or association that a word or phrase may arouse. Connotation is distinct from **denotation,** which is the literal meaning of the word. The word *snowstorm*, for example, may arouse emotions such as fear or excitement.

Context: the words and phrases that closely surround a word and affect or suggest its meaning. Often, the intended meaning of a word can be determined from its context, as in the following examples.

> "The customer refused to buy the table because the edges were too *rough*."
> "The students felt that the last two questions were too *rough*."

For an event or incident, *context* includes the situation and circumstances that surround the event. For example, we often speak of a specific event in its historical context.

Contrast: a striking difference between two things. In literature, an author may contrast ideas, personalities, or images to heighten or clarify a situation. (See also **Comparison and Contrast.**)

Denotation: the literal or "dictionary" meaning of a word. (See also **Connotation.**)

Dénouement (dā•nōō•män'): that part of the plot that reveals the final outcome of the conflicts.

Description: any careful detailing of a person, place, thing, or event. Description is one of the four major forms of discourse. Descriptions re-create sensory impressions: sights, sounds, smells, textures, or tastes. Some description is direct and factual, but more often, description helps to establish a mood or stir an emotion.

Dialect: the speech that is characteristic of a particular group or of the inhabitants of a specific geographical region. In literature, dialect may be used as part of a characterization. The characters in Helen Norris's story "The Singing Well" speak southern dialect.

Dialogue: the conversation carried on by two or more characters in a story.

Diction: a writer's choice, arrangement, and use of words.

Episode: one of a series of significant events in the plot of a story.

Exposition: that part of a story or play in which the author provides background material about the lives of characters and about events that have taken place before the story opens. As a form of discourse, exposition is writing intended to explain a subject or provide information.

Fable: a brief narrative in prose or verse intended to teach a moral lesson. Many fables, such as those of the Greek writer Aesop, are beast fables, in which animals speak and act as if they were human.

Fantasy: a work that employs highly imaginative elements and that involves a departure from reality. A fantasy might take place in a dreamlike world, present unreal characters, or project scientific principles into the future (as in *science fiction* stories such as Ray Bradbury's "The Pedestrian"). A fantasy can be a whimsical form of entertainment or can offer a serious comment on reality. It often has more than one level of meaning.

Figurative Language: language that is not intended to be interpreted in a literal sense. Figurative language consists of imaginative comparisons called *figures of speech.* **Simile, metaphor,** and **personification** are among the most common figures of speech.

Flashback: a device by which an author interrupts the logical time sequence of a story or play to relate an episode that occurred prior to the opening situation.

Foil: a character who serves by contrast to emphasize the qualities of another character. For example, the appearance of a particularly lazy, shiftless, and unenterprising character will strengthen the reader's impression of an active, ambitious, and aggressive character.

Foreshadowing: hints or clues; a shadow of things to come. The use of foreshadowing in a story stimulates interest and suspense and helps prepare the reader for the outcome. For example, in "Flowers for Algernon," Daniel Keyes foreshadows Charlie's fate in the descriptions Charlie gives of Algernon's increasingly odd behavior and eventual death.

Framework story: a story that contains another story. Saki's "The Storyteller" is an example of a framework story. The frame story is the story about the bachelor meeting the aunt and her rebellious charges in a railway car. The inner story is the tale the bachelor tells to the children to keep them quiet.

Hyperbole (hī•pûr′bə•lē): a deliberate exaggeration for the purpose of emphasis or humor; overstatement. "I'm dying to hear what happened" is an example of hyperbole.

Idiom: an expression that has a special meaning different from the usual meanings of the words. *To turn the corner, to carry out,* and *to pull* *someone's leg* are examples of idioms. When the term is used in reference to an overall manner of expression, it also refers to the language or dialect of a particular group of people.

Imagery: language that appeals to one or more senses and creates pictures and impressions in the reader's mind. Although imagery most often creates visual pictures, some imagery appeals to the senses of touch, taste, smell, and hearing as well. Imagery often involves the use of figurative language and vivid description. In the following passage from "A Worn Path," Eudora Welty uses vivid images that appeal to the senses of sight, hearing, and touch.

> "On she went. The woods were deep and still. The sun made the pine needles almost too bright to look at, up where the wind rocked. The cones dropped as light as feathers. Down in the hollow was the mourning dove—it was not too late for him."

Irony: a contrast or an incongruity between what is stated and what is really meant, or between what is expected to happen and what actually does happen. There are three kinds of irony. With *verbal irony*, a writer or speaker says one thing and means something entirely different. For example, a writer might say of a character who has just taken several clumsy falls on the ice, "What a fine skater he turned out to be!" With *dramatic irony*, a reader or an audience perceives something that a character in the story or play does not know. *Irony of situation* involves a discrepancy between the expected result of an action or situation and its actual result. Irony of situation occurs in O. Henry's "The Ransom of Red Chief" when Red Chief's kidnappers pay ransom to get rid of the boy.

Jargon: the special vocabulary of an identifiable group. This vocabulary may include terms used by people who share a particular occupation, art, science, trade, sect, or sport. For example, sports fans may use special football jargon. *Jargon* can also refer to language full of long words and circumlocutions that serve little purpose other than to impress and bewilder the average person.

Local Color: details of dress, speech, locale, customs, and traditions that give an impression of the local "atmosphere" of a particular region.

Metaphor: a comparison between two unlike things with the intent of giving additional meaning to one of them. Unlike a **simile,** a metaphor does not use a connective word such as *like* or *as* to state a comparison. For example, in James Ramsey Ullman's story "Top Man," the mountain is described as "a white-hooded giant."

An **implied metaphor** does not directly compare two things but suggests or implies the comparison: "the white untrodden pinnacle of K3 *stabbed* the sky."

Monologue: a long, uninterrupted speech by a character in a narrative or drama.

Mood: the prevailing feeling that a literary work communicates to the reader. Mood is often developed, at least in part, through descriptions of **setting** and by the author's **tone**. Edgar Allan Poe often establishes a mood of gloom and foreboding at the very opening of a story, as in "The Masque of the Red Death."

Motif: an image or phrase that recurs and thus provides a pattern within a work of literature.

Motivation: the reasons, either stated or implied, for a character's behavior. To make a story believable, a writer must provide characters with motivation that explains what they do. Characters may be motivated by outside events, or they may be motivated by inner needs or fears.

Myth: a tale or story usually focusing on the deeds of gods or superhuman heroes. Myths played an important role in ancient cultures by helping to explain the mysteries of nature and the universe. As a loose term, *myth* can denote any invented or grossly exaggerated story.

Narrative: a piece of writing that tells of a series of events or incidents that together make up a meaningful action; a story.

Narrator: one who narrates, or tells, a true or fictional story. The narrator may be a major or minor participant in the action of the narrative or simply an observer of the action.

Novel: a fictional narrative in prose, usually longer than a short story. A novel is similar to a short story in its use of characterization, plot, setting, mood, theme, and other literary elements. Because of its greater length, a novel may introduce several different groups of characters, a complicated plot or various subplots, multiple settings, or more than one mood or theme, while a short story usually focuses on one predominant effect.

Onomatopoeia (on´•ə•mat´•ə•pē´•ə): the use of words that imitate the sound, action, or idea they represent. Sometimes a single word sounds like the thing it describes, such as *cuckoo* or *twitter*. Sometimes several words are grouped together to imitate a sound, as in "murmuring of innumerable bees."

Paraphrase: a rewording of a line, passage, or entire work, giving the meaning in shorter form, usually to simplify the original.

Personification: a figure of speech in which a nonhuman or inanimate object, quality, or idea is given lifelike characteristics or powers. For example:

> ". . . the wind hunkered down in the hollow flinging the leaves, drumbeating the panes with fingers of rain . . ."

Plot: the arrangement of incidents, details, and elements of conflict in a story. Plot usually includes the following elements:
  a. the *conflict(s)*, or problem(s), usually introduced at the beginning of a narrative;
  b. the *complications,* or entanglements, produced by new or complex events and involvements;
  c. the *rising action,* or advancing movement, toward an event or moment when something decisive has to happen;
  d. the *climax,* or most intense moment or event, usually occurring near a narrative's major *turning point,* or crisis, the moment when the main character turns toward a (good or bad) solution of the problem;
  e. the *dénouement,* the final outcome in which the resolution of the conflict(s) is made known.

Point of View: the vantage point from which the story is told. Each viewpoint allows the author a particular range or scope. There are two basic points of view:
  a. **first-person point of view,** in which the narrative is told by a major or minor character in his or her own words. The author is limited to the narrator's scope of knowledge, degree of involvement, and powers of observation and expression. Daniel Keyes's "Flowers for Algernon" is an example of a story that uses first-person narration.
  b. **third-person point of view,** in which the narrator serves as an observer who describes and comments upon the characters and action in a narrative. In the *omniscient* third-person point of view, the narrator knows everything there is to know about the characters—their thoughts, motives, actions, and reactions. Jack London's "To Build a Fire" is told by an omniscient third-person narrator.

  Writers can also adopt a limited third-person point of view. An author using this point of view tells the inner thoughts and feelings of one character only, usually the main character. We are never told what other characters are thinking; we must infer this from their external acts. Toni Cade Bambara uses the limited third-person point of view in "Blues Ain't No Mockin Bird."

Protagonist: the main character in a story or a drama. The word, which comes from the Greek *protos* meaning "first" and *agónistés* meaning "contestant" or "actor," was originally used to designate the actor who played the chief role in a Greek drama. (See also **Antagonist**.)

Repetition: the use of the same sound, word, phrase, sentence, idea or effect to achieve emphasis or suggest order in a piece of literature. Repetition is most often used in poetry, but it is sometimes found in prose. (See also **Alliteration**.)

Rhythm: in poetry, the regular rise and fall of strong and weak syllables. In prose, although rhythm is often present, it is irregular and approximate; prose rhythm is the effective and pleasing arrangement of meaningful sounds in a sentence.

Rising Action: the part of the plot that leads to a turning point in the action that will affect the fortunes of the main character.

Satire: the use of ridicule, sarcasm, wit, or irony to expose, set right, or destroy a vice, folly, breach of good taste, or undesirable social condition. Satire may range from gentle ridicule to bitter attack. "The Mao Button" by Feng Jicai is an example of satire.

Science Fiction: a type of **fantasy** that includes speculation about the impact of science on society or individuals. Science fiction stories, such as Ray Bradbury's "The Pedestrian," usually have highly imaginative, futuristic settings.

Setting: the time and place of the events in a story; the physical background. The importance of setting as a story element depends on the extent of its contribution to characterization, plot, theme, and atmosphere. For example, in "To Build a Fire," the setting forms the basis for the plot, which focuses on a man's struggle to survive in the remote, deadly cold Klondike.

Simile: a stated comparison or likeness expressed in figurative language and introduced by terms such as *like, as, so, as if, resembles,* and *as though*. For example, Helen Norris uses the following simile in "The Singing Well":

> "The summer days . . . ran away like a rabbit flushed out of a blackberry bush."

Sketch: a short, simply constructed work, usually about a single character, place, or incident. A *character sketch,* for example, may be a brief study of a person's characteristics and personality.

Style: a writer's distinctive or characteristic form of expression. Style is determined by a writer's choice and arrangement of words, sentence structure, tone, rhythm, and the use of figurative language, and rhythm.

Surprise Ending: in fiction, an unexpected twist of plot at the conclusion of a story; a trick ending. It should be carefully foreshadowed to produce its striking effect. O. Henry often wrote stories with surprise endings.

Suspense: the feeling of curiosity, uncertainty, or anxiety that is created in the reader by events or complications in a literary work. Suspense makes readers ask "What will happen next?" or "How will this work out?" and impels them to read on.

Symbol: a person, place, event, or object that has meaning in itself and also represents or suggests something larger than itself, such as a quality, an attitude, a belief, or a value. For example, a heart symbolizes affection and love; a horseshoe, good luck; a lily, purity; a skull, death; and a dove, peace. In fiction, some symbols have *universal* meaning, such as the association of spring with youth and winter with old age.

Some symbols have a special meaning within the context of a story. A character's name, for instance, may suggest his or her personality. "Prince Prospero" may be a name associated with a wealthy, royal, and "prosperous" character. The action of a story may also be symbolic. A long trip might, during the course of a story, come to symbolize a person's journey through life.

Theme: the main idea of a literary work; the general truth behind the story of a particular individual in a particular situation. The theme of a story is usually implied rather than stated.

Tone: the attitude of the writer toward his or her subject, characters, and readers. An author may be sympathetic and sorrowful, may wish to provoke, shock, or anger, or may write in a humorous way and intend simply to entertain the reader. Tone is created through the writer's choice of words and details.

Understatement: the representation of something as less than it really is for the purpose of emphasis or humor. For example, in agreeing with a friend's praise of a new sports car, the owner might say, "Oh, it will do, I suppose."

Vignette: a brief but significant sketch of a person or event. The meaning of a vignette is usually subtly implied rather than stated. It often forms part of a longer work.

THE LANGUAGE ARTS PROGRAM
LIST OF SKILLS

Throughout the textbook, language arts have been integrated with the presentation of literature. The majority of language arts activities appear in the end-of-selection questions and assignments under the headings **Meaning, Method, Language, Composition,** and **Composition and Discussion.** Others are introduced and discussed in the general introductions, and still others, especially those concerning word origins and derivations, are covered in text footnotes.

The following indexes are intended to serve as guidelines to specific aspects of the language arts program in *A Book of Short Stories 1.*

VOCABULARY DEVELOPMENT

COMPOSITION